Brandishing Balance

M.E. Thornwood

Midnight Dreaming Publishing

M.E. Thornwood

Midnight Dreaming Publishing

P.O. Box 312 Elburn, IL 60119

Interior design by Atticus

Edited by: Cantina Book Club

Cover by: RJ Creatives

ISBN: 978-1-962688-11-6

ISBN: 978-1-962688-10-9 (e-book)

CONTENTS

I F YOU ARE MY family member, thank you for your support, I love you dearly, but DO NOT READ THIS BOOK. This is not for you. We will not be having an awkward conversation about the contents of this book.

Brandishing Balance is book 3 of a trilogy and must be read after Brandishing Beginnings and Brandishing Betrayals to make sense. It is a dark Reverse Harem/Why Choose romance, meaning the main female character will not choose between her loves interests. There will be group scenes and dark themes including Motorcycle Club Culture. This is a BDSM romance with on screen negotiations and themes that are not suitable for every reader.

READER BEWARE:

There is graphic, on page sexual assault in chapters 4 & 7 & 12. During these chapters there are suicidal ideations. If you need to skip them, it is perfectly OK. Please take care of yourself. Your mental health is important.

For the full list of trigger warnings please see the author's website.

To everyone who has supported me... thank you.

Marcos "Killer" Candella

"WE CAN'T JUST FUCKING go in there, guns blazing! That's my fucking son in there!" I yelled over the chaos around me. My motorcycle club, the Devil's Psychos—my brothers—were standing around Elaine Henderson's garage and were screaming over each other trying to decide the best course of action on how to rescue my son from our enemy.

Dax fucking Hillcrest, leader of Las Serpientes, had kidnapped my son right out of the fucking school locker room after his football game that ended not even an hour ago.

My phone rang, and I pulled it out of my pocket and answered immediately when I saw it was Maya Henderson, the mother of my child. "Maya, I'm sorry about the yelling. We'll be done soon."

"Marcos," she breathed my name. "I'm sorry." There was something in her voice that immediately set me on edge.

"What do you mean, Mi Vida? This wasn't your fault. Give me a minute to finish up with the guys and I'll come in there."

"I left, Marcos. I'm not there." A pit of dread settled into my stomach.

"What the fuck you mean you left, Maya?" I shouted over the arguing voices, silencing them.

She sniffled as if she'd been crying. "I got a text from Hillcrest. He said if I turned myself over to him, he would release Luke. A simple trade," Maya explained.

"What the fuck, Maya! It's a goddamn trap! Turn around now!" I screamed through the phone.

"I'll text you the address, but I'm already here."

"Maya—"

Maya hung up on me before I could yell some more.

"MAYA!" I screamed into the phone as the love of my fucking life said she was going to trade herself to our enemy in return for our son Luke, and then hung up the phone.

I immediately called her back as all the men standing around me in the garage, who had been yelling just moments before, quieted down to listen.

"What happened?" Jason "Stone" Langford demanded, limping closer, pain and anger making his face pinch. His gunshot wounds in his leg and shoulder were only a couple days old, and today was the first time Jason had gotten out of bed since he had been gunned down by Hillcrest's men. It was supposed to be family day at Luke's football game, and was quickly turning into a living nightmare.

"Maya got a text from Hillcrest. He told her to trade herself for Luke. She went to him. She texted me the address. She's already there."

"Where?" Nico "Dagger" Gage demanded, stalking across the garage toward me.

"The address is in The Edges. Nico, call Seratelli. He's closer; see if he can either get men there or back us up. We need to move fast."

Nico was already pulling out his phone and dialing his cousin Leonardo Seratelli's contact. The Seratelli family were family by blood on Nico's mother's side, and his recent reunion with them just might come in handy.

I turned to Jason. "I'm coming," Jason said before I could say anything.

"You can't ride." It came out harsher than I intended. I didn't have time to sugarcoat things for feelings right now. My woman's—our woman's—life was on the line here.

"Then I'll fucking drive," Jason snapped.

I nodded and tossed him the keys to my truck. We were wasting time here. "Let's roll!" I shouted to the rest of my club. My MC brothers would follow me into battle anywhere, and it meant everything to me as president of the Devil's Psychos that I trusted these men to have my back.

Maya Henderson

I hung up on Marcos before he could yell some more. I forwarded the text message from Dax so Marcos would have his phone number as well, but I knew full well that it was likely a burner cell and nothing traceable.

My phone rang immediately after, and I quickly silenced it. I didn't outright shut it off, but I turned off the ringer so I couldn't be distracted from my mission. Tucking the phone in my back pocket, I walked the final two blocks to the house and waited on the sidewalk in front of the run-down house that looked more like a shack than a home.

Huge sections of the roof were missing. Clearly, it hadn't been lived in for quite some time. This was obviously just a meeting place, and that was it. They probably wouldn't keep me here very long at all. I would likely be moved to a different location.

I would need to stop them from moving me. My life would depend on it. I had called Marcos, though. They were maybe five minutes away by motorcycle, so they would get to me before I got moved. I was sure of it.

Swallowing hard, I steeled my spine and then walked up to the front door. It opened just as I stopped on the front step. Dax Hillcrest stood with my son held in front of him and a gun trained on his head. "You came alone?" he demanded, his milky white eye catching the light and making him look more deranged.

"Yes," I muttered, my eyes on my son's bruised face.

Hillcrest motioned me closer with the gun, but I held my arms out for Luke. Hillcrest pushed him into my arms, and I held him tightly, bending down to whisper into his ear. "My phone is in my back pocket. Grab it and run as fast as you can. Call your dad."

"Mom," Luke cried.

"You do this, Lucas." I whispered fiercely into his ear. "Now." I snapped a little louder and shoved him to the side. I felt my phone get lifted out of my pocket and then heard the pounding of Luke's feet as he ran as fast as could.

Hillcrest aimed the gun at me and smiled wickedly. "You stupid bitch. You'll pay for that."

The gun fired.

And everything went black.

Marcos

THE DEVIL'S PSYCHOS MOTORCYCLE club raced through Mourningside and over the Evermore bridge into Creekton, or the area right before Creekton city limits better known as The Edges. The address that Maya had texted us was barely a ten-minute ride away, and we *flew* the distance on our bikes.

A little over five minutes later, we pulled up into the neighborhood of the address. I commanded my guys via the Bluetooth intercoms in all our helmets to break off and surround the block.

I slowed as I approached the block the house was situated on. The Edges were run down and mostly vacant. Most houses around here were condemned or foreclosed on. There weren't many families still hanging on.

Someone yelled behind me, and I jerked my head around. "Dad!" I heard it again and whipped my head around.

I found Luke. He was bruised and bloody, but he was running toward me, still in his lower football pads from the game.

Pulling the bike to the side of the road, I dropped my kickstand and jumped off the bike. I ran toward Luke, yelling his name. "Luke!"

I fell to my knees as Luke crashed into me, wrapping his arms around me tightly. "Dad! Mom came! I think he shot her!" Luke said between gasps of breath. He was crying hard.

I pulled away, cradling Luke's face in my hands. "What do you mean?"

"She came for me. He told her he would trade me for her. She gave me her phone and told me to run. To call you." Luke was still panting hard, tears pouring down his face.

My heart dropped into my chest.

Nico ran over; his eyes wide.

"Find her," I ordered.

Nico took off toward the rest of the club and started forming a plan.

Jason pulled up in the truck, and I immediately picked up Luke and walked toward the Silverado. I opened the front passenger door before Jason could climb out. "Take him home," I ordered while buckling Luke's seatbelt. "Now."

I watched Jason's jaw clench as he ground his teeth, but I stepped back and slammed the door before he could say anything.

Jason sped off up the block to the intersection, where he flipped a wide U-turn and then barreled past us again.

With Luke now safe, I joined my brothers headed for the house. Nico already had our guys surrounding the run-down shack of a house. I drew my Glock from the back of my pants, not giving a damn who might see it in broad daylight. The Edges was the kind of place where people kept their mouths shut, because they already knew the horror of loss.

When I reached Nico, I patted his shoulder and nodded. Nico kicked in the front door, and I followed behind him.

The ramshackle house had a massive hole in the roof, and there was no furniture inside. It was clear that this was just a meeting point. There was no one there. We took the time to search every square inch thoroughly, but there was nothing.

"Fuck!" I roared. I turned and punched the wall, breaking through the drywall in my fury.

Nico kicked in the closet door, yelling in anguish.

Maya was gone.

Nico "Dagger" Gage

I was furious and heartbroken all at the same time. We had *barely* been seven minutes behind Maya. Between organizing the crew, the five-minute drive and then deciding the plan of attack, barely seven minutes had passed from the time Maya had called Marcos and our arrival to save her.

It hadn't mattered though. She was gone.

We searched it all again, but it was pointless.

Our guys started shouting outside, and I ran out the door, only to come up short beside Marcos. Six heavily armored SUVs had pulled up, and men clad in suits were climbing out of the vehicles.

The Seratelli crime family.

I stalked toward my cousin, Leonardo Seratelli, the head of the family and business. Our Don. "You're late."

Leonardo's head whipped toward me. He buttoned his suit jacket and clenched his jaw. "We got here as soon as we could." Leonardo was the same age as me, at forty years old. He had a full head of black hair that was coiffed back away from his handsome face. He was tall and broad shouldered with tanned olive skin and the same blue eyes that I had. "I've brought you thirty men."

I couldn't even feel gratitude for the fact that my cousin had dropped everything and brought me a small army of trained killers. It hadn't mattered. "She's gone," I muttered. "We got here too late. We found Luke, but she had already traded herself to free him. Hillcrest had already moved out, taking her with him."

Leonardo clenched his jaw and grabbed me by the shoulder. He pulled me in so our foreheads were touching, and we were staring into each other's eyes. Leo's gaze was hard as he met mine. "I promise you, cousin. We will do everything we can to get your woman back."

Tears welled in my gaze at the intense promise from Leo. I nodded. "Yeah."

Leo nodded as well. He squeezed my shoulder before letting go and turning away, immediately barking orders to his crew. "Spread out. Canvas the neighborhood. Knock on doors. Find out if anyone saw anything. You tell them Leonardo Seratelli is looking for Dax Hillcrest!"

The weight of Leonardo's words barely registered. My cousin was declaring open war on Hillcrest on behalf of me and the Devil's Psychos. It was monumental, and I should be more grateful. But I couldn't wrap his mind around the fact that Maya was gone—*again*.

"Thank you," I murmured in a daze. I wasn't sure if Leo even heard me as he was already on the phone a few feet away.

Marcos walked over and pulled me into a hug. "I need you to stay strong, brother." Marcos hand wrapped around the back of my neck, holding me tight, grounding me.

"I just got her back," I breathed.

"I know, brother. I know." Marcos's voice was tight, emotion choking his throat.

"We'll get her back, if it's the last thing we do."

Chapter Three

Jason "Stone" Langford

ANGER RAGED INSIDE ME, blocking out most of the pain that radiated from my gunshot wounds. I was pissed that I wasn't out there helping search for Maya, that I had to play babysitter to her son. Guilt coursed through me the second I thought that, though. Luke was the most important thing to Maya, and she would want one of us watching him and keeping him safe.

My injuries shouldn't be taken lightly either. It was the first day I was even conscious, let alone up and about. I really needed to go lie down.

Luke was a nervous wreck, though. He kept pacing the living room, tears rolling down his face. I at least at the sense to clean the cuts on Luke's face and hand the kid an ice pack to help with swelling. We would need to teach him how to fight as soon as possible. He needed to know how to defend himself.

Elaine Henderson had also been beside herself since I hobbled into the house with a crying Luke. I had to break the news to Maya's mom that she'd been kidnapped by the very man that had been stalking her for the last ten years. "She never should have come back here," Elaine muttered to herself.

I ground my teeth, clenching my jaw to keep from snapping at the woman. She'd been nothing short of horrible to Maya most of her life. Even when Maya dropped everything, put her own life at risk to come back here and take care of her injured parents after a car accident almost killed them, Elaine had still treated Maya like a servant.

"I should call Jenna," Elaine said.

"Not yet," I snapped. "Let's hold off on notifying anyone yet. I don't need another hysterical woman to deal with."

Elaine turned to me with a death glare. "You will not sit in my house and disrespect me."

"I'm not trying to be disrespectful. I'm just saying, let's hold off before you call her. There's nothing she can do from up in Chicago, and she's just going to rush right down here and put herself in danger. Hillcrest would love nothing more than to grab another Henderson sister. Especially if he could use Jenna against Maya."

Elaine's face paled as her eyes widened in shock. *Yeah, she still doesn't want anything to happen to her precious Jenna,* I thought.

"When is my dad coming home?" Luke asked.

I shifted from my prone position on the recliner to look over at Luke as he paced the living room. "I don't know buddy, he and Nico are going to look all over the city. They have friends helping and Nico's family."

Luke started to get teary-eyed again. "I really want my dad."

"Come here, buddy," I said, lowering my voice, making it softer. I knew I wasn't the best person to be comforting the scared and nervous family right now, but for Luke, I would try.

Luke walked over and stood next to my recliner.

I pulled him over the arm of the chair and onto my lap, wrapping an arm around his waist and holding him tight. "Let's FaceTime your dad and see where he's at, alright?"

"Kay," Luke whimpered, trying to be brave.

I pulled out my phone and quickly started a FaceTime call with Marcos. He didn't answer right away, and just when I thought he wasn't going to answer at all, he did. "Hey buddy," Marcos said, seeing Luke's face on the screen.

Luke broke down in tears immediately upon seeing Marcos. "Dad!"

"Aww buddy. I know you're scared, but your mom's going to be alright. I promise you we're doing everything we can to find her."

Marcos tried to reassure him. "I'll be home by bedtime, ok? Give me a couple more hours and then I'll come home."

Luke nodded, seemingly appeased by that. He wiped his eyes and took a deep breath. "You promise?" *Way to break a dude's heart, little guy,* I thought.

"I promise, Lucas. I will be home," Marcos said.

"'k."

"Alright, we'll see you later," I said, turning the camera toward my face before I hung up the call. I rubbed a hand over Luke's back, and the kid melted into my side. I hugged Luke to me and settled in for the long haul.

Elaine put on some mindless action movie, something we'd all seen a million times, and the three of us settled down, trying to relax.

Twenty minutes later, there was a knock at the front door, and I jerked my head at the sound, cursing myself for being so distracted. Looking through the large picture window that took up most of the front wall, I saw Kara and Kevin standing at the front door.

"Auntie Kara!" Luke exclaimed. Kara gave a little wave, and Luke jumped up to unlock the door.

"Hey buddy," Kara greeted with a sad smile on her face. She immediately bent over and hugged him tightly to her.

Kevin "Rockstar" Adams walked past her into the house, arms laden with heavy grocery bags. I nodded to the man as he walked by. "How's the wounds?" Kevin asked, and I thought that was more tactful than asking how I was doing. Because anyone would know, I wasn't doing well.

"Sore," I answered.

Kevin set all the grocery bags on the dining room table.

"Have you taken anything?" Kara asked, looking over at me.

I shook my head. "Not since we left this morning for the game."

Kara frowned. "Where are the pills?" She didn't wait for me to answer though; she headed down the hall and into Maya's bedroom like she'd been here before.

It took me a minute to realize that Kara probably had been here before. She'd been friends with Maya since college, and even if they had a falling out in the last decade, they had still been close once.

Kevin busied himself in the kitchen, and Luke started helping him unload the grocery bags, keeping up a steady stream of chatter with the other man.

Kara returned a moment later, her long blond hair draped over her shoulder and the bottle of pain pills in her hand. She went into the kitchen and poured a glass of water before she returned to the living room. "Here," she said, handing me the pills and the water.

I didn't argue with her. I downed both pills and the glass of water, drinking the whole thing down in two large gulps.

Kevin entered the living room carrying a plate.

I took the plate that I was handed and looked down at the sub sandwich and chips. "Thanks," I muttered.

"Elaine, you hungry? We brought dinner." Kara spoke gently to the older woman.

Elaine shrugged and slowly stood from the couch. "Maybe just a bit," she admitted.

Kara smiled and set about making up plates.

After we finished eating dinner, Kevin caught my eye and nodded at the backdoor. Catching his drift, I slowly stood up, feeling better after the medicine and food. Instead of going out back though, I walked over to the garage door and headed out there instead. I hit the button for the overhead door to open, then grabbed a couple of the lawn chairs stacked in the corner.

"Let me," Kevin said, grabbing the chairs before I could lift them.

"Thanks," I grunted.

"That shoulder has to be killing you."

"Bit better now."

Once we were both seated, Kevin pulled out a bag of joints from the front pocket of his leather Ravager Knights cut. He opened the baggie and pulled one out. Kevin slipped the joint between his lips and held a lighter to the end, sucking on it while he lit up. Once the joint was good and lit, he passed it to me while he slowly blew out the smoke.

"Thanks," I muttered. Taking the joint, I took a long, slow drag. I passed the joint back while I held in the smoke, letting it settle into my lungs.

We were silent for a while, both of us puffing on the joint and passing it back and forth. It was the kind of comradery you'd expect from people that were friends for years and didn't need small talk to fill the silence. It didn't matter that Kevin and I were barely acquaintances; we shared a like mind and the same traumatic pain. It wasn't that long ago that Kara had been kidnapped by Las Serpientes.

"I hear you've got the Seratelli's helping out."

I nodded slowly, my eyes watching the street beyond the driveway. It was a beautiful late summer evening, and the weather didn't reflect the pain I felt inside.

"Yeah. Nico's cousin is Leonardo."

"Thought I heard something along those lines."

"They're newly reacquainted. After some shit went down years ago, they had stopped talking. Nico went to him not that long ago, trying to set up the sit down between them and the Knights, and for help with Carmichael. He had to pay some dues to the family, but it worked out in the long run. Let's hope Seratelli keeps his word."

"He will." Kevin nodded his head once. "I don't know him, but just in the simple dealings we've had with him, he's honorable."

I nodded slowly, my brain fuzzy as the Mary Jane worked its magic on my mind and body. The throbbing in my wounds had finally diminished enough that I almost forgot they hurt at all. "How'd you handle it? When Kara was gone?"

Kevin hissed out a breath and shook his head. "I didn't. We didn't, not really." He ran a hand through his black spiky hair, making it stick up more. "It was the hardest time of my life."

"We haven't been in a good place," I admitted.

"Kara filled me in a little. Hillcrest has been harassing Maya for the last ten years?"

"Pretty much. Come to find out that he was the reason she left, and Buckley might have been involved even back then."

"Shit," Kevin hissed.

"Yep."

"That's a lot to wrap your head around."

"Yeah. How do you just move past the pain of that? Do you just get back together like nothing happened?" I mused through the thoughts that had been plaguing me. "Nico seems to think so."

"That's a tough one. Clearly, you still care about her." Kevin pulled out another joint and lit it up, taking a long drag.

"I don't think that I ever stopped. Maya was it for me, back then. She's been the girl I've compared everyone else to. No one else ever measured up, never even came close."

"Then I guess you have to figure out how to move past that heartbreak in your mind. But brother, I'm telling you—at the end of the day, it doesn't matter. Especially after she comes out of this ordeal with Hillcrest. When their life is in danger, nothing else matters but holding them alive and well in your arms. You'll see when you get her back. Things like this put life into perspective, and you realize life is too short to hold on to heartbreak." Kevin passed me the joint as he slowly let out a stream of smoke.

I accepted the joint and mulled over his words while I took a drag. It was sage advice, offered from a levelheaded man who understood explicitly the pain that I was feeling—at least the shared misery and fear of our loved one being kidnapped. "Thanks."

"No problem." Kevin nodded slowly. "Our clubs may not be on the best of terms, but we're still family. Kara and Marcos ensure that regardless of the colors we wear. We're here for you guys."

I appreciated that more than I could admit. "Thank you," I nodded. "We'll get the club shit figured out too. Nico is working on Seratelli to get you guys a sit down."

"Appreciate that," Kevin said. "Things got more complicated when we started dating a lawyer, and all the shit Mac signed us up for before he passed. It wasn't a club vote."

I huffed out a laugh. "Yeah, we're seeing a lot of that in the clean-up from Buckley's death. It's been a pain in the fucking ass."

Kevin also huffed out a laugh, and I felt the unease lift off my heart for at least a bit. I was still worried and terrified that something was happening to Maya, but being injured, there wasn't much I could do to add to her search. "It would really help if we had a tech guy who could find Hillcrest. He's been a ghost."

Kevin's mouth slowly opened, then closed again. "I may have someone who can help with that."

I raised an eyebrow at the man as he puffed on the joint.

"My brother is a tech guy. He helped find Carmichel when we were looking for him last year. I'll give him a call."

Relief had my shoulders sagged; there may be hope for Maya yet.

Maya

P AIN. PAIN ERUPTED THROUGH my body. It was my first thought as I slowly came back into consciousness. It radiated outwards from my shoulder and ribs. The rest of my body throbbed as well.

I'd been shot.

The memory had my eyes snapping open. Bright light blinded me, and I immediately closed my eyes, groaning.

A nasally laugh greeted me, forcing me to focus on my surroundings. I tried to open my eyes again, but there were bright lights aimed at me, forcing me to keep my eyes down, unable to take in my surroundings. "Welcome back, whore."

Fear raced down my spine. I knew that voice. The voice of my nightmares.

I looked around wildly, eyes squinting, trying to find him.

He laughed, as if he were taking joy in my terror. "Finally, I have you right where I want you."

I tried to sit up, tried to move, and realized I was strapped down to some kind of hospital bed or gurney, because I was angled up, so I was almost standing, and I was naked. Very fucking naked. I couldn't move, no matter how much I pulled or yanked my limbs. My breathing labored as I began to panic. I was trapped.

Hillcrest laughed again, his voice coming from somewhere in the shadows of the room. I could make out the brief outlines of the tripods of the construction lamps that were aimed at me. For some reason, I was lit up like I was on stage.

"Please," I murmured.

"Oh no, my little whore," Hillcrest moved through the room. "Your men have cost me a lot of money, so I'm going to use you to make that money back."

My head fell listlessly to the side; my mind swam. I had no idea what he was talking about.

Hillcrest was one who enjoyed the sound of his own voice—despite that it was nasally and of a higher pitch than most men—so I didn't have to wait long for him to explain things. "You see, I've had a deal with the Devil's Psychos president, Larry Buckley, for years. He made me money. In return, the bastard got what he wanted: his dogs kept on a tight leash and you out of the picture."

I frowned, my eyebrows pulling together as I tried to work through what he had just told me. Dax Hillcrest had been working with Buckley? For years?

"It was like the stars aligned for me that night you witnessed me murdering the mayor. When I told Buckley who you were, he told me how much you'd been a problem for him. How you distracted his top guys. How you shook things up in the clubhouse on party nights. How your little disrespectful mouth kept starting fights between the sluts at the clubhouse. Buckley was fucking over the moon when I told him my plan to drive you away. Granted, he wanted me to kill you, but I knew I could use you one day."

I felt like my mind was treading through water as I tried to keep up with what he was saying. Hillcrest and Buckley had been friends for the last decade? Buckley had wanted me gone? I always knew he was a snake, but to actually be connected to Las Serpientes for so long? He really had been their snake.

"Why?" My voice was raspy and low.

Hillcrest laughed evilly. "Why what, little whore? You'll have to be more specific, because I already told you why Buckley wanted you gone. As for me?" He laughed again. "Because it was fun? Because seeing the terror in your beautiful amber eyes every single time you got a new bouquet was like a hit of dopamine to the brain. And I became addicted."

Fear ran down my spine. He was deranged. He got off on my fear. There would be no saving me from this man. I would not be able to play on his baser instincts to plead for release. He wasn't wired like everyone else.

"Please, God," I begged.

Hillcrest's evil laughter was my only answer.

Marcos

D ESPAIR WEIGHED ME DOWN as I pulled into the Henderson's driveway. I drove my Harley all the way up the long driveway and turned it around near the garage, parking it with its front end facing the street so I could make a fast get-away if I needed to.

The sun was just beginning to set, but I could feel the weariness settling into my bones. Nico had decided to stay out with our club brothers and the Seratelli's, which was good, because I needed to be home for Luke, and relieve Jason.

Finding that my sister, Kara, and one of her guys were still at the house alleviated some of my burden. I had called her after getting off the phone with Luke, explaining what had happened and asking if she wouldn't mind checking in on them.

Jason was in no shape to take care of a child, and Elaine was never all that motherly to begin with. I couldn't imagine how she was coping with everything. The last thing Luke needed was to hear her brand of *love* being spouted in front of him. No.

I was grateful my sister had said she would head right over; I was even more happy that one of her guys had accompanied her. The last thing I needed to worry about was her safety while I tried to find Maya.

The garage door was closed, and a faint smell of weed drifted from under the door. I hoped it had helped Jason calm the fuck down. I used my keys to open the front door before anyone in the living could get up.

Luke jumped up from where he was cuddling Kara on the couch and flung himself into my arms. He immediately began to cry while he clung to me.

Tears welled in my own eyes as I held my son tightly, picking him up completely. "I know, buddy, I know." I met Kara's gaze and saw that tears were already slipping down her face.

Kevin wrapped his arm around Kara and pulled her against him, giving me a nod. "We should go; give you guys some space."

"No!" Luke shouted! "Auntie Kara, please don't go!" Luke scrambled out of my hold and ambled over to her, climbing into her lap to wrap his arms around her neck.

"Oh, buddy," Kara breathed, holding him closer. She rubbed his back while she rocked him slightly.

Marcos sighed heavily. "Luke, baby. She can't stay. She has to get home to her baby."

Luke wailed louder, his sobs wracking his small body.

Kara's face scrunched in pain, as if Luke's misery was killing her.

It was killing everyone.

Elaine looked on with tears in her own eyes. "There's an air mattress in the hallway closet," she murmured.

Kara met Kevin's eye. An unspoken conversation passed between the two of them before Kara nodded slowly. "It's alright. Luke, I'll stay the night, ok?"

Luke nodded through his tears, his face pressed into the crook of her neck.

I sagged with relief. God, I didn't know what I would do without my little sister.

Kara wiped her cheeks as she rocked Luke. "I'll need to run home for a bit though. Do you want to see your cousin, Lilah?"

"Can we? Please?" Luke asked, pulling away from Kara to look over at me.

Kara eyed the weary expression on my face. "We could take him with us. Give you guys some time to talk. We took my Lincoln."

My face must have dropped at the suggestion, because Kevin immediately sat forward. "I'll guard them with my life."

I took a deep breath and rubbed my hand over my buzzed head before I nodded slowly. Kara lived in the same neighborhood as Maya's mother. The house she shared with her guys was right around the corner and there would be three big burly bikers there to look after my son. Technically, I had nothing to worry about, but everything was hitting so much harder with Maya kidnapped.

"Yeah, ok," I murmured softly. Seeing Luke perk up had been worth it. I would do anything to help ease the pain my son was feeling.

"I have to pump, so we'll be a little while," Kara said.

I nodded. "I'll change the sheets in Maya's room. You guys can take her bed. We'll crash in Luke's room."

Kara reluctantly agreed.

After they left, I sat heavily on the couch where my sister had been sitting. I leaned forward, resting my elbows on my knees, and hung my head.

Jason and Elaine eyed me warily. "Nothing?" Jason prompted.

"No." I shook my head. "It's like they fucking vanished. We checked all of Las Serpientes known hang outs. The whole fucking gang has gone a ground."

Jason swore and shook his head. "And the Seratelli's?"

I leaned back against the couch and shrugged a shoulder. "They're helping, they're doing everything they can. The extra manpower has been amazing, but still, it's not enough."

"Kevin called his brother, Jack. Apparently, he's some big tech guy in Chicago. He's searching the dark web for Hillcrest."

I felt my spirits lift a bit at the news. "Yeah?"

Jason nodded. "Kevin said Jack was the one that helped them find Kara. So he should be able to help this time around."

"Thank fuck," I sighed, letting my head fall back against the couch and closing my eyes.

"When you say, 'the Seratelli's'" Elaine's voice broke through my thoughts. "You mean, the mafia?"

My eyes snapped open. Fuck. I had forgotten she was in the room.

"Yeah," Jason answered, before I could respond. "The Don is Nico's cousin."

I shot Jason a look that said, *what the fuck dude?*

Jason shrugged a shoulder.

Elaine nodded, as if she expected that. "Well, let's hope they can help. Now, the air mattress is in the hallway closet. Marcos, you'll have to grab it. It's much too heavy for me. You can set it up in Luke's room, but I'm sure Jason would feel better sleeping in the recliner. I know when I had my shoulder surgery, laying down made the pain worse. I slept in that recliner for weeks."

I felt dumbfounded by Elaine's easy-going demeanor and acceptance to the news of the mafia helping to find her daughter. The woman sitting before me was a far cry different from the one that used to berate and belittle Maya growing up. "Right."

"Come on, the sooner you get the air mattress set up, the quicker you can relax." Elaine stood from the loveseat and limped toward the hallway.

I stared after her in shock.

"She's right," Jason grunted.

Shaking my head, I got to my feet and followed after Elaine.

Chapter Six

Nico

I PUNCHED AND JABBED and punched the bag in front of me. Each hit making my knuckles bloodier. Each hit reverberated through me, the pain in my knuckles echoed the pain in my heart.

Our search had been fruitless. We had searched the neighborhood for forty-eight hours straight, taking shifts to sleep, eating only when someone shoved something at us. In the end, Leonardo had called off the neighborhood search. He ordered his guys home and told me to do the same.

I had argued immediately. I had gotten in my cousin's face, almost ruining the tentative relationship we were reforming. In the end, Leo had pulled me into a tight embrace and told me to fight it out at the gym. So I found myself at the family's boxing gym, sparing with a bag for the for the first time in years.

I'd hung a punching bag in my garage at home, but I'd fallen out of practice. Now I was hurting in all the right places, bleeding out, just like my heart.

Forty-eight fucking hours without the love of my life. I couldn't imagine the hell Maya was facing, enduring. I was living in a nightmare every second that passed by without her in my arms.

Fuck my cousin for calling off the neighborhood search. Fuck Marcos for agreeing.

We needed to keep going, keep pushing on. Someone somewhere was bound to crack. They had to have seen something. No one in that neighborhood had loyalties that couldn't be bought. That's what we needed to do; we needed to announce a reward for any information on Maya's whereabouts.

"Nicolai!" Leonardo's deep voice rang out from behind me. His yell indicating he'd been trying to get my attention for a while now.

I stopped hitting the bag, but didn't turn to face my cousin. I grabbed the bag to stop it from swinging and rested my forehead against it as I panted hard and caught my breath.

"Nicolai. You've been here for hours. You need to go home." Leonardo's voice was soft and gentle, yet firm. He was used to getting his way and expected everyone to listen to him, family especially—family specifically.

I had already fucked up my relationship with Leo and the family once, I didn't really want to do so again—not when we were finally back on speaking terms. "I can't." I huffed a sigh, my body deflating at the admission.

"Then go to Marcos or Jason." Leo's patience was something of legend. I never understood how Leo put up with half the stuff he had over the years without lashing out or snapping. He was a firm and steady Don, someone that was easy to respect—but God help the person who did piss him off. Where his patience was legendary, his wrath was fearsome and alarming. They wrote nightmares about the times my cousin had lost his temper.

I never wanted to be on the receiving end of that anger. I shook my head slowly. "They're with Luke. I can't be around him right now. Not like this."

Leo's hand rested on my sweaty shoulder. "Then come with me. You shouldn't be alone right now."

I huffed a humorless laugh. "The mighty Don, stooping to take care of a lowly associate?" I asked, sarcastically.

"No dumbass. A cousin offering assistance to his family in need. Stop looking a gift horse in the mouth and let's go." Leo's tone brokered no argument, but I was too tired to move. I leaned against the bag, feeling the weight of the world crushing down on me as my body slowly succumbed to the lack of sleep and strenuous workout, I just put it through. "Nicolai," Leo said again.

"Yeah." I nodded my head.

"Come on." Leo tugged on my shoulder and dragged me away from the punching bag.

I let my cousin drag me away from the bag. I was dripping with sweat, yet Leonardo didn't seem to mind as he gripped my shoulder and led me away. The boxing gym was twenty-four hours, but the place was empty besides a worker at the front desk. I hadn't even come in with any workout clothes, I had simply peeled off my Devil's Psychos cut and white t-shirt, setting them on the front counter, before I'd stalked over to a bag and began beating the hell out of it, bare knuckles and all.

I was realizing the error of my ways as I slowly uncurled my fingers and flexed my fists over and over. My knuckles were bloody, but nothing felt broken, despite the utter beating I had bestowed upon them.

My cousin handed me my shirt and cut, but I chose not to wear either. I was too sweaty and the idea of slipping into the leather without the shirt sounded like a nightmare to clean. It would only make shit smell. I draped both items over my arm and followed my cousin out into the night.

The humid night air did nothing to cool me down, and I briefly thought about turning around and heading back inside the gym to plant my ass in front of one of the industrial sized fans they had aimed around the place. I knew though that if I sat down, I wouldn't get back up again. I hadn't slept in two days.

There was a blacked-out Escalade waiting for Leonardo, with a motorcycle trailer hitched up to the back of it. I paused in my steps as I realized what Leonardo had planned. "What?" I asked, my mind struggling to keep up.

"You can't ride. Come on, I'll help you strap it down." Leonardo was already pulling off his fancy as fuck suit jacket. He tossed the thing into the Escalade before he rolled up his shirt sleeves.

I felt like I was living in an alternate reality. There was no way my posh as fuck, mafia Don cousin was about to get dirty and help me strap down my Harley to the trailer. How the fuck did he even get his hands on a motorcycle trailer in the first place?

"Marcos called looking for you earlier," Leo said as a way of explanation. "When I found you, I called him for the trailer."

I shook my head in disbelief.

"Come on." Leo nodded toward my bike.

Snapping out of it, I tossed my shirt and cut into the backseat of the Escalade before I turned toward my bike. I pulled the keys out of my pocket and started the engine quickly. It roared to life, loud and unforgiving in the dead of night. Taking a seat on the bike, exhaustion and fatigue weighed severely on me, making the idea of backing my bike out of the parking spot and driving up the short ramp of the trailer feel monumental.

"Come on, cousin. You've got this," Leo said, walking over.

I nodded slowly. Yeah, I could do this. I had to. I sat and put the bike into reverse and slowly eased out of the spot, keeping both feet planted on the ground as I walked the bike backward. When I was clear of the spot, I switched gears and drove up the ramp of the trailer, lining up my wheels between the metal brackets that would hold the bike upright.

"Good," Leo said. He walked up the ramp of the trailer while I put the kickstand down on the motorcycle and shut it off. The silence that fell was deafening, causing my ears to ring.

It didn't take us long to strap down my Harley, ensuring the motorcycle wouldn't move during transit. I was still shocked that my cousin had thought ahead to call Marcos in the first place. "Thanks," I muttered, when we were done.

"Don't mention it," Leo said, his voice gentle. "Come on, get in." He nodded toward the black SUV.

I sighed and followed orders. I had a feeling it wouldn't be the last time I followed my cousin's directions.

Chapter Seven

Maya

I GROANED IN PAIN, my vision blurring. I didn't even try to blink to try to focus my gaze. I didn't need to see what was going on. I've seen enough in the last forty-eight hours. Felt enough.

The lights, the camera, and the toys that had filled and fucked each of my holes. My ass and pussy were sore, my throat scratchy from screaming and pleading. But the worse part of all were the drugs that he kept pumping into my system. A little prick of pain and I was floating above it all.

Dax had started filming me while he fucked me with all sorts of different toys, but I knew it was only a matter of time before he grew bored. He had been live streaming my torture sessions, saying I needed to earn back the money I cost him. Money that he apparently had been getting from President Buckley, but that had dried up when he'd been killed.

I was living in a nightmare. I lost count of how many orgasms he'd forced out of me. Not only did I have the pain of being raped by his toys, I also had the pain of the unhealed gunshot wound in my shoulder. I had a feeling it was infected. It would be just my luck too: kidnapped, shot, an infected wound, and filmed in a revenge-porn plot. All because Buckley didn't like me taking Marcos's, Jason's, and Nico's attention away from the club.

So much pain and heartbreak over the years, all because of greedy fucking men. I had endured so much pain. I just wished for it to be over. The years of psychological torture had worn me down, and now that he had his hands on me, I didn't want to give him any pleasure in my torture.

Not for the first time, I wished he would kill me.

Just end it all.

I would be free.

I didn't even feel guilty anymore as I thought of Luke. He had his father and Jason and Nico. He had a full family unit that would take care of him. He would be ok without me.

Fire erupted in my shoulder and I screamed in agony, jerking against my bindings. White hot fire raced through me as someone poked and prodded at my gunshot wound. "Stop!" I yelled.

"No can do, little whore," Hillcrest crooned, laughing lightly like my pain amused him. "This wound is looking mighty nasty.

We've got to get that bullet out of there." He dug around in my wound again and I screamed and flailed against my bindings. "That's it, little whore. Scream now for the subscribers, they're asking for blood."

Dread barely registered in my mind as the brutal pain overtook me.

Maya

When I woke again, the pain in my body had dimmed. There was a floating feeling again, and my pussy throbbed with need. My pierced nipples ached, a clear sign that clamps—weighted this time—were fastened to them again.

I looked around and realized I was no longer on the medical gurney. Instead, I was draped over U-shaped steel pipes that rose from a floor stand. The pipes came up to waist height, forming a sick and twisted version of monkey bars turned BDSM rack that was meant to exploit and torture.

Between the two metal pipes, my breasts were firmly clamped, with my shoulders and ribs bearing down on the cold steel. With my legs dangling, my hips were uncomfortably supported by a third pipe that pressed painfully into my hipbones. With my arms outstretched across the first bar supporting my shoulders, my wrists were fastened to the steel.

When I tried to move my legs, I found there was a spreader bar holding them apart, and it only slid wider the harder I struggled.

"Well, well, well," Hillcrest said as he walked over to me, holding a hand-held camera. "Our little whore is awake again. Smile prettily for the camera, whore." The camera zoomed in on my face, getting a close-up. I was grateful he hadn't used my name, but I knew it wouldn't last. This man was out to ruin me.

I closed my eyes in shame.

Hillcrest laughed obnoxiously. "Our viewers have been asking for more. And we're here to give the people what they want."

I didn't make a sound. I learned early that Hillcrest enjoyed my whining and crying and begging. He wanted to break me. He wanted my blood and my tears—it made him more money. I prayed to God that whatever dark website that he was uploading to or live streaming on, that my guys never saw them. I didn't want them to see the pain and torment Hillcrest was putting me through. Nico especially. It would break him.

Hillcrest set his phone into the holder on a ring light tripod, and I glanced up wondering what his plan was. He flashed me a wicked grin that made me quickly look away. "Time to up the ante, little whore." He strode around behind me, and I heard the metal clicking off his belt. "Should I just plunge straight into this cunt dry? Or should I make you suck my cock first?"

"Dry," a deep male voice spoke from behind me. There was someone else in the room. That was new. "Get her screams on camera."

I couldn't see whoever was speaking, but it didn't matter. They clearly weren't going to help me. He laughed, "The audience agrees." I heard the *click-clacking* of what sounded like a keyboard before he spoke again. "Oh yes. User TruckerDaddy84 will pay extra if you make her bleed on your cock and then make her lick it clean."

Hillcrest's nasally laugh was the thing of nightmares and it would be sure to haunt mine for the rest of my days. His meaty palms gripped my hips before his heavy cock slid over my ass. "Make it bloody? We can certainly do that, right little whore?"

I squeezed my eyes shut tight. I bit down on my lower lip and dug my fingernails into the metal bars supporting my chest, trying to brace myself for what I knew would be an onslaught of pain.

The scream he tore out of me when he shoved into my bone-dry pussy ravaged my throat. Agony ripped at me. I could feel the tissue shredding as he pulled out and forced himself back in. Every single thrust drove my hipbones harder against the steel pipe they rested on, bruising me bone deep.

Tears poured down my face as I screamed.

Hillcrest laughed as he pulled out, "Look at that blood."

The other man chuckled. "Have her clean it now, then fuck her some more. Here we'll get a close-up."

There were footsteps as the man rounded the rack I was trussed up on. All I could see were baggy blue jeans and heavy work boots. He must have grabbed the camera, light and all, and moved it closer as Dax grabbed a fistful of my hair and yanked my head up from where it had been dangling.

Dax pressed the head of his cock against my lips and I whimpered, but kept my lips closed in a firm line, my teeth clenched behind them. "Oh little whore, you want to be difficult? We have ways around difficult."

He dropped my head and shuffled away momentarily, before he returned. He shoved a pair of hooks on to one side of my cheeks before a rubber band wrapped around the back of my head. I tried to struggle, to no avail, as he yanked my head back by my hair and shoved the other two hooks of the Claw Hook mouth spreader into my mouth on the other side.

I cried out as he tightened the strap behind my head and my cheeks were pulled open wide. No longer able to close my mouth, I cried earnestly as Dax shoved his cock into my awaiting mouth. He was rough and gripped my head hard, "Clean it, little whore."

The other man laughed as Dax thrust his cock deep into my mouth, hitting the back of my throat, gagging me. "Choke on that cock, whore."

I tried to zone out, tried to force myself to dissociate, but the pain was too great. The laughing, the lights, the taste of fucking iron in my mouth as I was forced to clean my blood from his cock would stay with me for the rest of my life.

44

Chapter Eight

Jason

I STARE AROUND THE empty house. It had been over a week since we closed on the property and the painters had made great progress. In fact, they were finished, and I could move on to the next stage of updates I wanted to make to the home: new counter tops.

The granite installers were due any minute. They were going to replace the kitchen counters and bath vanity tops in the bathrooms.

That was how I found myself standing in the empty house, staring at all the blank walls, wondering what the hell I should do next. What would Maya want to change? It was a painful thought, though.

It had been four days since Maya had been taken and we still weren't any closer to finding her. Four long, horrendous days. Nico was a mess. Marcos was barely holding it together, trying to keep Luke on schedule with school and homework and football practice.

And Luke... Luke was not having any of it. He didn't want to go to school, or practice, or do homework. He was argumentative with everyone, but with Marcos especially. Kara seemed to be the only that could get through to him, but she still had her hands full with a baby at home.

We needed Maya back. Fuck, did we need Maya back.

I was pulled from my thoughts at the sound of the back door opening. Turning my head, I watched a dazed-looking Nico walk into the kitchen. His eyes were bloodshot and I wondered if he was stoned or hadn't slept in days. "What the hell man?" I asked.

Nico met my gaze and sighed. "Leo dropped me off. Said I needed to get my shit together and face my family."

I snorted. "Yeah, sounds about right."

Nico nodded, not even the slightest bit offended by my gruff response. "Yeah. So what's next? We're waiting on Jack Adams to find something. We're waiting on Leo's people to find something. Our guys are searching everything we know as well. What are we supposed to do in the meantime?"

"I've been standing here thinking the same thing. Paint is done; the granite guys should be here any minute. I found myself asking what would Maya want?"

"New carpet," Nico answered immediately. "She loved how fluffy the carpets were upstairs when we first moved in. They had been brand new. Re-carpet upstairs and the living room here. Re-finish the hardwood everywhere else."

I hmphed and shook my head. "I've been standing here for forty minutes trying to figure that out, and you knew it immediately."

Nico carded his fingers through his blond hair and shrugged a shoulder. "I just remember everything from back then. I relived it as much as possible, trying to figure out what went wrong and to never forget her. She was my everything."

I hung my head, staring at the floor. Nico's dedication to Maya was admirable and humbling. It reminded me that I treated her like complete shit for the last seven months that she had been back and kept pushing her away.

The part that killed me the most, though, was that Nico had seen through her bullshit. He had known she was lying the whole time, but he didn't push through her boundaries. I thought I had been able to read her pretty well back then. I should have seen the lies this time. Fuck. I had seen the lies; I just couldn't get her to talk to me. Instead, I had lost my fucking temper and choked her in the dining room after a family dinner. Great way to fucking get her to trust me.

And while Nico was busy remembering everything there ever was about Maya, reliving their past, I had been busy trying to forget her by drowning myself in pussy for the last decade. It wasn't until she had returned last January that I stopped fucking around as much. After the Devil Chaser I had fucked on the side of Kara's house at the spring party, I hadn't touched another slut since—not after I saw the pain firsthand on Maya's beautiful face.

It had ripped my heart out.

I had fucked up so epically where Maya was concerned, I didn't know a way to begin fixing things. So I threw myself into the remodel of the house. It was the only thing I felt like I had any control on. I didn't care if I drained my savings doing so. I would make this house the home of Maya's dreams.

"Carpet for sure," Nico murmured. "We should also start working on Luke's room. I think she'd want him to have a cool bedroom."

"Yeah." I nodded. "Yeah, we could get him involved, maybe? Maybe it will give him something to be excited about?"

"How's he been doing?"

"Not good. He's arguing constantly with Marcos and Elaine. He doesn't want to go to school or do homework. e's more aggressive at football practice. The coach said he might have to bench him for the game if he doesn't cool it."

Nico sighed heavily. "I wondered if that might happen."

"Yeah. Marcos doesn't know what to do. Kara's been around a lot, helping out. Luke really likes her, but she's got Lilah too."

Nodding, Nico folded his hands behind his head and locked his fingers together. "What if we took him to the gym? I hit the bag for the first time in a long time again, and Leo's gym offers youth classes. What if we taught him to box? MMA?"

"You want to teach an angry kid how to fight?" I countered.

"I want to give an angry kid a safe outlet to release that pent up rage. Come on, Stone, he's hurting. We're all fucking hurting here. Let's teach him to defend himself. He's old enough, and I bet he rocks at it."

"We should run that by Marcos first, but yeah."

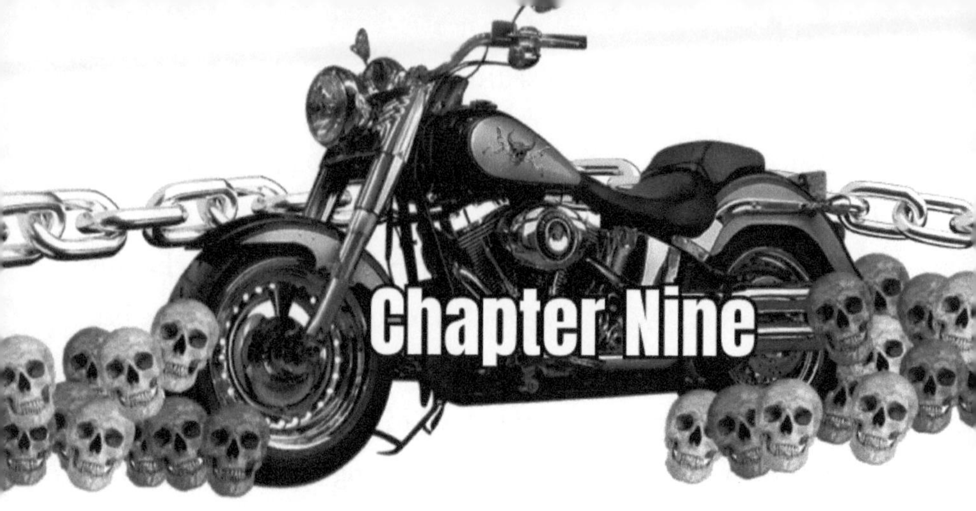

Chapter Nine

Marcos

I WAS WORKING ON my laptop in Elaine's dining room, going over bills and bank statements for the clubhouse, when Elaine walked in from the living room carrying a piece of paper. I eyed her warily, wondering what she was up to.

Elaine had been cordial enough in the last five days that we had invaded her house. She'd said she didn't mind the company, was grateful for it with Maya gone, but she was still curt with us at times. Neither Jason nor I were much for small talk, but we had to be there for Luke. We wanted to keep him comfortable and in his own home.

Despite the occasional awkwardness of being in Elaine's house, we tried to be supportive and understanding of her inability to drive due to a spinal injury from a car accident last autumn. I had club prospects driving her to doctor appointments and grocery shopping for us. Nickle's old lady had dropped off a couple cooked meals, so there was always something to eat.

I did my best to treat her with respect, even if she was a cranky old broad sometimes. "Whatchu got there?" I asked, nodding at the paper in her hands.

Elaine looked up at me and gave me a pensive look. "I went through Maya's sock drawer," she admitted, shuffling the paper in her hands. "Tomorrow will be a week, and I don't know if she's still coming back or not, but I think you should have this."

"Elaine, we have everyone in the county working on it. We'll get her back. I promise," I said, frowning.

Elaine forced a smile on her aging face and shrugged a shoulder. "Either way," she spoke softly. "I think you should have this." She handed over the folded paper she'd been holding.

I took the paper, frowning. Slowly opening it, my eyes widen in shock at what I read on the document. *Official Cook County Birth Certificate.* I scanned the paper in disbelief. There in black and white it spelled out, Lucas Nicolai *Candella*, with his birthdate for November 11th, almost ten years prior. And under the father's name? *Marcos Candella.*

"Holy shit," I let out a heavy breath, rubbing a hand over my head. "Did she just do this?"

"No, she's always had your name on his birth certificate. It's been my biggest argument for telling you sooner. Why keep it from you if she was going to name you as his parent?"

"Why indeed," I muttered.

"I thought you should have that in case anything happens at the school. She listed you as his father on his registration papers too, if anything were to come up."

I looked up and met her gaze with my own watery stare. "Thank you, Elaine."

She patted my hand and nodded her head. "I'm sorry I'm difficult most of the time, but I saw the way you treated her back then. How the three of you cherished her. I would see you all around town sometimes and Jenna kept me updated. Maya was happy with you."

I cleared my throat and blinked away the tears that gathered in my eyes. I hadn't expected this from Maya's stoic mother. "Thank you." I nodded.

Marcos

"Have you heard anything from your brother?" I didn't wait for preamble as I walked into Kara's house later that night. It was a

Friday evening, and instead of heading to the clubhouse, I was taking Luke to meet Nico at the boxing gym. But first we had to stop by Kara's so Luke could see his aunt for a bit.

It was the perfect excuse for me to check in with Kevin. Once again, I found the black-haired man washing bottles at the kitchen sink. "Nothing good," Kevin sighed. "He's struggling to find Hillcrest, meaning Hillcrest has some high-tech firewalls, or someone in the government covering for him."

"The government?" I snapped. "Like the damn mayor?"

"No, like the fucking FBI," Kevin elaborated. "Someone who is able to erase and hide information. Jack hasn't tried hacking them yet, but he will if he has to."

"Fucking hack them already! Find my fucking woman!" I growled.

Kevin nodded. "Yeah, man. He'll get on it."

I stalked passed Kevin, grumbling to myself about not beating the fuck out of the guy because it would upset my sister, when I turned the corner and ran smack into a wall of muscles. Johnny "Mayhem" Taylor had been walking toward the living room when I ran right into him. "Easy," Johnny muttered, gripping my shoulder.

Wrenching my shoulders out of Johnny's grip, not in the mood to deal with the temperamental biker, I tried to push past him and search for my sister. Only Johnny wasn't having it. "You're not going to come into this house and bring your shitty attitude around my woman and my kid, you hear me, *brother*?" Johnny growled, getting in my face.

All fight drained out of me at the reminder that the two of us had unfinished business. I had forgotten all about the fact that I shared a father with Johnny. It was something we'd learned last year. It hadn't seemed all that important in the grand scheme of things, though. It had explained some of the backstory regarding my mother's history and the history between Vince Carmichael and Mac Taylor. It also explained why Carmichael had it out for Mac Taylor.

Johnny had given me our father's journal, but I had only glanced it over. I never had a burning need to know who my father was or track him down growing up. I had been raised by a very strong woman, and while she had made some mistakes when she was younger, I didn't fault her. Not one bit.

"Yeah, brother," I conceded. I didn't need to be starting shit with Mayhem. Not when things had finally settled down between the two clubs, and especially not when my sister was practically married to the guy.

Johnny's metaphorical hackles lowered and he patted me on the shoulder. "We're here to help man. We'll get her back. I promise you, I know how it feels."

I hissed and turned away. Even that little reminder to when my sister had been kidnapped was not something I needed at the moment. "Yeah, but my sister was held as collateral. Hillcrest has been obsessed with Maya for the last ten years."

"We'll get her back, man," Johnny said again, his tone brokering no argument.

I could only nod. "Hey, uh, I'm sure Adams already told you, but I thought you should hear it from me too. The Seratelli's are working heavily with us on this. Nico made peace with his family."

Johnny rubbed at his bearded jaw with his knuckles and nodded slowly. "I appreciate the transparency. Any word on a sit down?"

"I'll press Leonardo myself for it after Maya's found."

"Understood."

"The bratva giving you a hard time?" I asked.

Johnny shook his head. "Not yet. They're icing us out currently, which isn't great either. But Tarasov said he wouldn't talk to us unless we cut ties with the Italians. So I'm not expecting anything until afterwards."

I sighed and rubbed a hand over my head. "Yeah."

Marcos

Luke's first lesson at the boxing gym was a thing of beauty, and a learning experience for me too.

Nico was an amazing fighter and had the patience of a saint. He walked Luke through each move step by step. Teaching him how to land his hit on the bag as to not break his own knuckles or wrist.

Seeing Nico in his element, teaching and boxing, had shown me how much being stuck at the clubhouse working on cars was draining him. It was like life was being poured back into Nico. Despite our current worries, Nico was happy teaching Luke how to box.

Luke had taken to boxing like a fish to water. Once his hands were in gloves, that Nico had pulled out of his duffle bag, he had immediately tried swinging on the bag, only to realize how fucking hard it actually was. Filled with sand and covered in layers of leather, it was not an easy hit.

I stepped away while Nico taught, letting both Luke and Nico get lost in the lesson. I hung back for a while watching, before he headed over to the weight machines and started lifting. I could at least burn off some energy of my own while they worked.

I was on my back, doing bench presses when a shadow loomed over me. Turning my head to the side, I saw none other than Leonardo Seratelli standing before me in a black three-piece suit that was clearly tailored and perfectly coifed hair. I would think he was a pansy if not for how ruthless the motherfucker was known to be. "Seratelli."

"Candella." Leo nodded his head in greeting.

I racked the bar and sat up. Facing Seratelli, I rested my elbows on my knees. "Find anything?"

"One of the mothers in The Edges came forward. She said she saw a young woman being shot before she was thrown over a shoulder of a guy with a jagged scar across his face and tossed into a trunk of a late model white Buick Sabre."

"We knew most of that already." I didn't need to hear the gruesome details on how my woman was hurt and kidnapped. I already knew she was. I needed to know *where* she was.

"Yeah. It's about all we got though. People are talking at least."

I could only nod. I was drowning in misery and didn't know how to track down Maya anymore.

"I've got a tech guy on it," Seratelli continued, before I could say anything. "He's searching for any cameras in the area and hoping to trail after the Buick. The Edges aren't known for the security cameras though."

"Only two ways out of The Edges, though," Marcos said.

"Exactly. My guy is good. He'll find the car, eventually."

"I've got a tech guy working on it too. Looking into a possible FBI connection. Looks like Hillcrest is highly protected from someone high in the government."

"Who's your guy?" Seratelli asked.

"Who's yours?" I countered, meeting his gaze.

Seratelli's lips twitched slightly. "My brother, Stefano."

I didn't know if I was surprised or not by Seratelli's confession, but I met him on the transparency front. "My sister is dating the Ravager Knights' vice president, Kevin Adams. He reached out to his brother, Jack. He's some big tech guy in Chicago."

Seratelli let out a surprised bark of laughter. "Jack Adams is looking for Dax Hillcrest? I'm surprised he hasn't found him yet."

"Like I said, Hillcrest is being protected by someone in the FBI—according to Kevin—but he's going to hack the FBI and see what he can find. I guess it's why it's taking so long."

Seratelli shook his head, falling serious again. "How does a fucking gangbanger get so powerful?"

"No idea. He'd been working with our dead president for the last decade or so. Pushing Maya away, framing Nico, killing Mac Taylor. Whatever deal Buckley and Hillcrest had, it earned Hillcrest a lot of money."

"Big money and big protection," Seratelli surmised, shoving his hands into his pockets.

"Yep."

A lull fell between us and Seratelli looked over at his cousin teaching Luke how to box. "He's yours?"

I turned to watch the pair as well, nodding. "Yeah. He's nine."

"Nico looks good teaching. Relaxed."

"Yeah." I huffed out a breath. "He's been miserable the last ten years. I just hadn't realized how miserable."

"Hopefully when Maya is returned, he finds happiness again."

"Yeah, hopefully."

Chapter Ten

Axel Jones

I SURVEYED THE BUSTLING warehouse, my gaze sweeping from the scantily clad women to the shirtless fighters weaving through the crowd near the fighting ring. Men and women offering the promise of something a little *more*, for the right price.

Bookies hung out in the corners making deals and taking bets, while dealers weaved in between the throng of people, offering party favors of the harder variety. Along one wall there was a make-shift bar area, selling overpriced drinks to uncaring patrons.

Over all it was a cluster fuck of epic proportions and my boys and I were right in the middle of it.

Blaze Thomas and Phoenix Kendrick had been by my side since we were kids growing up in a lower middle-class neighborhood in

Creekton. In the kind of neighborhood where our parents worked their asses off to provide a roof over our heads and look picture perfect to the public. But things behind closed doors weren't what they seemed—at least in my case.

I had a picture-perfect home life until I hit high school and my younger brother, Andrew, had been killed by Dax Hillcrest and Las Serpientes. My brother, who had been the light of our family, had been in the wrong place at the wrong time. We had stopped by the convenience store after school, something we probably did almost every day, only to walk into an armed robbery.

Hillcrest had just been an upstart back then, but he had been spooked when the door of the store opened. He shot off two rounds right into Andrew's chest. My brother had been dead before the ambulance even showed up.

And fucking Hillcrest had ran away.

There had been no camera's, no proof, and it was mine and my friend's word against ghosts. Literal ghosts. The police had never found the men that been in the store. It wasn't until Blaze, Phoenix, and I had joined up with the Devil's Psychos did I learn the truth. Using the club's connections and another fight night—similar to this one—did I discover who had killed my brother.

Now we were here to find out anything we could on Hillcrest's whereabouts.

The underground fighting scene had been around for years, but no one knew who ran it. With how organized everything was, I could only assume they were mafia run, but Nico had never said anything. The fights changed location every month, with the location only being texted out an hour or two before they started.

It was very much a *who you knew* situation.

"Spread out." I kept my voice low, and despite the loud music pumping through the speakers, my brothers heard me. Like a unit, the three of us went our separate ways.

I slid through the crowd toward the bar. Slipping my hands in my pockets, I waited for someone to notice me. I felt naked without my cut, but it was the rules: no colors. No one was allowed to wear anything that showed which gang or MC or crew they were affiliated with. Not that it mattered when half the men in the room had tatted their colors on their bodies.

Listening to the surrounding conversations while I waited, I crossed my arms over my chest, trying to appear nonchalant. My plan was apparently working when I picked up a conversation to my right.

"Yo, have you guys seen the live streams?" a man asked.

Another man laughed heartily. "You mean the whore he kidnapped?"

Douche number one laughed. "Hell yeah. She's a hot little thing too. Curves for days, tattoos, tits pierced, like damn. It's a shame a chick like that got picked up by the snakes."

I had to clench my jaw to keep from saying something. I needed to hear more. I pulled my phone out of my pocket and shot off a quick text.

"Probably taken from some unsuspecting sucker. Shoulda had her on a leash." Douche number two said.

Douche one laughed. "Or she's right where she's meant to be."

"Oh man," I forced a hearty laugh. "You guys talkin' 'bout the new videos?" I inserted myself into the conversation with the men to my right, turning to face them. I scanned their faces, taking in every detail and committing it to memory.

Two men that were too skinny and lanky with stringy hair. One had dark hair while the other was a dirty shade of blond and oily. Both were probably barely old enough to drink. I wondered how the hell the two of them even got invited to the fight, let alone knew about the website.

The two twerpy derps smiled as they looked over at him. "Yeah, bro. It was insane. He had her up on this rack, with weights hanging from her tits. Fuck dude."

"Did they change the link again? I tried to get in and was moved." I played it cool, for the two idiots that had no idea what they were in for.

Only one of them seemed to hesitate, but the other immediately laughed and nodded. "Always do, don't they? Here, I can send it to you. What's your number?"

Like a damn idiot, douche one pulled out his phone and sent a link to me. I checked that I received it before I forced a grin to my face and nodded like a fool. "Hell yeah, man. Thanks for this. His live streams are the best."

"They really are! Hey man, I'm Jimmy and this is Pete."

"Steve," I replied, shaking Jimmy's hand.

Jimmy and Pete were so distracted by me; they didn't even see Blaze and Phoenix come up behind them. Both men tagged a small, barely there tracking device into the back pockets of thing one's and thing two's jeans.

"Steve, bro! Where you been?" Phoenix grinned broadly, pushing between the two twerps to shake my hand and slap me on the shoulder. "Fights are about to start! We should head up front!"

"I was gonna get a drink, but service sucks up here." I shrugged and laughed. "Come on!" I patted Phoenix on the shoulder and turned away, only to glance back at his new friends. "Hey guys, you wanna check things out from up front? We've got VIP!"

"Hell yeah, we do!" Jimmy cheered.

It took everything in me not to punch the dude in the face. I turned my back on the twerps and stalked off toward the ring in the center of the room. Fights were about to start and while I hadn't lied about VIP, I also didn't want the twerps to know why we had ringside seats.

Walking up to the rope, I sped up to meet the guard first. I slapped hands with Nick, the guard, and pulled him in close. "Name's Steve tonight. Working some recon."

Nick didn't even bat an eye. He laughed and slapped me on the back. "My man, Steve!" he greeted, his voice booming.

"Hey, man." I forced a grin. "I brought a couple friends with us, that cool?"

"Oh yeah, yeah! No problem. You got it!" Nick said.

"Dude, this is so cool!" Jimmy yelled over the crowd.

"Totally!" Pete cheered.

"Yeah man. Anything for a couple of like-minded guys, like yourselves. It's rare to find people that also enjoy the darker aspects of life."

Jimmy and Pete took the compliments and ran with it. "Yeah dude! Like I love it when a bitch is put in her place! You should watch the latest video from last night. It was so sick. He had her up in this rack, while he fucked her raw."

I clenched my jaw to keep from responding.

Phoenix saw me struggling and slapped Jimmy hard on the back pretending to be playful. "That's fricken awesome, dude! I can't believe I missed it."

Jimmy stumbled forward from the force of Phoenix's smack, his eyes watering. He tried to play it off though.

I didn't want them to think they were being bullied, so I waved over a ring girl, "Let me get a bottle of Don Julio 1942 and four shot glasses." I saw Jimmy's eyes widen out of the corner of my eye—that was exactly what I was looking for here.

"Shiiiit," Pete smirked.

I shrugged a shoulder. "I like what I like. Now tell me more about the latest video."

"Oh man," Jimmy said, grinning. "It was epic!"

I didn't know how I managed to sit through Jimmy and Pete's idiotic rambling most of the night, while also watching the fights from the sidelines. It wasn't something I usually did; most of the time I watched from backstage while my boys were ringside, or at our merch table.

Didn't matter though, because we were here on a mission and I had a job to do. Slowly Blaze, Phoenix, and I fed Jimmy and Pete shots. The two idiots didn't even realize the three of us weren't drinking and they kept running their mouths, describing in vivid detail what the girl in the video was going through.

Pete had described Maya down to the tattoos. It may have been a while since I had seen Maya—the Spring party at Johnny Taylor's place—but the girl Pete had described was Maya. There was no doubt in my mind.

With the drunken idiots tagged for location, my boys and I finally said our goodbyes and headed out of the warehouse. It was late, but I texted Marcos when we were back by our bikes.

Axel:

I suggest you NOT watch this. Give it to your tech guy. I'm serious.

I waited a minute, expecting a text back right away, but it was late and I was sure Marcos was probably burning the candle at both ends. Hopefully he was sleeping.

Marcos:

Thx

I knew the chances of Marcos listening to me were slim to none. I wouldn't have listened if anyone sent me a link and told me not to look.

Maya

I FADED IN AND out of consciousness. Thoughts no longer consumed me as dehydration and starvation plagued me.

Still trussed up on the mattress, the men of Las Serpientes crew took their turns fucking me. I lost track of how many and how long.

Someone poured lube on me whenever I started to dry out. I had become swollen and desensitized, that despite the amount of lube and cum sloshing inside my cunt, I was still feeling friction burns and tearing.

"Such a dirty whore." Someone laughed.

"See if you can fist her," someone else said.

"Look it! Get the camera in there!"

Pain exploded as someone's fingers pushed into my cunt, followed by their knuckles. A chorus of loud mocking cheers could be heard as his fist slipped completely inside me.

Overwhelmed by the agony, I fell unconscious, my mind seeking refuge from the torment.

Marcos

I SENT THE LINK Axel had given me to Jack Adams immediately, hoping that Jack could track down something—anything. Then I called Jason into Maya's bedroom at her mother's house, and together we began to watch the videos of the last week of Maya's captivity. Despite Axel's warning not to, I needed to know.

I grew sicker and angrier the longer we watched. Both of us sat on Maya's bed, leaning back against the wall while we watched the shit on my phone. Thankfully Luke was asleep.

"Dude, no more," Jason finally snapped. He stood from the bed and began to pace in front of it. "I'm going to kill that motherfucker."

I was numb, I was beyond reaction at this point. I needed to watch them all, because every little detail I committed to memory. I would find Dax Hillcrest and repeat each and every touch, every hit, every fucking thrust into Hillcrest myself. The man would experience the hell he put Maya through tenfold.

Hitting play on the next video, I ignored Jason's pacing and continued watching.

"I can't sit here anymore." Jason stalked from the bedroom.

I heard the front door close quietly a couple seconds later. I thought briefly about following Jason, knowing he likely went around the corner to the new house, but decided against it. Jason needed to calm down, and I wasn't done with the videos.

There was a knock on the bedroom door that had me pausing the video and locking the screen. I looked up to see Luke standing there rubbing his eyes. "Hey, buddy. What are you doing up?"

"I heard Jason's voice, then heard him leave. Where's he going?"

I sighed and patted the bed next to me. "He was having problems sleeping. He was going over to the new house to check on things."

Luke frowned as he took a seat next to me on the bed. "When are you moving in there?"

"Not sure yet. Jason called around to get the floors done. He wants new carpet upstairs and the hardwood refinished downstairs. Could still be a couple weeks."

"Why doesn't he ask Uncle Johnny? He owns a construction company." Luke was so matter-of-fact; I was caught off guard.

"Uh, guess we hadn't thought about it." I huffed a laugh and rubbed a hand over my head. "Yeah, definitely forgot about that."

Luke giggled softly, sliding onto his side, next to me on the bed. "Well, ask him tomorrow, I bet he can get it done ASAP."

"I'll talk to him." Silence fell between us, both of us lost in thought, zoning out on the wall in front of us. I let it linger for a few more minutes before I spoke softly. "You did good tonight, at the gym."

A slowly smile pulled across Luke's face. "Thank you."

I chuckled softly. "I'm proud of you, Luke. I know this is hard. I know it hurts, but it's going to be ok. I'm going to get your mom back."

The smile slowly faded from Luke's face. He nodded his head once, but didn't reply.

I frowned, knowing there wasn't anything more I could do for Luke to reassure him.

Maya

I didn't know what day it was or how long I'd been captive. I didn't know if it was day or night, or when the last time I even ate anything.

I knew only this: a bone deep exhaustion, pain of unimaginable levels, and I wished for death.

My eyes were puffy and swollen from both crying and the slaps to the face that I'd endured for the sake of *their viewers*. The fact that even my teeth ached, told me the fever coursing through my body was serious.

Lying on the threadbare mattress, my mind drifted to Lucas, as it often did, then to Marcos and Jason and Nico. My precious Nico, who had forgiven me explicitly and loved me no matter all the heartache I'd put him through.

I wondered how Luke was doing without me, but knew that Marcos would take care of him. Was my mother enjoying the peace and quiet? Or was she upset that something happened to me? We might have had a rough relationship over the years, but I had hoped we had moved past it.

Did Jenna know I was gone? My sister would have sped down the highway to raise hell if she knew. Was she causing a shit storm for Marcos to deal with? I almost smiled at the thought of my tiny, yet older sister wreaking havoc on my guys. Jenna had loved the stories I had told her over the years. She had always been adamant that I should have told my guys the truth, but Jenna also hated that they never came to Chicago. Never fought for me.

Would they come for me this time? Would they even be able to find me?

There was a bang as the steel door slammed against the wall. I barely flinched as Dax Hillcrest stalked into the room. I didn't bother to look at him, still lost in my mind as I zoned out on the concrete wall in front of me.

"Up an at 'em, little whore," Hillcrest said, amusement in his voice.

I didn't move.

He grabbed my foot and roughly yanked my body down the mattress. I immediately began to flail and fight him, but two other men walked in the room. They moved quickly, helping Hillcrest grab me. Despite my thrashing, I was too weak to get away, and the three of them quickly subdued me.

I was carried out of my cell and down the hall to the filming room. It held all their torture equipment and lights, though knowing Hillcrest, one of the men was filming me even now. They always had a camera on me.

They tossed me onto another mattress and I stayed where I landed, too exhausted to move. It wouldn't matter; they would move my body where they wanted me. Sure enough, a moment later, hands were on me. The men rolled my on to my back and slid my body to the edge of the mattress.

Leather cuffs bound my hands and stretched them taut above my head. I barely uttered a sound as my legs were bent back and my ankles landed somewhere near my head. Somehow, they were tied in place and I was left contorted on a bed with bright lights shining from every angle.

"Fantastic," the camera man said. It was the same guy, always the same guy that gave orders on how to arrange my body, how far to push me, how to give the audience what they wanted.

"Where are the nipple clamps?" Someone asked.

"Here," Hillcrest responded.

I closed my eyes and zoned out, falling deep into my mind as the male voices around me spoke about me and their viewers. I felt a prick of pain in my neck before I was floating. A low moan escaped me as someone started massaging around my pussy.

"Dude, what are you doing? Fuck her already," someone said.

"Not into dry pussy. It's better when its gushing for you."

"Then go last, by the time we're finished with her, she'll be gushing for you." Male voices snickered around the room.

I didn't know how many men there were, but I had a feeling I knew who they were: Dax's crew. He was going to share me with them after all.

I couldn't help the moan that escaped me as he continued to massage my pussy lips and mound. Again, laughter echoed around the room, but I was too far gone to care. Whatever it was that they injected me with kept me feeling nice and floaty, everything was heightened.

"Keep going," the camera man said. "The viewers are into it. They want to see her squirt."

The other guy chuckled. "Sure thing."

I was helpless to stop him as his fingers danced over my skin. Rubbing and pulling, he plucked gently at my labia and clit, before he slowly inserted a finger inside me. It was torture in a different way as he slid his finger in and out, swirling it around before he slipped in a second finger alongside the first.

I moaned loudly as he worked my core.

More laughter around the room. "Play with her tits."

"Clamp them."

"Nah, let me play first."

I didn't know who was speaking, there were too many men in the room. Someone plucked and pulled and pinched my nipples. Arching my back, I tried to get more from them as I moaned loudly.

"She fucking loves this. Such a dirty whore."

The fingers in my cunt abruptly changed their rhythm from a slow sliding fucking, to a concentrated circling as they hooked upwards inside me and pressed against my top wall. "Ohhhh." I moaned low in my throat, throwing my head back in pleasure.

"That's it," the guy in front of me murmured. "So close now." He pressed his fingers harder to that spot inside me and jerked his fingers faster.

I screamed as I came with an earth-shattering orgasm that crashed over me, and a very large amount of fluid gushed out of me, soaking the hand between my legs and the bed beneath my ass.

Cheers were yelled around the room, both in excitement and in awe, like they'd never seen a woman squirt before. "She fucking likes it!"

I was lost to the pleasure and the drugs in my system as my entire body shook in ecstasy from the powerful orgasm.

"Fuck yeah. The tips are pouring in! Thank you, whore!" the cameraman shouted.

"Enough of this," Dax snapped.

The fingers were pulled away and someone slammed into my pussy. I didn't even feel any pain. I arched in pleasure and moaned loudly.

Guilt and shame warred within me. This was so much worse than when they were hurting me. The pleasure, the orgasms, those were supposed to be good things. They weren't supposed to be associated with this nightmare.

The drugs they gave me this time, though, made everything feel ten times better. It didn't help that the guy who had been massaging me and gotten me so worked up so quickly, that I was dying for another release already.

Someone started playing with my tits again, massaging and squeezing, getting on board with pleasure and not pain. It was hell. I moaned loudly and the room laughed.

"Fuck yeah, she's making more money tonight than she has with the torture," the cameraman said.

Imagine that, pleasure sold. Even on the dark web, I thought.

Dax kept fucking me roughly, slamming in deep. I was so keyed up by whatever they gave me and the attention they were giving me, that I quickly came again, arching my back and screaming out.

A moment later Hillcrest grunted, as he followed me over the edge.

My vision swam in and out of focus. I blinked lazily as I glanced around. Despite the excessive brightness, I could distinguish enough to count the men. There were four to my left and another four to my right. Behind Dax, I could make out another two or three.

It was too many.

The men were all in various stages of undress, with wicked gleams in their eyes. Some were already jacking off while watching the show in front of them, while others were holding handheld cameras, getting the action from all angles—including close ups of where Hillcrest was slowly pulling his cock out of my cunt. "All yours, boys." He smirked down at me. "Run on a train on her."

Dread coiled in my stomach as his words filtered through the haze of my drugged mind. A low moan escaped my lips. "Nuuu—" I tried to say no and pull away, but it was no use. My tongue felt heavy, as did my limbs, and I was tied too tightly to move.

Laughter echoed around the room.

Someone else gripped my hips and slammed into my cunt.

With a new wave of suffering, another groan escaped my lips.

Marcos

Saturday morning dawned bright and early, because I forgot to close the curtains in the bedroom. Luke stirred in the bed beside me, grumbling about the curtains and it being too early.

I felt his pain, but now that I was up, I wouldn't be able to get back to sleep. I never could once I was up. Patting Luke's back, I got up and shut the curtains for him, letting him sleep. Despite it being Saturday and a game day, I wasn't going to make the kid play if he wanted to sleep. There wasn't much of a point.

Real life had swooped in and everything else could wait.

I hit the bathroom to relieve myself before I walked out into the living room. I found Jason sleeping in the recliner, a blanket pulled across him.

Creeping past him, I went into the kitchen to start up the coffee pot, only to find it already full. Elaine was sitting at the dining room table, sipping her own cup, while staring out the back patio door. "Morning," I grunted.

Elaine murmured her own greeting that was sufficient.

Guilt ate at me every day that went by that we didn't bring Maya home. Staying with her mom was hard on everyone, but no one wanted to be alone. If Nico wasn't spending the night here, he was crashing at Leo's place.

My phone pinged on the counter with an incoming message.

Jack Adams:

Found him.

Hope soared in my chest.

Marcos:

Where?

Jack Adams:

Meet me at Kevin's at 9. I'm headed there soon. I'll show you everything I have.

Bracing my hands on the counter, I let my head hang as I let out a breath of relief. We had a lead, *finally*.

"Bad news?" Elaine asked, her voice scratchy with sleep.

My head shot up. I had forgotten she was sitting there. "No. We finally have a lead. Our tech guy just texted. He's got something."

Relief shone on Elaine's face, and I didn't want to crush it. We had a lead on Hillcrest, but we didn't know what shape Maya would be in after all of this. The videos were brutal and I would never tell Elaine about them.

I moved around the counter and over to where Elaine sat. Crouching down beside her, I put my hand on her shoulder and met her gaze. "It's just a lead on Hillcrest's whereabouts; we don't know that he's holding her there. I'll find out more in a little while. Jack's going to meet me at my sister's house."

Elaine patted my hand on her shoulder and gave me a nod. "I trust that you'll do everything you can to find her and bring her home."

"I will. We will do everything we can to bring her home, no matter what stands in our way."

Nico

I woke up in a plush bed and slowly opened my eyes. Glancing around, I took in the opulent surroundings of my cousin's guestroom. My phone buzzed on the nightstand, and I reached for it blindly as I rolled over in the large bed.

Marcos:

Jack found something. Meet us at Kara's house at 9. Grab something to share for breakfast.

Nico:

10-4

I sat up in bed once I realized it was 8:05 and I still had to shower. I took a quick shower, washing rapidly, then put on the same clothes I'd worn the night before.

In the dining room, I found my cousin Leo sitting at the table with a large spread of food in front of him and an iPad propped up right beside him. "Morning." Leo nodded.

"Morning. Marcos texted; Jack found something. Said to meet him at Kara's." I cut right to the chase.

Leo looked up from his iPad to meet my gaze. "That's great. You gonna sit and eat?"

"No time. I've got to stop and pick up something to share for breakfast on the way. I'm assuming that came from Kara."

Leo smirked and stood up, setting his napkin on his chair as a sign that he would be returning. Ever the gentleman, even in his own home. I followed Leo into the kitchen. "Gustavo, can you put together a tray of those chocolate croissants for Nico? He's going to brunch."

The chef—a portly man with a jolly face—turned away from the stove to face them. "Of course, Mr. Seratelli!" Gustavo shut off the burner and moved the pan off the heat before he walked over to the opposite counter.

I watched as the chef boxed up a dozen chocolate croissants in one of those fancy pastry boxes you'd get from a bakery. Of course, Leo's personal Chef had them lying around the house. "Thank you, I appreciate it." I nodded at Gustavo as he handed over the box.

"Not a problem! Happy to help." Gustavo smiled broadly before turning back to the stove to continue whatever he was cooking previously, dismissing us.

I took the hint and left the kitchen, heading back into the dining room. Leo followed me and walked over to his plate of food. "Thanks for this." I held up the box of croissants.

"Not a problem, cousin. Keep me updated on what Adams found. And if you're going to move in on Hillcrest, let me know. We'll back you up."

Gratitude and relief rolled over me. I was constantly being surprised by the lengths my family was willing to go to help me. The tips alone that had poured in the last week alone had been amazing, even if they were useless in the grand scheme of things. The fact that people in the community were willing to help Leo Seratelli because he said he was looking for someone, was astonishing.

The man had authority, there was no denying that. Authority and ruthlessness.

The ride over to Kara's house from Leonardo's was about twenty minutes. I pulled into the long driveway just before Marcos and Jason. Jason still couldn't ride his motorcycle yet, due to his healing injuries, but he was getting closer every day. He only slightly limped as he walked now.

I greeted my brothers with a nod as we all walked in the back door of Johnny Taylor's house, each man carrying a bag of what looked like bagels from the local shop. We all took off our boots in the mudroom, knowing how upset Kara got when we wore our shoes in the house.

We were met by the three Ravager Knight men, plus Kara, and someone who I assumed was Jack Adams, Kevin's brother and the resident tech guy. He looked just like Kevin, but slightly scrawnier if that was a thing. His face was narrower, sharper cheekbones, his shoulders didn't have as much muscled packed on like his brother. Jack also had a touch of gray around the temples of his black hair, showing he was probably older than Kevin as well.

Kara walked into the kitchen, barefoot and in cut-off shorts and a tank top. Her precious baby Lilah was held in the crook of her arm cooing softly, and Kara quickly handed her over to Derrick. "Morning," she greeted them with a forced smile. They knew this wasn't a social call, but Kara was ever the hostess as she grabbed the box from me and started laying out food on the breakfast island. Bagels and cream cheese, chocolate croissants, bacon and sausage, and scrambled eggs. There were even jugs of juices laid out.

It was an amazing spread for a last minute get together and I was impressed, but Kara had that effect on most people. Even on the weekend, dressed in cut-off shorts and a Harley Davidson tank top, Kara looked beautiful. Her blond hair was pulled back into an artfully messy bun and there was a light sheen of makeup dusted over her cheeks.

"Thank you, Kara. This looks fantastic." I pressed a kiss to the side of her cheek.

Marcos looked on edge—shit we were all on edge—but he looked like he didn't want to play nice and have brunch. I knew he was probably crawling for answers but couldn't snap right out and ask for them because it was Johnny's house, and Johnny wouldn't tolerate bullshit.

"Jack, what did you find?" Kara asked, cutting to the chase as she began to make a plate.

Thank God for small mercies and for Kara, I thought.

Jack chuckled as he grabbed a plate. "The link was the best thing. I was able to track his IP address and then jump through the hoops. He was too well hidden before. Hacking the FBI hasn't exactly been hard—but it's cumbersome. There's no good way to search for anything regarding Hillcrest that might have been covered up, but I did find the case for when the Mayor of Creekton was killed ten years ago. It led me to the agents that were working that case. Particularly, Agent Rick Bolton, out of Chicago."

"Why the fuck is an agent out of Chicago dealing with shit down here?"

"Technically, it's still his jurisdiction," Jack said.

I shrugged a shoulder, cause what did I know? Jack was clearly the expert here.

"Anyways," Jason grunted.

"So I started digging into Bolton. Turns out his brother is Illinois State Senator Bradley Bolton," Jack continued.

"No fucking way," Kara muttered.

Marcos tensed and locked eyes with his sister. "You know him?"

Kara shook her head. "D.A. Winters has mentioned him a time or two. He's been giving her hell regarding my father's case. She's not letting it go, and he's pushing for it to be thrown out."

"What the fuck?" Nico asked.

"Yeah." Kara nodded. "He went as far as to send the Attorney General down here. Thankfully Winters and AG McNeil went to U of I together, so McNeil smoothed things over with the Senator. But he almost cost me the firm."

"I'm sure Hillcrest has been pushing Agent Bolton, who's been pushing his brother," Kevin surmised.

I nodded. I grabbed a paper plate and quickly stacked food on it. The conversation paused for a few minutes while everyone followed after me, loading up their plates with food, before we took a seat around the table in the breakfast nook. It was a tight fit for the eight of us, but we made it work.

"I'm surprised your father even made it to sentencing then," I admitted, glancing at Kara.

She frowned, pursing her lips. Her father was a sore subject for her, their relationship having grown rocky over the last several years, but she still cared about him. "I know. And with this shit with Hillcrest and Maya, I have a feeling any move to rescue Maya means my father's life."

"Kara—"

"Rescue Maya, obviously," Kara snapped, meeting Marcos's eye. "I'm just preparing myself."

Marcos clenched his jaw, the vein in his temple pulsing from the strain of gritted teeth. "Have to find her first." Marcos met Jack's gaze.

"Yeah. So tracking Hillcrest's IP address has proved difficult, but I did find some dummy corporations and shell companies. I dug through all that and got a location for a warehouse down in Sparland," Jack said.

"Sparland, where the fuck is that?"

"About an hour south of here. Along the Illinois river, middle of nowhere," Jack replied.

"How'd you get his IP address?" I asked.

"Axel went to one of the underground fights last night and met some people. He got a link to a website on the dark web," Marcos said. He hesitated and shared a look with Jason.

I stopped eating and watched my two best friends, my brothers. We didn't keep secrets between the three of us, ever. Clearly, I had missed something.

"The website has videos posted of women being—"

"The videos are of Hillcrest assaulting Maya," Jason cut off Marcos who was trying to say it gently.

My heart sank and Kara gasped.

"Dude," Johnny snapped, glaring at Jason.

My stomach churned.

Tears immediately gathered in Kara's eyes. "He's raping her and posting the videos?" Her voice cracked.

"Yeah," Marcos grunted, unable to meet his sister's gaze.

I sat back in my chair in a daze, my eyes staring unfocused on my uneaten plate of food. Hillcrest was actively hurting my woman and we were sitting here eating brunch like fucking idiots. Snapping out of my daze, I jerked my gaze to Jack Adams. "You have a location?"

"Yes."

"We go tonight," I ordered, turning to Marcos.

"We can't just go in there, guns blazing," Marcos tried to reason.

I stood up abruptly and slammed my hands on the table, rattling the silverware, as I leaned over the table to get my point across. "I don't give a fuck, Marcos. I will take the fucking Seratelli family and get my fucking woman back without you."

Marcos met my gaze evenly, but before he could say anything, Kevin spoke up.

"Easy now." Kevin's hands raised in a placating gesture. "You're not going alone with the Seratelli's. We'll be there too."

I finally broke my stare off with Marcos and turned to Kevin. Johnny and Derrick were watching me with varying degrees of contempt for causing a scene, but it was easy to see they were just as angry with Jason when they both glared at him.

As Kara got up from the table, Johnny watched her go, concern etched on his face. "What the fuck is wrong with you?" Johnny rounded on Jason.

I took my seat, watching the argument unfold.

"I fucking told you about bringing that bullshit attitude into my home. Now you upset my fucking woman," Johnny growled, rounding on Jason. "After Maya is found, the three of you will answer for this bullshit in the ring."

"Agreed," Marcos answered immediately. Jason and I echoed the sentiment.

"Go home, gather your club. We'll meet you at your clubhouse at nine." Johnny made the executive decision for all of us. He turned to me, "Call your cousin. Have him meet us in Sparland. Jack will find us a safe place to meet up and discuss entry."

I nodded once, meeting Johnny's gaze. His natural dominance made him easy to follow. No longer hungry, I stood up again and left the breakfast nook. I slipped into my boots in the mudroom and headed out the backdoor. I didn't even bother to lace up my boots until I was at my bike. Even then I only bothered to tuck them in my boots and started the bike.

Rage and anguish clawed at me as I rode away from Johnny Taylor's home. Betrayal and disbelief welled within me. Marcos should have called me last night when he got the link, or even this morning at the very latest. Giving me the information for the first time while we were at an acquaintances' was unacceptable.

Worst of all, it hurt. Marcos had left me out of the loop. Kept me in the dark. Purposely.

I didn't know how long I rode for, didn't know where I was going. Eventually I turned my bike around and headed back toward Creekton. I found myself outside of my mother's house, staring up at the McMansion while lost in thought.

"Nico!" Gulia's voice shouting over the engine snapped me out of my daze.

Jerking my head, I looked over to see the housekeeper staring at me with a worried expression on her face. I shut the engine off and put down my kickstand. Shutting off the bike, the deafening silence greeted me as I slowly pulled my helmet off.

"Nico, you've been out here for ten minutes with that engine roaring. Are you alright?" Guila asked, her hand on her heart.

"Not really." I shook my head.

"Come on. I'll put coffee on. Your mother's in the sunroom."

Of course she is, I thought, but I followed Guila up the grand stairway to the house wordlessly.

The house was as beautiful as always, Guila's hard work apparent as there was not one thing out of place. We strode down the hall and through the living room and out into the sunroom beyond. My mother was already seated at the table, a lightly breakfast set before her. I would have laughed at the idea of the leaving one breakfast to go to another one instead, but I was too far gone to care.

"Nico!" my mother greeted me with a smile. "What a pleasant surprise." Her face fell as she took in the anguish that was clearly on my face.

I fell to my knees before her and buried my face into her stomach as a heart wrenching sob tore out of me.

"Nico." My mother's voice was soft. "What happened? What's going on?"

"It's Maya," I choked out. "She's been kidnapped. They're hurting her."

"Oh, Nico." My mother's soft gasp, paired with her shaky fingers in my hair made me lose control over my emotions. Heavy sobs wracked my bodies as I held onto her for dear life.

She didn't say anything more, just held me and ran her fingers through my hair, stroking gently. I eventually stopped crying and caught my breath, but I kept my head on her lap, basking in her comfort.

Marcos

I FELT LIKE SHIT. I should have told Nico before I brought it up at the goddamned breakfast table. I never should have said that shit in front of my sister either. Kara had been through her own fucking torment with Hillcrest. Thankfully she hadn't been raped, but that didn't mean her own ordeal wasn't traumatic as well.

And here I was, fucking it all up.

Johnny was right to call me out.

I felt listless as I stared out the front picture window of Elaine's house. I wasn't sure if I was waiting for Nico to show up or not. Or if I was just hoping the fucking answer would drive down the road and so I didn't have to make these big decisions.

Not that I even had to make any decisions—Johnny was taking charge of it all.

I shook my head, trying to clear my thoughts. I couldn't even muster up the energy to be angry about it. It was like a heavy fog weighed me down and I was struggling to get to the surface, drowning.

Nico was the only one of us who was fired up, but then again, he had been right about Maya all along. He was the only one fighting right now. It was the reason I had named him Vice President all those years ago. Nico was the only level-headed one of the three of us. He was the only one that tended to look deeper into things before making a decision.

Jason was too stubborn. He had denied that anything was wrong with Maya for so long, that he was now having issues coming to terms with just how badly he'd fuck things up.

"Get your head out of the clouds, boy," Elaine snapped from behind me, pulling me out of my endless musings. "You have a lead. Do something about it."

I startled and looked over my shoulder to find Maya's mother standing in the doorway from the kitchen into the living room. She was holding a dish towel in her hands as if she had just finished washing them. The hard stare in her gaze was nothing new, but it hit different knowing she was right.

A moment later, Jason walked out of Maya's bedroom, riding boots and jacket on, with his cut pulled over the leather jacket. He looked ready to ride. "She's right, let's go to the clubhouse and get our club ready."

"You're gonna ride?" I asked, struggling to keep up.

"Yes. It's been two and a half weeks. I'm riding out with you when you rescue Maya."

"We're gonna need the truck."

"We're going to need an ambulance with a fucking doctor on board. I already made some calls. Nickle is dating an EMT and Griff is going to ride with her. They're gonna be on standby tonight." Jason was so direct and matter-of-fact that I could only blink at him.

Seeing the blank stare, Jason moved closer. Resting his forehead against mine, Jason gripped the back of my neck. "Come on, man. Time to snap out of it. We need you fired up and ready to roll. Maya needs you."

Hope flared to life inside me, making me realize for the first time all morning that we had a shot at getting her back. I nodded. "Let's go get our girl back."

The clubhouse was packed. I had ordered a lock down, meaning all the immediate families of the patched club members were current-ly behind the locked gates and doors of the clubhouse compound. Fear of retaliation was high, with Hillcrest being a loose cannon.

Jack Adams had gotten us the location along with a wealth of knowledge we could use later. But tonight we were focusing on the location we believed Maya was being held. Once Maya was safely returned, we would set about destroying Dax Hillcrest and Las Serpientes as a whole.

The Ravager Knights MC was a lined up out front, ready to roll out.

All that was left to do was to speak to my crew. With Nico and Jason by my side, I addressed the barroom as a whole, not caring if family were present. "You all know why you're here. We're going after Maya Henderson, our Old Lady who has been kidnapped by Dax Hillcrest and Las Serpientes. I know many in this room have their own vendettas against Dax Hillcrest." I paused to make eye contact with Axel, Blaze, Phoenix who were standing against the wall to my right, and then with Johnny, Derrick and Kevin who were standing near the door. "After the torture Hillcrest has put my woman through, I'm claiming his death by hands."

Johnny and his boys glared, but didn't say anything. Axel and his boys only nodded once, in agreement. Axel had gotten me that video. He had heard first-hand what Maya was being put through by Hillcrest and his men. He knew that Maya's torture was horrendous.

"I want him alive. He doesn't deserve a quick death," I continued. "Let's roll out."

The bar exploded in a deafening cheer.

Marcos

We rode the hour and fifteen minutes to Sparland in formation. I was at the head of the pack with Johnny by my side. Behind us were Nico and Kevin, our respective VP's, with Derrick and Jason next in line. The line up of bikes down the highway was a sight to see.

I could feel the anger raging in my veins the closer we drove to Sparland.

When we arrived at an empty warehouse, a mile north of where Maya was being held, we pulled over and broke into smaller groups. We would ride in from all different directions and surround the warehouse. We needed to be quick and stealthy. We needed the element of surprise if we wanted to get Hillcrest, but more importantly Maya.

We also needed the Seratelli's manpower to boost ours. Leonardo Seratelli had delivered us an army of one hundred men who would follow us into the warehouse.

Once we were into the smaller pre-planned groups, we hit the road again. In less than five minutes we were surrounding the building, dismounting from our bikes and pulling out our guns.

The comms unit in my ear crackled to life when Griff and the ambulance were in position.

I motioned forward and our guys used explosives to blow the doors off the warehouse. From there, things moved quickly. We stormed the building almost silently. Down a dark and long narrow hallway, we ran toward the lights at the end. Shouting could be heard all around us.

My heart raced in my chest. We were so close.

"Marcos!" Nico shouted from down the hall.

I pushed passed the guys in front of me and took point, racing down the hall. I burst through a doorway, into a nightmare of a scene. Bright lamps were pointed at a bed in the center of the room, satin sheets covered the mattress, and in the middle of it all, was a very bruised and battered Maya.

She lay on her side, her body curled up as she slept—I hoped she slept. "Maya!" I shouted, falling to my knees besides the bed. I reached out gently to tuck her hair behind her ear and feel for a pulse. "Gracias a Dios." I let out a relieved sigh. It was faint, but it was there.

"Maya," Nico spoke softly. He climbed on the bed beside her and gently turned her on her back. "Maya, baby. Little Dreamer, wake up."

She stirred and blinked her eyes open.

"Come on, Little Dreamer. Come back to me," Nico murmured.

Out of the corner of my eye I saw Leonardo walk into the room, followed by Jason. Jason slid to his knees on the other side of the mattress, watching as Nico coaxed our girl awake.

"Nic." Maya gasped his name, a light breathy sound that showed just how weak she was.

"I've got you, Little Dreamer. Come on, let's get you out of here."

Her body was limp as Nico lifted her into his arms. "Maya, stay with me," he murmured to her unresponsive body.

Nico

M Y HEART POUNDED IN my chest as I raced through the halls with Maya in my arms. Marcos and Jason were hot on my heels, but the only thing I could think about was getting Maya to the waiting ambulance. It was a stroke of genius that Jason has reached out to Griff to have him on standby. Maya was in horrible shape.

Outside, the cool night air nipped at my arms, and I knew it would be worse on her naked body. I didn't have time to wrap her in my leather jacket; I ran as fast as I could to the ambulance that was backed in. The back doors opened and our club doctor Griffen was jumping out.

I carefully stepped into the back of the ambulance and set Maya down on to gurney. Dr. Griffin jumped back into the ambulance as a lady dressed in an EMT uniform walked in the back bay from the driver's area. "Hey, I'm Marlene. How's she doing?"

"Not good. Were you filled in?" I asked.

Marlene nodded. "Yes. I know the score. So I'm asking was she responsive when you picked her up?"

"She woke up long enough to say my name before she passed out again," I said.

"That's good," Griffin said.

The ambulances back doors slammed shut and someone got in the driver's seat. I looked over to see my cousin, Giovanni, behind the wheel. He gave me a nod. "We ready?"

"Hold on," Griffin said. Him and Marlene got to work hanging bags of fluid from an IV pole before they slowly and carefully arranged Maya on the gurney. Marlene covered her in blankets while Griffin stuck the needle into a vein at the crook of her arm.

"What's that?" I asked.

"She's severely dehydrated, so basic saline and then antibiotics. There's not too much I can do from the back of a moving vehicle, but we'll keep her stable," Griffin said, before he turned to the driver. "You know to take us to the back door of Mourningside General?"

Giovanni nodded. "Yes, and I'll turn everything off as we get closer."

"Good," Griffin nodded. "Let's go."

Giovanni put the ambulance into drive and slowly moved forward.

I sat down out of the way, while Griffin and Marlene attended to Maya. They had to hold on to the overhead grab bars while Giovanni drove us out of the bumpy parking lot, but soon we were on a smooth highway and racing home.

Maya moaned as Griffin pressed on her belly through the blanket. "Maya, does that hurt?" Griffin's voice was commanding.

Maya moaned again, her eyes blinking open. "Please," she muttered.

"Maya, it's Dr. Griffin. I need you to tell me if your belly hurts when I press down."

She jerked and cried out.

I moved to her side. "Easy, Little Dreamer. I'm here."

"Nic," Maya panted my name.

"I'm here, baby. I'm here."

Tears lined her eyes as she reached for my face.

"Can you answer Griff? You remember him? He came by when Jason was hurt."

Maya blinked and looked up at Griffin. "Yeah, Katalina's friend."

"Good, Maya. Now, does it hurt when I push here?" Griffin asked again.

"Yes! Stop!" She cried out, arching her back as she threw her head back in pain.

Griffin immediately dropped his hands and fell onto the bench behind him. Meeting my gaze, his face was grim. "We need to hurry. With her trauma it could be anything from bad to worse and I won't know until we get images."

Unease settled into me, but I pushed it down as Maya turned toward me. She reached through the gurney railing for me and I quickly grabbed her hand, lacing our fingers together. I bent over our joined hands and kissed her knuckles as I squeezed her hand tightly. "I'm here, Little Dreamer. I'm here."

"Nico." She sobbed my name, and it broke my heart.

"Shh, baby. Just rest now. I'm here."

"I love you."

"I love you too, Little Dreamer. Always." I kissed her knuckles again and held her hand as she drifted off.

"How bad do you think it is?" I asked Griffen when I was sure Maya was asleep.

"Possible perforated bowel. But I won't know until we get imaging, or I get in there and see. Let's see how she responds to antibiotics on the way and if we can get imaging done, it would be preferred."

"Step on it, Gio," I said to my cousin.

"On it."

Nico

Maya slept the whole way to the hospital. Or she was unconscious? Hard to know, but it was a blessing, because she wasn't in any pain.

Gio cut the lights and sirens two miles out from the hospital and drove around the back to reach the private VIP entrance where Griffin treated his VIP clients.

"She's stable for now. We'll get her blood drawn and get her into imaging immediately." Griffin jumped out of the ambulance the second the doors were flung open.

Staff from the hospital rushed out to assist and I sat back, staying out of the way as they pulled the gurney out of the ambulance and rolled Maya away. I scurried after her, trying to keep up, when Marcos and Jason fell into step with me.

"How's she doing?" Marcos demanded.

"Not great. She's stable enough for bloodwork and imaging, but he thinks there's a possible perforation in her bowel."

"The fuck?" Jason growled.

I could only shrug. I didn't want to think about how the injury may have happened, or what it might mean in terms of her healing.

Just as I was following Griffin and Maya down the hall, a perky middle-aged woman with short black hair and horn-rimmed glasses cut them off. "Hi, I'm Darla. I'll be taking you to Dr. Griffin's private waiting room."

I stopped so hard that Marcos crashed into my back.

Darla smirked and raised an eyebrow, as if waiting for one of them to snap at her.

"Lead the way, Darla," I said, before my guys could snap off.

Marcos

"THERE WAS A SLIGHT tear in her colon, but we managed to repair that laparoscopy. It was a very minor tear, but she was leaking gastrointestinal liquid into her body, so sepsis has set in. We're treating her with high doses of antibiotics, but she's heavily sedated for the time being," Griffin said. "Basically, we've induced a coma to help her body heal. Because of that, we've had to put her on a ventilator just to help her lung function easier."

I stared at the doctor, not comprehending what all he said.

"Thanks, Griff," Jason grunted beside me.

Griffin nodded. "I'm gonna get cleaned up and grab something to eat, but I'll be around if you have any questions. Darla will escort you to Maya's room. Give her a few minutes to get everything situated."

I nodded numbly.

Nico sat back down on the leather chairs we were occupying before Griff came in the with the update. The VIP waiting room was like nothing I had seen before, leather couches and recliners, with table lamps set low to give a cozy vibe.

Jason began to pace the small waiting room, like he had for the last several hours.

I forced myself to ignore him, before I snapped at him.

A few minutes later Darla walked into the waiting room, with a bright smile on her face. She'd worn the same bright smile all night, despite it being the early hours of the morning. While it immediately eased our fears and settled our nerves, I had to imagine it grew tiresome. Had to be hard to keep a happy smile and inform families when their loved ones weren't doing well.

"Alright, gentlemen. If you would follow me, I'll take you back to Maya."

Nico and I jumped up from our chairs, ready to roll.

"I want to prepare you for what to expect though. It can be a little overwhelming for families when they first see their loved ones hooked up to so many machines and tubes. The main thing to remember is she's doing well, despite the infection. All those tubes and wires are just to help her get stronger." Darla spoke gently and met our gazes with compassion.

"Yeah," Nico murmured, nodding.

Darla turned on her heel and lead the way out of the room. My brothers and I followed her down the hall and around the corner. Darla walked into the second door on the left, right across from the nurses' station, and I followed right behind.

Inside, I didn't know where to look first. The room did not look like the typical hospital room. To the right was a living area, with two couches and a recliner facing a wall mounted big screen TV. To the left of the room was what one would expect to find in a hospital room. The hospital bed was centered on the left wall, with real nightstands on either side.

There was still hospital equipment in the room, though. The breath was sucked from my lungs as I stared at Maya lying prone on the bed, tubes and wires coming off her. "I know it looks scary," Darla spoke up, pulling me out of my thoughts, "but she won't need them for long. A couple days at the most. Doctor Griffin will make sure she makes a full recovery."

I nodded numbly.

Nico walked past me and right over to the far side of the bed where a comfortable-looking recliner was. He pulled the chair as close to the bed as he could get it and sat down. Lacing his fingers with Maya's, Nico looked like he was settling in for the long haul.

"The call button is right here," Darla pulled out the standard issue bed remote with nurse button.

"Thank you, Darla," Nico said.

"Not a problem, dear. Over here you'll see is the VIP suite. You get a living room, and through this door here," Darla opened the door, "Is your bedroom. There are two queen beds here and the bathroom just to the right, like a standard hotel room. If you need another bed, the couches in the living room pull out and there are extra linens in the closet here."

I watched her go through the quick tour and nodded my head mechanically. Standard hotel shit, in the middle of a fancy as fuck hospital suite. Got it.

"Alright darlings, try to get some rest. Maya's going to be sedated for the next twenty-four hours or so," Darla said, before she left the room.

In her absence, a deafening silence fell over the room. The only sound was the constant beeping of the heart monitor, reminding us that Maya's heart was still beating. Nico was zoned in on Maya, staking his claim at her side.

Jason stood a foot from me in the center of the suite, looking as lost as I felt. What the fuck were we supposed to do now?

Marcos

I woke up to my cell phone buzzing on my chest. I'd fallen asleep on the couch in the living room area of the suite, after hours of texting in the early hours of morning, updating everyone that needed updates. Seeing Kara's picture on my screen, I sat up and answered immediately. "Hey, Lil Manita."

"Hey, Marquitos," Kara greeted, her voice soft. "How are things this morning?"

I cleared my throat. "She's uh, she's the same. Griff said it would be a day or two before they took her off everything."

"That's rough." Kara sighed. "How are you doing?"

I glanced around the suite to see that Jason sleeping in the recliner near him and Nico in the recliner beside Maya. I switched to Spanish, so I could speak freely and stood up and headed for the bedroom suite for some privacy. "Mal. La verdad es que estoy hecho un desastre. No sé cómo hacer esto. ¿Qué hago?" *Not good. Honestly, I'm a mess. I don't know how to do this. What do I do?*

"Oh, Marquitos. It's ok to be a mess. It's hard. No one should have to live through the trauma that Maya lived through. The important thing right now is to remind yourself that she's alive. She's alive, and she going to recover. You just have to be there for her."

"Yeah," I mumbled, switching to English. "What do I do about Luke?"

"You can't tell him what happened to her, not the exact truth. He's too young," Kara said. "But he knows she was with Hillcrest and that he hurt her. That's enough for him. I wouldn't wait to bring him to her. Even if it's a lot right now. It's been a week since he's seen his mother."

"Yeah." I grunted the word and had to clear my throat as my voice choked with emotion. "Yeah, I—"

"How about I bring him by this afternoon?" Kara suggested.

I thought about it for a minute. "No, no. I should be the one to drive him up here. Elaine too. I'll run home and shower and change my clothes and all that. Get some food and I'll bring them up here. Can you come too? Say around one?"

"Yeah, I can do that. I'll probably have one of the guys with me," she warned.

"Wouldn't expect anything less, Lil Manita. You need to stay safe."

Marcos

I held Luke as he bawled in my arms. Seeing his mother like she was would be hard for anyone. But for a nine-year-old kid who knew his mother had been kidnapped—who had traded herself for her son's safety—it was excruciatingly painful.

I took Luke into the bedroom suite and held him tightly as he cried. Kara came and sat down next to us on the bed, rubbing Luke's back as I rocked him gently. "It's ok, buddy," I murmured softly. I kissed the top of Luke's head and held him tighter.

Elaine stepped into the bedroom suite, wiping tears from her eyes. She walked past us and over to the window, looking out at the city of Mourningside below. "I called Jenna this morning. She should be here soon."

Luke pulled away slightly to look over at his grandmother. "Aunt Jenna is coming?"

"Yeah, honey. She's on her way." Elaine confirmed.

"That's a good thing, huh, Luke? Another Aunt here," Kara smiled at Luke and patted his hand.

Luke nodded and climbed off my lap and into Kara's. He curled up around her on the mattress and sniffled as he tried to control his breathing. "I know mom looks bad right now," I said, trying to keep my voice even, "but she's only going to look like that for another couple days. Doc Griffin is keeping an eye on her and giving her the medicine she needs to get stronger."

"You promise?" Luke voice is so small, so soft, it broke my heart.

"Yeah, bud. I promise. Your mom is going to make a full recovery." I could only hope and pray to God that I kept that promise to my son.

Chapter Seventeen

Jason

I HAD TO LEAVE the room. There were too many people around. Even with Marcos in the bedroom suite with his sister and Luke and Elaine, it was too much. Nico hadn't moved from the recliner besides Maya all night, except to hit the bathroom. Otherwise he sat silent vigil beside her, keeping her hand in his.

When Kara had shown up with Derrick in toe, I left the room. I couldn't handle all the emotions flying around—not when my own were hanging on by a hair-trigger. Derrick took one look at my face and nodded toward the hall. I told Nico I would be back and then took off with the Ravager Knight.

Outside, in the parking lot, far from any doors or cameras, I pulled a joint out of the inside pocket of my cut and quickly lit it up. Taking a long drag, I sucked the smoke back before I offered Derrick the joint.

"How you hanging in there?" Derrick asked. He took the joint from me and puffed on it.

"Not good," I spoke around the smoke I held in my lungs.

Derrick nodded as he inhaled the weed and handed me the joint. I exhaled a slow cloud of smoke, before I brought the joint back to my lips again. We stayed that way until the joint was finished: passing it and smoking, not talking.

When the joint was smoked down to my fingertips, I put it out on my shoe and tossed it under a car but didn't make a move to head into the hospital. Instead, I stared off into the parking lot around me as my mind grew fuzzy from the Mary Jane. "How was Kara when she came home?" I asked, my voice low.

"You mean after she was kidnapped by Hillcrest's men?" Derrick clarified.

"Yeah."

Derrick blew out a breath and ran a hand over his shoul-der-length brown hair. It was pulled back into a ponytail, but pieces still hung loose. "Shit, man." He stuck both hands in the front pockets of his blue jeans and shrugged. He rocked on the balls of his feet while squinting his eyes against the sun to make eye contact with me. "Not good. But Hillcrest never touched her. His men... they never touched her either. She was held in a room with a guard in the corner staring at her for all hours of the day and night. It was psychological more than physical."

I nodded and looked away from the guy. It wasn't the same—not that what Kara went through wasn't traumatic, because it was—it just wasn't the same. What Maya had lived through... shit, I couldn't even imagine the pain. I took one look at those videos and couldn't stomach them.

I had no idea how Marcos watched every single one.

"Kara had a lot of nightmares when she came home. She started seeing a therapist. She still can't sleep in complete darkness, needs a nightlight. We still haven't let her out of our sight and make sure one of us are with her all times. We hired a security company for her office, on top of her beefing up security for the building itself... I dunno, man. It's still hard. There are still times when it hits us how much we could have lost if things were different." Derrick's voice is gruff with emotion.

I nodded numbly. "How did you deal?"

"By punching people," Derrick answered immediately.

A surprised bark of laughter exploded from me and I jerked my head to look at Derrick. The man had a slight smirk on his face, but he was otherwise serious. "You're serious."

"Yeah. The Knights host fight nights, there's always some grievances with brothers, and then Brawlers Night is great too, if more dangerous. But you need to be in with the right people."

"Mmm, yeah. Axel knows people. He fights there with his boys."

"Yeah, I've seen them around. Phoenix really knows how to put on a show," Derrick chuckled.

I smiled faintly, my thoughts still in a dark place. "So fighting?"

"It helped me and Johnny. Kevin...I don't know. He's gone to therapy with Kara a couple times—ok we've all gone to therapy with Kara a couple times—let me make that clear. She wouldn't put up with us not going, made it clear we weren't going to work out if we didn't all talk some shit out. But did it help? Maybe, probably. Having an outside opinion to walk us through some of those doubts and emotions that still hung on, probably helped some. Was it a load of shit? Half-way maybe. The main thing was it got the four of us talking about the heavy shit, and that's what we needed. To talk about the heavy shit."

Rubbing my hand along my scruffy jaw, I vaguely wondered if I should shave or let it grow while I thought over Derrick's words. "I think I need to fight first."

Derrick shrugged. "Probably. I know I did. Maya's got a tough road ahead of her. She's going to need you to be strong for her. You can't let her see that you're breaking—not yet at least. Do that shit in private. Later, when she's strong, then you can break. So you guys can build each other up, together."

No truer words had ever been spoken.

Chapter Eighteen

Maya

Fire seared up my body, licking at my sides and across my chest. My throat burned with every breath I took. I tried to swallow, only to find it felt like glass tearing me to shreds. It was agony.

There was an incessant beeping that grated on my nerves. It grew louder and faster the more agitated I became. Something was holding my arm down, I tried to jerk it free, but it held tighter.

"Maya?" It was a man's voice, laced with concern.

I lashed out, trying to push them away.

I couldn't see anything.

I tried to scream. Something was blocking my throat; only mumbled noises came out.

"Maya!" That voice again, he was yelling this time.

The fucking beeping wouldn't stop.

I tried to lash out again, but hands were holding me down.

Hands were everywhere.

Agony ripped through me.

A searing scream ripped from my throat, setting it ablaze.

My head pounded.

Then there was nothing. Sweet, peaceful silence embraced me as I floated away.

Maya

"Griff said she shouldn't have woken up so quickly, that her body likely burned through the drugs faster, because of what she was on before."

I heard the male voice speaking softly, but didn't really understand. What drugs had I been on? Where was I? Why did everything feel so heavy?

I felt like my limbs were weighted with concrete.

My throat hurt, but I felt like I could swallow easier, despite the pain.

"So now what?" Another male voice asked.

"Now we wait. He said she should wake up any time. It's up to her," the first voice said.

It was up to me. Of course, it was up to me, dipshits. I would do whatever I damn well pleased.

"At least they took the tube out of her throat. I bet that freaked her out when she woke the first time," Nico said, his voice laden with emotion. He wrapped his fingers around my left hand and squeezed.

I squeezed back.

"Maya?!" Nico's voice got louder.

I squeezed again.

"What's going on?" the first voice—Marcos asked.

I heard Marcos. Fuck, I heard him. Did that mean? Was Jason there too?

"She awake?" Jason asked. Yes! My boys were here. Wherever here was.

"She squeezed my hand twice now! Maya, can you open your eyes?" Nico asked.

I tried to open my eyes, but it was too bright. *The lights! Fuck, the lights. Hillcrest's lights were blinding me. Was he still filming?* My thoughts raced a mile a minute to catch up.

The incessant beeping was back again, growing louder and more frantic as my heart rate increased. *My heart rate!* That's what the beeping was, a heart rate monitor. Was I in the hospital?

"Maya, calm down, Little Dreamer. You're safe now. We've got you. You're in the hospital," Nico's voice was soft and soothing, hands slid across me as he pressed a kiss to my forehead.

I squeezed his hand for dear life. "Nic." A strained breath escaped me, his name but a whisper.

Nico's hand squeezed mine tighter, his forehead leaned against mine. "Yeah, baby. I'm here. We're all here."

Someone else grabbed my other hand. "You're safe now, Mi Vida." Marcos's voice was a thick gravel. "We've got you."

"We're all here, darlin'," Jason murmured from my right. He wrapped his hand around my foot, squeezing gently. "We're not going anywhere."

I felt the tears leak out but was too exhausted to stop them.

"Get some rest, baby. We'll be here when you wake up." Nico kissed my forehead before he pulled away.

But I couldn't, I needed to know. "Luuke," I gasped.

"He's safe, Mi Vida. He's at home with your mom. He's been here a couple times, but we're trying to keep him in school," Marcos said.

I squeezed his hand in a silent thanks.

"Rest now, Little Dreamer. We'll be here when you wake up," Nico murmured.

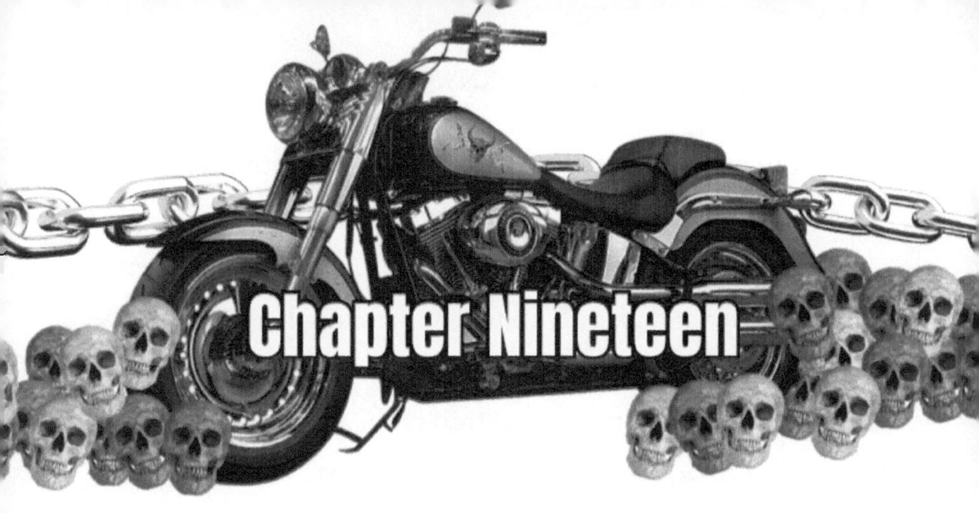

Chapter Nineteen

Nico

Relief washed over me as I took my seat in the recliner besides Maya. She had woken up and spoken to us. She was all right.

All right may have been a relative term, but she was alive and with us. She would pull through his. I knew it. I would make sure of it.

Marcos and Jason both let out a heavy sigh of relief as Maya's hands grew lax and she drifted off to sleep again. The heart rate monitor, slowly returned to normal, and I glanced at the doorway to find the daytime nurse Jaylin watching from afar.

I flashed her a thumbs up and she smiled and nodded. I knew she was monitoring everything from her computers out in the nurses stand, but the check in was always nice. Even though there wasn't much she could do for her.

Griff was scheduled to come in a couple hours. He would check her over and give an update on weaning her off the pain meds. After the last time she woke up, they took her off the ventilator and took out the breathing tube. He had scaled back her meds a little after that, but warned that she would still be in a lot of pain. Thankfully, she was no longer sepsis. The antibiotics were doing their thing to fight off the infection.

It really was just a waiting game, as Griffin had told us. Maya needed the time to rest and heal before she woke up.

I was an impatient bastard though.

So I started doing things that would encourage her to wake up, like reading to her. Only once I started reading, Jason snatched the book away that I had chosen—a popular romantasy series—and replaced it with her favorite Why Choose novel. And instead of letting me read it, Jason took over reading.

Jason took a seat on the hard-as-nails chair across the bed from me and settled into read.

Jenna had said that it was good for her, to hear our voices. It was the one thing she had agreed with since she arrived the day before. Jenna was as feisty as her sister and had ripped Griffin a new one after Maya had woken up with the breathing tube still in her throat.

Things had finally calmed down since then, but the two doctors often debated her care.

It made me happy that they were both giving their best efforts, and when Jenna agreed with something Griffin did or said, it reassured me that we had the best care for Maya.

The fiery woman was a carbon copy of her sister, but with black pin straight hair that was cut into a no-nonsense bob. She had laid us all out on our asses when she walked into the room the day before.

We were still licking their wounds while we waited for Maya to wake up.

Nico

Three days later, Maya was still unconscious. It had been a full six days since her rescue, and I was growing impatient. Griffin had said it was up to her at this point, but I couldn't help but want to shake her ass awake. I needed to see her beautiful amber eyes. I needed to know that she was still in there.

I was sitting with her alone on a Friday night while Marcos and Jason were making an appearance at the clubhouse for the usual Friday night party. Neither man had wanted to go, but as VP, I had pointed out that either me or Marcos needed to put in an appearance, and I wasn't leaving her side.

Marcos had grumbled about it, but when Jason agreed, they left the room, vowing to only be gone an hour. It was just the opening I needed, both men left after Jenna headed back to her mother's house for the night, leaving me alone with Maya.

"Maya, my Little Dreamer, I need you need to wake up. I'm going crazy here without you. I need to see your eyes, hear your voice. I need to know you're still with me." I kissed her knuckles and squeezed her hand.

There was a faint squeeze back and Maya's eyelids fluttered open.

"Hey, there, Little Dreamer."

"Hi." Her voice was soft, barely a breath.

"Welcome back. I was told if you wake, we need to try to get you to eat."

Maya's lips twitched in the corner of her lips. "Jello?"

"Good ole hospital Jello," I smirked. "Maybe some ice cream too, but I'm sure the nurses want you to eat some protein shake. It's been a week since you've been here."

Maya frowned. "How...long...was...I...gone?" She was panting with the effort it took for her to get the words out, but she did so well.

"You were gone a full week."

"And...it's been..."

"And it's been six days since your rescue," I said, filling in the gaps.

Maya gasped softly.

"Don't worry about that right now," I said, waving my hand away. "Let's worry about getting you some food. Do you want to sit up a bit?"

Maya nodded.

I smiled and raised the head of the bed up with the remote. Then I pressed the call button for Darla, our friendly night-shift nurse. I was just getting Maya's pillows situated when Darla walked smiling. "Well, there's my pretty patient finally awake. How we doing?"

"Okaaaay," Maya said, speaking softly.

Darla grinned. "Alright. Doc said we need to get you eating. How about we start with a protein shake and see how you do? Then we get some Jello in a bit."

"Told you so," I chuckled.

Maya rolled her eyes, a faint smile pulling at her lips.

Twenty minutes later, we had the TV playing some car action movie we'd both seen a million times, while Maya sucked back a protein shake. It almost felt normal, though we both knew it was far from it.

"Where are...Marcos...and Jason?" Maya asked.

"They had left right before you woke up. It's Friday night. They had to make an appearance at the clubhouse."

Maya wrinkled her nose.

I chuckled. "Yeah. They've been here as much as they can. Marcos is president though, so he's still needed, and I kicked Jason out. He kept reading to you, when it was my idea."

Maya's mouth dropped open in shock. "His...voice..."

"Yeah, I bet you heard his voice. It was why he did it. Took my idea and ran with it, because he knows you love his damn voice." I laughed and shook my head. "So he read you spicy romance in that sultry voice of his."

Maya laughed, and at first, I thought she was coughing, so I leaned forward to help her, only to realize that she was silently laughing, her shoulders shaking with glee.

My heart swelled in my chest; fucking pounded as I saw her beautiful smile. God, that was a sight for sore eyes. "Yeah, you love that shit." I smirked and shook my head.

Darla came in to check on things when Maya's heart-rate monitor started beeping like crazy again. She smiled when she saw Maya laughing and came over and shut the monitor off. "I think we're good on this for a while. How's that shake doing?"

Maya gave her a thumbs up and a grin.

My heart felt lighter than it had in the last two weeks. Shit, it felt lighter than it had in months. I knew the road to recovery would be hard for Maya, but I hoped that this was a good sign at least.

Maya

I WAS FINISHING UP my protein shake when the hospital room door opened, and Marcos and Jason walked in. Both men stopped in their tracks when they saw me sitting up and coherent.

"You guys weren't even gone a full fucking hour. I thought you were gonna STAY there for an hour!" Nico complained loudly to his brothers.

Both men were still staring wide-eyed at me, not blinking. It was making me feel self-conscious, and I realized for the first time that I had no idea what I looked like. I assumed I looked like hell.

"Well, you just gonna stand there? Say something! You're making her uncomfortable." Nico's annoyance had me shooting him a wry smile. Leave it to Nico to call out those two.

"Uh, hi," Marcos said after a moment's hesitation.

"Hey," I replied softly. Why were they being weird? Why was this so hard?

"You're awake," Marcos said, stating the obvious.

I nodded, saving my voice.

Both men looked so out of place and neither one seemed to know what to do. Not like Nico, who had been talking almost nonstop the last hour, carefully avoiding the topic at hand. I didn't want to think about the elephant in the room, and the last thing I wanted to do was talk about it.

Thankfully a moment later, Darla walked into the room with my Jello. Who would have thought I'd get excited over the thought of Jello? Darla walked right through the tension in the room with a smile on her face. "Here you are honey. Let's see how this goes, and if you're still up in a couple hours, we'll do another shake. Otherwise in the morning you can have soft foods."

I nodded gratefully and took the container of orange Jello and the spoon from her.

"Now boys, take a seat, you're kinda in the way." Darla winked at them.

Snapping out of their stupor, both Marcos and Jason startled at her words and headed for the other two chairs besides her bed. Both of them looked like your standard hard as fuck, typical plastic hospital chairs. Not like the recliner that Nico had claimed for himself.

Darla left the room and silence once again descended on us. Marcos and Jason were still staring at me unblinkingly and it was beginning to unnerve me. "Stop," I mumbled the best I could with my sore throat. Nico had explained it was because of the breathing tube, but it still sucked. I vaguely remembered waking up with that still in.

"How are you?" Jason asked, then winced as if he realized what he asked.

"I'm...alive," I murmured the words the best I could.

Jason's eyes closed for a moment before he opened them. He nodded solemnly.

"But we're not talking about that right now," Nico jumped in. "We have all the time in the world for depressing shit. We're talking about this dumb movie and whatever dumb shit happened at the clubhouse. I'm sure Nickle or Phoenix got up to something in the short time you were there."

Marcos chuckled and nodded. "Nickle and Phoenix were doing burlap sack races...naked."

My mouth dropped open and Nico burst out laughing. "Yes! Not that anyone in their right fucking minds wants to see that, but yes!"

I started laughing and dug into my Jello with a smile on my face, ignoring the two idiots that were staring at me in awe.

Maya

After the movie ended, I yawned and started to drift in and out, but I didn't want to fall asleep just yet. I was basking in the presence of my boys and didn't want it to end. There was rustling to my left and I looked over in time to see Nico reach across me and hand Jason a book. "What? No." Jason tried to push Nico and the book away, but I perked up.

"Please?" I asked, my voice soft.

Jason startled and looked over at me. His gray eyes were a storm that peered into my soul. He looked so raw and unsure of himself. It was different. I couldn't ever recall a time when Jason wasn't sure of himself.

"Please?" I asked again, my voice a little stronger this time.

He sighed softly, but grabbed the book from Nico. He leaned forward in the chair, so he was resting his elbows on his wide-spread knees, and opened the book at where the bookmark was shoved in. It was then that I realized it was my favorite Why Choose novel, about a girl that found her fated mates after a war tore them apart.

Jason's voice a smooth honey that sent shivers down my spine as he immediately picked up from where he left off. I fucking missed his voice. I fucking missed *him*. All of them.

Jason

I never felt so uneasy or out of place as I did in that moment. Marcos and Nico were watching me expectantly as I started to read the book. I tried to ignore them and was just getting into the story when I glanced up. Maya was watching me through lidded lashes, her head turned toward me as she hung on to my every word.

My heart exploded in my chest at the sight of her amber eyes watching me with such devotion. I kept reading, glancing up at her once in a while, catching her gaze until her eyes slid closed. I paused, wondering if she had fallen asleep.

"Keep...go...ing," she murmured.

I continued, knowing my words were helping her drift off to sleep.

I didn't know how long I read for, but when Nico let out a quiet snore, I looked up. Nico was sound asleep in the recliner next to Maya, and Marcos had left the room completely, probably to the attached bedroom suite that we had been using for the last six days.

When I turned back to Maya, I found her eyes open again, watching me silently. "Hey," I murmured.

She gave me a faint smile, just her lips tipping up in the corners.

"Maya...shit," I grumbled, unsure where to begin. I needed to apologize.

Her hand reached out toward me, palm up and open.

I furrowed my brows as I stared at her hand in confusion, but I reached for it, anyway.

Maya laced our fingers together the best she could and gently tugged me forward. I leaned toward her, resting my elbows on the mattress as I got closer to her. "Come here," she whispered.

I frowned and tried to see how I could get any closer. She tugged me toward her. "May—"

Maya tugged my hand harder.

"Alright, alright, already," I muttered and stood up. I kicked off my shoes and Maya hit the button on the bed to lower the head down. I waited while the bed moved, glancing at a slightly snoring Nico before I looked back at Maya. She was rolling onto her right side and scooting over to make room for me in the hospital bed. Maya even went as far as to pull back the blanket and sheet for me to get under.

I shook my head slightly in disbelief, before I slid into the bed with her. Once I was covered up, I slid my arm under her neck and pulled her against me. It took some maneuvering, but we eventually got her comfortable with her head on my shoulder and her arm with the IV's in it resting on my chest. She even draped her leg over mine.

I wrapped my arm around her and reveled in the feeling of her in my arms. It was fucking heaven, and I wasn't going to let go ever. Loosely, I laced my fingers with hers on my chest, stroking gently over the top of her hand. "Darlin'," I breathed the endearment I used for her.

"Not now, Jase." Her voice was hoarse, but getting stronger.

"When?" I had so much I needed to say, to get off my chest. I needed to apologize and beg for her forgiveness, grovel if I had to.

"When I'm ready."

I sighed and pressed a kiss to the crown of her head. Maya was completely within her right, but it was hard to accept that. It was hard to keep my damn mouth shut when all I wanted to do was explain and pour my damn heart out.

She tensed momentarily in my arms, before she relaxed. Melting against me, she nuzzled her cheek a bit against my shoulder before settling in.

Maya

SEEING LUKE HAD BEEN more emotional than I expected. The pain in his eyes when I gave him my phone to call Marcos and made him leave without me. I would never forget the look in his eye. The fear.

The heartbreak on his face when he walked in the hospital room and saw me sitting up in bed, eating breakfast, would forever be engrained in my mind. He rushed toward me; Nico barely moved my food tray out of the way as Luke flung himself into my arms. I didn't even care that it hurt to hug him, I had my baby boy back safely in my arms, and that was all that mattered.

"Oh, my baby." I cried and hugged him tight.

Luke sobbed in my arms and refused to leave for the rest of the day. And I wasn't making him. Instead, I ate my food with one hand and held him with the other. We watched movies and hung out with my guys, and when Darla came in that night, she brought with her a package of fresh-baked cookies from the local bakery.

Later that night, Luke was half-asleep lying in bed with me when Marcos told Luke it was time to go. I frowned at Marcos but didn't say anything. I didn't like the idea of him leaving though. I didn't want him so far away.

Luke immediately started protesting. "No! I'm staying with my mom! I'm not leaving!"

"Luke, your mom needs rest, buddy." Marcos tried to coax him away from me.

Luke started crying as he clung to me. My heart broke into a million pieces. Jason and Nico looked as lost as I felt. Darla must have heard the commotion because she walked in a moment later. "Can I suggest the family bedroom? He can get his rest and so can mom?"

Ever the fucking lifesaver, I thought. I caught Marcos's eye and shrugged. Marcos nodded slowly, as if admitting defeat. "It's ok, Luke. I'm ok." I rubbed my son's back, speaking softly while trying to sooth him. "There's a bedroom here, you can stay in the suite with Dad."

"I can?" Luke's head shot off my shoulder to look back at his father.

"Yeah, buddy. We can stay. But you need your rest, and so does mom," Marcos said.

Luke looked back at me and I gave him a warm smile. "You need to sleep," I said.

"Alright," he reluctantly agreed.

Once he was in the bedroom suite and Marcos closed the door behind them, I let the first tears fall.

"Oh, Little Dreamer." Nico sighed and sat on the edge of the bed next to me, pulling me into his arms.

I silently let the tears fall down my face, sniffling here there into the tissue that Jason handed me.

"It's ok to let go," Nico said.

I shook my head. I couldn't do that yet. Just like I couldn't dwell too much on what had happened during my week with Hillcrest. I couldn't think about it yet. I wanted to be physically strong again before I let emotions weigh me down.

It was only a matter of time before my emotions got the better of me and completely crashed around me, but I wasn't ready for that yet.

"Maya." Nico breathed my name like he was disappointed in me.

I vehemently shook my head. "No."

"Leave her alone," Jason snapped at Nico.

Nico huffed and slid off the mattress and returned to his recliner. I had quickly discovered since waking that morning that the recliner was *his* and no one else was allowed to sit in it.

Jason shook his head and grabbed my hand, wrapping his fingers through mine. I squeezed his hand appreciatively. I didn't want to be coddled right now and was grateful that coddling was never Jason's default.

Needing to change the subject, I turned to Jason. "What did you get up to this week?"

"You mean, when I wasn't by your side every hour of the day?" Jason shot back, immediately rising to my bait.

I smirked. "You weren't."

He rolled his eyes. "I was organizing shit at the house. Contractors and all that."

My eyebrows furrowed together. "House?"

Nico shifted in the recliner next to me but didn't say a word.

Jason shrugged a shoulder. "Yeah, I bought a house. I'm remodeling it right now. New carpet upstairs, redoing the hardwoods downstairs."

I nodded absently, wondering if there was something I was missing. I didn't remember him saying he bought a house, but it wasn't like we were talking much until the night before my capture. And we definitely weren't talking mundane shit like house renovations. No, we were calling a truce.

A truce that didn't matter in the grand scheme of things, not when things like life and death were involved. I was glad that he wasn't angry with me anymore, though. Being able to hold his hand, or listen to him read my romance novels, was something I was thoroughly enjoying. It would be better if I could shower and change into comfy jammies, but Griff wanted me to stay in bed as much as possible.

When the day nurse had taken out my catheter and I'd hobbled into the bathroom, I found I couldn't look at myself in the mirror. So I avoided looking at it. I probably looked atrocious, but it didn't matter. Peeing had burned, but that was probably from the catheter being removed versus any kind of infection, because they still had me on IV antibiotics. But being wide awake like I was now, I found that bed rest was getting old.

My body was healing slowly. The sepsis had taken most of my energy and strength, as had not moving for days after a week of abuse. I wasn't thinking about that, though. I needed to think about something else, so I dove into the reno project with Jason. "What kind of carpet?" I asked.

"Plush, extra padding underneath." He answered me immediately, a slightly smirk tugging at his lips like he was sharing a secret with me.

I nodded, finding his answer acceptable. "And what color on the hardwood?"

"Dark stain."

It sounded like something I would choose for my own house. I hated that I was jealous that he was putting everything I wanted into his home. I really didn't know what else to ask after that, and Nico had shut down completely when Jason snapped at him, which wasn't like him at all.

Looking over at Nico, I found him watching the TV silently, ignoring Jason completely, which was also unlike him. It made me wonder just what the hell was going on with the two of them, but I also didn't want to think about it. I didn't want to deal with anything heavy or emotional right now.

All I wanted was to recover and go home. I wanted my own bed, my own shower, and my own damn food. Darla was nice and all, but I really wanted to be left the fuck alone for a while, and Nico had made it clear that he wasn't going anywhere.

The idea of Jason buying a house made me wonder about too many things. Like, did he buy the house alone, or with Marcos and Nico? Did he buy before or after Marcos decided he needed a paternity test court ordered? Was Marcos planning to take Lucas from me? Was that why they bought the house?

"Maya," Nico's voice broke through my twisting thoughts. "Don't do that."

"Do what?" I asked almost petulantly.

"Let the darkness consume you." He squeezed my knee reassuringly.

That was easier said than done, I thought.

Maya

B y Monday, I was chomping at the bit to get the fuck out of the hospital. Jenna and my mother were driving me nuts. Nico—bless his heart—was also driving me fucking nuts. Sunday Jason and Marcos had left for most of the day, taking Luke with them, leaving me with the three of them hovering over me. By the time Marcos and Jason came back that night, I was ready to lock myself in the bedroom suite.

Jason took one look at my face and had kicked everyone out. Thankfully Luke had been fine to go with Jenna and my mother. When Nico finally left, Jason had climbed into the bed with me and pulled me into his chest.

Monday morning was different though. Nico hated being away, so he was being clingy again. Marco and Jason had to leave for a job for the day, so my mother and Jenna had swooped in again. "I love you all, but I can't take you guys anymore," I finally said, putting my hands on my head. "I need quiet. All of you need to leave."

"But—" Nico said, looking hurt.

"Nicolai, I love you, but you gotta go. For a couple hours, at least, please," I said, exasperated.

Nico gasped in a fake outrage, holding his hand to his heart acting a fool. "You're kicking *me* out? What about—"

"Please!" I shouted, my fingers wrapped around my hair, pulling at the roots. I was getting overwhelmed and over stimulated; I was about to freak out on all of them soon if they didn't leave me the fuck alone.

"Alright, Little Dreamer. I hear you," Nico finally relented. He held his hands up in surrender and stood from his recliner.

When I was finally alone, I took a deep breath and fell back against the bed. I wanted a shower, a *real* shower, and I wanted my own damn bed, with no nurses coming in the middle of the night to check my vitals despite the damn computer I was hooked up to telling them everything they need to know. Darla had been fantastic, but on the nights she was off, the other nurse, the younger one, was a little less tactful. I had already complained to Griff several times.

I had also begun to text Griffin frequently, complaining about still being in the hospital. I needed peace and quiet, I needed my normal routine again—and Luke NEEDED to be in school. He was throwing more and more of a fit every time he had to leave me. While it broke my heart, it was getting out of hand.

We needed our fucking normal back.

I would fight tooth and nail to get my ass back home.

"How you doing?" Darla asked.

I slowly opened my eyes to meet the gaze of the older woman standing in the doorway and gave her an exasperated look that said it all.

Darla laughed and walked closer. "They mean well, at least."

"I know. I know they do. It fucking sucks though. I haven't time to fucking process everything yet and they're watching me to see if I'm gonna fucking break down. Like they're waiting for it."

"Yeah, meeting other's expectations of grieving is hard. Everyone processes pain and grief in their own way." Darla took a seat in the hard plastic chair to my right that Jason usually sat in.

"I haven't even had a chance to think of what happened, I've been refusing to let myself think about it, to be honest. Not while they're all here and watching—waiting," I grumbled.

Darla chuckled. "Have you thought about a therapist?"

"Yeah, I've thought that I'll probably need one when I finally let myself think about the week of hell I went through. That's about as far as I've gotten with that line of thinking though," I admitted.

"That is honestly way more emotionally cognizant than anyone could expect after what you endured," Darla nodded.

I shrugged. "It's more of an avoidance than coping method, if I'm being honest. Anytime I start to think of what happened, I keep telling myself that now is not the time. I'm not ready to unpack all that yet—if I'll ever be ready."

"No," Darla shook her head. "I don't think anyone would ever ready to unpack that."

I chuckled sardonically. "I'm gonna need therapy just dealing with my family."

Darla barked a laugh. "They do seem a little *much*, at some points."

I grinned widely. "Met my sister, have you?"

"Oh, Doc Jen is great." Darla grinned. "Your mother on the other hand?"

I laughed and slapped my thigh. "I know. Tell me about it."

"She was going off on another nurse for the size of the ice cubes. I mean, you were unconscious still. Ice wasn't a worry." Darla shook her head.

Again, I found myself laughing. "You don't know Elaine Henderson. Everything has to be perfect. It's all about appearances."

Darla shook her head, a knowing look in her eye. "That had to be tough growing up."

Nodding, I wondered how much to reveal. In the end, Darla had already seen all of me, so why not bear the ugly truths. "She was never a good mom to me. Jenna was the favorite, and that was that. Jenna always tried to include me, always tried to make mom see reason, but it didn't matter when Elaine got what Elaine wanted."

"I can see that about her," Darla admitted.

"I will say in the last five years or so, she's turned things around. She is actively trying, and she really is great with Luke, but it doesn't change much for me. That relationship was already strained. I think with my dad's passing recently, and my... kidnapping... she's seeing how short life is and is trying harder this time around. But it's almost like, too little, too late, you know?" I asked.

Darla nodded her head, a thoughtful expression on her face. "I get that. That's totally acceptable to feel that way—valid even. But what about letting go of the past? I'm not saying to forgive and forget—never that—but to let go of the pain you felt over the past and start anew. You can hold her at an arm's length if makes you feel better, but you could also give her a chance again."

I sat silently, mulling over Darla's words. "I'm not saying I won't try, but I'm tired of always having to."

"Tell her that. Spell that out to her. She has more to lose now."

"Jenna said the same thing years ago. When Luke was two, my mother showed up in Chicago on Jenna's doorstep one night. Jenna hadn't spoken to her in a couple years, not since my mother had kicked me out of the house after college. I hadn't been dating the guys very long then, barely a couple weeks, and she kicked me out because I got home later than I thought. Though I had told her when to expect me. She was so set in her ways back then, and so fricking rigid in her thinking. Unreasonable, honestly.

"But yeah, she showed up at Jenna's house and saw me with a baby and just started bawling. She apologized for everything and went on all these tangents, and I just let her. I kinda just let everything go in one ear and out the other. Over the years, I kept things cordial, but always at a distance. Then they got in their accident last year and needed someone to take care of them. I volunteered because Luke had been asking about his father, so I figured two birds with one stone..." I shook my head, trailing off.

"Things go back to the way they were before?" Darla asked.

"Not really? But kinda? Like it was weird being back in that house again. She was great with Luke, but kinda cold and standoffish with me? I know she was stressed, taking care of my father—seeing him that way was hard—but I dunno."

"It still hurt?" Darla supplied.

"Yeah, yeah it did." I nodded, then shook my head. "I don't know what to do about it now. And I keep getting on Griff to let me out of here, but realistically heading back to her house doesn't sound all that great either."

"Why not? Wouldn't somewhere familiar be better than not, right now?"

I thought about it for a moment. "Sure, but it's a small three-bedroom house and my sister is in town, Luke has his own space, and Nico and the guys..."

"Are very clingy?" Darla chuckled.

"Yes. Is it too much to ask for some space?"

"No. Not at all. You need to set boundaries with them. Communicate."

I laughed and shook my head again. "We used to be so good at that—or so I thought."

"What do you mean?"

I played with the Band-Aid from where my IV needles had pierced my skin, debating my words. "What do you know about BDSM?"

"Quite a bit, you'd be surprised." Darla winked at me.

I let out a started laugh and nodded appreciatively. "Alright, Darla!"

Darla just smiled and waited for me to continue.

Looking down and toying with my bandage, I explained. "When we started dating, we negotiated everything. Full out kink lists, likes and dislikes, hard and soft limits, the whole nine yards. And we would check in with each other weekly, see if things weren't working any more or if there was something new that we wanted to try. It worked well for so long... then eventually the lines began to blur, and we fell into this twenty-four/seven relationship that we never negotiated. At the time it felt natural. But looking back, I realize that it had gotten harder for me to speak up, to speak my mind. I didn't want to upset the status quo, I guess."

"How old were you then?"

"I was twenty-four when I left. We were together for two years."

"You were still really, really young," Darla said. "You gotta give yourself some grace. Being in full-time, D & S relationship is hard for anyone, let alone a twenty-year-old kid still figuring out how the world works. They're older than you?"

"Yeah. They're all forty now."

"And you're thirty-four?"

"Yep." I nodded.

"Yeah, you gotta cut yourself some slack. You were in over your head and probably managed well. Maybe you did great, but lines were blurred and things happen. Add in the outside forces you were dealing with and of course you felt overwhelmed. I think you should kick those boys' asses for letting things escalate the way they had. They were your Doms and there were three of them. They had a say in how things progressed as well. They should have either backed off or initiated the conversation themselves regarding the relationship. Had you felt comfortable enough to bring things up back then, maybe you would have gone to them about the stalker thing."

I frowned as I contemplated what Darla had just said. It wasn't the first time I had heard something along those lines. I'd gone searching for answers in the local BDSM community when I was in Chicago and online forums. There had been too much left up in the air, and that last night I'd shared with my guys in the forest hadn't sat right with me for years after. It was how I found my therapist—a friend from the BDSM club I frequented had recommended her.

Sighing, I nodded. I had a lot to think about and not enough time to figure it out. Everyone was gone, so I was going to take advantage of the quiet to take a shower. "Can I shower?" I asked, changing the subject.

Darla smiled easily and nodded. She stood up and patted me on the hand. "Sure, can, kiddo."

Axel

I LOOKED AT THE three men standing in front of me and frowned. Marcos, Jason, and Nico, aka Killer, Stone, and Dagger were at the gym where I trained with Phoenix and Blaze, and not at the hospital taking care of their woman. "What's up?" I asked, sitting up from the shoulder press and looked up at the three men surrounding me.

"Hey man, we just wanted to thank you for your help getting that video," Dagger said.

"Yeah, it's what finally found her. Without it, our tech guy couldn't pinpoint their exact location," Killer added.

"Yeah, no problem. Glad I could help." I nodded.

"Seriously, though. Thank you," Stone said as well.

I only nodded, because now it was getting weird. I didn't do big shows of gratitude. I was a quiet guy that stuck to the shadows, unless I was fighting. "Look, I know you guys have more claim to killing Hillcrest at this poi—"

"We all have a claim," Killer—Marcos, interrupted me. "He killed your family, your brother, that means something. You have a claim. He kidnapped my sister. He kidnapped my woman. He was stalking Maya for months—years. We all have a claim. I know you want to kill Hillcrest, but the best I can offer at this point is being there. The Ravager Knights—Johnny and his boys especially—want dibs on killing Hillcrest too. At this point we need to wipe out their entire crew."

"Fuck yes," I growled and stood up. I clapped palms with Marcos before we shook on it.

"Dagger's going to meet with his cousin and set up a sit down with the Knights. We'll get the coke trade figured out, then we'll talk about Hillcrest." Killer explained.

I nodded, because what else could I say? They had everything all figured out. "Yeah."

Marcos walked away and Dagger followed him. Both men glanced back over their shoulder when Stone stayed behind, but he waved them off.

I waited patiently until Stone said what he needed to say. "I need a fight."

Shifting on my feet, I turned to meet the stone-cold killer, not surprised to see the stoney expression on the man's face. Emotions locked down, no flicker of anything across his gray eyes, the man was a fortress. I eyed him warily, for as stone-faced as the club enforcer was, he was also known for being a hair-trigger away from erupting into violence.

"Not sure I'm the one you should be talking to. Ask Johnny Taylor," I said, offhandedly. This was not the direction I thought this conversation was going to.

"No." Stone grumble. "I want in at fight night."

"Taylor's fights are legit; there's big money there. Go fight there." I tried my best to push by Jason, but true to his road name, he was a solid as stone.

"I don't want to fight over at the Knights's compound. I want in at Roadies," Jason snapped.

"Man, you don't know the bullshit that goes on at Roadies fight nights. They're dangerous—they're one step away from prison fights. You don't know if you're going to walk away from them—a lot of people don't."

Jason narrowed his eyes at me, a spark of anger igniting in those stormy gray eyes. "You and your boys fight there."

I barked a sardonic laugh. "Me and my boys don't have anything to lose. We don't have much to live for, if you catch my drift. Fighting and the club is all we have. And each other."

Giving me a once over, his stony expression shifted into something else, something too close to pity that I didn't fucking like. "You wanna fight? Come on, let's hit the ring right now."

Stone glared, but nodded his head.

I was going to enjoy this. It was about time someone knocked Stone fucking Langford on his ass.

Ten minutes later, both of us were shirtless and in gym shorts as we stepped into the practice ring, while we both pulled gloves on to our hands. "This a smart idea?" Blaze mumbled from behind me.

"He asked for it," I murmured back.

"Still, is it smart? Shouldn't you have pushed him toward Taylor or something? Shit, even Dagger would be better than this," Blaze grumbled.

"He keeps asking about Roadie's." I pulled my gloves on tight, eyeing Jason from across the octagon as he spoke softly with Marcos and Nico.

"Not good," Phoenix muttered.

"Yeah, I know. Figured this would be better than anything. He's hurting, needs an outlet."

"And you think it's smart that you're the one to do that? He's a brother, Ax," Phoenix said.

"I know, dude, I fucking know. But you go change his mind." I shook my head exasperatedly at my brothers.

Jason finally turned away from Marcos and Nico, and I had to remind myself that they were his president and vice president respectively... and Jason was the club enforcer. He was no weak fighter. He could hold his own, though no one had seen him get dirty in a while.

"Go easy," Blaze suggested softly.

I nodded.

"Give him hell," Phoenix chuckled.

I smirked slightly and stepped toward the center of the ring. Jason met me in the middle and we pounded our knuckles together by touching gloves. "Typical rules apply, knock out or tap out. Everything else goes," I said.

"Got it," Jason agreed with a nod.

I glanced to the right and saw Marcos's son standing ringside. "You sure you want him here?"

Jason glanced at the kid and nodded. "Marcos will take him away if it's too rough, but he could use the demonstration. We're teaching him to defend himself."

Shrugging, I smirked and made the first jab, tossing a sucker punch right to Jason's jaw.

Jason's head snapped to the right, and he swore, before he laughed, and then we were fighting. Jason came at me with a solid one two punch that I blocked and ducked easily.

I swung my leg out and aimed a roundhouse kick right into Jason's ribs. The thud of my foot connecting with flesh echoed through the gym. Jason grunted with pain and came at me with vengeance.

We danced around the ring, both of us hitting and dodging, striking and kicking. I was slowly wearing him down. Jason was starting to lag on his feet. Both of us had sweat pouring down our muscular bodies.

I went in for the kill. A one-two punch to distract Jason while I swiped my foot out and took out Jason's legs, sending him sprawling to the mat. I didn't let up though, I dropped my elbow and my body weight on top of Jason in one of those TV professional wrestling moves that had Jason bouncing up in pain. I didn't let up though; I wrapped my thighs around his torso and locked my elbow around Jason's neck in a chokehold.

The men around the octagon ring started yelling and shouting, but I held tight. Jason knew the rules, he could tap out at any time. "Tap out!" Nico called.

"Jason!" Luke shouted.

Finally, after hearing the kid's voice, Jason tapped the mat twice.

I immediately let go and Jason rolled to his side, gasping for breath. "You good, man?"

"Yeah, thanks for the fight."

Laughing, I slapped Jason on the shoulder before I stood up and walked away. I walked over to where Blaze and Phoenix were waiting with a bottle of water ready. Taking the bottle, I sucked back half of it in one large sip.

Chapter Twenty-Four

Maya

GETTING RELEASED FROM THE hospital felt surreal to me, because I didn't have anywhere to go. Griffin had made it fucking clear that I wasn't allowed to be alone for long periods of time. I was still in pain from a broken rib, and my abdomen still hurt from the surgery. But I was otherwise getting around alright, albeit slowly, and I was managing alright on my own.

Doc Griff refused though, and my mother said she didn't like the idea of me at the house because she still needed help of her own. She said she didn't feel comfortable knowing we were both too weak in the house.

Marcos had offered to stay at the house a while longer since apparently, he'd already been doing that to take care of Luke. Elaine

155

was being a finicky fucking bitch, and said she was tired of all the company. She wanted her peace and quiet back.

I was just supposed to find new accommodations after being released from the hospital? It was fucking bullshit. Elaine was kicking me out all over again.

So fucking Nico had swooped in and saved the day and offered up his place, saying Luke and I could stay with him. I was still in disbelief that my mother had refused to let me come home, and had agreed like an idiot instead of arguing with her.

"This is ridiculous. I don't know why she's such a fucking bitch all the time," I muttered to my sister while she helped me pull my clothes on for the first time. It hurt to move my arms with broken ribs, and Jenna had been a life saver, grabbing me a button-up shirt to wear.

Jenna sighed. "I don't know, Maya. I think the separation might be good for both of you. You've been through a lot, and I'm not sure that house is the best place for you right now."

I frowned. "Why wouldn't the house be a good place for me?"

"I just mean, being around her in general. You need to heal in a safe environment, and while the house is fine, we both know mom can be ridiculous and not realize how cruel she's being," Jenna said, holding up a sleeve to a sweatshirt for me to slip my arm into.

I moved slowly, sliding my arm through the sleeve. Mourningside felt the approach of autumn as September brought a cold front and the reminder that winter was making its approach quickly.

"What makes you think being with Marcos, Jason, and Nico will be good for me?" I countered.

"I think we both know that Nico will move heaven and earth for you. And the other two...I say give them a chance. They've both realized just how fucked up the situation is. They're trying. They want to make amends. It's clear they still love you."

I frowned, watching as my sister moved about the room, picking things up and gathering the last of my belongings. Nico had already grabbed most of my things that morning, taking them back to his place, but there were still odds and ends left behind.

Where the fuck were they? After a sold week of all of them—Nico especially—breathing down my neck and hovering nearby, they were gone. Only Nico had come back to the hospital the night before, after I had kicked the three of them out for annoying the shit out of me.

Nico didn't offer an explanation, and I didn't ask.

Marcos and Jason hadn't been by this morning, and Nico had taken off right after having breakfast with me. He said he had some stuff to do to get ready for my arrival, but he would be back in time to drive me home.

"How am I supposed to make amends with men that see me as fragile and breakable? Like, what the fuck Jenna? Do we just go back to how we were? I can't do that. I'm not that same person anymore! I've been through too much—seen too much. It's not possible." I felt like I was ranting and took a deep breath, shaking my head.

"You don't, sweetheart. You fucking don't. You have to have the hard conversations. You need to break down what happened after you left them, and how you felt about that last scene. Most of all, you need to fucking talk to them about *everything*," Jenna stressed.

I looked away, feeling disheartened. "I'm not sure I can," I admitted.

Jenna sighed and sat beside me on the hospital bed. Reaching for my hand, she squeezed my fingers gently. "Have you called your therapist yet?"

I shook my head.

"What about your friends at Niche?"

My brows furrowed at the thought of the BDSM club I used to frequent. The friends I had made there had been a lifesaver when I had hit rock bottom after leaving Mourningside/Creekton all those years ago. The friendships I had, had opened my eyes to things in my relationship with the guys that wasn't all right.

I hadn't talked to any of those friends since I moved back down here, not truly. We kept up through text messages in group chats, but nothing substantial. The thought of talking to them anytime soon and having to explain what happened only made my anxiety skyrocket. So I shook my head, shaking the thought away.

I refused to think about it right now.

There was a knock on the door, and I looked over to see Nico standing there, his blond hair around his shoulders and bright blue eyes sparking as he grinned. "Hey, Little Dreamer. You ready to break out this joint?"

I couldn't keep the smile off my face if I tried. Nico was a goofball, but he was my goofball. "Yeah. Let's blow this popsicle stand."

"Right on!" Nico said.

Darla walked in with a wheelchair a moment later and I turned to Jenna. "Are you following us?"

"No, I'm gonna go check on mom. Then I'm probably going home tomorrow afternoon. I'll come by in the morning before I leave to say goodbye." Jenna squeezed my fingers again.

"What about Luke?" I turned to Nico.

"Already at my place with Marcos. We've got him covered, no worries." Nico grinned.

I frowned, feeling like that was all I did anymore. "Got it all figured out, huh?"

"Sure do, Little Dreamer. Now, let's get you out of here, and you can relax in a real bed."

"I mean... this is no normal hospital bed," I said, motioning to the fancy as fuck bed I was propped up against.

Nico just smirked and Darla wheeled over the wheelchair.

After shuffling around and only a small grunt of pain from shifting from the bed to the wheelchair, I was on my way out of the hospital. Hopefully I would be on my way to happier beginnings.

Chapter Twenty-Five

Marcos

I LOOKED AROUND THE house in awe. Jason had out fucking done himself with all the work he had done in the short amount time since we closed on the property. The newly redone hardwood floors were a dark stain that made the freshly painted white kitchen cabinets pop. The new counters in the kitchen and bathrooms made the house feel brand new. Add in the extra plush cream carpet Jason added up the stairs and onto the entirety of the second floor, I barely recognized the place anymore.

It was our home, but new. A fresh start.

I couldn't wait for Nico to pull up with Maya.

Jason and I had spent the last two days moving in, including setting up a bedroom for Luke and moving Maya into the primary bedroom. Luke would still have his bedroom at Elaine's house, as would Maya, but the plan was to move them both into the new house. It was their home as much as it was mine, Jason's, and Nico's.

Jason still wandered the place aimlessly, looking around, like he was searching for something else to replace or fix. "Maybe we should—"

"Maybe you should chill out. It's going to be fine," I said, trying to console my brother.

Jason shook his head but didn't reply as both our phones dinged with an incoming message.

Nico:

Just leaving the hospital.

"Fuck," Jason grumbled. He put his phone in his pocket and left the kitchen. Probably in search of something else to fix or fluff or add to the list to remodel.

I shook my head. I really couldn't fault Jason for being nervous, shit I was nervous too. What if Maya hated the house? What if she didn't want to stay with us? Nico hadn't exactly been up front when he invited her to stay with him. She'd been to his condo before, but she had no idea that we bought a house together.

I could only hope that she would be happy to see the old house. We had two years of wonderful memories here, or so I thought.

Hopefully Maya thought the same.

Maya

I glanced at Nico for the hundredth time as he drove through the streets of Mourningside. He was being shifty, and for Nico that was saying something. Any time I asked where Marcos and Jason were, he just said they were 'at the house'. Whatever the hell that meant.

"Hey, isn't your condo back that way?" I asked, when Nico turned the opposite direction than he should have to get home.

"Just have to make a stop, really quick."

I narrowed my gaze on him but didn't respond. Instead, I watched as he drove toward the older unincorporated area south of the industrial district on Mourningside's Southside. Where my mother lived. Maybe we were just picking something up at my mom's house? Nico had said they grabbed my things, though.

I hated the cloak and dagger. The fucking secrets. It was utterly pointless and just drove up my anxiety. After all the shit we've been through over the years, I wanted nothing more than to have an open dialogue between us, at all times. Open communication.

It was the only way anything was going to work going forward between us. After all the shit I went through in last couple weeks regarding Hillcrest, I was honestly surprised that he still wanted me. But I wasn't questioning it. I didn't want to think about it, just like I didn't want to think about everything else going on.

Processing could wait.

Nico turned into the neighborhood my mother lived in and I frowned. I didn't really want to see my mother, not if Elaine was being a bitch again and not going to let me recover at home. Only, Nico didn't pull onto my mother's street. Instead, Nico pulled on to the road past my mother's street. Our old street, from the rental house days when the four of us lived together: Primrose.

Our old rental house had been two blocks from my parent's house, and Nico looked like he was driving right toward it. I turned in my seat to watch him. Nico was a shit liar when it came to me, I could see right through his bullshit nine times out of ten. There was only the smallest tweak at the corner of his lips, and I fucking knew.

"What have you done?" I asked, my voice soft. My throat still hurt from being intubated with the breathing tube, despite it being several days without it.

Nico's face broke into a full-blown cheesy-as-fuck grin that sent my heart racing thunderously in my chest. He looked so fucking proud of himself. We were a block away from the old rental house and I just knew in my heart, that's where we were headed. "This one wasn't all me. Marcos spoke to the relator about the house. Jason delt with all the financial shit. I just helped pay for shit and pointed Jason in the right direction when he got stuck on the remodels."

I sat in silence, completely speechless as I listened to him explain everything. He had spoken so matter-of-factly, like it was nothing life-altering.

My guys had bought a fucking house. Our fucking house.

I had loved that old farmhouse and every day of our lives there. Even on the bad days, I had loved our life together. I often wondered what had happened to the old house back then; the guys still haven't said what exactly went down after I left.

I gasped as Nico pulled the car into the long driveway that passed the house on the right side to the large pole barn of a garage in the back. The wrap-around porch and the beautiful shutters were in need of a paint job, but it looked the same. It looked fucking amazing.

Nico pulled Marco's pickup truck in front, where two very recognizable Harley Davidson's were parked. "Nic," I breathed his name when he shut the truck off. "What are we doing here, Nicolai?" I needed to hear him say it.

Nico turned to me with a cheshire grin on his face. "Welcome home, Little Dreamer."

Tears welled my eyes. My hand covered my mouth as it sank in.

He brought me home.

Marcos and Jason walked out the back door onto the deck. Standing at the railing next to the driveway, they both waited for me to get out of the truck. I couldn't move though. Tears began pouring down my face as the reality of what they had planned crash over me. "Nic, I can't." I barely got the words out before Nico was unbuckling his seatbelt and getting out of the truck.

I watched him walk around the front of the truck, still in a daze as he reached my door and opened it. "Come on, Little Dreamer. They're waiting for you."

I didn't want to think about how I was going to get down from the truck, I had barely been able to climb up into it at the hospital. Nico didn't seem to have those same worries though, because he slid his hand around my waist, and undid my seat belt. Once it was back in place, Nico slid his arm under my legs and the other one around my back, and carefully lifted me out of the truck.

I immediately looped my arms around his neck, holding on. "Nico," I muttered.

"I got you, Little Dreamer."

I turned my attention toward the three steps up to the deck from the driveway, and to where Marcos and Jason were watching. Both men had their eyes on my face and I didn't bother to wipe the tears away. They wouldn't stop falling, anyway.

"Mi Vida," Marcos said, moving toward us.

"I got her." Nico shook his head.

"I can walk." I complained.

"I'll put you down inside," Nico conceded.

I glanced at Jason, finding his intense stare to be a little much for me right now. I was emotionally raw and was already tearing up, I was afraid if I looked deep into his stormy gray eyes, I'd see too much emotion there that would break me.

I wasn't ready to break. Not yet.

Nico walked through the backdoor, into the mudroom and then carefully set me down.

I was in awe as I stared around the small laundry slash mud room. It was completely different from when I lived here ten years ago. It was white and modern and airy. A wooden countertop was set atop the washer and dryer and there was a set of cabinets and open shelving. All empty. A blank slate. It looked fantastic.

I turned away from the mudroom and walked through the door into the kitchen—the completely remodeled kitchen. My breath caught in my throat as I took in the room. The upper cabinets were painted white, while the lower cabinets were painted black. There were granite counters now with a marbled finish and a white subway tile backsplash. It was modern and clean and sleek. Everything I had wanted back then.

Stainless steel appliances—and were those new floors?

I turned to face my guys, only to be startled when all three of them were watching me intently. "What is this?" I asked, my voice hoarse.

"It's your home," Jason said. "We thought we would update things while it was empty, before we all moved in."

"All moved in?" I asked.

Marcos nodded. "Yeah, Mi Vida. We're all moving in here. Together. Like it was before."

I didn't know what to say, so I didn't say anything. Wiping away my tears, I turned back to Jason. "Nico said you've been remodeling the house?"

He nodded and rubbed a hand over the back of his neck, looking sheepish. "Uh yeah. Well, calling crews in and directing them to do shit."

"Like what?" I asked, wanting the full break down of everything he had done to the house.

"The kitchen for one, the bathrooms too. Had the whole house painted, the floors down here redone, and new carpet upstairs," Jason explained.

I stared at him in awe and disbelief. Turning to the kitchen again, I just took in all in, trying to absorb the fact that I was even standing in this kitchen again. "Why?" The word was barely audible, but all three of my men flinched as if I dealt them a physical blow.

"Because it's our home," Marcos said. "When the relator told us it was available, it occurred to me that I wanted nothing more than to raise Luke here. When Griff said you shouldn't be alone when you go home, we thought it would be perfect to bring you home with us. Because this isn't a home without you."

A sob burst out of me that I couldn't hold in. Arms wrapped around me and I crumbled against whoever it was as my legs gave out. Emotions consumed me and I finally broke down. Everything poured out of me in heart wrenching sobs that tore through my body.

I clung to whoever grabbed me—Marcos I thought—as he carried me up the stairs in the living room. I didn't even get a chance to look at the rest of the house before I broke down. Marcos carried me into our old bedroom and laid down on the large mattress, pulling me with him.

My throat hurt as I wailed and screamed through my tears, letting out the pain of the last couple weeks. A body pressed into my back and arms wrapped around my waist tightly as they snuggled in close.

Nico

WATCHING MAYA FINALLY BREAK down was both a blessing and a curse. It needed to happen, it was long overdue in my opinion, but it still broke my heart. I curled around her on the mattress—the Alaskan King that Kara had delivered as a housewarming gift—spooning her, while she sobbed into Marcos's chest.

Jason stood at the foot of the bed awkwardly, before he put his knee on the mattress and crawled toward us. He pushed Marcos away and Marc shifted over to make room for Jason to lay between him and Maya. Jason pressed his face into Maya's stomach, while her face was buried into Marcos's chest.

The position was familiar, in a nostalgic way, and seemed to calm Maya down a bit, as she slid her fingers into Jason's hair. Jason's hands slid up under the back of her shirt, exposing bare skin. He kissed her stomach softly, nuzzling his face against her.

Slowly, Maya calmed down to just soft sniffles, before her body relaxed and she finally fell asleep.

I let out a soft sigh when her body went lax and let my own eyes drift shut. The rest of the world could wait; we had our woman in our arms again and she needed us.

Nico

Three hours later, Maya shifted between us, groaning softly as she tried to roll over. "What's wrong?" I asked, opening my eyes in time to watch Marcos's eyes snap open.

"I have to pee." Maya's voice was scratchy and hoarse, likely from screaming and sobbing. Hopefully she hadn't injured her already sore throat.

I made a note to make her hot tea later. Or should it be cold ice cream? I didn't know, but I made a note to offer both to her and let her decide.

Patting Jason on the shoulder, I shook him awake. "Jase, man. Let her go," Nico said.

Jason grumbled and slid his hands up her back. He pressed a kiss to her bare stomach before he pulled his hands out from under her shirt and let her go.

I rolled away, going as far as to roll off the bed and stand up.

Maya tried to the do the same thing, but ended up gasping in pain. "Fuck," she groaned.

"Shit," I swore. "I'll go get your meds. You need to eat too. Someone should make dinner."

"I'll order something. Maya what do you want?" Jason asked.

"Pizza," she murmured, holding her hands to her stomach as she panted softly.

"Can I carry you?" Marcos asked.

Maya shook her head. "I just need a minute, or help up, or a new body. I don't know."

I snickered as I walked out of the room. I pounded down the stairs glancing out the front window to see the darkening sky. September was in full swing, and the days were growing shorter. We'd slept the afternoon away, and I hoped that after we fed Maya and gave her more pain pills, that she would pass out again.

Just because she was home didn't mean she was fully healed. Her colon was still healing from her surgery. It would take time, and she needed to take it easy.

In the kitchen, I found the pharmacy bag sitting on the counter with Maya's other bags from the hospital. I grabbed everything and a bottle of water out of the fridge, and brought it all upstairs.

Marcos was hovering outside the ensuite bathroom door, while Maya was inside doing her business. I heard her opening and closing drawers and cabinets, likely taking in everything of hers that we had already moved in—as in everything from her mother's house, just like how we'd grabbed everything of Luke's and put it in his room just down the hall.

In the week that she had been in the hospital, Jason had not only gotten the floors and carpeting done, he'd also arranged our moves. Marcos hadn't had much from his small one-bedroom apartment, and Jason had been living at the clubhouse for years.

I on the other hand, had a whole two-bedroom condo to pack up. Jason had arranged not only movers but also people to pack up all of my shit. I'd never been more grateful for how strategic and focused my brother could be, because I had not been in the right mind to think of all of that while Maya had been lying unconscious in the hospital.

Jason hung up the phone as the bathroom door opened and Maya stepped out, looking pale, but she'd brushed her hair and pulled it up into a ponytail. "Pizza will be here in thirty minutes."

Maya nodded and then yawned, covering her face. "Show me the house," she murmured. She started walking toward the door before anyone could say anything.

Jason followed after her and I let him. It was his project; he deserved the credit for all of his hard work.

Jason

Sitting at the kitchen table, eating pizza like we had so many times before, I couldn't keep my eyes off Maya. Even as pale as she was, she was utterly beautiful. She chewed her food and looked around the remodeled space in awe, like she was trying to see every inch of it.

"You said you all moved in?" Maya asked after she swallowed her bite.

"Yeah. I only had my one-bedroom apartment, so it made sense," Marcos said.

I noticed how he conveniently left off the part about doing so because they needed the space for Luke. "I've been staying at the clubhouse since we moved out of here last time." I shrugged.

Maya frowned and her eyes narrowed on the table in front of her. She didn't say anything, but I could see it on her face. She didn't seem to like that. Ignoring me, Maya turned to Nico and waited for him to speak up.

"I still have my condo, but everything is here now. I'll probably rent out my place and use it as an income property," Nico said.

"Where's Luke?" She finally asked, glancing around the kitchen again, like he would appear out of thin air.

"He's at your mother's still. We thought we'd give you the night to settle in and he would come home tomorrow," Marcos said.

Maya frowned again. "Did my mother really have an issue with me going back there?"

"No, Darlin'," I said, immediately. I hated seeing her hurting so badly, and I knew the strained relationship with her mother was a trigger point. "She didn't have any issues with you going home with her. She expected you to, but... well—"

"We wanted you here," Nico cut me off. "We wanted you home, and didn't want to wait. So we underhandedly asked your mother to help us. I'm sorry, Little Dreamer. It was a low blow and we shouldn't have done it. We know how much it bothers you that things with your mother aren't always that great."

"It really hurt to think she was kicking me out after everything." Maya's voice was so soft, so dejectedly broken, my heart ripped to shreds in my chest. *We* did that to her. It was our dumb idea that hurt her and caused her pain.

"I'm sorry, Maya. That was my idea," Marcos said.

"It was all of us. I'm sorry too," I added.

Nico sighed and ran a hand through his hair. "I'm really sorry, Little Dreamer."

Maya looked so fucking lost as her eyes jumped between each of us. "I don't know—I can't fucking do this."

Pain flared in my chest. I couldn't blame her though—I really couldn't—but it still fucking hurt. "Can't do what, Darlin'?" I asked, my voice gravely.

"I don't know how to trust you guys again. I don't know to do this—" she waved a hand around her, gesturing at the house at large, "all of this again."

I swallowed thickly and nodded slowly. I'd expected this, I could work with this, hopefully. "We get that, Maya. We know. We don't expect you to just jump into anything. We have a truce, remember?" I asked.

She nodded slowly, swallowing.

"Just trust us enough to take care of you, ok?" I pressed. "The bedroom is yours, just like before. Kara gifted us the bed, but we all still have our old bedrooms—except Nic who took Kara's old room downstairs, so Luke could be upstairs."

"How can I trust you, when you don't ask my consent?" She leveled her stare on me.

I swallowed and seemed at a loss for words.

Marcos shifted in his chair. "It was my call," he said, taking the blame. "I knew if we asked you, you'd say no." He cleared his throat, glancing away momentarily. Running a hand over his buzzed head, he met her gaze again. "I'm sorry. We can take you back to your mom's at any time you want. I'm asking now, will you please stay here—at least while you recover—so we know you're safe. Hillcrest is still out there, and the safest place for you and Luke is here with us."

I continued up when Marcos finished. "I know we have a lot to work through. I know things are up in the air, but we want to work through things with you. If you want to, of course."

Maya eyed us both warily, her eyes flicking between Marcos and I while she thought it over.

I waited, wondering if she was going to hand us our asses or not—the old Maya would have. Maya had changed a lot in the last ten years, and one of those things had been her fiery personality. It was something I noticed the first time I saw her again. Life had been very hard for her, and I wished that we had known sooner.

I wished for the hundredth time, that things were different.

Chapter Twenty-Seven

Maya

THE NEXT DAY, I was sitting on the couch in the living room, waiting for Marcos to come home with Luke. Marcos had made sure that Luke was still going to school while I had been both held hostage and in the hospital, for which I was grateful. It made me wonder what would come of his court order.

We hadn't talked about it yet. We hadn't talked about a lot of things yet.

It was an unnerving feeling being back in this house—our home—and not being *with* them. My heart hurt and my head was conflicted as to why I was there. I placed a lot of trust in Nico, believing above all, that everything would be alright.

"It'll be alright," Nico said beside me, resting his hand on my knee.

The backdoor opened before I could respond, and Luke called out, "Mom!"

"In here!" Nico yelled.

Luke's feet pounded on the wood floors as he ran into the living room. Just as he was about to pounce on me, Nico stood up and caught him. "Easy, man. Gentle." He shook his head.

Luke grinned sheepishly as Nico let him go. "Sorry," he said to me.

I grinned and raised my arms for Luke, as Nico walked out of the room to give me privacy with my son. Luke gently slid into my arms and hugged me. I held him tight as tears welled in my eyes; I never wanted to be away from him like this ever again. "Hey, buddy. I missed you."

"I missed you too, mom." He held me tighter. "I'm glad you're home."

"Me too, buddy. Me too."

Luke slowly pulled away and sat on the couch beside me, leaning against me and looping his arm through mine. "Are we living here now?" Luke asked softly.

I rested my head on top of his and grabbed his hand. "Would that be ok? I mean, at least for a little while?"

Luke turned and looked up at me with a massive grin. "Yeah, I like the idea of living with dad."

My heart pounded in my chest at Luke's words. I didn't know how I would ever take him away from Marcos again. If things didn't work out living here, all of us together, I would never be able to break Luke's heart—or Marcos's—and separate them.

I would never be able to do that to them.

"Alright, buddy. We'll give it a chance," I agreed.

"Awesome! I can't wait to set up my room! Dad said we could go shopping! He already painted it my favorite color! Did you see?" Luke hopped off the couch, talking excitedly.

I grinned and nodded. "Yeah, I did see. I saw there was a big bed in there too! And they got all new furniture!"

"Yes! Can we grab my stuff tonight?"

"Uh." I was surprised Marcos and her guys hadn't already grabbed his stuff, as they had already grabbed all of mine.

Before I could respond, Marcos walked into the living room from the kitchen, like he'd been standing there all along, just out of sight. "We can grab whatever you want tonight, and whatever we can't get, we can go for this weekend."

I stared at Marcos, wondering if I even had any say. This whole co-parenting thing was going to get interesting if we had issues talking to each other. I didn't even know if we had issues talking to each other, because I hadn't been able to really talk to any of them since my rescue.

And before my capture... things were way different between us all. I was struggling to keep up with the status quo.

I felt lost... adrift at sea, unable to anchor.

Marcos took one look at my face and stopped. "Hey Luke, why don't you head outside with Jason. I'll be right behind you, ok?"

Once Luke was out of the room, Marcos crouched down in front of me and rested his hands on my knee. "Maya, are you, ok?"

"Hmm?" I asked, snapping out of the stupor of emotion I'd been in.

"Mi Vida," Marcos murmured, rubbing his large hands over my knees. "Are you ok with this? Moving Luke in here?"

"I—of course," I stammered.

"Maya." Marcos's voice was gentle and soothing. "Talk to me."

Tears welled in my eyes at how gentle and caring he was being. "I don't—this is just all so fast." My voice broke as I choked on a sob.

Marcos immediately pulled me into his chest, holding me close while sobs wracked my body. "Shh," he murmured, rubbing my back. "I know it's fast, I know we're rushing you. I'm sorry, I should have thought of that beforehand. You being taken by Hillcrest, it killed me, baby." Marcos choked up and took a moment to get this own breathing under control. "The idea of being without you and Luke, not having you two close and *home*, didn't sit right with me. I'm sorry for moving things too fast and practically forcing you in here. Like I said, we can bring you back to your mom's at any time."

I shook my head. "After you already told Luke he could have both parents living together like all the other kids at school?" I pulled away from him to glare at him. "So I can be the bad guy and take him away from his father again?" I shook my head.

Marcos sighed. "There's a lot we need to talk about, but I know now that you didn't know you were pregnant when you left here. There were outside forces at play, I get that. I know you wouldn't take him away from me. Even if we don't work out, we'll figure out the co-parenting thing. I promise you, Maya."

I sighed, wiping my eyes and nodded. *Why the fuck did he suddenly have the answers for things now?* "Ok."

Marcos nodded slowly. He slid his hand up my arm and over my cheek. "Luz de Mi Vida," *Light of my life* "you are still the light of my whole fucking world. I hope you know that."

I gasped, my eyes widening as I met his intense dark brown eyes. I traced his face with my eyes, taking in the crow's feet at the corners of his eyes, his buzzed hair, and the stubble that covered his chiseled jaw—a permeant five o'clock shadow that only enhanced his features. He'd always been an attractive man, but he seemed to have aged like fine wine. His Mexican heritage shown through his complexion and dark eyes, had only served to make him even sexier.

The fact that his name of endearment for me was *Mi Vida*, and it literally translated to *my life*, only made him hotter. I had never stopped loving any of my men in the ten or so years we'd been apart. That was never the issue. The issue was just everything else.

"Dad!" Luke shouted from the back door.

I jumped, whipping my head toward the doorway to the kitchen, expecting to see someone standing there. Marcos's hand slipped from my face and he sighed. "This conversation isn't over," he said, before he stood up.

I didn't respond, I didn't know what else to say. We had so much to talk about...one day.

Chapter Twenty-Eight

Nico

WALKING INTO THE LOUNGE at the Seratelli family house, I weaved through cousins and family members, friends and acquaintances that loitered in the space, sipping cocktails and liquor. I greeted everyone that slapped me on the back as I walked by, giving pleasantries as I went.

It was a far different welcoming than my first night back at family dinner, and I didn't know how I felt about it. I was grateful to all of them, of course, but I still wasn't used to being back in the fold after so many years away.

I walked to the bar and ordered a whisky neat. Resting my elbow on the bar, I turned to face the room, just as my cousin stepped up beside me. "How's your girl doing?" Leo asked.

Turning my back to the room, I sighed. "She's...alright, I guess? She's hanging in there. It's hard to say, really. She's surviving."

Leo nodded solemnly, "That's to be expected, right? I mean, she lived through something no one should ever endure."

"Yeah," I muttered despondently. Thankfully the bartender set down my whisky at that moment and another for Leo, before he walked away.

"You know, I'm here for you. If you need anything at all, even a fight, I'm here." Leo squeezed my shoulder reassuringly.

I barked out a laugh. "You still get in the ring? God, what would the family say if I bruised their precious don?"

"Your don too." Leo nodded at me. "I'm still your don, too."

I swallowed roughly, meeting my cousin's blue eyes. I jerked my head once in agreement, the emotion clogging my throat made it hard to speak.

"But yes, I still get in the ring occasionally," Leo continued. "And who says you'd even get close enough to land a hit, let alone bruise me?" Leo smirked at me and raised his whisky to his lips.

Chuckling, I shook my head. "Alright, cousin mine. I'm game. Let's do it."

Leonardo grinned and nodded. "After dinner?"

"Yes. At the gym?"

"Yes."

Both of us clinked our whisky glasses together, agreeing to the plan.

"Invite the Knights. Let's get that finished too," Leo said before he tossed his whisky back and walked away from me.

Marcos

I had just sat down on the couch in the living room when my phone pinged with an incoming text message. Glancing around the room at Maya and Luke watching a movie, while Jason finished up the dishes from our dinner in the other room, I hoped the message wasn't anything that would pull me away from family tonight.

Dagger

Leo agreed to a sit down with the Knights. Tonight. At the gym, after family dinner.

"Shit," I sighed, glancing at the clock. It was almost seven p.m. Family dinner with the Seratelli family started at seven p.m. sharp. It was usually a two-hour affair and then drinks after. But with a fight on the table—judging by the meeting being held at the gym—I bet they would be done by nine, and at the gym by nine-fifteen.

I needed to call Johnny.

"What's wrong?" Maya asked, her voice soft as she looked over at me.

I glanced at Luke who was engrossed in the movie, before I met her eye. "Just club stuff." I nodded my head toward the kitchen.

She got the hint and stood up. Maya walked into the kitchen where Jason was finishing up the dishes. Jason looked over at her as I followed behind her.

I got straight to the point, knowing Luke would notice our absence sooner than later. "Nico texted. The Seratelli's agreed to a sit down with the Ravager Knights. Tonight. We gotta head out in a bit." I told both Maya and Jason at the same time.

"Where?" Jason asked, shutting off the water. He reached for the dish towel to dry his hands.

"The Seratelli's gym," I responded, my eyes on Maya. Her face was hard to read; she looked sad and almost worried. "Maya?"

She met my gaze, but the dazed expression on her face had her looking a million miles away. In the five days since she'd been home, I'd watch her go in and out of these dissociative 'zone outs' as I referred to them, but it was like her brain was struggling to keep up with the events in real time. "You're leaving us alone?" Her voice, as it always was since the attack, was soft.

The instinctive protective urges flipped on inside me, and I let out a low growl, as I stomped toward her. She didn't back up or cower away from me—thank God, because I realized how aggressive I was being after the fact—no, she looked up at me with a trembling lip and unshed tears in her eyes that broke my damn heart.

I hated how Hillcrest had fucked with her confidence and self-worth. Every time she cried, I wanted to tear Hillcrest down and fucking torture him to death.

I vowed that Hillcrest would pay for every single fucking tear that Maya shed.

I put my hands on either side of her face, cupping her neck and jaw. I made sure to speak gently, but firmly to her. "You are safe here. The house is wired with the alarm system and no less than thirty cameras all over the place. The three of us will receive a message on our phone if there are ANY issues. There will be two prospects outside, and I have a police cruiser parked down the street with someone on our payroll watching the house. You know how to use a gun and where we keep them. Your own gun is in the nightstand too. This is not at all how I wanted to leave you, but we have to go to Nico."

Maya took a shuddering breath and a tear slipped down her face.

Jason moved behind her, his hands wrapping around her waist and she only startled a bit, until she looked over her shoulder at him. He wrapped her tightly in his arms while I gently massaged her neck and jaw.

Maya's eyes closed as she tilted her head back against Jason's chest, giving me more room. I smirked and slowly massaged her jaw and neck muscles in long, slow swipes down her neck. Watching her relax in our arms was a sensual thing.

Jason rubbed his hands over her stomach and up her sides and back down her hips, being careful to keep his touch sensual and stay away from anything that might make her uncomfortable. "You are a brave, strong, woman." Jason dropped his voice low, making it gravelly as he spoke into her ear.

Watching the goosebumps roll across Maya's skin, just from listening to Jason's voice was always a sight to behold, and I would be lying if it didn't make me a tiny bit jealous. But watching them now, after so long, just filled me with happiness.

"You can handle anything that life throws at you," Jason continued.

Maya's eyelids fluttered, but remained closed.

I couldn't help myself; I held her chin between my thumb and forefinger and pressed a gentle kiss to her lips. Maya gasped, and I felt the puff of air hit my lips. I backed away only slightly, watching as her eyes snapped open. "Wha—"

"You are the strongest person I know," I said. "You can handle *anything* that life throws at you." I repeated Jason's words. "You can handle this. We will only be gone a couple hours and we'll be back as soon as we can."

Maya swallowed as tears once again lined her eyes.

I felt sick. I was doing this to her this time. Once again, I was leaving her, and she was silently begging me not to. Why the fuck was I doing this? My phone buzzed in my pocket. I clenched my jaw to keep from lashing out at the damn thing as I met Jason's gaze over Maya's head. He had that stone-face look about him, that said he was in business mode.

"I have to go, Mi Vida. I will see you later." I pressed another kiss to her lips and turned away. I walked into the mudroom without looking back; despite knowing I was breaking her heart right now.

A moment later, Jason was joining me in the mud room as we both laced up our boots. I heard Maya's stifled sob before I walked out the backdoor.

Maya

I COULDN'T BELIEVE IT. I should believe it—but I couldn't. They fucking left me alone. They left me AND Luke alone, not even a fucking week since I got home from the hospital. The fucking club always came before me. Always.

I was so sick of it.

I left the kitchen before they even left the house, trying to stifle the sob that escaped me as I moved through the living room. I had to put on a brave face for Luke, despite the fact that my heart was being crushed into a million pieces.

All I fucking wanted was to be put first for once my fucking life, have them choose ME over the fucking club. Was that too much to ask?

I had to slow my breathing and concentrate. Hearing two Harleys fire up on the driveway shook another sob free from me.

"Mom?" Luke asked, turning away from the movie to look out the window. "Where's dad going?"

I covered my mouth with my hand, trying to calm my breathing.

"Mom? Are you ok?" Luke turned to me, catching my tears.

I quickly swallowed my sobs, took a deep breath and wiped my eyes. Forcing a smile to my face, I nodded. "Yeah, baby. I'm just really tired and not feeling that well. What do say we go finish the movie upstairs?"

Luke eyed me cryptically, but as the motorcycles roared away down the driveway, then the street, drawing Luke's attention to the window again, I saw him frown. "Dad didn't say goodbye."

My heart couldn't take much more. Marcos was a selfish fucking ass, and now my son was seeing it for the first time too. "I know, baby. I'm sorry. He said he had to go and he'd be back later tonight."

Luke frowned, clearly not buying my white lie.

"Come on, let's go upstairs." The house suddenly felt a lot less safe when it was just the two of us in it.

Luke nodded and I stood from the couch. I went to the backdoor and made sure it was locked and dead bolted, then I checked the patio door, and the front door, before I turned off all the lights and followed Luke upstairs. I made a stop into my bedroom for my handgun, tucking it the back of my yoga pants, before I went down the hall to Luke's room.

Luke set up the movie on his TV in his new bedroom, super proud to have his own big screen. The guys had even set up his gaming system for him, so he could play whenever he wanted, much to my dismay.

"Are you sad that dad left?" Luke asked once we were settled onto his queen mattress and wrapped in blankets.

"Yeah, buddy. I am. I'm scared too," I admitted.

"We're safe here, right?" He looked worried as he met my gaze.

"Yeah, buddy. We're safe. I'm just still nervous after everything that happened." I tried to be as open as I could with my son about everything. Luke was a smart kid, he knew I traded myself to make sure he was home safe, and he knew the toll it took on me.

"I wish dad didn't leave," Luke said.

"Me too, buddy, me too."

"It makes me mad. You feel better when he's here. He should be here, taking care of you."

I couldn't say anything to that, not without crying, so I kept my mouth shut and let Luke vent his frustrations.

Maya

I must have dozed off, because I startled awake a while later. I didn't know where I was as first. Looking around in a panic, the soft glow of the TV gave off just enough light for me to see Luke sleeping in the bed beside me.

I slowly got up, sliding from Luke's bed. I made sure my son was tucked in under the covers before I slipped out of his room. Heading down the hall toward my bedroom, I frowned as she realized all the lights in the house were off. Did Marcos and the guys come home? Or were they still gone?

Walking into my bedroom, I flipped on the light, only to be disappointed. My bed was empty and still made from when I changed the sheets earlier that afternoon. Upset, and feeling let down, I couldn't stop the tears that immediately welled in my eyes. Closing the door behind me, I walked over to the bed. I slid under the fresh sheets of my massive empty bed and grabbed the remote for the ceiling fan and light and quickly turned on the fan while shutting off the light.

Once I was in the cool darkness, I let the tears flow down my face as sobs wracked my body. As tired as I was of being weak and always crying since coming home from the hospital, I wasn't ready to stop. I needed to get the emotions out.

I still couldn't believe that they left us alone. My guys should have known better. I knew—or thought I had known—back in the day that the club always came first. I naively assumed that now it wouldn't be the case, not after spending a week with Hillcrest using me for his sick pleasure.

Why weren't Marcos and Nico and Jason here?

The club always came fucking first.

I would never be good enough for them, no matter what pretty words they threw my way. I would never be first.

Gut wrenching sobs tore through me and I lost myself into the self-doubt and the dark memories of being held captive with Hillcrest.

Nico

I danced around the ring at Telli's, the Seratelli family's boxing gym. The place was packed with Devil's Psychos and Ravager Knights and members of the Seratelli organization. It was louder than all hell, as everyone yelled and cheered. Leo smirked at me from across the ring as we danced around each other.

I gave Leo the first hit, letting my don set the pace. I smirked and got moving, letting the crowd fuel my fight.

Leo grinned wickedly as we both jabbed and dodge one another's punches. We had been raised together, trained together. It may have been over a decade since we were in the ring together, but we still knew how the other one moved.

I shook off a rough hit to the jaw and smirked. "Game on, cousin."

"Took you long enough," Leo shot back.

Movement in the corner of my eye caught my attention, and I glanced over to see both Marcos and Jason standing in the corner of the ring. "The fuck?" I growled, mostly to myself.

Leo landed another punch, this time to my ribs, and I grunted in pain.

Attention still on Marcos and Jason, I shouted at them. "You left them alone?"

Marcos shrugged a shoulder.

I narrowed my gaze on my president as anger flared within me. Leo still swarmed me, but he sensed my shifting mood and quickly went on the defensive as I turned to my cousin to end the fight quickly. I had another fight to get to—namely kicking my brothers' asses.

"What happened?" Leo asked, eyeing me as he blocked a particularly nasty punch.

"They fucking left her alone," I growled. "They're both here."

Leo turned just enough to see Marcos and Jason out of the corner of his eye. "Alright, then we call it. You can't go after your president here, but call Jason into the ring."

I paused mid-step and nodded. The crowd yelled around us, clearly confused by the fight stopping. It was for the best anyway, I didn't want to get into trouble with my family, not when I just got them back. Not that I cared much about the others, but I did care about Leo, and Giovanni and my other cousins.

Stalking toward the corner of the ring, I ducked through the ropes before and jumped down to the floor below and got right in Jason's face. "You fucking left her?" I growled.

"Shit," Jason muttered.

"It was my call," Marcos spoke up.

"It's always your fucking call," I growled.

"Not the place, brother," Jason muttered.

Rage roiled within me. "Maybe not for him, but it is for you, motherfucker." I grabbed Jason by the collar and yanked him forward roughly, tossing him into the ring aggressively, before I got in Marcos's face. "I'll deal with you in private," I vowed, before I turned back to the ring and climbed in after Jason.

Jason had already rolled to his feet and was getting up as I stormed toward him. The surrounding crowd cheered loudly, but I ignored them all. I had a beef to settle with my brother, and I didn't give a fuck who witnessed it. I was sick and fucking tired of Jason and Marcos leaving Maya alone. She'd only been home a couple days after the most traumatic thing someone could go through—in my mind—and she was home alone.

I hit Jason in the face—hard—without Jason even putting up a fucking arm to stop me. I didn't go easy on my brother, despite the man not fighting back, I laid into him like he was a fucking punching bag. "Fight back, motherfucker!" I growled.

"No," Jason grunted, absorbing another hit—this time to his ribs. "You're right, absolutely right. We shouldn't have left. I should have told Marcos to leave without me. He's president, you're VP, it makes sense that you're both here. I can stay back, one of the other guys could have watched Marcos's back."

I landed another punch to Jason's face. "You got that right, motherfucker. Stop. Fucking. Leaving. Her. Alone!" I growled the words, landing a punch with every word I said, emphasizing my point.

Jason was a bloody mess before I finally backed off. Swaying on his feet, blood pouring out of his bruised and battered face, Jason nodded at me. "You're right."

I shook my head and walked away. I didn't give a fuck about being right. I needed to get home to my woman and make sure she was ok, both physically and mentally. I could only imagine the toll this was taking on her.

Marcos

REGRET FLARED WITHIN ME, not for the first time that night. Ever since I left Maya and Luke back the house, I'd been having second thoughts. I had set up every precaution in place to ensure their safety, but after seeing Nico's rage, I knew I fucked up. Nico was clearly looking out for her wellbeing and I was only doing further damage.

Jason slid out of the ring, his father Jerry Langford—another patched member of the Devil's Psychos—helped him down.

I watched them walk over to the locker rooms and sighed. Add another thing to my running list of epic fuck-ups. Nico was walking toward the door, his cousin Leo walking beside him. They stopped at the door, Leo grabbing Nico into a hug before patting him on the back. Clearly, Seratelli was the better man at this moment.

Johnny Taylor of the Ravager Knights slid up beside me, snapping me out of my daze. "What was that about?" His voice was sharp, the anger evident in his tone. This was not how tonight was supposed to go down. Taylor needed a sit down with Seratelli, and after witnessing the don take sympathy on his cousin, I wondered if Leonardo would still allow anything more to happen tonight.

"I fucked up—again." There was no point in denying it. Johnny was my fucking brother at this point, both by blood and marriage practically.

"Well, you better make this fucking right. I need this fucking sit down, and you still owe me a fucking turn in the ring," Johnny snapped.

I nodded. "You'll get your chance in the ring. Let me go talk to Seratelli." I walked away, heading for the don.

Johnny followed me and I wondered how this would play out. Before the two of us could even get close to Leonardo though, his men closed ranks. Two of his brothers stepped in front of Leonardo, blocking my path. "I just want to talk," I said, holding up my hands in surrender.

"I'm getting really sick of you, Candella," Leo snapped. His brothers moved out of the way so he could step forward, getting into my face.

"Yeah, I'm pretty sick of me too," I agreed.

"Good. Fucking fix shit with Nicolai." The order was clear, despite the *or else* being unsaid, I knew it was there. Leonardo Seratelli would protect his family, *all* of his family, and I knew without a doubt, Maya and Luke were now considered his family.

Leo looked away from me, clearly disgusted. His eyes landed on Johnny. "Taylor, good. Get your VP and let's hit my office." Leo walked away before either of us could say anything.

Johnny turned away, leaving me behind.

Another one of my fuck-ups added to the list.

Marcos

At home, I unlocked the back door, helping Jason stumble in the house. How he had rode home with his eye swollen shut was beyond me, but Jason had.

The house was quiet and dark when we walked in after midnight. We both kicked off our boots and headed straight for the stairs. In Maya's room, we found Nico curled around her sleeping form.

I sighed and went into my own bedroom, leaving them to their privacy. Jason must have decided the same thing, because his bedroom door closed a moment later. I had no idea how I was going to get any sleep, but I lay on my bed and stared at the ceiling, knowing it was going to be a long sleepless night.

Not even twenty minutes later, Maya's yells pulled me from my thoughts. I jumped out of bed, my heart racing, wondering what the hell was happening. I burst into her room at the same time as she sat up abruptly in bed.

"What happened?" I demanded.

Nico also sat up in bed. He put his hand on her shoulder and she flinched away.

"Don't fucking touch me!" Maya snapped.

Shit, I thought, watching Nico's face fall.

"Maya," Nico tried.

"No!" Maya's voice cracked, as she became overcome with emotion.

I carefully stepped into the room, watching her warily. "Maya?" I asked.

She turned to glare at me instead. "What?" she snapped.

"Are you ok?" I asked her, trying to keep my voice gentle.

"Clearly not. Why the fuck do you care?"

Regret sank my heart to my stomach as her anger rolled over me. I deserved that, absolutely. "I'm sorry I lef—"

"Fuck off, Marcos," Maya cut me off. "I don't want to hear your shitty excuse for always leaving me the fuck alone."

Holy shit, I thought. She sure the fuck was letting me have it. For the first time in like ever—I could see a hint of the old Maya in her anger.

Glancing at Nico, I could see he was just as dumbfounded as I felt. At least it wasn't just me, then. "You're absolutely righ—"

"I know I'm right, Marcos. Just go already. I don't want to see you right now. You too, Nicolai," Maya snapped at both of us.

I immediately felt bad for Nico, though. His face fell as he turned to her. "Maya."

"Please, Nic." She didn't even look at him.

I backed out of Maya's room as Nico slowly slid off her mattress. I gave them their privacy if Nico was going to try to talk to her again. It was clear that I was an issue, and I didn't want to create more issues between the two of them when they had been doing so well before—well before everything happened.

Back in my bedroom, I threw myself on my mattress before my door opened and Nico stormed in. "You're a fucking dick all the fucking time," he announced.

I could only nod in agreement, because my brother was right of course. "Yep."

"Going forward, you don't get to call the shots when it comes to her. She's MINE, not yours anymore. I get the say on what happens, and we will NEVER leave her alone. Ever. Again. You fucking hear me?" Nico was towering over me at the edge of the bed by the time he finished his rant.

I nodded. "Of course, brother. You're absolutely right."

Nico shook his head, clearly upset at my easy agreement. "Fuck you," he snapped, before he turned on his heel and left my bedroom.

"Yeah," I agreed numbly. "Fuck me."

Maya

Sitting alone in the bedroom in the middle of night after I kicked both men out, I silently cried, tears pouring down my face. It wasn't fair. I hated how things had ended up between all of us. I hated that I'd been raped and used and fucking filmed for some revenge fucking porn by Hillcrest. I hated that I was too fucking weak to fight back and that I couldn't kill the mother fucker myself.

Most of all, I hated that I was back in this fucking house like the ten fucking years of torture and torment hadn't happened. I hated how Marcos and Jason were just acting like shit wasn't still all fucked up between us.

Nico hadn't treated me like the other two had when I came back. Somehow, he knew from the get-go that I hadn't left of my own accord. Marcos and Jason though, they had believed every lie I told them. I shouldn't blame, but I couldn't help it. They took me at face value and didn't dig deeper. They saw what I showed them, and that was it.

It hurt. It hurt more than I cared to admit. I think back to all those years ago, when I was last in this house, hiding something from them that they never realized... and I can't help but wonder if they hadn't been so invested in other things, would they have noticed back then?

It was something I've brought up to my therapist several times over the years, and she always gave me the same answer. *You can't live your life in the what-ifs.* The fact of the matter was, they hadn't noticed, and I hadn't told them. Can't expect them to suddenly be mind-readers.

It still hurt. And I still didn't want to deal with them. There was too much fucking history there and the what-ifs broke my heart.

Watching Nico walk out of my bedroom just now had been hard. It wasn't his fault the other two left me—us—home alone. He had gone to a family dinner. It was a Sunday night and Nico was required—though I wished he wasn't. The events that happened after dinner, that could have been different.

I lay back down on my side in bed, staring blankly into the dimly lit room. I made Nico install a nightlight the first night we were here. I couldn't handle the dark anymore, not after Hillcrest. I couldn't handle bright lights either anymore, because of Hillcrest. Flashes, cameras, groups of men. It was all fucking bullshit.

How was I going to survive if I couldn't get over myself and my trauma?

Simple answer was: I wasn't.

I lay there all fucking night, thinking and wondering, and fucking plotting in my head. I didn't see the sunlight peeking through the blackout curtains. I didn't see Luke come in and talk to me. I didn't hear Nico as he bent down to get in my face.

Tears silently slid down my cheeks, as I got lost inside my own head. Disassociating like I had desperately tried to do while I was with Hillcrest.

I was so tired of having to be strong for others, only to find out I wasn't strong enough. It was fucking exhausting. I wanted someone else to take care of me for a change. I wanted to be put first for a change. Was that so much to ask for?

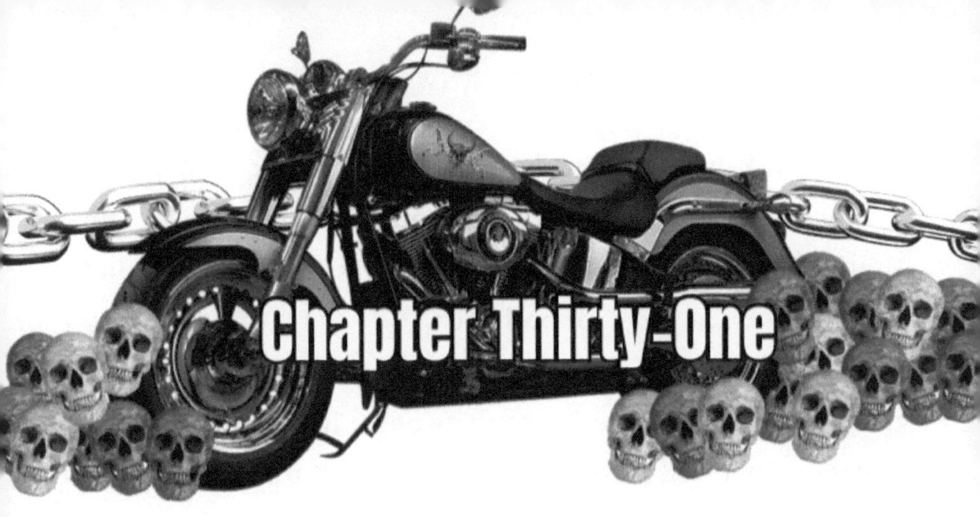

Chapter Thirty-One

Nico

I STORMED OUT OF the house, anger radiating off me. I wanted to hit Jason again. I wanted to fucking beat the shit out of Marcos. How dare he fucking leave her alone again? Just because she was a strong fucking woman, didn't mean she should have to be. She had three fucking men to lean on, and yet, we all fucking left her alone.

Stalking into the pole barn garage, I flipped on the lights before I bee-lined for the punching bag in the corner. I didn't bother to wrap my knuckles or grab my gloves. I attacked the bag with everything I had, letting my rage and anger overcome me.

I growled deep in my throat as I slammed my punches into the heavy bag. I briefly thought about calling Leo, but after the shit storm that happened at the gym, I really didn't want to add more fuel on the fire where my cousin was concerned. Leo already didn't like Marcos and Jason, but the more he found out, the less he cared for both men.

Not that I could blame him after tonight. Leonardo Seratelli was extremely protective of the women in his life. His own damn sister had a bodyguard on her at all times. I was half tempted to stick a prospect on Maya permanently—if I ever felt like I could leave her again.

Nico

The following morning, Luke's yelling down the hall caught my attention as I stepped out of the shower. "Mom!" he shouted.

I barely wrapped the towel around my waist as I ran down the hallway to Maya's bedroom. Luke was standing in front of his mother, shaking her, but she wasn't responding. My heart jumped into my throat as I rounded the bed, just as Marcos and Jason ran into her bedroom as well. "What's going on?" they asked.

I gently pushed Luke out of the way as I stared down at Maya. Her eyes were open, but she wasn't home. Her eyes were vacant and lifeless. My heart plummeted into my stomach. "Maya!" I shouted, shaking her.

She didn't blink or acknowledge that I was even there. Scared to fucking death, I pressed my fingers against the pulse point in her neck. Her pulse was strong, and she was breathing, but she wasn't fucking home.

"Fucking hell, Little Dreamer." I groaned and dropped to a crouch in front of her, trying to get her to focus on me. "Maya." I snapped my fingers in front of her face.

"What's wrong with her?" Luke asked, the panic evident in his voice.

"Dissociating," I said, my eyes snapping to my brothers.

Jason frowned while the vein in Marcos's jaw throbbed as he clenched it.

"What does that mean?" Luke's voice rose in a panic.

"It means, she's lost in her mind right now." I sighed and stood up, clutching my towel to keep it from falling down. Turning to Luke, I wrapped my arms around him and pulled him into a hug. "It'll be ok, buddy. Your mom is just trying to figure some shit out right now."

"Like what?" Luke's voice was muffled against my chest.

"Like how to handle things right now. After everything that happened with Hillcrest, she's just going to need a little time to figure it all out." I tried to tell Luke and myself that it would be ok, but it wasn't working well.

I shot a glare at Marcos and he snapped out of his own daze. "Come on, buddy. We got to get ready for school."

Luke hugged me tighter, his little arms squeezing me tight. "I don't want to leave her. She's always alone."

My heart broke hearing my own words echoed back by the nine-year-old. "I know, buddy," I said, rubbing his back, "but we both know your mom wouldn't want you to miss school. You've already missed a lot the last couple weeks. She would yell at all of us if she was feeling better."

Luke sighed and slowly pulled away. "I hate this." The anger his voice was poignant.

"I know, buddy. Me too," I murmured.

"Come on, Luke. I'll take you to school," Marcos said, motioning him to leave the room.

Luke clenched his fists and stared at his father. "No."

"Luke." Marcos dropped his voice, deepening it.

Luke stalked toward Marcos and cocked back his arm, stepping into Marcos as he threw a punch right into Marcos's jaw.

"Shit!" Marcos swore as his head snapped to the right.

I couldn't help but laugh at the balls on the kid for doing the very thing that I had wanted to myself. "Nice, punch, Luke!" I congratulated him. He was taking all my teachings to heart. The wind up on that punch, the fucking execution! Fantastic! It was a proud fucking Papa moment, and I almost said he could stay home from school, but I knew I needed time to coax Maya out of whatever spell she had fallen into, and I needed him to not be here while I did that.

Luke pushed past Marcos, shoulder checking him as he went.

I glanced at Jason, whose face was swollen and beat to hell from my own punches last night, and smirked. Clearly me and Luke were on the same side here. The right fucking side: Maya's.

"Is she ok?" Jason asked.

"No. She's fucking not," I snapped back.

"Yeah." He nodded like a dumbass and walked away.

My own rage fired up again at my brothers' blatant incompetence—both of them.

"I'm gonna talk to Luke, you've got Maya?" Marcos asked.

"Yep. Always." I let the double meaning hang in the air.

Marcos sighed heavily and nodded, before he turned away to go search for his son down the hall.

Holding my towel to my waist, I crouched down in front of Maya, and brushed my knuckles over her cheek. "Little Dreamer, you missed a hell of a punch by Luke. He just cracked Marcos in the jaw."

She doesn't even blink.

"Oh, Little Dreamer." I sighed, shaking my head.

I walked over to the bedroom door and closed it, locking it for good measure. I didn't want interruptions today. I was going to get my girl back, if it was the last thing I did.

Nico

Hours later I was still sitting with a catatonic Maya. I had gone so far as to call her therapist looking for help. The therapist lady, Dr. Burns, had been very concerned when I explained the full details behind Maya's capture. She had immediately wanted to call the police, but I explained that the police were already involved and that now Maya needed to recover. I might have lied to the woman, but I couldn't have her calling the cops.

I needed to get Maya to snap out of her dissociative episode so we could fucking talk shit out. With Dr. Burns on a video call, I just start talking to Maya about everything. "I'm sorry I had to leave last night, Little Dreamer. I had a family dinner and you know how demanding my cousin can be about those things. I thought I was leaving you in good hands with Marcos and Jason. I didn't know they would you leave you and Luke alone. I thought they knew better by this point."

I glanced at Maya; she was still staring off in front of her. "I beat the shit out of Jason. He was the one that was supposed to stay with you. I needed Marcos last night, but Jason was supposed to be here. So when you see him, he's rocking some colorful bruises to his face."

Still no response from Maya.

"Keep going," Dr. Burns said, softly.

"Luke is pissed at Marcos. He punched Marcos this morning, right in the jaw. Marcos didn't even see that shit coming, it was glorious. His head snapped to the side and everything. Luke remembered everything I taught him."

"You taught him how to fight?" Maya's voice cracked.

I didn't bring attention to the fact that she was back, I just continued my conversation. "Yeah. He's pretty good at it too. We brought him down to my cousin's boxing gym in Creekton. Letting him get his anger and aggression out in a healthy way, showing him how to hit the punching bag."

Maya blinked at him. "You taught my son how to fight?" Her voice was stronger now, a little more aggressive.

I pretended like I didn't hear the anger leaking through. I smirked slightly at the doctor on the phone. "Sure did! He's a fucking natural too. You should have seen him clock Marcos this morning. Bad ass little dude, for sure."

Maya sat up abruptly. "Nicolai. Randall. Gage. What the fuck?"

Fucking finally. "Welcome back, Little Dreamer."

"Hello, Maya, how are you feeling?" *Dr. Burns to the fucking rescue*, I thought as the doctor spoke up.

Maya's eyes flashed to the phone in my hand. Her mouth dropped open in shock as she stared at the face of her therapist on the phone. "Dr. Burns?"

"Hi, dear," Dr. Burns said. "Nico, be a dear and give Maya your phone, then skidaddle so we can have some privacy."

I laughed and handed over my phone to Maya. "Sure thing, Doc. Maya I'm going to make you something to eat." I pressed a kiss to her forehead and turned for the door.

"I'm not finished with you, Nicolai," Maya called after me.

"Never, Little Dreamer. You're mine for life," I called over my shoulder.

I went downstairs to the kitchen. Marcos and Jason were lounging on the couch and both men perked as I came down the steps. "How is she?"

"She's talking to her therapist," I said, as I rounded the bottom landing. I passed them and headed into the kitchen, otherwise ignoring them. I was still pissed off at the pair of them and wanted to kick their asses—Jason had gotten off easy in my mind.

Both of them got up and followed me into the kitchen. "But she's talking at least?" Marcos asked.

"Yep," I deadpanned. I glance over my shoulder at him as I walk to the fridge and laugh as I take in the split lip and the bruise forming on his jaw. "Luke got you good."

"Yeah." Marcos huffed.

"How did you get her out of it?" Jason asked.

"I told her that Luke punched Marcos and how I was teaching him to fight down at Leo's. She didn't seem too happy about it." I shrugged. I pulled out sandwich stuff from the fridge, taking stock of what was in there. I could send one of them for a grocery run, because I was not leaving Maya alone anytime soon.

Marcos shook his head.

Jason stared out the back window.

Both men were fucking wallowing in their own self fucking pity and it pissed me off. They needed to get their heads out of their asses and fix shit with Maya...and soon.

A moment later I heard Maya's feet pounding on the stairs before she burst into the kitchen. She stopped in her tracks when she saw both Marcos and Jason standing there, but she ignored them and focused on me. "I want to go to Chicago this weekend."

"Can you handle sitting in a car that long?" I ask, not saying no. I will never say no to again.

"I don't know, but if we have to stop, so be it. I'm going to Chicago this weekend."

I fucking love the fire in her voice. "Alright. I'll drive you."

She nodded her head once, like she already thought about that. Then she looked down at the sandwich I had just finished making. "Is this for me?"

"Sure thing, Little Dreamer." I pushed the plate toward her.

A faint smile tugged at her hips. "Thanks."

She grabbed the plate and walked away, heading back upstairs.

I smile, staring after her. I'll get my woman back, one way or the other.

"You can't go to Chicago." Marcos sighed.

"Fucking stop me." I turned and stared him down.

He rubbed a hand over his hair; the buzz was growing out and made him look younger. Weariness plagued at him though. "I mean you can, of course, but fuck."

"Yeah, about sums shit up with you anymore man," I shake my head. "Maybe while we're gone, you can get your head on straight, figure your shit out? Both of you?" I glanced at Jason. "Maya needs us, now more than ever. I already told you; I'm all in with her. So figure out if you are or not too, then fucking grovel your way back into her good graces."

Chapter Thirty-Two

Maya

THE NEXT COUPLE DAYS were hard. I got up and helped Luke get ready for school, I made his breakfast and packed up his lunch box, and I walked out with him to the bus stop, but when he was gone, I would go back to my bedroom and cry.

I thought briefly about my job, but didn't reach out. Nico said he had spoken to my boss, and I didn't have to worry about it—so I didn't. Nico was a fucking angel though. He gave me space when I asked for it, and cuddled me when I needed him to. We watched movies and binged TV when I needed to keep my mind off things, and I called my therapist daily.

Jenna called me every morning and evening, being almost as clinging as Nico, in her own big sisterly way.

In the evenings, I ate dinner with Luke and the guys—they rotated who cooked—and then helped Luke with his homework. He told me that he stopped going to football practice and I told him it was ok. He could figure out if it was something he wanted to do again when we both felt better.

I also signed Luke up for counseling. We had gone through a terrible ordeal, and though Luke didn't know the full extent of what I went through, he still knew I was kidnapped and tortured by their enemy. Thankfully, Kara mentioned that one of the Ravager Knights old ladies was a therapist, so we were able to get Luke in with her; someone who was familiar with the club life and what had truly happened to me so she could help Luke the best way possible.

After he finished his homework, Luke spent his evenings in my room, watching TV with Nico and me.

Things with Marcos and Jason were strained and distant. I kept my walls up around them, not sure where we stood, and neither man seemed interested in trying to break though those walls. They mostly kept to themselves, while staying accessible by always being around. Once in a while I thought they tried to say something, but when I'd look over at them, they'd close their mouth and look away.

It drove me bat shit crazy... and made me want to keep my distance even more.

I snuggled into Nico's chest, the movie Luke had picked was still playing, but it was some cartoon that I didn't really care about. I was tired and content, and Nico was warm and comfy. The fact that he had taken to sleeping in my room was not lost on me. He had started on the floor, but I quickly put an end to that. Now it didn't bother me to snuggle him with Luke around. I would explain to him my situation one day, but for now, Nico was my pillow, and that was that.

There was a knock at the door and I kept my eyes closed as whoever it was walked in. "Hey guys, I brought popcorn." Marcos's voice was low.

"Popcorn!" Luke cheered, oblivious to me pretending to sleep on the other side of the massive bed than him.

"Easy, dude. I think mom is sleeping," Marcos said softly.

"Oh oops." Luke sounded sheepish, and I almost felt bad, but I wasn't bothered by it.

"Whatcha watchin?" Marcos asked.

"Cloudy with a Chance of Meatballs," Luke replied.

I listened to them go back and forth a couple more times before the bed dipped at the foot of the mattress, meaning Marcos must have sat down.

Nico hand rubbed circles into my hip and I mumble sleepily about school nights as I nuzzled into Nico's chest. "He can finish the movie. It'll be ok," Nico whispered. He pressed a kiss to my forehead.

I honestly wasn't worried; I would likely be asleep soon enough as it was. Sure enough, I must have dozed off because I startled awake to a pitch-black room. The fan was on, but there was not a light on in sight. "No. No, no, no!" My heart rate exploded in my chest, as my breathing becomes labored. Panic claws up my throat, and I thrash about as the sheets become tangled with my legs, tricking my mind into thinking I'm being restrained.

"Maya!" Marcos turned up the lamp on the nightstand, before he grabbed my arms and held me still. Getting in my face, he cupped my jaw and forced me to tilt my head back and look up into his warm chocolate eyes. "Maya, it's me." His voice was deep and husky, thick with sleep.

Still in the throes of panic, I gripped his arms painfully, digging my nails into his skin. "Marcos?" I asked, my voice cracking.

"Yeah, Mi Vida. It's me. I've got you. You're safe," he said and pulled me into his arms.

The sobs that broke out of me hurt my chest and stomach, as I wrapped my arms around him and buried my face into his chest. My soul poured out in the sobs that tore out of me, and I clung to him harder. I hadn't realized how much I needed him to hold me. Nico had been great, but my body, my soul was missing Marcos—and Jason—and badly I needed his arms around me.

"I'm so sorry, Maya. I've got you, you're safe now. I promise, I won't let anything happen to you," Marcos murmured in my ear.

"What happened?" Nico asked from behind me, somewhere near the door.

"I don't know. She woke up and started panicking," Marcos said.

"Did you shut the light off?" Nico asked, his voice getting closer.

"Yeah, shit, I didn't even think. I'm so sorry Maya," Marcos said, rubbing my back.

"What's going on?" Jason's deep voice sent shivers down my spine.

"I shut the light off to sleep," Marcos said.

"She's afraid of the dark now," Nico added softly.

I shuddered in Marcos arms, hating that they were talking about me like I was a child that need taking care of. I hated that I was so broken after everything that happened. Pulling away from Marcos, I took deep breaths as I wiped my eyes. "Maya?" Nico asked, sliding on to the bed next to us. "How you doing, Little Dreamer?"

I laughed sardonically and shook my head. "Fine."

"Yeah," Nico deadpanned.

Looking over at the door, I watch as Jason walked away and frowned.

"Don't worry about him," Nico said, trying to cheer me up.

I shake my head, not wanting to hear excuses.

"Do you want to talk about it?" Marcos asked, his voice tentative.

I narrowed my eyes on my lap, wondering if he was being serious. He'd practically avoided all conversation about anything important in the last couple of days. Even in the hospital, Marcos had been present but distant at the same time. Face value only, nothing below the surface.

Granted, in the hospital I had Nico by my side constantly, my mom and Jenna visiting, even fucking Jason read a damn romance novel to me every night. And where was Marcos? Present, but not.

It drove me up the fucking wall and I was about done with it. "Do you want to hear it?" I shot back, looking up at his handsome face. His usual trimmed, dark goatee was longer, thicker, and the beard had grown in on his cheeks. I loved how ruggedly handsome it made him look. I would have to tell him, so he wouldn't shave it off.

His eyes flashed to mine. "Of course I do, Mi Vida."

I shake my head and hang my head. "You say that, but then you avoid me."

"I'm not avoidi—"

"You're distant. You're here, but you aren't, not really." I look up and meet his gaze again, his dark eyes are tortured looking—wide and emotional, glassy. "You've been here physically, Marcos, but you're not really here mentally. Why? Where are you?"

He lets out a shuddering breath as a tear slipped down his cheek.

I reached up and slid my hand over his cheek, brushing his tear away with my thumb, as I wait for him to respond.

Marcos's eyes slid shut. "Mi Vida." My name leaves his mouth on a whispered breath.

"My life." I murmured in return.

His eyes snap open, the intensity of his love for me pouring out of them. "I can't stop thinking of what happened, how I almost lost you. I saw the videos o—"

I jerked away from him abruptly. "What? You saw—how?"

"He filmed you…"

"I know he fucking filmed me," I snapped. I slid off the side of the mattress and pace around the bed from him, needing some space. I whirled back to face him. "How did *you* see the videos?"

Marcos stood up slowly, acting as if I'm some cornered animal about to lash out at him. "Axel, our brother from the cl—"

"I know who Axel is!" My heart started pounding in my chest.

Marcos started talking faster, as if realizing I needed the information faster. "He got the link to the dark website that Hillcrest uploaded them to. It was through the videos that we were even able to track you down. Kevin's brother Jack is some tech guru."

My heart hammering in my chest, I clenched my fists and tried to steady my breathing. "So you're telling me, that not only have you watched those videos of me being completely violated, but so has half your club? The Knights as well?" I pant as my breathing grows labored. Panic surges in my veins.

"No, Maya. No." Marcos shook his head vehemently. "I promise you, no one else saw them but me and Jason. Jack was able to use them to back door hack into Hillcrest's system and Axel never looked at it. I promise you." He moved closer and my vison blurred around the edges. "Maya, Mi Vida, please. I need you to breathe. Come on, now." His hands landed on my shoulders, sliding down to my elbows as he pulled me into his embrace.

I took a gasping breath as a sob tore out of me. Shuddering as deep guttural sobs destroyed me, Marcos wrapped me tightly in his arms. "Let it out, my love." He murmured, pressing a kiss to my temple. "Get it all out."

I screamed in rage as I clung to him. The idea of other people watching me be so thoroughly debased and humiliated tore at me. That the videos were floating somewhere out there on the internet forever. What if Luke somehow stumbled across those videos when he was older? My heart broke all over again as I cried.

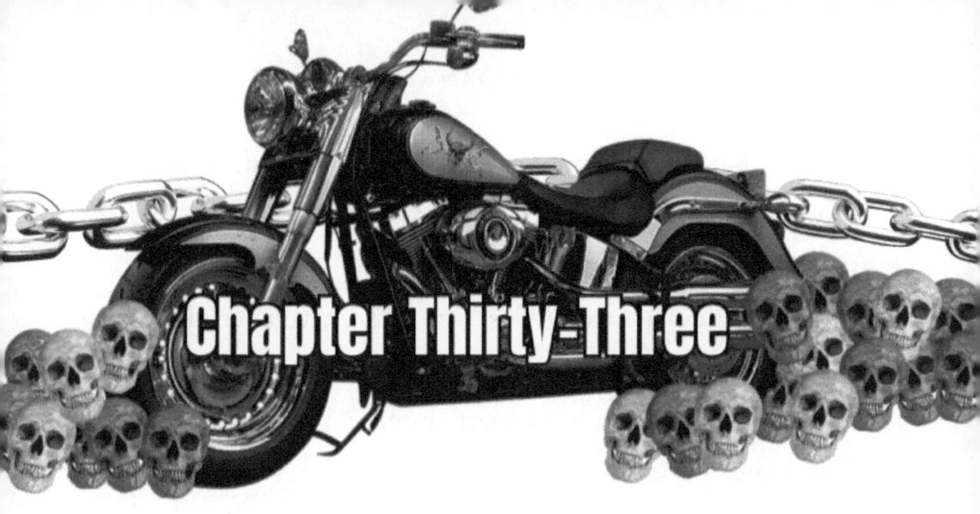

Chapter Thirty-Three

Marcos

I NODDED AT JASON as he plugged in a small lamp on the nightstand. It was half the size of the regular lamp—meant to be a nightlight—and then walked away. Nico hovered in the doorway, but must have realized that Maya and I had some shit to work through. So he left as well, closing the door behind him.

I held Maya tightly, pulling her onto my lap as she cried. Her head fell into the crook of my neck and rubbed her back soothingly, letting her get her emotions out. "That's it, Mi Vida," I murmured. "Get it all out."

When her sobs eventually slowed and only little sniffles remained, I grabbed the tissue box off the nightstand and set it beside us. I pulled out a tissue and waited until she slowly pulled back.

Handing her the tissue, I waited patiently while she grabbed it. Wiping her eyes and nose, she reached for another tissue; tears still streamed down her face.

"I don't know how to do this," she said, her voice cracking with emotion.

Fear and anguish made my heart plumet at her words. "Can't do what, Maya?" I needed her to clarify.

"This! Survive this! I don't know how to be this vulnerable—this fucking broken!"

"You're no—"

"I fucking AM! Stop trying to brush it under the rug! I am broken!"

I leaned back against the headboard, arranging with her in my lap and watch her. She doesn't look broken, there's a fire in her eyes that hasn't been there in a long time, since before she came back to Mourningside nine months ago. "You're not broken." I shook my head and placed my finger over her lips as she went to argue. "You. Are. Not. Broken." I stare into her amber eyes. "You are fierce and strong and brave. You fought as much as you could. I saw that."

"I begged them to kill me."

"I know," I murmured.

"I wanted to die."

"I know."

"I wished for it every day."

"I know."

"I still sometimes wish that I died there." Her voice broke again as she choked on another sob after admitting that hard truth.

My heart breaks in my chest as I gripped her chin between my thumb and forefinger, I forced her to meet my gaze. "You listen to me, and listen good," I demanded, my voice low. "You are a survivor. You are fierce and strong and brave." I repeated my earlier words, hoping they sank in. "There is nothing in this world you can't do if you put your mind to it. Dax fucking Hillcrest will not ruin you. He will not get the best of you. You will be the one that ruins him. Do you hear me, Maya? Hillcrest doesn't win. You will—by living your life to the fullest."

Maya's eyes shine bright as she stared at me intently.

"I need you to live, Mi Vida. Luz de mi vida, amor de mi vida, te necesito a VIVIR," I growled the words in Spanish to her. *Light of my life, love of my life, I need you to LIVE.*

Another sob broke out of Maya at my words, but I knew she didn't understand what I said. She didn't speak Spanish.

"Tú también eres el amor de mi vida, pues uno de ellos." *You are also the love of my life, well one of them.*

I gasped at her words, my mouth dropping open at her perfect enunciation and accent. "Maya." I breathed her name.

"Ya han pasado diez años, Marcos." (It's been ten years, Marcos).

I didn't know what to say. Obviously, it had been ten fucking years, but what the fuck? "Why?" I asked, utterly stunned that she had learned Spanish in the last ten years.

"I missed you."

My hand slid from her chin and cupped the side of her face. I pulled her toward me and crushed my lips to hers without a second thought. She moaned and wrapped her arms around my neck, leaning into me. She opened her mouth, and I slid my tongue against hers, massaging it as our kiss turned more passionate.

Breaking the kiss, I pulled away from her gasping. "Maya," I murmured.

She opened her eyes slowly, her brows furrowed in confusion, the cute little line between them.

"I missed you, Maya. Every fucking day. My heart bled for you. My soul wept for you. Every. Fucking. Day. I woke up every day and wondered if I would ever see you again."

Sobbing again, she wiped her tears away as best she could. "I saw you every single day. I saw your face looking back at me in our son, and it killed me that you didn't know him, that you had no idea that he existed."

I felt my own tears well up in my eyes and did nothing to stop them. Watching her, listening to her was all I wanted. If I cried while doing so, who cared. Maya needed to see my emotions too, I had always been too closed off with her back then. I couldn't afford to do that this time around. "I understand why you stayed away, and I'm glad, Maya. I'm glad you protected our son."

Again, she sobbed, and I pulled her against my chest. I held her as she let out the pain and suffering, she'd endured the last ten years—the heartbreak and stress and harassment.

"I was so scared," she admitted.

"I know, baby. I know." I rubbed her back.

"He'd randomly send flowers up north, to my hospital in Chicago, just to remind me that he always knew where I was and how to find me. Keep me in my place."

Anger raged inside me. Every time she told me more of what she'd endured over the years at the hands of Hillcrest's mind games, I wanted to bash his fucking skull in. I vowed that one day soon, I would. I would beat the holy shit out of him, then serve him up on a silver platter to Maya, so she could finish him off if she wanted.

Maya would be the one to kill Dax Hillcrest.

"I just wished I told you guys years ago."

"We can't do that, Mi Vida." I shook my head. "The what-if game will eat us alive. We can only move forward." I squeezed the back of her neck so she would jerk back from the pressure point tickling her. I needed her eyes on me. Once she was looking up at me, those beautiful amber eyes locked on mine, I continued. "You and I have a lot to work through, but I believe in us. We can figure this out, I promise you."

Tears slid down her cheeks as a hint of a smile tugged at the corner of her lips. "How do you forgive ten years of pain, Marcos? Because I *know* I hurt you. I left you... and then I didn't tell you I had your kid, for ten fucking years. Marcos," she gasped my name. "How can you forgive me for that? I betrayed you."

I closed my eyes as her anguish and heartbreak hit me hard, mixing with my own. God, it fucking hurt when I first learned about Luke, that she'd had my son and never told me, but I knew the truth now. I saw the reasoning. I could understand now. "Maya," I murmured her name, opening my eyes. "I can't lie to you and tell you it didn't hurt, because it did—so fucking much—but I understand now."

Another sob tore out of her and she closed her eyes in pain. I grabbed her hands and pulled them between us, resting them on her lap as she sat upon mine. Lacing our fingers together, I squeezed her fingers tightly. Her eyes popped open. "I don't blame you, Maya. And I need you to stop blaming yourself too."

She shook her head, as more tears fell down her face. "I can't do that. How can you not? After all the fucking lies, I told you—fuck! I even told you Hillcrest was Luke's father at one point!"

Maya tried to climb off my lap, like she was going to go pace the room again, but I didn't let her. I held her hands with one hand and wrapped my hand around the side of her throat with the other. I wasn't going to let her walk away right when we were getting somewhere, hitting the nitty gritty of our issues. No, she would stay here in my lap and look me in my eye as we had this conversation.

"You did say that. Then you told me you were in a relationship with the man torturing you for a decade and willingly kissed him," I reminded her none too gently.

Again, Maya sobbed and closed her eyes, unable to face me. "That one killed me," I admitted. "All I knew at the time was that was the man who kidnapped my sister and you were choosing *him* over me and Jason and Nico."

I squeezed the side of her neck, adding just enough pressure to make her gasp and look at me. Her amber eyes were wide, despite the tears flowing down her cheeks. I wrapped my hand fully around her thin throat and squeezed just a little tighter, now that I had her attention. "I wanted to kill you," I told her, dropping my voice to a menacing gravel. "You came back here after years of being away, then acted all aloof and standoffish the last half a year, and then I found you fucking with that scum of the earth?" I squeezed her neck just a little more, making her gasp. "But I couldn't, because you fucking told me that I wasn't on the birth certificate. Then you fucking said Hillcrest was the father." I released her throat, roughly pushing her backward enough that she had to throw a hand out to catch herself.

"Marcos, I'm sorry." She bawled through the words, choking them out.

I had to take a deep breath to calm the rage that simmer inside me. "I told my sister I was going to take custody of him if you were going to be with that bastard. I wanted to take Luke away from you, because I didn't want him near my son."

Maya nodded through her tears.

"Kara told me because I wasn't on the birth certificate that I didn't have many options. So she hooked me up with a friend of hers, to try to establish paternity." I had to tell Maya my side of the events that happened between us. I didn't want any more secrets, any more lies. We needed a fresh slate. In order to do that, we'd have to air all the dirty laundry.

"They served me at work," she murmured, her voice thick with emotions.

"I know. I told them that was the best place to find you."

She nodded, resigned. Sniffling, she reached for a tissue from the forgotten box next to us. "I understood why you did it." Her voice was scratchy.

"I had to do what I felt was right for Luke. The thought of that monster around you was bad enough, but you made that choice—or so I thought—but the idea you were subjecting our son to him too—fuck, Maya. I lost my damn mind." I wrapped my hands around her waist and pulled her closer. Bending my knees, I forced her weight to fall toward me.

Her hands landed on my bare chest; her hands cool against my warm skin. She watched me warily, waiting.

"I'm sorry that I tried to take Luke from you, even if it never got that far, I'm sorry that was my intention."

"Marcos." Maya shook her head. "Don't—"

I shook my head cutting her off. "We're airing our dirty laundry tonight, Maya. We're getting it all out there."

She sighed softly. "I don't think we can do that in one night."

"No, we probably can't. Not when a lot of what we need to talk about involve my brothers too." I sighed, thinking of Jason and Nico. We would need to discuss what happened in those last couple of days together, but that was a conversation for a different night.

"Marcos, I am truly sorry for everything I've said or did since I've come back." She sighed heavily. "Everything was intended to hurt you intentionally, to keep you away. I needed the distance. I couldn't have you guys looking at things too closely—Nico especially."

I laughed dryly, "Fucking Nico."

A smile tugged at her lips. "Yeah, ever the persistent one."

"I'm sorry I didn't think to push or fight harder. It felt like every time I tried to get answers, you pushed me away harder."

"I did." She nodded. "I had to."

"Yeah," I deadpanned.

Silence fell between us as I held her in my lap, her hot core pressed against my dick. I rubbed circles into her the sensitive area just inside her hipbones, absentmindedly as I stared into her eyes. Her fingers traced over the tattoos on my chest, tracing over her name on my heart. The tat I got after our first year together, when I knew she was it for me.

Needing to get all the truths out there, I continue our conversation. "Your mother told me the truth. Elaine gave me a copy of his birth certificate; she thought I should have a copy in case anything happened to you and I needed to get custody of Luke."

Maya gasped, her eyes flying to mine.

"Yeah. I saw you listed my name as his father on his birth certificate. When did you do that?"

Her eyes softened as she met his gaze. "I did it from the beginning. Your name has always been listed as his father. I took one look at him, and I knew he was yours."

I leaned forward and kiss her softly, sensually, needing the connection between us. I slid my hand up her side, grazing her breast before I cupped the side of her face and held her against me, deepening the kiss.

Maya's hands on my chest slid up and around my neck and she leaned into me, pushing me back into the headboard with her weight dropping on my chest. It was a delicious feeling, holding her on top of my body after so many years. She'd lost weight though the last couple weeks, and I didn't like how light she was. Her ass wasn't as round.

Moaning, Maya pulled away and yawned deeply, making me realize it was still the middle of the night. "Sorry," she muttered, sheepishly.

I can't help but grin. "Don't worry about it. Do you want to try laying down again? Jason brought in a night light." I nodded my head toward the mini lamp on the nightstand.

Her smile was a bright cool balm on my broken soul.

"I don't think I can sleep yet."

I nodded, knowing that was probably the case, despite her yawning. Enjoying the closeness of having her in my arms, I slid down the mattress and held her tight against me as I laid down with her on top of me.

Shimming us around, trying to grab the sheet and blankets, Maya chuckled as I jostled her slightly. Finally, I managed to grab everything and pulled the covers over us. I hit the remote on the nightstand for the overhead light and shut it off, plunging us into darkness. "Shit, sorry," I muttered, when Maya stiffened against me. Blindly, I reach out for the mini lamp and turn it on, basking us in a dim light.

Maya relaxed atop me and let out a heavy sigh. "Thank you."

I rub my hand over her back while I squeezed her hip with the other. "Anything, Mi Vida." I spoke softly, as if the dim lighting created a more intimate setting between us. "Now tell me about learning Spanish."

A startled laugh burst out of her and I felt myself breathe easy for the first time in a while. She was alright—would be alright. We would be alright.

Together, we'd figure it all out.

Chapter Thirty-Four

Maya

I WOKE TO THE shrill sound of a cell phone ringing. Still wrapped in Marcos's arms, I grumbled when he jostled me to reach for the phone. The room was still dimly lit, but there were thick blackout curtains covering the windows, so it was hard to tell. All I knew was that I was exhausted still, considering we lay awake talking to the early hours of the morning.

"Yeah," Marcos grunted as he answered the phone. "What?" He slid me off of him and sat up.

I sighed, curling on my side to watch him. He looked concerned.

"Alright, see you soon." He hung up the phone and stood from the bed. "That was Kara, she and her guys are on their way over here."

I sat up and frowned. "What happened?"

"Kara's father was killed in jail." Marcos ran a hand over his head, his fingers sliding through the hair that was growing out.

236

My heart hammered in my chest at the news. Kara had to be devastated. I got up on my knees and walked across on the mattress toward Marcos, taking in his messy bedhead hair and scruffy beard thinking he never looked so hot. It wasn't the time, but I needed to say something, anyway. "Hey," I murmured, reaching out for him.

He wrapped his arms around me immediately. "Hey," he murmured.

"I know it's not the time, but I gotta tell you before you do something rash," I started, rubbing my hand over his bare chest while I looped my other arm around his neck.

"Tell me what?" he asked, raising an eyebrow.

"I like the longer hair and beard. They're sexy as fuck. Please don't cut or trim them," I told him.

The devilish smirk he gave me had butterflies erupting in my stomach. My heart skipped a beat as he wrapped his hand around the back of my neck and pulled me in for an open mouth kiss. I moaned pressed closer into his shirtless body.

He pulled away before things could grow more heated and slapped my ass. "Get dressed, they're already here," he said, as a truck rumbled into the driveway.

I got up and finally looked at the clock on the nightstand. It was already after nine in the morning. "Fuck, I didn't get up with Luke!"

"I'm sure Nico got him up and ready. Don't worry," Marcos said as he walked out of the bedroom.

I headed into my walk-in closet and pulled on the first outfit I could find. A pair of jean shorts from the day before and a clean bra and tank top. I dressed quickly before I walked into my attached bathroom. Running a brush through my hair, I sighed in defeat at unruly curls before I grabbed a hair tie and put my hair up in a messy bun.

My body was feeling better after my ordeal. It had been over a week since I've been home from the hospital and my stomach didn't as much hurt now. Besides my mind being all fucked up, my body was mostly healed.

I left the bedroom and headed down the stairs to the first floor. I could hear the rumble voices as I descended. Johnny Taylor, Kevin Adams, and Derrick Halson of the Ravager Knights MC stood in the kitchen in their menacing leather cuts. Kara was with them, her baby girl in the car seat carrier on the floor at her feet, the little lady wide awake and cooing softly.

Kara looked up when I walked in and all conversation stopped when they realized I was standing there. "Hey," Kara smiled. "You're looking better."

"Bitch, I look like shit," I grumbled, earning laughter from the guys, but I walked over to her and hugged her tightly. "I'm sorry about your dad," I murmured.

"Thanks." She whispered as she hugged back.

"How you doing?" I asked softly, as I pulled away from her.

Kara sighed heavily and gave me a watery smile. "I didn't think I would feel like this, you know?"

"It's a hard situation all around," I muttered, "Things with your dad were never easy. It's natural to be upset."

Kara wiped away a tear and nodded. "They weren't, that's for sure."

Nico walked over and handed us both a cup of coffee.

I smiled gratefully and kissed him softly. Turning back to Kara, I asked, "What happened?" I glanced at Marcos over my shoulder too.

"He was killed in prison," Kara said.

I turned to face the rest of the room, leaning back against the counter and sip my coffee as I watch them, waiting for someone to say something. "Who was it?"

"Hillcrest," Marcos answered. "One of his guys."

My face paled and my heart sunk into my stomach. "Was it retaliation for me?"

"No, Maya, don't think that," Kara said immediately.

"Retaliation for a lot," Marcos nodded his head once. "We killed a lot of his men that night."

"Did any of your men die?" I asked, feeling foolish for not thinking of it sooner.

"None," Marcos said immediately. He walked through the kitchen toward me, the other guys stepping out of his way, so he could stand in front of me and grip my jaw between his thumb and forefinger. He tilted my head back, so I was staring up at him. Marcos eyes were intense, but I held his gaze. "This was not your fault." His voice was a low gravel that rumbled through his chest. "You hear me? This was not your fault."

I blushed slightly at the intensity in his words and the fact that everyone in the room was watching us. "Marcos..."

"No, Maya. Hillcrest has terrorized you for long enough. He doesn't get one more piece of you. He did this because he's a sadistic fuck, not because you did anything wrong. You can't let him win anymore." Marcos was so adamant, I could only blink back at him and swallow thickly as tears lined my eyes.

"'k," I breathed.

His eyes searched mine, as if looking for the lie. Then he kissed me, in front of everyone, his tongue sweeping in and devouring me whole. I clung to his cut, holding him against me.

"Damn, brother. Get a fucking room," Kara said.

I tried to pull away, but Marcos still gripped my chin and he only held me tighter, refusing to let me go. I moaned softly before I pushed him away, blushing. Feeling the eyes of everyone in the room on me, as I met Marcos's smirk. I buried my face into Marcos's chest as several guys snickered.

"Don't be embarrassed, Maya," Kara said, chuckling. "I was giving my brother shit, not you. You do whatever the hell you want, damn the consequences."

I pulled away from Marcos's chest, my face red, and smile at her. Shrugging, I say. "I plan on it."

Picking up my coffee again, I walked over to the kitchen table and sat down. "So what's the plan?"

Johnny had an amused smile on his face as he glanced between me and Marcos. Scratching at his thick blond beard, he looked to Marcos. "Guess we're waiting to hear how you want to handle Hillcrest."

"We're going to find him and his entire organization. We're going to wipe them all out, but leave Hillcrest for last," Marcos said.

"What the fuck?" Derrick groaned. "Why?"

"Because I'm going to serve him up on a platter for my old lady. Maya gets that kill." Marcos said.

I gasp as his words register. My mouth slowly opened, only to close again when I find I have nothing to say.

Again, all fucking eyes are on me.

I met Jason's eyes first, wondering what the hell he was thinking, as he was being his usual stony self. "You deserve it," he said, his voice commanding.

A shiver went down my spine at the cadence of his voice. Every damn time that man spoke, it made me shiver. I loved his damn voice so fucking much... just about as much as I loved his stupid face and self. If only me and him could work past our shit.

Nico walked around the side of the kitchen table to kneel beside me, "This is your decision, Little Dreamer. Whatever you choose, I'll be right beside you."

I smiled and cupped the side of his face with my palm. "I would expect nothing less, Nicolai," I murmured, then leaned forward and kissed him softly.

"You'd be ok with that? Killing Hillcrest?" Johnny asked, pushing the issue.

I pulled away from Nico and sighed. Scratching at my messy bun, I shrug a shoulder. "I don't know," I answered honestly. "But I know that if I can't do it, one of my guys will."

"Amen," Marcos, Nico, and Jason said in unison.

A smirk tugged at Johnny's lips as he studied me for a moment before he nodded. I didn't know what he saw, but I felt confident in my decision. I wanted the chance to at least *try*. If I couldn't do it in the end, then I knew my guys would make him suffer. I hoped they fucking tortured him first.

Chapter Thirty-Five

Jason

I WATCHED MAYA FROM across the kitchen. Sitting at the table with her coffee mug, she looked utterly regal. A fucking queen addressing her court. I could tell that Johnny felt it as he watched her, even Kara never took her eyes off of Maya.

Maya had always had a way with people, a charm about her. It was fucking magnetic and immediately drew us to her way back then. She hadn't understood, and I hadn't had the words to explain it, but something cosmic had drawn us to her, from the very first meeting.

Now, as she perched on her chair and addressed the room, her spine straight and that easy confidence back, I felt myself fall in love with her all over again. Not that I ever truly stopped, but damn, was she fucking sexy.

Nico still kneeled beside her, his hand on her thigh, eyes watching her reverently.

"How do we find him now?" I asked, glancing around the room at the men all staring at my woman.

"My brother is already searching," Kevin said. "Jack said he's found some leads and is digging deeper. The IP address for the warehouse helped him dig into financial records and find Hillcrest through other business ventures. Jack's working on it."

"I also reached out to Stephanie," Kara said, looking to Maya. "She has her own forensic accounting firm—"

"Stonewall Financials. I know," Maya nodded.

"Right," Kara nodded, looking a little put out.

I wondered if Maya kept in contact with Stephanie after all the years, and if that was why Kara seemed upset? Just because Kara hadn't kept up with most of her friends, didn't mean that Maya hadn't.

Shit, just because Maya hadn't kept in contact with me and guys, didn't mean she didn't keep up with all of her friends. Her ink was testament to that. The fucking wall of photos at Slade's booth at Skin of a Different Breed was testament to that too.

Clearly, Maya had kept up with people over the years.

"So yeah," Kara continued. "Stephanie is digging into what she can find publicly. And Jack's getting her what he can find *not publicly*."

I read through the lines on what Kara was trying to say—Jack was getting her records and accounts by hacking into systems illegally. I didn't give a damn how Jack Adams found the information, as long as it led him to Hillcrest's fucking location so we could go in there and wipe the bastard off the face of the fucking planet—after torturing him for a week straight, maybe longer, like ten fucking years.

"What happens now, with your dad? Does that mess up things at the firm for you?" Maya asked Kara.

Kara shook her head. "No, it shouldn't. The plea deal he accepted gave me the guilty verdict that I needed to gain the firm. With my father's guilty verdict, his ownership shares in the firm were transferred to me. I now own sixty percent of all shares in the firm." Kara shrugged a shoulder.

Maya laughed lightly. It was a balm to my tortured soul. I was so fucking glad she was able to laugh still, after everything that happened. "Good for you. Bad ass bitch."

Kara's daughter fussed in her car seat and Kara bent down to pick her up. "Are you bored? Did you think we forgot about you?" she cooed at the baby.

I watched Maya as she watched Kara intently. The yearning in her gaze about did me in. "Can I hold her?" Maya asked, and my fucking heart exploded in my chest. I need to work my shit out with her ASAP, because I had things I needed to work into her.

I don't know where my need to have kids came from, but seeing Kara with her daughter so often, and then hanging out with Luke daily too, it really drove home the idea of having a baby of my own.

Nico stood up from where'd still been kneeling next to Maya and backed away.

Maya also stood up though, confusing me. I thought she wanted to hold the baby. "Let's go sit in the living room, I'm kinda sore."

Kara only nodded and followed Maya into the living room, where she waited until Maya was situated at one end of the couch, before she handed over her child.

Maya's bright smile warmed me from the inside out. The wonder and awe on her face only added fuel to the fire—I wanted to have a baby with Maya as soon as possible.

I eyed my brothers, wondering what they were thinking, but saw it clearly on their faces as they both froze and stared in awe at Maya cooing softly to the baby in the other room. Yeah... they were on board alright.

Johnny chuckled and shook his head. "You guys are fucked."

"Yep," We responded together.

Nico

The clubhouse was quiet when Marcos and I rolled in later that afternoon. Jason stayed behind with Maya—because I told him I'd kick his fucking ass if he ever left her alone again—but I was wishing I had been able to.

As vice president for the club, I couldn't do that though. Not when Marcos was president, and he was going to call church in a couple hours after most of their guys got off work. Lots of them still had day jobs, as the club wasn't earning enough to make ends meet anymore. Not since the bullshit Buckley pulled over the years, and not since we stopped running coke for the Seratellis.

All of that was changing though. Marcos and I were on it. In the meantime, though, we had to wait. So we headed into the clubhouse early to see what we could hear, and when Luke got out of school, Jason would join us for church and the vote, bringing Maya and Luke along. They would wait in one of our dorm rooms while the meeting commenced.

It would be different having Maya back here again, but I couldn't wait. She had run the Devil's Chasers when she'd been with us before. Maya had been the only old lady at the time, and while we never inked her, she always wore her 'Property Of' patch showing that she belonged to the three of us.

None of the Devil's Psychos had old ladies—except for Nickle—we weren't as sophisticated as the Knights. I was pretty sure every member over there was wifed-up. It made me yearn for more with Maya. I wanted her tatted with my ink, permanently showing my ownership of her. She was mine, and I was never letting her go again.

Watching her this morning with Kara's baby only confirmed that. I never used to understand Marcos's obsession with knocking her up back then, even going as far as to tamper with her birth control. But now I got it, completely. The urge was strong, but I knew I couldn't act on it.

Maya needed time to recover, and we all needed to discuss limits and way too many other topics before we could ever discuss having a baby together. The urge was there, though.

I followed Marcos into the president's office and closed the door behind me. "Dude, I never got it before, the birth control tampering, but I get it now."

Marcos whirled on me, "What the fuck?"

I held up my hands in surrender, "I'm just saying, back then I didn't get it. I get it now though. Seeing her with a baby... I want that." I admit the words that have been in my heart all morning.

Marcos softened and sighed, running his hand through his messy hair—that he was slowly growing out because Maya asked him to, same with the newly thicker goatee. It oddly made him look even more menacing.

Chuckling softly, Marcos shook his head and walked over to his desk, settling in the chair behind it. I took one of the chairs in front of it, like we were in some white-collar office downtown and not some dingy ass biker office. We should get the Devil's Chasers in here to clean up now that Buckley's been gone a while.

"I guess we'll be talking to Maya about more kids after everything settles down?" Marcos asked.

I nodded immediately. "Doc Griff said she has an IUD, so they weren't worried about pregnancy after everything with Hillcrest. They gave her a dose of basically liquid Plan B in her IV to be safe, but yeah, it's something we're going to have discuss because she'll need it removed."

Nodding thoughtfully, Marcos smirked. "When the time comes, we'll bring it up to her. We're going to have renegotiate *everything*. I need to make sure what happened back then never happens again."

I sighed. "I don't even know how much of that scene affected her, so much as what happened after? Like obviously the hypothermia was nothing to play at and we won't do that again, but was the suspension play an issue? The extreme punishment? Those are things we need to ask her."

"Yeah." Marcos sighed.

"So I take it then, you're all in? The four of us—shit you moved her in with us immediately. That was a far cry from trying to establish paternity and trying to sue for custody."

"I know. Fuck, I need to call that lawyer and tell her to stop moving forward. Elaine gave me a copy of Luke's birth certificate. My name is already on it... and I have no plans of living without both Luke and Maya going forward. Yeah, I'm all in."

I grinned and nodded approvingly. "So now we just need to get Stone on board."

"He's there, he's just stubborn as fuck. He never stopped loving her. Stone is just being hardheaded, but you saw his face today—he's team *knock-up Maya*." Marcos laughed at his own joke.

Jason

"Alright Luke, I need you to listen to your mom while we're here today. It's important," I told Luke as I pulled into the parking lot of the clubhouse. It was early still, just after four p.m.; the clubhouse was mostly quiet, but things would pick up as more brothers got off work and headed over.

Church was scheduled for six that night and we needed to be ready. It was going to be a rough session, and we needed to have our ducks in a row in case shit went sideways.

"Ok," Luke agreed.

As we all climbed out of Marcos's truck, I caught Maya's eye. She was staring at the clubhouse with apprehension written on her beautiful face. "Hey," I murmured, "it's going to be ok."

She forced a smile on her face, but didn't say anything.

We both closed the truck door, and as we walked toward the main entrance, I grabbed her hand and laced her fingers with mine. Shit may still be rocky and up in the air between us, but I would physically make sure she knew I was here for her.

She looked up at me, a confused expression on her face. I didn't comment, but squeezed her hand and lead the way inside.

Luke was looking around wildly, taking everything in. It made me pause and take a deeper look around the main bar room, trying to see things from his point of view. It was still dark and slightly run down, but Marcos was having the Devil's Chasers clean things daily. I knew he wanted to paint and update things, but we had also talked about moving the clubhouse out of the downtown area.

"This place is so cool!" Luke announced as he looked at the art on the walls—the half-naked women that I hadn't thought about before I brought him.

"Uhh," Maya said, looking around. Not much had changed since she'd last been here, but the place being almost utterly empty, really put things on display. "Let's get to the dorms."

I nodded and quickly led them to a hallway in the back that led to the dorm rooms. Up the stairs and down another hallway till we reached Marcos's dorm. He recently claimed the president's dorm room, but it wasn't all that. It was the only suite though and had the most space.

Nico and I had pulled pieces from our own dorms to furnish the living room area of the suite, and the prospects had painted everything fresh. We'd moved Marcos's bed and dressers from his old dorm into the bedroom here, so it at least looked a little put together, despite the man never sleeping here if he didn't have to.

"Hey guys," Nico called from behind us as we opened Marcos's door.

I looked back to see both him and Marcos walking toward us with bags of food and trays of drinks from the diner down the street. "Hey beautiful," Nico grinned as he greeted Maya.

"Hey Nic," Maya practically preened and tilted her head to meet his kiss.

"Little Dreamer." Nico all but growled against her lips.

I rolled my eyes and push further into Marcos's dorm room. I don't need to see that shit, not when my own jealously flared to life. I never used to be jealous of my brothers' relationships with her, but since I'm still on the outs with Maya...I can't help but feel a bit out of sorts about the whole thing.

Luke followed me into the room and we quickly headed over to the dining area. We managed to set up the living side of the suite with both a living room and dining room in a sense, but really it was a dining room table behind the couch. It fit and it worked, and I doubted Maya would mind.

Eventually they all filed into the room and joined Luke and I at the table. Marcos and Nico set down the bags of food and trays of drinks, and Luke cheered happily. "Yay! I'm starving."

"This looks awesome guys." Maya smiled happily as a cheeseburger was set in front of her.

Another pang of jealously hit me. Simple things like this always made Maya happy, and yet I couldn't seem to be the one to do that. Resolution settled within me; after we had church and the conversations we needed with other brothers, I was taking my girl home and romancing her in my own way. I just needed to figure out what that looked like.

"This was Buckley's room?" Maya asked a while later while we're all still stuffing our faces. She looked around the room with a curious eye.

"It was," Marcos answered. "I had it painted and then Jase and Nic helped me furnish it. I haven't even stayed here yet since it became mine. But there's a bed and bathroom in the other room."

Maya frowned but didn't comment.

"We bought the house, and I gave up my apartment, so I don't really need this place, except for times like this." Marcos shrugged.

"I like it, Dad!" Luke grinned.

"Thanks, buddy," Marcos murmured.

As if sensing that Marcos was a little out of his element, Nico immediately jumped in. "We got you guys hooked up with TV and internet. You can watch movies while we conduct business, and as soon as we're done, we'll head home, ok?"

"Ok," Maya agreed.

"After talking with Maya about things that had happened in the past before she left, and what happened during those ten years she was away," Marcos addressed the club, "We discovered something we didn't know back then about Buckley. He was working with Dax Hillcrest, even back then."

Grunts and cursing went around the table as the group of leather clad bikers grumbled over their old president. All of them had voted to kill Buckley, and let Johnny Taylor have his revenge, but you never knew who still had hard feelings over things. It was good to see the group was upset about Buckley and Hillcrest teaming up.

"Maya told me that Buckley was feeding Hillcrest to drive her away. We have reason to believe he was behind Trish coming into the clubhouse that night before Maya left and started the fight with her. Hillcrest has been threatening Maya for the last ten years, because she witnessed him kill the mayor," I said, drawing all eyes to me.

My father cursed and shook his head. "We heard," he motioned to Bear beside him, "what Trish said to Maya that night, talking about Dax, how he wanted to make her his plaything. Maya was shook-up really bad. She also told Maya that Hillcrest couldn't wait to kill the three of you and share her with his crew."

Marcos growled.

"She also mentioned," I pressed on, ignoring Marcos, "that Hillcrest sent her flowers in Chicago as reminders to stay away. And when she finally got the courage to come back here, and started looking at apartments, Buckley had Marcos and I arrested for those bullshit battery charges—from when Buckley told us to go after Davies. He set the whole thing up. Hillcrest informed Buckley that Maya was getting ready to move back, and Buckley sent us after Davies. They organized our arrest at the same time they knew Maya would be in the bank across the street," I concluded.

"What. The. Fuck?" Axel growled.

I nodded solemnly.

"All this fucking time, that fucking bastard has been working with the snakes?" Axel went on.

"Yes, seems like it," Nico said.

"I need to know what else you guys know about Buckley's relationship with Hillcrest. Any side jobs you might have done because your president asked you. I don't care about the ancient history, I'm looking for clues to anything that might lead us to Hillcrest now," Marcos ordered.

"I had always wondered why Buckley had killed that girl before you guys got a chance to question her yourselves," Bear muttered. "It was like he was covering something up."

"Yeah, his fucking involvement," I spat.

Grumbles went up around the table.

"He once had me deliver a payment to a house in Dixon. It's about an hour north of here. It was a mansion in the middle of nowhere," Phoenix said.

"I've done that run before." Nickle nodded.

"Us, too," Trick said, motioning between him and Ransom.

"Gonna need that address," Marcos demanded.

"I'll text you aft—"

"Get your phone now," Marcos ordered. There were no phones allowed in church when a meeting was in session, so Trick had to get up and grab his phone from the table outside the door.

While we waited, I thought of all the ways I was going to hurt Hillcrest when we finally got our hands on him. Maya might get the last kill, but we were going to torture the shit out of him first.

"Also," Marcos said, turning to look at Axel, Phoenix, and Blaze, "We think Maya should be the one to kill Hillcrest in the end."

The three of them clenched their jaws, Axel especially, but in the end they nodded.

"We're not going to just kill Hillcrest, we're going to torture him, and then we're going to wipe Las Serpientes off the board. I want every last fucking snake six feet under," Marcos growled.

The room erupted into loud cheers.

Trick texted Marcos the address to the house in Dixon, and Marcos immediately shot it over to Jack Adams.

"The next thing we need to discuss—Kara came over this morning with her guys to tell us that her father, Vince Carmichael, is dead. Hillcrest had him killed in prison," Marcos said.

"For fucking Christ's sake," someone snapped.

I felt the same. As we sat here lining up all the shit that Hillcrest has done over the years, it was fucking bullshit that the man was still alive this long.

"It doesn't really affect us now, as Kara had already given us the green light to kill Carmichael; but it should have been our kill, not Hillcrest's," Marcos continued.

There were rumbles around the room, but no one really had anything else to say.

"Another thing you guys should be aware of is the Ravager Knights. I kinda pissed off Johnny the other day at my sister's house—his house—and then again with Jason and Nico too," Marcos admitted.

A couple of the guys chuckled.

"What'd you do?" Nickle asked, smirking.

"It doesn't matter," Marcos shook his head. "What matters is we disrespected them in their home and Johnny wants us to answer for it in the ring."

"What the fuck?" Phoenix grumbled. "I thought things were good between us and the Knights?"

"This isn't a club thing," I jumped in. "It's my fault. I spouted off some shit and Kara got upset; the guys took offense."

"It's a brother thing too," Marcos added. "Johnny and I never addressed the blood status between us, and lately it's come up when I visit my sister. And if I piss off my sister, Johnny takes offense. I think him and I need this."

Blaze chuckled. "Yeah, I'd say so."

Nico laughed and shrugged. "It'll be ok. We'll all be standing at the end and if anything, it'll give clubs something fun to root for."

Fucking Nico, always looking on the bright side things.

"I'm having Kevin's brother Jack Adams dig into Hillcrest, so if there's anything more you have, we need to know. Between the warehouse in Sparland, and now this address, I'm hoping Jack can dig deeper. Turns out Hillcrest has not only and FBI agent in his pocket but also state Senator Bradley Bolton."

"Jesus fucking Christ," someone muttered.

"Yeah." Marcos nodded, running his hand over his head. "He's connected and they've buried shit deep. Jack was having a hard time before, but I think he's getting some solid leads now that he can connect it with the two of them."

"What do you need from us?" my father asked.

"Keep thinking of anything Buckley might have said or done over the years that might give us a lead. Be ready to go when we go after Las Serpientes when its time. We do need to vote on who kills Hillcrest though. We may think that Maya deserves the kill," Marcos said, motioning between him, Nico, and I, "but the club still gets a vote."

"It's a no brainer, man." Axel sighed. "Yeah, I wanted that kill for my baby brother, but the hell that Maya lived through..." he trailed off shaking his head. "She deserves that kill."

"Aye," coursed around the room as each and every one of our brothers agreed that our woman should get to kill Dax Hillcrest.

It made my heart swell with pride that these ten other men had my woman's best interest at heart, and they would protect her with their lives.

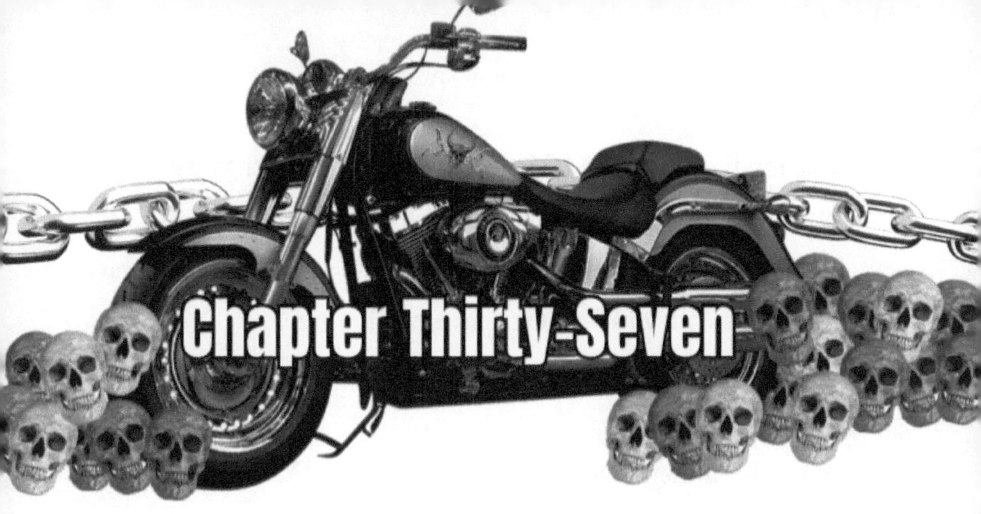

Chapter Thirty-Seven

Maya

IT WAS GOING ON eight p.m. when Marcos, Jason, and Nico walked back into Marcos's dorm room. Luke was engrossed in the Transformers moving we were watching, while I kept glancing between the book I was reading on my phone and the movie.

Same shit I'd be doing at home, except at home I'd be more comfortable and not in the jeans I squeezed my ass into just to come here. Ok, that's a lie, I'd lost a lot of weight in the last couple weeks and all my clothes were baggy now—including my jeans.

"Hey, Mi Vida," Marcos murmured tiredly. He walked over and pressed a soul-sucking kiss to my lips, his tongue immediately invading my mouth as his hand cupped my jaw.

"Ewww," Luke groaned.

I immediately pushed Marcos away, shocked that we forgot about Luke sitting a few feet away. "Luke—"

"Are you guys like *together*?" Luke asked, his precious face watching us with a hint of excitement in his gaze.

"Would that be ok with you?" Marcos asked, before I could respond.

A bright smiled bloomed on Luke's face. "Yeah... I mean... I guess." He tried to play it off. "It'd be alright, I guess, to have parents that are like other kids' parents."

My heart broke for what my son has been forced to endure in his short nine and half years. "Luke, you know it's ok to not be like everyone else, right?"

"Yeah, I know. Tommy likes boys, but I like girls." Luke was so serious as he spoke, a wry smile pulled at my lips.

"Yes. And like most other parents there's usually only two people in the couple, either the man and the woman, or sometimes two men or two women," I started, figuring this was the best lead in I could get. "But for some families there are multiple partners."

"Like how Auntie Kara is with uncle Johnny, Uncle Kevin, and Uncle Derrick?" Luke asked.

"Yep, exactly. I'm also with Nico and Jason." I don't look at him as I add his name to our relationship. Shit with him was still rocky as fuck, and we might have only had a truce, but I believed in my heart that he still loved me—we just had a shit ton to work through.

Luke's mouth dropped open. "Really?" he asked, looking around at the three men that stood to my left.

"Really," Marcos answered.

"So if you see me kiss your mom, don't freak out. We just all love her very much," Nico added.

"Yes, your mom is the very center of our family, and we can't live without her," Jason said.

I snapped my gaze to his and stifled a gasp. His stormy gray eyes were watching me intently. His usual stone-cold mask was gone and in its place was a yearning emotion that I hadn't seen from him in years.

"Huh," Luke said. He glanced at the four of them before he shrugged and went back to watching his movie.

I smirked and shook my head at his resilience. He never ceased to amaze me.

Jason cleared his throat, drawing my attention to him. "Do you think you'd be up for a ride?" he asked me.

My mouth dropped open in shock. "Um," I shot a quick glance at Luke then Marcos.

"Its fine, we got him," Marcos said.

Feeling apprehensive, but knowing Jason and I need to talk, I got up from the couch and walked over to Jason.

"We ran back for my bike before we came up here, so Marcos will take Luke home in the truck. Think you can handle a ride?" he asked.

"Um, maybe? I guess we'll see." I answered as honestly as I could. I had no real way of knowing how my body would react. My internal stitches had dissolved already, according to Doctor Griffin, but I still had moments when I got too sore if I over-did something.

Jason nodded. "Alright, we'll try to keep things short then."

I said goodnight to Luke, before I kissed Nico and Marcos goodbye and then turned back to Jason. He was watching me and clenching his jaw in anger. Was he mad at me? Trepidation rolled through me. Did I really want to go somewhere alone with him if he was angry?

Probably not, but mostly because I didn't want to cause a scene if I ended up bitching him out for being a dick. We needed to talk though, so I pushed past him out the door.

"Hold on," he said grabbing my hand.

I looked up at him and his stone-cold mask was back in place.

"You're not inked yet, or wearing a 'property of' patch. You gotta stay with me," Jason said as a way of explaining grabbing my hand.

I rolled my eyes, I knew the rules around here. It may have been a decade since I left here, but I remember how things went. I often wondered why they never inked me back then, but I often wondered about a lot of shit from our relationship in those days.

Jason led me down the stairs, through the barroom and out the front door. The cool night air had me stopping in my tracks. I was dressed in jeans and a t-shirt, and despite it being late September in northern Illinois, it had been warm when we drove over in the truck. I was not dressed for riding on the back of a bike at night.

"Here," Jason said, motioning me forward. I watched him pull a wad of black fabric out of his left saddle bag before he handed it to me. I grabbed it and unfolded it, discovering it was one of his hoodies. Quickly pulling it over my head, I embraced the warmth that settled around me. It was a thick sherpa lined hoody that the man would not be getting back, ever.

Jason opened another saddle bag on the other side of his Harley and pulled out a spare helmet. I pulled it over my head and as I started doing up the straps under my chin, Jason slapped my hand away.

I smirked, though he probably couldn't see it, and to mess with him I tried again to do my own straps. Not only did he slap my hand away again, he gripped the base of the helmet and jerked my face up to look at him. "Darlin' you want to be a brat, that's fine, but let's not forget who's in charge here."

Still smirking, because I know I have him, I chuckled softly. "If that's what you gotta tell yourself," I said.

He growled deep his chest, "You and I are gonna figure this shit out between us tonight, then I'm going to spank this ass for that sass."

I laughed lightly. "Bring it on, lover boy," I taunt him.

The smile that broke across his face had butterflies erupting in my stomach. His stormy gray eyes were crinkled at the corners, making my heart pound in my chest. He really was fucking hot as hell; he just had to be a dick half the time.

He finished up my buckles on my helmet, then slammed my visor closed for good measure, before he turned away from me to grab his own helmet. A few minutes later he was sitting on his bike that he had started and waiting for me to climb on. I grabbed his shoulder and used his body to mount the bike, putting one foot on the peg before I climbed up and swung my leg over.

It was a magical feeling being on the back of a motorcycle again. Feeling the rumble of the engine beneath me, my man between my thighs. It felt like coming home after a long ten years away. I had to remind myself not to cry, because I wouldn't be able to wipe my tears away with the helmet—not easily at least.

"Are you ready?" Jason's voice crackled to life in my ears and I shouted, jumping in alarm.

His rich, melodious laugh rang through the apparent speakers in my helmet, sending shivered down my spine.

"Holy shit." I breathed hard, hand on my heart.

"Gotta love technology. Bluetooth speakers and mics in both helmets." He spoke normal, his voice a soothing balm for my ears. "We didn't have these back then."

"These are fantastic," I murmured.

"They are—they let you listen to the music too. One day, if you're a good girl, I'll give you the remote to the radio," he crooned.

The moan that escaped me was obscene. I had already forgotten that he could hear me, because I blushed bright red when he started laughing.

"You ready, darlin'?"

"So ready, si—Jason," I said, slipping up and almost calling him sir.

"Oh baby, you and I aren't going to talk things out if you keep that up, and we have a lot to talk about," Jason said. He didn't wait for me to respond before he revved the engine. He was still in park, so I quickly leaned forward into his body and tightly wrapped my arms around him.

Jason slipped into first gear and took off a moment later. Music filled the speakers in my helmet and I slipped into the zone, enjoying the night air zooming by me.

A while later, Jason pulled into the parking lot at Quinnlyn beach my heart immediately skipped a beat. He really wanted to talk about our relationship, our future, at such a romantic spot at night?

The sun had long since set, and the moon and stars were out, shining in full force. There was no one else here, as the beach was technically closed the public after dusk. But since when did my guys care about the law?

Jason pulled into a spot and shut off the bike, killing the music in my ears as well. The silence was deafening, and we both sat still, watching the waves roll on the massive lake. It might not be as big as Lake Michigan, but Lake White Buffalo was no small body of water either. It would be warmer than Lake Michigan, though, should we choose to stick our feet in it—especially at this time of year.

And I kinda wanted to stick my feet in it.

"I'm sorry you couldn't go to Chicago this weekend," Jason's voice is soft over the speakers in the helmets.

I startled nonetheless. Needing to be face to face with him, I made quick work of the helmet straps and pulled it off my head. I fixed my messy hair as Jason pulled his own helmet off. I slid off the bike and set my helmet on my seat and stepped away so Jason can dismount. He quickly swings his leg over in a practiced motion while undoing the straps of his helmet. Once he placed his own helmet on the handlebar, he looked over at me.

"Are you upset?" he asked.

I shake my head honestly. "No. I knew tonight was important for the club—for you guys. I just saw my sister last week, and I never told her or Luke I was going, so it's not a big deal."

"But you wanted to go and had to cancel because of us. That still means something."

I shrugged.

"Don't do that." Jason stepped closer to me, shaking his head. "Don't just disregard how you feel."

I snort out a disbelieving laugh and shake my head. "Jason, it's not the first time I've had to put aside my wants or needs because of the club. And with the way things are going, it won't be the last time either."

Jason hissed out a breath. "I don't like that."

I shrugged and looked away from his intense gaze. He could not like it all he wanted; the fact of the matter was, in this life, that was the luck of the draw.

Jason grabbed my hand and turned toward the beach. I went easily with him, wanting to move on from this argument and check out the water. "Shit, hold on." He dropped my hand and headed back to the bike.

I waited, watching him pop his trunk and pull out a blanket and a cooler. *Be still my aching heart.* What the fuck was this man up to? Jason rarely did romantic gestures, but when he did, he did them in spades.

He handed me the blanket when he reached me, and I quickly tucked it under my other arm while reaching for his hand again. I fucking loved holding his hand.

"That truce didn't last long," I said.

"What do you mean? We're still under a truce." He shot me a smirk.

I rolled my eyes and a smile tugged at the corner of my lips. I refused to give him more than that though.

We walked for a little while, until we found an alcove in the grassy knoll that formed a u-shape cut out in a sand dune, giving us a sense of privacy. Jason set down the cooler before he reached for the blanket and unfolded it in a whipping flourish and laid it down on the sand.

Settling down, we both watched the waves in the moonlight, letting the quiet fall between us. It was so soothing, so fucking romantic, and the jerk with me always had one card up his sleeve, just waiting to spring on me.

"You told Luke we were together," he murmured.

I nodded slowly, the knowledge that we were going to have this conversation weighed on me. It needed to happen, but I still felt like a lead weight settling onto my shoulders. "Yep."

He turned his head to meet my gaze. "Why?"

"Why do you keep holding my hand?" I countered.

He huffed and reached for my hand again. I rolled my eyes and laced my fingers with his as we both looked back to the ocean. "I know shit is rocky right now between us, but holding your hand is the only way I know how to show you I still care, even if I can't express the words."

I knew that already, I did, but it was still nice to hear him say it.

"Truth is, I never stopped loving you and it tore me to pieces when you left us without a word." His voice is low, sending shivers down my spine.

Tears welled in my eyes and I knew they're only the first of many. I nodded, "I know, I never doubted that."

"Yes, you did, I put that doubt in your head, just like you put the same doubt in ours."

I nodded, a sob escaping me.

"I don't know how we do this, how we move forward... but I know I don't want to live another day without you by my side. I don't want that doubt between us anymore." He reached over and wrapped his arms around my knees and waist and physically hauled my ass onto his lap. I barely settled, straddling him, when he grabbed my chin between his thumb and forefinger, and jerked my face so I'd meet his gaze.

I fucking loved when they manhandled me. Looking him in the eye, I waited for his next move.

"I don't think you understand how important you are to me." His voice grew gravellier as it clogged with emotion. "I tried to erase you from my heart, tried to fuck you out of my system, but I couldn't. None of them were ever you."

I choked out a half laugh-sob, and felt oddly satisfied about that. "That's not what it looked like at Kara's party all those months ago."

He at least looked contrite. "I couldn't come after you left. In fact, I haven't been able to come with anyone else since you came back in January."

Shit, if that wasn't romance, I didn't know what was. Funny, how such a stupid thing could ease my jealousy. "That had to hurt your ego."

"It did... and probably fueled my rage. I'm sorry again for wrapping my hand around your throat. That was uncalled for."

I tried to looked away from him, but he still held my chin in his grip and immediately nudged me back when I moved. "I've never seen you look at me like that before—that rage and utter hatred for me—I've never been afraid of you before that moment." My voice was soft as I admitted the truth.

He finally let go of my chin as horror washed over his face. I could see the shame in his eyes. I reached up and put my hand on his cheek, needing to touch him. "Maya..." Tears welled in his stormy gray eyes, and I rubbed my thumb over his chiseled cheek bone and waited, giving him the time to think out what he wanted to say. "I'm so sorry. I never—fuck." He cleared his throat. "God, baby." He groaned and his tears fell down his face.

I wiped his tears away, bringing my other hand up to his other cheek.

"I'm so fucking sorry, Maya." Jason muttered, closing his eyes.

"I'm not going to say *it's ok*, because it really isn't," I murmured. "I will say that I know things have changed since then, and I know you feel worse about it than I'd ever want you to feel. I can forgive it this one time, but Jason," I shook my head sadly, "if you ever do something like that again, I'm gone. Even if I'm still with Marcos and Nico, me and you would be done forever. I won't be another domestic abuse statistic."

A sob broke out of him and his eyes closed. His body shook as he began sobbing in earnest. I dropped my hands from his and wrapped my arms around his back, leaning into him. He buried his face in the crook of my neck and pulled me tighter against him. We sat that way for a long while, my own tears trailed silently down my face as I rubbed his back.

Eventually he pulled back and wiped his own tears away. "I promise you, Maya. You don't have to worry about that ever happening again—it won't. And I'll spend the rest of my life making it up to you."

I nodded my head once, reaching up to brush his tears away again. "Ok."

He nodded himself once, as if unsure of what else to say.

"Tell me about not being able to get off with the Devil's Chasers." I smirked up at him.

"Ah fuck." He groaned and shook his head. "It happened on and off over the last ten years, any time I'd think about you, really. If I tried to erase your memory with another woman, it happened. And then when you moved back in January, it's been since then."

I laughed wryly. "Good."

He grinned brightly, his white teeth sparkling despite the dim light of the moon.

"I wanted to bash that bitch's face in, anyways."

"Always my little brawler." Jason chuckled.

I rolled my eyes.

"How do we do this?" Jason asked, changing the subject. "How do we both just forgive and forget?"

"We don't forget." I shook my head. "We can't—the pain is too real. We won't ever forget it." I sighed heavily, taking a moment to compose my thoughts. "Honesty. Honesty is the only way forward. Both of us need to be open with each other, communicate our feelings constantly. I know that's hard for both of us, but Jason, there's no other way at this point. We both need to work constantly, every single day going forward on our relationship if we want this to work. I've said the same thing to the other two, being open and honest is the only way forward."

"Yeah," he grunted.

"I need to be a priority. I hate that I even have to ask for that; I feel like it should be a given in a healthy relationsh—"

"You *are* a priority. You always were."

"The club *always* came first. And I know it will again, and most of the time I will understand that..." I shook my head and trailed off. I needed a minute to gather my thoughts again. I swallow thickly as emotions choke me up again. "My son will always be my number one priority," I settled on. "His happiness and safety will always come first, as will the happiness and safety of any more children we may have down the line."

"You want more children?" Jason asked, his voice higher than normal.

I rolled my eyes, "Please, like I didn't see the three of you salivating at the thought of it when you saw me with Lilah this morning."

A sheepish smile pulled across Jason lips and I swear if I could see the color of his cheeks, I bet he'd be blushing. He cleared his throat. "I know you think that we didn't make you a priority last time, and maybe we could have tried harder back then. But I promise you, Maya, things are different this time around."

"How so?" I questioned, raising an eyebrow.

"Marc's pres now. He runs things differently than Buckley. We're still cleaning up a lot of Buckley's mess, but I promise you, all the bullshit and drama you had to go through back then, it's not an issue now." Jason sounded so sincere, so earnest, it was hard not to believe him.

I had to look away from him. I was baring my heart too much and I needed a minute.

Chapter Thirty-Eight

Jason

"Was it so bad being with us back then?" I asked, almost regretting it immediately.

"No." Maya didn't hesitate, not even for a second. My heart calmed for a moment, but my mind still raced a million miles a minute.

"I know the club is important to you guys, and I'm glad Marcos is now president, but that also terrifies me because of the expectations of time and attention. He's married to that club as are the two of you, and I don't know where I fit in all of that." Maya took a deep breath, before she continued on. "Being with you guys painted a giant target on my back, and I unfortunately fell victim."

"May—"

"I *should* have been smart enough to speak up," she spoke louder, emphasizing her point. "All I can think about is how intense everything was between us, especially in those last couple of weeks. I should have used my safe word and made you guys listen to me, but the timing always seemed to not be right, or you guys weren't home. Working nights didn't help either."

"Maya." I breathed her name like it was a prayer. My heart lay in shambles around me as I heard her very clearly tell me how I failed as a dom. She may not have said those words, but she spelled out each and every failure on how my sub couldn't come to me with life-threatening news, how she didn't feel comfortable talking to me. How she thinks she should have used her fucking safe word just to get my damn attention, because I was too far up my own fucking ass to realize something was wrong with her.

"This really is a conversation that we need to have with Marcos and Nico present. There's much we need to discuss as a group if this is going to move forward," she said.

"Yeah," I grunted, lost for words.

She went to climb off my lap, but I squeezed her tighter against me. "Jason," she muttered.

"Having you close heals my broken heart. I can't breathe without you. Please, just stay." The words come out in a low rumble, and I can feel Maya shiver as my words wash over her. She always did have a thing for my voice; and if I sometimes used that to my advantage, who would ever know?

"Alright," she murmured softly. Her voice was low and husky and had me thinking dirty things. "Can I turn around? My knees are starting to hurt."

"Yeah, baby," I mutter. I help her slowly turn around, so she's sitting on the blanket between my legs. I held her close, her back to my chest, enjoying the warmth of her body against mine. Savoring the feeling of her in my arms, I pressed a kiss to the side of her neck.

"What's in the cooler?" she asked, breaking me out of my reverie. I had forgotten all about the cooler.

"Dessert. Shit." I tried to lean forward and reach for it, but with her firmly between my legs, I couldn't reach.

"I got it." She pulled away from me, and I immediately missed the warmth of her body pressed against mine. The cool night air was seeping in through my hoodie, but her body heat was keeping it at bay.

Maya grabbed the small cooler I packed and pulled it closer. She turned on the flashlight on her phone and opened it. Her squeal of excitement sent shivers down my spine. I fucking loved when she got excited about something. "Strawberries and dips?" she asked, inspecting all the containers.

"Yeah. There's chocolate and cool whip and that one fruit dip you like. There's also apples and caramel."

"Fuck. Yes." Maya settled back between my legs and opened the snack box I packed with our desserts.

Silence fell between us, as Maya dug into the snacks. I grabbed an apple slice here or there and at one point she turned around to feed me a chocolate-covered strawberry, but mostly I let her snack in peace. We'd both bared our hearts and souls tonight; a breather was much needed.

After a moment, I grabbed a strawberry from the container, dipped it in chocolate, then topped it with cool whip before I grabbed Maya's jaw with my other hand and turned her to face me. The startled gasp that left her lips was the opening I needed to paint her lips with chocolate and cool whip, before I slowly pushed the strawberry between her lips, fucking her mouth with it.

Her moan was lewd as fuck and had my cock immediately standing at attention. My balls were already throbbing, just from watching her eat, but this was a whole other level. Finally, she bit down into the strawberry, groaning.

"Fucking hell," I muttered.

She chuckled softly around her bite of fruit.

I held the fruit to her lips until she finished the whole strawberry and sucked my fingers into her mouth. "Maya," I groaned.

"Mmm."

"You keep doing that, you're gonna regret it."

"No, I don't think I will." She grinned brightly, even in the moonlight, I could see her smile.

"Baby," I moan, dropping my head against hers. I needed to get myself under control. There was no way we could have sex tonight. Not after everything she'd been through not even a month ago.

"What, Jason?" Her voice was a soft sing-song melodic tone that drove me fucking wild.

I took a deep breath and let it out slow. I was rock fucking hard, my cock digging into her lower back. I loved how she fit in my arms, but it was not the time for anything sexy. We still had things to talk about; she was nowhere near ready. This couldn't happen.

"You're driving me fucking crazy." I purposely added gravel to my voice, so I could watch those beautiful shivers dance across her skin. Kissing her neck, I ran my hands over her stomach and up, under her shirt, cupping her breasts.

Maya moaned throatily as my hands kneaded her flesh. "Jase," she gasped, arching against me. Her ass dug into my cock and I groaned low in my throat.

"Tell me to stop," I panted as I pinched and twisted her nipples.

"Mmm uhh," she moaned.

"I should stop, Maya," I said, letting go of her nipples. "I don't want to push you into anything you're not read—"

"Don't you dare stop," she snapped. She grabbed both of my hands and pushed them back to her tits.

I chuckled softly and continued toying with her nipples, pinching and plucking at them, switching it up to kneading her breasts like dough every once in a while.

She moaned again and I smirked, sucking a kiss into the crook of her neck. "Ja-son," her voice was a broken gasp.

"Yeah, darlin'," I whispered in her ear.

"I need—I need more."

"How much more?"

"Fingers," she panted. "I need—I need your fing...ers inside... me."

I froze, wondering if I should keep going. Was it safe? Griffin didn't mention anything about waiting for sexual activities because we were all pretty sure Maya wouldn't be interesting in anything like that any time soon. Was I pushing her boundaries? Would she come to regret this? "Maya."

"Jason Michael." Maya all but growled at me.

"I'm serious, Maya. I wouldn't be able to live with myself if I pushed you into something you weren't ready for. Fuck, baby." I dropped my hands from her body and ran them through my messy hair.

Sensing my distress, Maya turned around and faced me. "Ja-son." She grabbed my face with both hands and pulled me closer to her. "Hey," she murmured when I was a few inches from her face, the dim lighting giving me just the outline of her face to work with.

"Hey," I muttered.

"I'm ok. I promise you. Right this moment, I am ok." She stressed the words.

I nodded dumbly. We just got her back; I didn't want to be the one to fuck this up with her.

"Right now, I want you to touch me. Not fuck me, not yet, not here. I want your hands on my body and want your fingers inside me, ok?"

I loved that she fucking spelled it out for me. No questioning where the line was. "Ok."

She kissed me hard and I groaned, pulling her hard against me. Her mouth was magical and I needed more of her special kisses. I angled her head with my hand and deepened the kiss, groaning low in my throat.

Breaking the kiss breathlessly, Maya chuckled softly. "Keep kissing me like that, and I just might rethink my no fucking rule."

"Nuh uh." I shook my head vehemently. "You gave me a boundary—drew the line in the sand—I will respect that."

"Even if it means shitty puns?" she asked.

I laughed, feeling my heart grow lighter. "Absolutely if it means shitty puns."

Maya laughed lightly. "I can live with that...I guess." She turned back around and settled back between my thighs. Popping the button on her jeans, she leaned back into my chest and I wrapped my arms around her.

"Fuck, Maya, I don't think you understand what you do to me, the effect you have on me. You're so heart wrenchingly beautiful."

Maya's head fell back against my shoulder and she closed her eyes as I trailed my hands over her body, tracing down her sides and skimming over her breasts before I skated down to her opened jeans.

"Jason." She panted my name.

I smirked against her neck before I nipped her skin, making her moan loudly. "Good girl," I crooned softly.

My fingers slid into her damp panties and parted her slick folds. Sliding my other hand under her shirt again, I pinched a nipple while I nipped at her neck. "So fucking perfect, you have no idea, Maya. The love of my life."

She moaned my name again, setting off a raging inferno under my skin.

"Take a deep breath for me," I said, preparing her for my fingers to penetrate her perfect body.

Maya does as she's told and takes a deep breath.

I slid a single finger into her wet, hot passage.

"Jase," she gasped.

"How you doing, darlin'?"

"So... uh..."

I fucked my finger in and out of her slowly, twisting and twirling as I went.

"Mmm." She arched back against me.

"Still with me?" I asked.

"Jassssuuuuuuhhhhhnnnnn."

I chuckled softly and slipped in a second finger.

"Oh, yes."

I twirled my fingers inside her before I fucked her slow and steady, dragging the pads of my fingers along the top wall of her cunt, finding that spongy spot everything single time. I circle my fingers over it and press down on her clit with the palm of my hand.

"Jasseee," she hissed. Her legs clamped closed around my fingers, and she arched against me again as her body shuddered with her orgasm. "Mmmmm." She stifled her scream of pleasure.

I kept twirling my fingers, riding out her orgasm until she jerked against me, and I stopped. Pulling my fingers out of her gently, I made sure not to startle her or cause any discomfort to her over-sensitive body. "So beautiful, darlin'. So fucking perfect for me. I love you."

I pulled my hand out from under her shorts and grabbed her face, roughly pulling her face toward me so I could kiss her soundly. She was boneless against me as she kissed me back passionately.

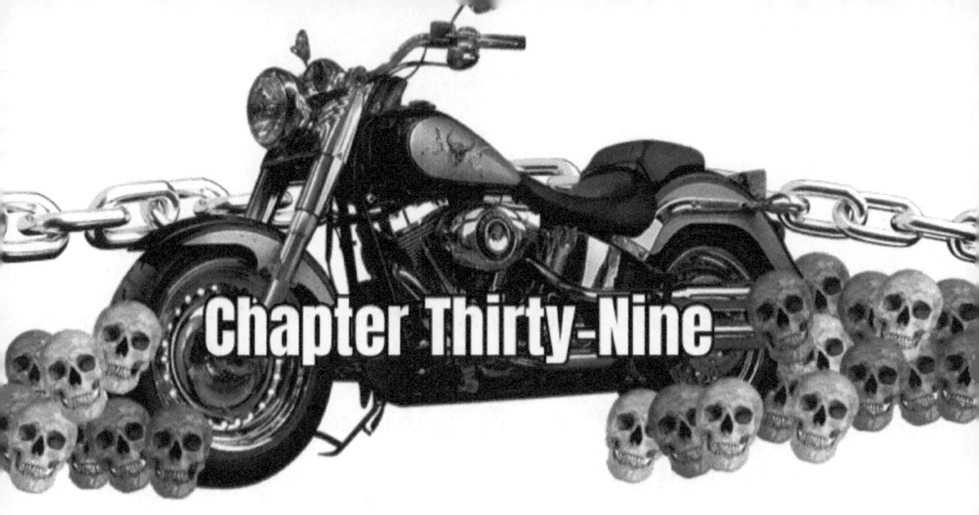

Chapter Thirty-Nine

Maya

IN THE DAYS SINCE my date with Jason, things around the house had calmed down and all of us settled into a routine of sorts. I got up with Luke every morning to make him and everyone else breakfast for the day. Then I packed up Luke's lunch and made sure he got on the bus. After Luke was gone, I changed my clothes and got ready for the day myself.

I started taking a kickboxing class in the mornings at Telli's Boxing Gym. The gym offered all kinds of kickboxing and self-defense classes. The self-defense classes were amazing and geared toward training muscle memory with a lot of repetitive motions and hitting the trainer holding pads. It made me feel empowered and really lifted my mood by the time I left. It helped that the trainer was usually assisted by one of my guys dressed in pads—that was very cathartic.

After my usual two hours at the gym, whichever one of my guys that had joined me that day took me home. I would then shower and eat a light lunch, before I settled for a video call with my therapist. We were doing daily calls for a while—my idea—until I felt strong enough to move on to every other day.

When I finished therapy, I relaxed on the couch either reading a book or watching a show or movie. It was my down time for the day before Luke would get home and I started cooking dinner.

My guys were fantastic about being with me and staying out of my way. They weren't leaving me alone by any means, but in the afternoons after my therapy, they would disappear upstairs or outside. It was fantastic, to be honest. I had been worried about them being up my ass after everything was said and done, but they were figuring things out.

I was never left fully alone, though, since the last time.

Jason and Marcos often left for work, leaving me with Nico a lot. They were in the process of changing their automotive shop over to specialize in motorcycles - something they both enjoyed more than working on cars. Nico didn't really care for either, though. He really came alive when he assisted the trainers at Telli's. He had a knack for both personal training and teaching classes, especially with kids.

Twice a week after school we brought Luke over to the gym. He joined the youth boxing league and was training for a match coming up in December. Luke also went to therapy twice a week and was just recently talking about joining football again.

In the evenings, we watched a movie or TV together as a family in the living room. We took turns on who picked, but usually it was between Luke and I, and half the time I let him pick because he watched it more than I did. I spent the time cuddling someone—either my guys or Luke—and split between watching whatever was on and reading my book.

It was relaxing. Things felt normal for once.

My mother and I finally hashed out a couple things since I moved out, and while we weren't close, we weren't estranged either. The biggest thing was that I didn't like how I ended up at the guys' home without a conversation from her. It felt like she'd kicked me out again, and that broke my heart.

In the end, Elaine told me I would always be welcomed back home, but she was glad that I had a place with my guys. Therapy made me realize that while my mother would never change, our relationship didn't need to be one of contention. Marcos and my mother's relationship was interesting, though. He checked in with her once a day and had prospects driving her around and delivering groceries. The Devil's Psychos prospects were becoming a whole geriatric service in themselves, and Elaine made sure to tell Marcos any mishaps that might have transpired—by her own machinations or the prospects fucking up.

Life was finally settling into *normal* and I loved every minute of it. The only thing that was still *not quite right* was our lack of sex life. We still had so much to discuss regarding that last scene from ten years ago and how to move forward as a unit.

Thankfully, my guys were on the same page, because Marcos scheduled for Luke to spend the weekend at Kara's this weekend. We dropped him off early this Saturday morning and Kara had plans taking him to the zoo with Lilah and her guys. Luke would spend the night, giving us some much-needed privacy.

October had rolled in and the leaves were changing colors and spooky vibes were in the air. My old Victorian home felt magical as I spent the late morning decorating for the season. "Hey, Little Dreamer, it's almost lunch time. I thought we could eat together, then sit down and have that conversation."

I sighed and nodded, looking away from the spider webs I was separating to wrap around the porch at some point. The conversation was the whole point of today, but I had distracted myself by decorating and now I was in the zone.

Nico laughed. "We'll help you after we talk."

"Yeah, yeah," I grumble playfully.

We needed this conversation to happen; we couldn't keep putting it off.

In the kitchen, Marcos had a pot of shaved roast beef simmering in au jus on the stove. There was an open bag of sliced French bread and a bag mozzarella cheese on the counter beside the stack of plates. "Smells good." I smiled as I walked into the kitchen. Marcos and Jason were already sitting at the table eating.

"Got yours here," Marcos said.

I looked over to see a plate already made up in my usual spot at the table. "Thanks, I'm suddenly starving." My stomach let out a loud grumble as I walked over to the sink to wash my hands.

During lunch we mostly talked about Luke and Halloween. We discussed his upcoming birthday a little, but short of inviting his Chicago friends down for the weekend and having a party at the house, there wasn't much to figure out yet.

I ate quickly, needing to get to the conversation part of the day. This felt all too much like our first negotiations all those years ago, and my heart ached for the nostalgia. I was no naïve going into that negotiation. This time around, I was more jaded—for sure—but also way more knowledgeable.

Finally, we sat down at the sectional in the living room, all of us spreading out to give each other space. I sat in the corner of the sectional and picked up a throw pillow to play with the tassels on the edges to give my hands something to do while we dug deep into the emotional conversation.

"How do you want to start this, Little Dreamer?" Nico asked, crossing one leg over the other and resting his ankle on his knee.

He sat closest to me, but gave me space to spread my legs out if I wanted.

Jason and Marcos sat to my right, with Marcos closest. Both men turned to face me and I sighed, knowing this was going to my show—my negotiation this time around.

"I think we need to start at the beginning with the night the mayor was shot and move on through that last scene we had. I think I need to explain where my head was at throughout all of that. That last week I was here was hard." I took a shaky breath.

"OK, Darlin'," Jason murmured, his eyes on mine as he nodded once.

Nico's hand landed on my knee and I gave him a grateful smile before I turned back to Marcos and Jason. I was more worried about their reactions than Nico's, honestly. Not that I was worried about Marc or Jase not believing me, but more like the devastation I was about to cause them. They hadn't seen all sides back then, not like Nico had.

"Can you guys just let me get it all out first, before you say anything? I just really need to get this out in one go...otherwise I don't think I will."

"Of course, Little Dreamer. We'll be quiet," Nico said.

Marcos and Jason nodded as well.

I swallowed thickly. "Most of this we've already talked about, but for the sake of starting at the beginning, I'm just gonna start there. The night the mayor died, I had gotten off shift in the middle of the night. It was pouring rain and I needed gas. I texted you guys that I was leaving and headed out, only to witness the mayor and Dax speeding into the gas station while I pumped gas. I was terrified when I saw Dax shoot the mayor. I didn't know who either one of them was at the time, only that I had witnessed a hit. I found out a couple days later who exactly he was and that it was the mayor he killed." I take another deep breath and squeeze the pillow. "Anyways, Dax saw me and got into my space, threatening me. I was so fucking scared, and I believed him. Then a week later, you two were shot." I looked up at Marcos and Jason, meeting their gaze.

They both swallowed and nodded at me.

"That day when I left work, it was the first time I found flowers from Dax on my car. It was then that I knew how serious he was about his threats—he had left me a message at my place of work. There was a note in the bouquet; it was crude, but basically he told me that he knew who you guys were, and that I was acting suspicious. He threatened me that if I told you guys, he'd kill you and share me with his crew."

The guys cursed and shifted on the couch. I could see it was taking them everything in their power to just sit still and not jump up angry.

"While I was freaking out about the flowers and what to do and how to tell you guys...Nico called. He told me you guys had been shot and that I needed to hurry home. So I did...and then you told me that it was Dax that shot you guys." My voice choked up as tears welled in my eyes. I quickly tried to brush them away, but they fell down my face, anyway.

"I was so scared, I jumped at everything. I barely slept. I kept agonizing over when or how to tell you guys, but every time I tried, you guys were busy with the club and I just...thought it might be better—safer—to keep my mouth closed." I looked down at the pillow, watching my fingers card through the tassels, unable to meet their eyes.

"Maya." My name came out as a whisper on Jason's lips.

I felt my face scrunch up as I fought the tears. I took a shaky breath and Nico handed me a bottle of water. Opening it, I took a quick sip. "After you guys were shot," I glanced at Marcos and Jason quickly, "I tried everything I could to get you guys to stay home with me. You said you had too much going on at the club, especially because of the shooting, so you had to go." I paused as more tears fell down my face. "I couldn't stay home alone. I was crawling out of my skin. I was worried sick that something was going to happen. I couldn't be here anymore...not alone. So I called Karma to see if her and Arturo were having people over and sure enough, they were.

"A million thoughts went through my head. All I remember is thinking that I was going to get fucked up that night. I wanted to forget it all, so I ordered the rideshare. Yeah...I probably should have drove and spent the night, but I wasn't thinking rationally at that point. The stress and fear had torn at me all week." I shook my head and wiped away my tears.

"Mi Vida," Marcos murmured.

I gave him a shaky smile as his hand landed on my knee as well.

Jason stood up and sat on the coffee table in front of me. I was surrounded by my guys, and while it helped ease some of the pain, I knew it was only going to get worse as I continued. "The disappointment on all your faces that night killed me. Walking into this room and seeing the three of you lined up waiting, knowing I broke one our rules—not even that I broke a rule—it was that I put myself in danger...and I knew it. That drive home, it was all I could think about." I shook my head and took another sip of water.

The three of them waited silently, respecting my wishes to not interrupt, though I knew how much they wanted to. "The next day, when I woke up and saw that you guys weren't here and then the note...I knew I fucked up. I was so anxious, I couldn't eat that day. My anxiety was through the roof. I was so scared that I ruined everything between us and was still kicking myself for not telling you guys about Dax." I took a shuddering breath as more tears poured down my face. "I was shaky when we started the scene. I should have told you that I hadn't eaten yet, but I couldn't. There was a lot I should have told you before then, but I didn't know how to speak up at that point. My anxiety was killing me."

"Jesus Christ, Mi Vida," Marcos swore.

I couldn't meet his gaze. I kept my hands on the pillow tassels, pulling and straightening them, smoothing them out. Anything I could do to keep my fingers busy while my mind freaked the fuck out. "So yeah, then we had the scene."

"Fucking hell, Little Dreamer." Nico groaned.

I took another sip of water, the paper wrapping fraying like my nerves and will to continue.

"Keep going Darlin'. Tell us the rest," Jason said, his voice low and full of gravel.

I swallowed thickly. "I did mostly OK through it. Even with the drug use and being tied up outside...I was OK with it...until I wasn't..."

"What was the tipping point?" Marcos voice was low and rough, but his hand squeezed my knee.

A sob broke out of me. My chest felt heavy as I tried to contain it, stifle it. I took another sip of my water and Jason handed me a tissue. I took a deep breath and tried to steady my breathing. "During the scene, you said *'maybe we need to reevaluate our relationship? Maybe it's time to renegotiate things? Because this isn't working on our end'.*" I can't look at him, even as I hear his intake of breath.

Another sob tore out of me and I let it. I curled up and buried my face in my knees and hugged them. I felt Nico's hand rub down my back, but he didn't say anything.

"Reevaluate and renegotiate. Red," Marcos murmured, sounding dazed.

"Fucking hell," Jason groaned.

"Little Dreamer." Nico's voice was almost a whine. I could hear the emotion in his voice, his own heartbreak over everything that happened.

I forced myself to calm down though, to uncurl my body. I wasn't done. We weren't done. We had so much more to discuss and we desperately needed to. It was time for it all to be all out in the open. Past time. Calming my breathing, I wiped my eyes before I took a sip of my almost empty water bottle.

Jason stood up abruptly and headed to the kitchen while I gathered myself. I glanced up at Marcos to find him staring at the table in a daze. I squeezed his fingers on my knee and he turned to me, looking haunted.

"I was so heartbroken. I thought you were breaking up with me. I should have used my safe word. I should have stopped the scene so we could have talked it out right then and there, but I was so scared that if I did anything you didn't want that night, that I would lose you forever." I took a shuddering breath.

Marcos watched me with wide eyes.

Jason sat back down on the table in front of me and opened a new water bottle before he handed it over.

Nico's hand on my other knee was a solid comfort. He was watching me with a pained look on his face. I hated that we were all being torn apart right now, but God damn did we need to do this. We could never move forward, otherwise.

I stared at the pillow again. "After the scene, I must have gone into shock and the hypothermia set in...the next morning when I woke up alone, I was so upset. I didn't know what to think, not after what you said. You had texted me 'duty calls' and you were at the club. You guys left me alone while I was dealing with post hypothermic symptoms. I could have died." The words came choked out on a sob and I quickly cleared my throat to stop it as the tears poured down my face. "I could barely move; I was so dehydrated. I was barely functioning. I ended up getting sick—dry heaving—all I remember was needing to get to my bag. I needed IV fluids or to call 911."

"Fucking Christ." Nico's sob broke out of him and he grabbed me, hauling me into his lap. "I'm sorry, Maya. I'm so, so, sorry." His body shook as he held me tightly to his body.

Through my tears, I looked over at Marcos and Jason, and both of them looked like they saw a ghost. Regret and anguish shown on their faces. Marcos looked like he was on the verge of freaking out.

I couldn't help him through this though. He needed to hear it all. I hated that I was hurting them so deeply, but I was done keeping things from them to spare their feelings. It might keep them safe, but it didn't do us any good in the long run. We were a team. They could share the burden, the weight of the feelings I've been carrying for the last ten years.

The truth.

"Somehow, I made it downstairs to my bag. Once I had the IV fluids, I felt better. Then I was pissed." I laughed ruefully. "I went to make myself something to eat, knowing I needed nutrients, and the fucking refrigerator was empty. I had spent a week on nights and no one else in this house had gone grocery shopping. I was so fucking pissed when I dragged myself out of the house. My heart was broken that my Doms hadn't thought about aftercare, hadn't thought to even check on me or stay with me when it was clear that you knew I was hypothermic." I shook my head, unable to look at them. The pain and heart break resurfacing. "All I kept thinking about was *reevaluate and renegotiate*."

"Maya," Marcos gasped. He covered his face with his hands and hunched over as his shoulders shook.

Jason looked sick, pale and green, and wide-eyed as he stared at me.

"When I was at the grocery store, Dax found me. He cornered me against the freezers and told me to leave town." I looked Jason in the eye as I spoke.

Nico squeezed me tighter.

"He said that if I didn't leave town, then he was going to kill the three of you." I took another shuddering breath and then looked away from Jason and took a sip of water.

Nico rocked me gently as he sniffled into the crook of my neck. "Fucking hell, Maya," Nico breathed.

Marcos's fingers gripped his short hair—hair that he was finally growing out for me.

I swallowed the cool water and took a deep breath. "I was more angry, than I was scared after encountering Dax. I had told him to fuck off, and vowed to myself that I would tell you guys immediately. I went home and got ready for the party at the club. I still didn't feel that well, I was nauseas all day. I tried to call you guys and tell you that I wasn't coming, but none of you answered your phones."

"Darlin'."

I shook my head, cutting him off. I stared at Marcos instead. "I went down to the clubhouse then. My heart was already broken, I didn't know what to think, those fucking words were on repeat in my fucking head all day: *reevaluate and renegotiate.*"

Marcos finally raised his head to meet my gaze, as if he could sense my stare. He looked a wreck. His face blotchy and his eyes puffy. My heart hurt to see it.

I spoke to him as I continued. "I went down to the clubhouse then. I saw Trish touching you, hanging off your arm. I saw you *allowing* it. And I fucking snapped." I huffed a laugh and shook my head. "The whole time during our fight, she kept spouting off shit about Dax and how he was going to kill the three of you and share me with his crew. I was going to kill her. I wasn't going to stop until she was dead." My voice had grown hoarse as I spoke, a soft gravely rasp. I stared at Marcos with disappointment in my eyes. "All I could think about was how you allowed her to touch you, after leaving me for dead at home."

He flinched as if he'd been slapped.

"And then you pulled me off her and were yelling at me, like I was the one in the wrong. I realized that we had gotten so far off course in our relationship, I didn't even know if I wanted to save it." I let out a small sob and looked away from him.

"Baby," Nico whimpered and held me tighter. I curled up in his arms and rested my head against his chest, turning so I was tucked in the fetal position, facing Marcos and Jason.

"I got sick when I got home. I hadn't been able to keep anything down all day, despite the IV. Then after that you guys came home, Nico was arrested, and you guys left me alone—again."

Jason hung his head into his hands as he hunched over and rested his elbows on his knees. "Maya," he groaned my name, like he was in pain.

"The next morning when all I had was another text message from Marcos, stating that Dax had framed Nico, I knew I couldn't do it anymore. He was too powerful. He could get to us anywhere. My work, the clubhouse, on the street. I knew the only way to protect you guys, was to leave. So, I packed up everything I could...and left." My voice was dead by the time I finished. My heart is broken all over again.

The guys look utterly defeated.

"After I'd been at Jenna's a week and had been sick the entire time, she made me take a test. I didn't know what to do, and I was so fucking scared of Hillcrest...so I stayed away."

Marcos let out a deep, heart wrenching sob that tore at my soul.

I wanted to go to him, but I couldn't. I didn't know what to do.

He stood up abruptly and swiftly left the room. I heard the back door slam as he left the house.

I sighed and tried to get up from Nico's lap.

"Let him go," Nico muttered. "He needs space right now."

"I think we all do," Jason rasped. He looked up at me with tears pouring down his face. "Darlin', I need to go too. I'm sorry. I just need...I don't...I can't—" his voice choked off on a sob of his own, before he got up and walked away too. Thankfully, he headed upstairs.

"Nic," I muttered, my heart pounding in my chest as I heard Marcos's Harley start up on the driveway.

"I'm here, baby. I've got you." His voice was thick with emotions and he held me tighter.

Marcos

I DROVE AWAY FROM the house with tears still pouring down my face, knowing in my heart I was making the wrong decision. I was making a monumentally stupid decision.

I screamed at the top of my lungs and pulled the fuck over three blocks from the house. I couldn't see straight, I couldn't fucking think.

Pulling over along the side of the road, I slumped over my bike and sobbed. Fucking Christ. This was all my fucking fault. I almost killed the love of my life with my own fucking selfishness.

"Marcos man, what happened?" Johnny's voice grabbed my attention.

Lifting my head, I found the leather clad biker standing on the side of the street...barefoot. Something about the sight jolted me out my anguish. "Fuck." I wiped my face with both hands and tried to calm my breathing.

"Dude, what happened?" Johnny asked.

"Me. I fucking happened."

The sound of boots stomping on the pavement made me jerk my head to the right. Kevin and Derrick ran down their long driveway toward me. In the front yard, I see Kara with a baby monitor clipped to her thigh and one hand on Luke's shoulder as they stood there watching me breakdown on the side of the street.

"You OK, man?" Kevin asked.

I shook my head. "Not really."

Johnny nodded. "Come on, we'll grab a beer in the garage. But you gotta say something to Luke first."

I nodded, feeling utterly defeated. I was probably scaring the shit out of my sister and son. I needed to be strong...but I was so fucking tired. How could someone be strong, when they were the cause of the turmoil and heartbreak around them? When they were the reason people had suffered for the last ten years? So much could have been different, had I not fucked up back then.

Slowly, I turn my bike around and make my way up the driveway. As I shut off my bike, Luke comes running over. I stand from my bike quickly, making sure the kickstand is down before I grab Luke to me and hold him tight.

"Are you OK, dad? Did something happen to mom? Why are you crying?" Luke squeezed me as I lifted him from his feet and buried my face in his neck.

"I'm OK, buddy. Just a little sad. Mom's OK too. We were talking about the past and why she had to leave here before she had you. I just realized how much I missed out on, how much of it I could have prevented. It was my fault buddy. I should have been a better man. I'm so sorry, Luke."

Luke stiffened in my arms. "Did you leave her alone again?"

"What? No!" I pulled back to look him in the eye. His little face was so serious as he stared me back, so determined. "No. Nico and Jason are with her. I promise you."

"Then why aren't you?"

My mouth dropped open in shock. I found myself utterly speechless. He was right. With four words, my nine-year-old son knocked me on my ass. "I—uh."

"Luke honey, sometimes after hard conversations, people need their space. Sometimes it's easier to breakdown without anyone watching," Kara said softly as she walked over.

I glanced at my sister, grateful and slowly set Luke back on the pavement. "She's right. I didn't want your mom to see me like this. I didn't want you to see me like this."

Luke frowned. "Hiding your feelings won't help. Secrets are what started this. It's not good to keep your pain secret from your family."

How the fuck was this little boy so fucking wise? "You're absolutely right, son. The truth is...I'm scared. I don't know how to fix things, or how to be the kind of man your mother deserves."

"Only Maya can decide what she deserves," Kara said softly. "You can only choose to do better, be better."

"Yeah, dad. You're a great dad, now you gotta be a great boyfriend."

I can't help but chuckle at Luke's logic. "Yeah buddy."

"Are you going to go home?" Luke asked, as Johnny, Kevin, and Derrick walked up.

I nod slowly. "I will. I just need to talk to your uncles for a bit."

"Alright. I love you dad. Go home to mom, soon." Luke wrapped his arms around my waist and I had to close my eyes as another sob threatened to escape.

"Yeah, bud. Love you too."

Kara gave me a reassuring smile as she wrapped an arm around Luke's shoulders and led him away.

"Come on, man," Johnny grunted, squeezing my shoulder. He steered me toward their garage and through the side door. Inside, besides the tools and bikes, was a designated man cave set up in the back corner with leather couches facing a big screen TV. They had fridge stocked full of beer and a bar full of liquor.

"Want a beer, or something stronger?" Derrick asked, as he walked over to the bar.

I eyed my sister's Macallan for a second before I shook my head. "Just a beer. I need to go back soon."

Once the beer was in my hand, and Derrick and Kevin left the garage, I sat down and sighed heavily. Resting my head in my hands, I ran my fingers through my short hair. It still felt weird to me, but Maya liked it, so I would do whatever I could to keep her happy.

"What happened?" Johnny asked, taking a seat on the other couch to my right.

I popped the tab on the can and took a long pull before I answered. "We sat down and dug into the past. What happened ten years ago...what *really* happened."

"Learned some hard truths, then," Johnny surmised.

I nodded and took another pull from the can. "Yeah."

"Some things we can only learn from and move on. Try to be better."

"What do you know about BDSM?" I asked.

Johnny barked out a laugh. "Oh brother, you really don't want to ask me that question."

I looked up confused, and he shot me a look that said I *really didn't want to know.* "Alright, not talking about my sister, but then you get the principle."

"Yeah."

"Back then... we were in a twenty-four-seven relationship. It wasn't negotiated, but it happened. In fact, during negotiations we had explicitly stated that we would never expect her to be in a twenty-four-seven dynamic, but like I said, living together for two years, we just kind of fell into that." I paused to take a sip of my beer.

"Shit."

"Yeah." I sighed. "Things got out of hand. By the end, I think it was hard for Maya to speak up, to come to us. I think the three of us steamrolled over her sometimes. And we definitely didn't take care of her the way we should have. Put her first more." I shook my head. "Things with Buckley and the club were never easy and more times than not, she was left home alone to fend for herself."

"What was the deciding factor, then?" Johnny asked, cutting right to the chase.

I took a deep breath and stared off at the black TV screen, unable to meet my brother's gaze. "Our last scene...I took things too far. It was a punishment, but I should have cooled off more. I should have waited until I was level-headed and cooled down. Maya wasn't in the right headspace either—hadn't eaten all day, was way too anxious to do a scene and I...I took things too far. I strung her up, in the woods out back," I motioned toward the back wall of the garage, indicating the woods we shared in our backyards. "She handled the scene well, but she ended up getting hypothermia."

"Fuck." Johnny grunted.

I looked down and nodded. "I didn't realize how bad it was at the time..." I choked up but forced myself to continue. "She told us how she almost died that night. The next morning, she had to give herself IV fluids because she was so dehydrated. And I left her alone after the scene. No aftercare. Short of warming up her body with ours...we left her alone the next morning."

"Jesus Christ, dude," Johnny growled.

A sob tore out of me, hearing his disappointment. I don't know why I was looking at him as my moral compass, but something about the man—my younger brother—that just made me want to be a better person.

He didn't comfort me while I cried, but he sat in silence while I got it out of my system. Johnny had a calm magnetism about him.

When I calmed down again, Johnny spoke. "Look man. You can't change the past. Yeah, it was completely fucked up what you did—but you did it. All three of you did it, that doesn't just land on you. Neither Jason nor Nico stayed back to take care of her that morning."

"I didn't give them the chance. I was VP then. I ordered them out of the house."

Johnny sighed heavily and rubbed his bearded jaw with his knuckles. "Either way, they could have told you to fuck off. Her safety should have been the most important thing. The club could have waited a couple hours." He held up a hand before I could open my mouth. "Your sub's safety is the only thing that should have mattered that morning. As a Dom, she was your responsibility. If you couldn't give her the care that she deserved and *needed*, then you have no place being a fucking Dom, you hear me?"

I nodded, tears sliding down my face.

"You can't do anything like that ever again. I would just take all punishment scenes out of your dynamic completely if you guys ever go down that road again."

Again, I nodded. Dropping my head, I rest my elbows on my knees and stare at the floor as tears silently slid down my face. "Yeah."

"Look man, we're human. We all fuck up from time to time. You can't let it eat you up too much." I looked up to meet his gaze as he continued speaking. "You gotta learn from it, though. Marcos man, you can't ever fuck up that badly again." Johnny shook his head. "Have you ever been to Sinister?"

I shook my head. "Never heard of it. What is it?"

Johnny gaped at me, looking surprised. "Dude, we need to educate you. Sinister Desires. It's owned by the Seratellis—it's a sex club or BDSM dungeon. Whatever you want to call it."

"What the fuck?"

"Yeah, how did you not know about this? I thought Nico was a Seratelli by blood?"

I shrugged. "He's been estranged from the family for a while."

"Either way dude. I suggest you go and take some classes on aftercare and etiquette. It's clear you need some retraining in the ways of being a Dom."

"Yeah." I pulled out my phone and immediately looked up the club. It looked sexy as fuck and it was right in The Edges. No wonder I never paid it any attention.

"Go home, Marcos. Talk to Maya. She needs you right now."

I nod and stand up. "Yeah." I turn to face Johnny. "Thank you...for everything."

Johnny gives me a wry grin. "Go read Dad's journal while you're at it. You might find something useful in there."

Chapter Forty-One

Jason

LAYING IN MY BED, my head is a mess. All I can think about is Maya almost dying and it being my fault. Our fault, but mine too. We fucked up back then. I didn't even feel comfortable calling myself a Dom anymore. How could I hold that title when the number one responsibility of a Dom is to ensure their Sub's safety? I clearly couldn't do that right.

Nico was right all these years. He should have safe-worded. We both should have told Marcos enough was enough that night and one of us should have stayed with her in the morning. My mind raced as I heard Marcos's Harley race away from the house.

Maya's sobbing in the living room killed me. My dumbass had to run away. I couldn't fucking face her. I was a fucking coward.

I couldn't do it. Not like this.

I sat up abruptly and raced downstairs. I fell to my knees in front of her, still on Nico's lap and buried my face into her lap. "I'm so sorry, Darlin'. So fucking sorry. I know it doesn't change a damn thing."

I felt her fingers slide through my hair to my nape and she pulled me up toward her. I looked up at her tearful face before she wrapped her arms around me and pulled me against her. Nico grunted as I pushed her into him, as I hugged her tight.

She pushed me away after her sobs subsided and stood up. I watched her walk over to the kitchen and get herself a bottle of water from the fridge, while I took a seat next to Nico on the couch. "Now what?" I asked.

Nico shrugged. "We're not done talking...we still need to dissect that night, but not without Marcos."

"Any idea where he went?" Maya asked, walking back into the living room. She's not shy and squeezed between Nico and me on the couch. She snuggled in, getting comfortable before she looked around for the remote.

I grabbed it off the coffee table and hand it to her. She smiled in thanks and turned on the TV.

We sat there for half an hour, watching whatever she put on. I was mostly lost in my head, though, not paying attention.

When we heard a Harley come up the driveway, the three of us immediately turned to see Marcos ride past the picture window, to the garage. Maya slumped back on the couch. I hadn't realized how tense she'd been until she finally relaxed.

"Did you want to keep talking?" I asked her.

She looked up at me, her beautiful amber eyes earnest and slightly puffy from all the crying. "I think we need to. When else would we get the time without Luke around? I don't want him to see us all breaking down...and honestly, I think we all need this."

I nodded.

"I agree," Marcos said, as he walked into the living room.

"Where'd you go?" Maya asked.

"I got about 3 blocks down the road before I was sobbing too hard to see the road. I pulled over in front of Kara's; Johnny and the guys came out to get me."

I was a little shocked that he admitted that, but his gaze was intently on Maya's.

Her little gasp was all I needed to know that she forgave him. She reached out to him and he went to her, falling to his knees between her spread legs. "I'm so sorry, Mi Vida. I'm so sorry."

Maya slid her fingers through his hair and closed her eyes. I glanced at Nico and he shrugged. Both of us scooted down and rested our heads on Maya's shoulders.

A happy smile tugged at her lips and she turned her attention back to the TV.

Nico

After we finished watching whatever action movie Maya had put on, she sighed and nudged Marcos to get him to move off her.

He slowly pulled away and I saw up close just how torn up he was. His eyes were puffy from crying, and he looked so broken.

Jason didn't look much better either. His blond hair disheveled and sticking up randomly—he looked exhausted.

While Maya's eyes were puffy from crying, she seemed lighter somehow, relaxed in a way that I haven't seen her in years. It was breathtaking.

She was right. We needed this, despite how much it was hurting us. Maya deserved to get her truth heard, no matter how many years later it was. It was the only way forward for this relationship.

Marcos sat back on the coffee table and watched Maya.

Maya cleared her throat. "Look, I appreciate you guys apologizing, but that's only the first step of this relationship moving forward. If we ever want to have any kind of dynamic again—and trust me I do—we need to clear the air about what went wrong in that scene, objectively. And not just that scene—there was a lot wrong with our relationship back then that was never addressed."

I nodded. "Break it down."

"Yes." Maya nodded and took a deep breath. "I've spent the last eight years or so heavily involved in the kink community in Chicago. I joined a dungeon there, made some really good friends, but most of all, I educated myself in a way I wasn't back then. I've learned a lot over the years, and I learned how badly the four of us—yes me included—screwed up back then."

"The unnegotiated twenty-four-seven relationship," Marcos said, his voice thick.

Maya nodded. "Yeah. Yeah, that one is blazingly obvious."

"You weren't able to speak to us freely, not really," Jason added.

Maya sighed. "Yes, though I don't think I realized it back then."

"You were young," I murmured. "We were so much older than you."

"Six years isn't that much," Maya said.

"It is when you're only twenty-four," I shot back.

She shrugged a shoulder. "I didn't realize until years later how much that might have played a part in things. Slipping into the full-time dynamic was easy and something I hadn't realized until it was too late, but even then, I hadn't minded at the time. Not until I realized how much agency I felt I gave up. I had to use my safe word during phone calls with you guys while I was at work. Toward the end there, it became too much."

I swallowed, knowing she was right. Marcos and Jason looked contrite at least. It was mostly them she was talking about anyways.

"The number one thing I learned though, was you *never ever* renegotiate during a scene." Maya's voice was steady and calm as she met Marcos's gaze.

He gulped and held her stare, though I could see tears welling up in his eyes again.

"That was my biggest trigger during that scene and it sent me spiraling mentally. I thought you were breaking up with me. I should have called Red. I remember thinking if I called Red, and he really meant to break up with me, this is it. I told myself to finish the scene and you wouldn't be so upset, that you wouldn't break up with me if could just finish."

"Fuck, Maya." Marcos's body shuddered as he stifled a sob.

Maya wiped away her own tears and kept going. "So yes. No renegotiating during scenes. The other aspect was communication. I hadn't been honest with you about my mental state, or my physical state. I wasn't in the right headspace to have a scene." She turned to Jason. "I hadn't eaten anything that day. I tried, but I was too nauseous. At the time I thought I was too anxious, but looking back, I was probably already having morning sickness and didn't realize."

Jason sighed and grabbed her hand. "I should have saw that. I should have known that you were so emotionally distressed that your nerves would have been shot. It's not going to happen again; we're going to check in before any scene we have in the future."

Maya nodded. "It was also a very long scene, incorporating elements that we had briefly talked about, we never fully discussed."

"Had I known you hadn't eaten, or were pregnant, I never would have drugged you," Marcos said immediately.

"I know, Marc. I know." She took his hand and laced their fingers together. Tears till poured down his face, but he was watching her with unflinching loyalty. "From everything I've learned from being in the kink community, the scene we did that night was something that most people wouldn't attempt unless they've been in the community a long time. There were a lot of elements that, stacked together, just made things too long and maybe too much."

"I should have use my safe word that night." I finally spoke up.

Maya's eyes snapped to mine and she shook her head. "I should have myself. I know that now."

"You shouldn't have had to," I insisted. "It should not have gone that far." I shot a look at my brothers, both of whom looked ashamed. "As your Doms, it is our job to ensure your safety. It was our responsibility to look after you, protect you. It was our job to make sure you had everything you needed and were cherished. We failed you."

"He's absolutely right, Maya." Jason agreed. "I failed you as a Dom. You deserved better."

"You do deserve better." Marcos spoke softly, his voice raspy. "I'm going to try to be a better man for you and Luke. It's funny;

I talked to him at Johnny's - he told me I was a great father, but I needed to be a better boyfriend to you."

Maya gasped and covered her mouth as she both smiled and tears welled in her eyes.

"He was right. I need to figure out how to be a better man for you. Johnny told me about a dungeon or sex club here. I guess it's run by the Seratellis?" Marcos's raised an eyebrow at me. "Sinister Desires?"

"I've heard of it," Maya said. "I go to the sister club in Chicago, Delicate Desires."

My mouth opened to speak, but I didn't have anything to say. My cousin's empire had expanded vastly in the last ten years. There was a lot I didn't know anymore. I was shocked. I'd have to reach out to Leo about it.

"Anyways, Johnny told me I should go to a couple Dom classes there. Relearn some things," Marcos continued.

"I'm down," I said immediately.

"Me too," Jason added.

Maya laughed lightly. "I'd definitely like to check things out. Like I said, I frequented the Chicago location often. It's actually how I met my therapist - through a friend at the club. She's actually a sex therapist. She was able to help me break through some of the pain over the years and helped me deep dive into what went wrong back then."

"I'm glad you found a community you felt safe in, Little Dreamer." I squeeze her hand before I bring it to my lips and kiss the back of it.

"Me too," Jason said, resting his hand on her thigh. "I've been watching videos about things online, trying to relearn things as well. It'll be nice to be able to ask questions."

Maya smiled. "I'm glad you guys are open to learning more."

"Of course, Little Dreamer. Sexy education, here we come!" I joked, trying to get her to laugh.

It worked. Her light laughter was a balm for my weary soul. "Why don't we take a break? We can help you decorate the house, then maybe later we can do a nice dinner and talk about what our dynamic will be in the future?"

Maya smiled brightly. "Yeah, that sounds great. I think we all need a break." She looked at Marcos and Jason.

Both men sighed heavily and nodded. "Yeah."

Maya leaned in and hugged and kissed them both, before she turned to me with a bright smile. "You always know what to say," she murmured.

I leaned forward and kissed her soundly. I held her jaw to angle her face and deepen the kiss. "I love you, Little Dreamer. You're the strongest person I know."

She was breathless as she pulled away, a blush covering her cheeks. "I love you too, Nic."

Chapter Forty-Two

Maya

THE AFTERNOON WAS MAGICAL. We ran out to the hardware store to pick up more decorations. The guys were really feeling the vibe I was going for with the old Victorian home, and they even picked up one of those twelve-foot skeletons. When we finished, we washed up and changed our clothes before heading out for dinner—at an actual sit-down restaurant with tablecloths. I couldn't remember the last time I'd been out to eat without Luke.

After we ordered, we kind of sat there staring at each other, not talking—or rather, they were staring at me. "What?" I asked, feeling slightly embarrassed.

Marcos was the lucky one that won the wrestling match to sit beside me in the booth. He slid his hand over my thigh and grabbed my hand. Lacing our fingers together, he brought my hand up to kiss the back of my knuckles. "We're just happy to be with you, Mi Vida." His voice was a low rumble that sent shivers down my spine.

"Let's just talk about our dynamic now. No negotiations, just a conversation about what we want or hope for the future," Nico said.

I looked at Marcos and Jason, who were watching me earnestly. "Alright, let's keep it simple then," I began. "Twenty-four-seven is likely off the table. I don't see it working out now that Luke's there. I'm not answering questions about our sex-life from my son."

"Agreed," Marcos said almost immediately.

"We were never supposed to go full time, it just kind of happened. We'll make sure to check in more." Jason nodded.

I bit my lower lip and nodded. "What do you guys want going forward? What do you see our lives like it a year, five years?" I glanced up at Marcos, before turning to Jason and Nico.

"More kids," Marcos said immediately.

I barked out a laugh. "I figured that much. Yeah." I reached for my glass of vodka and took a sip.

"More kids, for sure. Might have to put an addition on the house though," Jason said.

"Why? You plannin' on having more than three?" I asked, raising my eyebrow.

"Three? Little Dreamer, you got plans over there?"

"And why three?" Jason tacked on.

I laughed. "There's three bedrooms upstairs, don't you think you guys will eventually just move into the master with me? Down the line? Like before?"

"Is that on the table?" Marcos asked.

I looked up at him confused. "Of course, why wouldn't it be? I'm not talking tomorrow, but in time. After we've worked through some things, I don't see why that wouldn't be on the table. I'm staying. I'm here. I'm not going anywhere." I squeezed Marcos's hand while I looked around the table at them. I reached across the table and both Jason and Nico linked their fingers with mine.

Their smiles were everything I needed.

"So more kids, huh?" Marcos asked, his voice low and his mouth right next to my ear.

"I might have a developed a breeding kink." I giggle at the heat in his eyes.

"Mi Vida, you have no idea what that does me."

"I have an idea, Mr. Somnophilia." I bump his shoulder with mine. We're quiet for a moment and I scratch my eyebrow as I think.

"What's on your mind, Darlin'?" Jason asked.

I took a deep breath before I spoke. "How do you guys feel about therapy? Like maybe together and on your own?" Again, I bit my lip, turning so I could face Marcos at the same time as Jason and Nico.

"I'm there, Little Dreamer. Whatever you need."

I gave Nico a grateful smile while I waited for Marcos and Jason.

Jason nodded slowly. "I talked to Kevin about how they handled things after...Kara." He sighed deeply and squeezed my fingers tighter. "I will try the group sessions with you...I can't promise you anything else...talking really isn't my thing. I'd rather be fighting."

I smiled softly and nodded. "Thank you. That's all I ask for, to try."

"I uh...I reached out to Sheilia," Marcos said. "She's involved in the club life and knows what happened. I scheduled a session with her already. We meet next week...We'll see how it goes."

I squeezed Marcos's hand tightly, resting my chin on his arm as I stared up at him. "I think that's a great idea."

Tears welled in my eyes as emotions overcame me. They heard me. They listened to me. It was all I fucking wanted in the last ten years. We still had a long way to go, but I felt like we were on the same page trying to get there.

Chapter Forty-Three

Maya

"ARE YOU GUYS COMING to bed?" I ask as the movie ended. I stood up and started cleaning up the popcorn bowls and boxes of candy on the coffee table, pilling the garbage in the empty bowls.

It was comical how fast the three of them froze. They all started to stand to help me clean up, and all three of their heads snapped up to look at me, while freezing in place. "You want us...all?" Jason asked.

"Of course I want you all, that's the point. Why choose, when I can have them all?" I asked him, raising my eyebrow at him, a smirk on my lips.

It took them a minute, before they busted out laughing. They fell back on the couch, clutching their stomachs and I felt great. I grinned and headed for the kitchen, carrying the bowls to the garbage.

My guys helped me clean up and then we headed upstairs to my room. In the last several weeks, they've mostly moved in here. Nico always slept with me, but Marcos and Jason have slowly started staying every night. Now that Luke knew about it, we didn't feel the need to hide it from him.

It was nice to have them to cuddle up to again. I missed them so much over the years. I was just so happy that we were finally moving forward. It made putting the heart break and betrayal in the past a little easier. I wasn't healed by a long shot, and I'm sure there were going to be a lot of setbacks still to come, but we were communicating again. We were making progress. It was everything I've ever wanted.

We still had to talk about how we moved forward in the lifestyle, especially with kids involved—but I don't think any of us want or need the same dynamic we had back then. Again, those conversations would happen when or if we needed them.

Tonight, I was focusing on having group sex with my guys for the first time since my assault. I didn't know how my mind or body would react, but I wanted to try at least. I hoped I was ready, because I felt like I was. Until we started, though, I wouldn't actually know.

In the bedroom, I slowly turned to them and waited. I still wanted them to take control.

Marcos looked nervous and Jason seemed out of his element completely.

I licked my lower lip and turned to Nico. He smiled easily and stepped forward. "I think for tonight, we'll leave the colors and protocol alone, no honorifics, no names. Just us. Tonight, no means no, and we'll keep it at that."

"That sounds good." I nodded.

"If we restrain your hands, will that trigger you?" Nico asked.

I swallowed thickly. "I think if it's just your hands for now, I should be OK. I don't know, though. Honestly, I don't know about anything. I just know I miss you guys and I want this." I look over his shoulder to Marcos and Jason. "I need this."

"Alright, Little Dreamer. Then we keep talking. You tell us immediately if you don't like anything. We're gonna take this slow," Nico murmured.

I smiled and stepped into him. "I'll tell you. Just kiss me, fuck me, love me." I murmured against his lips before I kissed him.

Nico groaned and wrapped his arms around me. I saw Jason move out of the corner of my eye before I closed my eyes and leaned into the kiss. Jason pressed behind me, his hands on my hips as he placed an open-mouthed kiss to my neck.

I moaned and shifted my hips back against Jason's growing erection. I heard rustling and opened my eyes to see Marcos slowly peeling his clothes off. Distracted, I stopped kissing Nico to watch Marcos. His body had only been honed with muscle over the years. Hard muscle covered his body, and I groaned. My guys had only aged like fine wine in the years apart.

Nico chuckled as he glanced over his shoulder to see Marcos stripping. "So easily distracted."

"So hot," I mumbled.

Marcos grinned and pushed Nic out of the way and stepped into me. "So are you, Mi Vida."

I shook my head. "I have stretch mar—"

"You are a damn Goddess Warrior that created and carried my son, and I shall worship at your altar." Marco tilted my head and kissed me thoroughly.

I moaned and clung to his warm body, his skin smooth beneath my fingers. "Kiss ass," I muttered when he pulled away to kiss down my throat.

He laughed against my neck, and I moan as he sucked my sensitive skin.

Jason's hands roamed up my body, sliding between Marcos and I. He cupped my breasts as he sucked a hickey on to the other side of my neck.

"Ohhh."

"That's better," Jason crooned in my ear, his voice sending shivers down my spine.

"I need—"

"You need to let us take care of you," Nico interrupted me.

"Please," I pleaded.

Jason's hands moved under my shirt and pulled it up. Marcos stepped back a step to help him pull it over my head. I was briefly self-conscious of the stretch marks on my belly, but Marcos didn't seem to mind. He tilted my head back and kissed me passionately again while Jason's fingers began sliding down my sweatpants.

"I should shower." I pull away.

"You should relax," Nico chuckled. He bent down and helped Jason pull my pants off my body. He nudged my feet one at a time to make me step out of them.

"I'm nervous," I admitted.

"Shhh, Mi Vida. Just give in to us." Marcos kissed me deeply again, this time sliding his fingers to the back of my head and wrapping my hair into his fist. He gripped my hair tightly, bordering on painful. I moaned into his mouth, my mind quieting as the pain overrode my thoughts.

"More," I muttered.

Marcos chuckled and pulled my hair a little more. "You will submit to us tonight, Mi Vida."

"Yes," I whimpered.

Jason undid my bra and Nico slid down my panties.

Marcos broke the kiss and spun me in his arms. He pushed my body against Jason's, his hand still fisted in my hair. "Get him naked." Marcos's voice was rough and deep as he ordered me.

I complied immediately. My hands were steady as I reached for Jason's t-shirt and pulled it up his toned as fuck body. All of my guys had only gotten hotter with time. I think Jason even had more tattoos than the last time I'd seen him without his shirt off at my mother's house. I suck an open-mouthed kiss to his chest but Marcos jerked my head back before I could get too distracted. "Pants," he growled in my ear.

I whimpered with need. *Fuck, this was so hot!* I missed this so much. My fingers quickly undid Jason's jeans and I pulled them down. His pierced cock sprang out immediately—he still went commando after all these years. "Fuck," I groaned when I saw it.

"Yeah, Darlin', that's the point." Jason stepped out of his jeans and wrapped his hands around my waist.

Marcos let go of my hair and I let out a surprised 'eep' as Jason picked me up and carried me to our large bed. He laid down in the middle and pulled me on top of him. I straddled his waist, just above his cock and leaned down to kiss him.

Jason slid his fingers into my hair to grab a hold of it tightly; he angled my head and deepened our kiss. His tongue slid along mine, massaging it. I whimpered into his mouth as I let myself melt against him.

"Such a good girl, Mi Vida." Marcos's voice was low as he came up behind me. The heat of his body seared my back as he kissed his way up my spine. "How you doing, Maya?"

I whimpered and pulled away from Jason. "I need you. All of you."

The bed dipped as Nico kneeled his way toward me. I turned toward him and smiled. Nico smirked and tilted my head so he could claim my lips as well. I loved how they were all being gentle, yet dominate in how they reclaimed my body. "Mmm."

Nico chuckled and turned to face Marcos. "Lift her up."

"Gladly." Marcos and Jason lifted me up and lowered me over Jason's straining cock. Nico reached between us and held Jason's cock up and steady.

"Fuck," Jason grunted.

"You like that, bro?" Nico smirked.

I watched Jason's face contort with pleasure, his eyes squeezing shut. I moaned deeply as Jason and Marcos slowly lowered me onto Jason's weeping dick. "Ohhhh." My breathing was labored as I stretched around Jason's massive cock. "Fuck," I groaned and reached for his chest to brace myself as he bottomed out inside me. Nico's fingers slid over my clit before he pulled his hand away.

"Fucking hell," Jason grumbled. His hands tightened painfully on my waist, but I didn't tell him to let go. It fueled my need for them, for more pain. Fuck, I knew I was a masochist, but this only reaffirmed my love for it. It drove me deep into the headspace that I used to crave.

"Yes," I moaned.

"Hold her steady," Marcos ordered. He let go of my waist and climbed off the bed. I heard the drawer in the bedside table open and looked over to see him pull out a bottle of lube. He smirked over at me as he climbed back on the bed. "You ready, Mi Vida?"

I licked my lips and grinned.

Nico forcefully pulled my head the opposite direction and distracted me with a soul-stealing kiss. I groaned and leaned toward him, twisting my hips. Jason moaned loudly and held me in place.

"Fuck, Darlin'," Jason panted. "Need you to stay still."

I giggled softly.

Marcos poured the cool lube down my ass crack and I yelped and jumped. Jason groaned and held me in place while Marcos chuckled and started toying with my asshole. Nico's hands cupped my breasts and he leaned in to kiss me again.

One of my hands wrapped around Nico's shoulders to hold him to me, while I steadied myself on Jason's chest with the other. Nico deepened our kiss, angling my head with one of his hands. Marcos slid one lubed finger inside my back passage and I whimpered, pulling away from Nic's kiss to pant heavily.

"How you doing, Darlin'," Jason asked.

"So good," I breathed the words like a prayer. "Ohhh."

Marcos slid in a second finger and I arched my back, spreading my thighs wider around Jason, making me sink even further onto his cock.

Jason groaned and thrust his hips up, his fingers tightening on my waist. "Fuck, Darlin'."

Marcos scissored his fingers inside my ass and I arched against him, his heat searing me from behind. "Marc." I moaned.

"You're being so good for me, Mi Vida. This greedy hole is just sucking my fingers in deeper. I can't wait to see my cock splitting this luscious ass open."

I whimpered as he added a third finger.

Jason wasn't doing much better, if his labored breathing was anything to go by. I was going to have his fingerprints embedded in my skin after tonight.

"Marcos." I tilted my head back on his shoulder.

"Almost there, baby," he murmured.

Nico captured my lips again, holding my head to the side while he kissed me deeply.

I was so close, on a precipice about to tumble over the edge. I whimpered into Nico's mouth.

Marcos pulled his fingers out and lined up his cock. He pushed just the tip inside me and paused.

I broke away from Nico panting. "Marc." I whimpered his name while Jason swore. Marcos was driving us both insane. We were trying to hold still for him, trying not to come without him, and he was being a fucking tease.

"Jesus dude." Jason groaned.

Nico slid off the bed and quickly pulled off his clothes, before he climbed back on the bed and positioned his body next to us.

Marcos finally slid home and I moaned lewdly as both holes were finally filled.

"Fuck," Jason cussed.

I tried to fall forward and lay on Jason's chest, but he wouldn't let me. His grip on waist was still so strong, and Marcos's hands joined Jason's, holding me upright as he bottomed out in my back passage. "Ohhhh."

"That's it, Mi Vida. Being so good for us, taking our cocks like the good girl you are."

I couldn't keep the smile off my face if I tried. "So good," I agreed.

The three of them chuckled. "So good," Nico agreed.

I licked my lips as I stared over at Nico's cock. "You gonna give me that?"

Nico smirked. "Little Dreamer, it's all yours. Come get it."

One of Marcos's hands left my waist and pushed down in the center of my back, forcing me forward. Jason steadies me as I lean forward and reached for Nico's cock. I held myself up with a hand on the mattress between us, but my other hand wrapped around Nico and guided his dick into my mouth.

I licked the head, swirling my tongue over the tip, before I sucked him into my mouth, making him hiss with pleasure.

"Bro, you gotta move," Jason rasped.

Marcos laughed softly. "Need me to fuck you both?" He swiveled his hips and I moaned on Nico's cock.

Nico hissed and laced his fingers through my hair. He didn't pull, just rested his hand on the top of my head, like a steady reminder that he was in control.

"Fuck yes," Jason muttered.

I giggled around Nico's cock and sucked him down deeper, making him hiss.

"Just like that, Little Dreamer. Always such a good cock sucker," Nico said.

Marcos started moving, slow at first, then he picked up pace. He kept one hand on the center of my back, holding me in place, while his other hand wrapped around my hip. He set a brutal, punishing pace that made giving head hard, as I was moaning and writhing with every thrust. "Jesus, bro. Those fucking piercings."

Jason chuckled and thrust up into me, joining Marcos in utterly destroying me.

It didn't take us along before we were falling over the edge and our orgasms poured over or out of us. I went first, unable to stop myself as my body crested that edge and I shuddered between Jason and Marcos. Pulling off of Nic's cock, I cried out, resting my head on his thigh as I caught my breath.

Nico didn't give me long though; he pushed his cock back into my mouth and started slowly fucking my face.

Marcos picked up the pace and Jason joined them. Their rhythm driving me between the two of them. I moaned around Nico's cock as he used my mouth freely, fucking deep into my throat. Tears poured down my face and I relished every single one.

This felt like therapy.

It felt like coming home.

My second orgasm tore through even faster than the first. My body shuddered violently this time, shaking and arching as I came hard. "There's a good girl," Marcos intoned.

"Fuck, so close," Jason groaned.

Marcos fucked me harder and Jason let out a low rasping moan as his fingers tightened on my waist and he held tighter as his own body shook. He came hard, pouring himself into my spasming cunt.

Nico's fingers dug into the back of head as he fucked my face in earnest. I sucked hard and tried to swirl my tongue around the tip of his cock as much as he'd let me. For the most part, Nico used my mouth as his own personal flesh light. "That's it, Little Dreamer. Taking my cock so well. Get ready to swallow."

I moaned as I swallowed his load, barely recognizing Marcos's stuttering hips as his thrusting grew frantic.

"Fuuuccck," Marcos and Nico rumbled together as they both came hard.

Both men held their cocks in place while they caught their breath. Nico kept his down my throat until he finally groaned and pulled out of my mouth. My lips were swollen and sore, my face was covered in tears. I felt used and abused, but so fucking free.

That glorious floating feeling spread over me and a goofy smile spread across my face.

"There she is," Nico crooned. "There's our sub, lost in the subspace. So good for us."

I giggled softly and nuzzled Nico's thigh.

"So good, Darlin'. So. Fucking. Good," Jason grunted.

Marcos kissed the center of my back. "Perfecto, Mi Vida."

"So good," I murmured.

My boys laughed.

I hissed as Marcos slowly pulled out of me. "Sorry," he mumbled, and helped lift me off Jason's cock, making us both hiss.

They laid me down on the bed between Jason and Nico, and I curled onto my side, resting my head on Jason's shoulder while Nico curled around my body. Marcos came back from the bathroom with a warm washcloth. He carefully cleaned me up, before he tossed the towel toward the hamper.

Marcos made us all move just enough to pull the covers down from under our bodies, then he pulled them back up. He turned on the fan from the remote on the bedside table, clicked on the small night light lamp, then climbed into bed next to Jason. I reached across Jason's body to lace my fingers through Marcos's. "I love you guys."

Marcos's fingers tightened around mine. He leaned in close to my face. "I love you with everything that I am, Maya. You are the light of my life. My reason for living."

I smile sleepily and let go of his hand to cup the side of his face. I pull him into a passionate kiss. "I never stopped loving you, Marcos. Any of you. You're mine." I kissed him again.

Marcos pulled away after a moment, giving me another peck to the lips before he laid back down.

Jason tilted my head up on his shoulder so I'd look up at him. "I love you too, Darlin'. More than life itself." He kissed me deeply.

"I love you too," I murmured as we broke apart.

I laid my head back on Jason's shoulder when Nico pressed a soft kiss to the middle of my back. "Love you, Little Dreamer."

I smiled and closed my eyes. A feeling of deep contentment washed over me.

I had my guys. I was home. I was safe.

Maya

IN THE WEEK SINCE we finally slept together, it was like the flood gates had been opened on our sex life. Every night after Luke went to bed, they were on me. Or I was on one of them, or sandwiched between two of them.

It quickly became one of the best weeks of my life. Luke even commented that I seemed happier. And I was. Life was great. I was getting stronger every day. My therapist mentioned that we could drop down to once-a-week sessions, and I didn't freak out.

Luke was doing well in school. He was going to his weekly therapy sessions and training for his upcoming competition.

Things felt almost back to normal.

Dax Hillcrest was still a lingering threat, but he was lying low.

I knew Marcos and the guys were still digging into him, still had people searching for him, but I didn't want to know. I needed to take a break from some of that worry.

My guys must have had the same idea, because they booked me a weekend getaway at the local spa hotel. They didn't just book it for me; they also invited all of my girlfriends.

I was shocked when they dropped me off at the hotel and I saw Kara, Slade, Stephanie, and Karma. I screamed and practically threw myself out of the car to tackle Stephanie and Karma. Life made seeing them so hard sometimes. "I missed you!" I hugged them both tightly. I kept in touch with my girls after all these years, but it had been about a year since I'd seen them last.

They were both crying as they hugged me tightly. Slade and Kara joined us, forming a group hug. "I fucking missed you guys, so much." I wiped my tears away as I pulled back to look at my girls. It had been a decade since the four of us—Kara, Stephanie, and Karma—had hung out together. Slade might not have gone to college with us, but she tattooed all my friends and I grew up with her. It was going to be a fantastic weekend with the five us together.

I turned away from the girls to look back at Marcos's truck, where all my guys, Luke included, were watching me. "Luke, come say hi!" I waved him over.

He enthusiastically jumped out of the truck and threw himself at the ladies. Slade grabbed him up first, hugging him tightly, before Stephanie and Karma also moved in. "Damn, I missed you, kid," Karma grinned.

"Same! How's Uncle Turo?" Luke asked about Arturo, Karma's husband.

"He's good. He's gonna be upset he missed you." Karma ruffled Luke's hair.

"You guys will have to come out and see the new house. I'm gonna do Luke's birthday party at home. He wants a Halloween themed party," I said.

"Hell yeah, little dude. We'll be there," Karma grinned. Her and Luke do some overly elaborate handshake that they've been doing for years.

I laughed and shook my head. I walked over to the truck where the guys were standing to say goodbye. "Are you sure this is safe?" I asked again.

"Yeah, Little Dreamer. Trust me, we've got it covered," Nico said, tucking my hair behind my ear.

"Let me guess, this is one of Leo's places?" I smirked.

"Nah, it's Tino's." Nico chuckled. He kissed me softly then stepped away so Jason could move in.

Jason gripped my jaw and placed a gentle kiss to my lips. "Have fun."

"Thank you," I murmured against his lips.

He stepped away and Marcos took his place, wrapping his arms around my waist. "Have fun this weekend. Try to relax."

"Thank you. I love you," I murmured and kissed him sweetly.

"I can't wait till you get home." He groaned against my lips.

I giggled and slowly pulled away. "You guys gonna pick me up Sunday?"

"Nah, you can ride home with Kara. One of her guys will follow you. Don't leave the hotel this weekend. Even if you want to go out, stay on site. There's enough restaurants and things to do here."

"Yes, sir." I smirked and backed away.

"Fucking hell, Mi Vida," Marcos groaned.

My girls all laughed, Kara included, and we waved to the guys. I gave Luke a big hug and kiss and then the girls and I were headed inside where a concierge was waiting for us to start a magical weekend.

Once the girls and I had all claimed our rooms in the penthouse suite that we'd been given in the prestigious as hell hotel, we settled around the living room with a tray of charcuterie and glasses full of liquor. "OK, so catch me up! I haven't seen you guys in a year," I said turning to Stephanie and Karma. "I mean, we've talked, but damn, I haven't seen you guys!"

"Well, running from a stalker kinda takes precedent—trust me, I know," Stephanie shot back.

The girls groaned in unison. "Fucking hell, I know man. But what about those hot as fuck body guards?" I asked.

"I thought you were trying for something with them?" Kara pressed.

"Yeah, that Noah sure was a sexy fucker," Karma laughed.

Stephanie frowned and took a long pull from her drink.

"Oh no, what happened?" I asked, sensing her turmoil.

"After I talked to you, Kara, I tried to make a move. I wore skimpier workout clothes and afterwards I would make my protein shake still dripping sweat...it seemed to be working. They were definitely *affected*," Stephanie hedged.

I bit my lip to keep from interrupting my friend. I had a feeling I knew exactly where my shy, introverted friend was going with her story.

"Noah and I had sex one night," Stephanie hedged.

We cheered and toasted to her.

She shook her head, blushing.

"And?" Slade prompted.

"And it was fantastic, amazing, so fucking hot. Like all the adjectives. It was the middle of the night, I was digging deep into your dad's files," she turned to Kara, "and needed to work out. Afterwards, I was getting a drink of water in the kitchen, and Noah was on patrol or I startled him or something. I don't know." She shook her head and took another pull from her drink.

"And thennnn," Slade prompted again with a grin.

"And then I asked him why he wouldn't kiss me. Fuck, you know how I get when I'm annoyed. I run my mouth and shit just comes out. I was blunt, and he seemed to like that. I mean our faces were inches from each other. Then he said he needed to remain professional on the job, that he—they—didn't date clients. I told him I didn't give a fuck and kissed him." Stephanie groaned and buried her face in her hands. "And then we had the best sex of my life. As soon we finished, like he was still fucking inside me, he said that it was mistake—"

We all booed loudly.

"Yeah. He said it was a mistake and that he didn't date clients. He made me promise not to tell the other guys too." Stephanie sighed heavily. "I still feel like an idiot."

I shook my head immediately. "Don't you dare feel like an idiot!" I growled, rising to the defense of my friend. "That was a bullshit move. Fuck that guy."

"That was a dick move," Kara said. "I get being professional, but he didn't have to hurt you like that."

"They're just so straightlaced," Stephanie groaned.

"I was going to say, 'leave it to Stephanie to find the one man who wouldn't break the rules', but that was not what I was expecting." Karma shook her head.

"Have you talked to them recently? Wait, what happened with the job and the threat?" Kara asked.

"The threat went away. I was digging into a case for your girl, Lacey Winters," Stephanie said.

"The District Attorney?" I asked, shifting on the couch.

Stephanie nodded. "She wanted me to dig into Mayor Johnson financials. She was prosecuting him for campaign finance fraud, but he was killed before it could go to trial. So the threats on my life stopped."

Dawning horror spread over me. "Who killed Mayor Johnson?"

"Lacey didn't know." Stephanie sighed.

I turned to wide-eyed to Kara. "Do you think?"

"I don't doubt it." Kara nodded solemnly.

"What's going on?" Karma asked, looking between us, bewildered.

"Hillcrest," I answered. "I saw him kill Mayor Timbolt ten years ago. Kara found out recently that Hillcrest has a friend in Senator Bradley."

"Jack Adams found it while digging," Kara clarified.

Stephanie closed her eyes looking stressed.

"What's going on girl," Slade asked.

"I've been helping Jack dig." Stephanie opened her eyes and took a gulp from her drink. "Lacey called the other day. She left a message and said she had a case and was hoping she could hire me again. I haven't called her back because I'm still trying to get over the last case I helped her with."

"Shit," I muttered.

"You think it's related?" Karma asked.

"She said it was HUGE," Stephanie stressed the word huge.

"Taking down a senator would be huge. Does she know what Jack found?" I asked Kara.

Kara sighed and nodded. "I had lunch with her last week. I brought her up to speed on everything. She asked to be kept in the loop on all things Dax Hillcrest."

I nodded and gave Stephanie a reassuring smile that I'm sure came out as a grimace. "Sorry girl, sounds like you're being roped into all of this again."

"You gonna take the job?" Slade asked.

"And let that dipshit Clide Tanners get it if I say *no*? Fuck that," Stephanie shot back immediately.

The four of us burst into laughter as our competitive friend showed her true colors.

"Soo, have you still talked to them?" Karma asked, directing Stephanie back on topic.

Steph shook her head. "No. Not since the job ended."

"Dude, why the fuck not?" Karma asked.

"Because the rejection hurt, OK? And he hasn't reached out either...none of them have," Stephanie murmured the last part and I immediately felt horrible.

"Their fucking loss. You dodged a bullet." I sit up and grab her hand. "I'm sorry girl, but it sounds like you're better off."

"Yeah...and how are things with Marcos, Jason, and Nico?" Stephanie turned the conversation back around on me. "I couldn't help but notice a whole lot of kissing going on when they dropped you off."

I rolled my eyes, laughing. "We're good. We're figuring things out, but yes, we're together. Luke knows and seems cool with it. We're just taking things slow and talking through everything."

"About fucking time!" Slade said.

"Agreed." Karma nodded and clinked her glass against Slade's as they toasted to me.

I rolled my eyes again. "Guess the moral of the story is to always be honest with your loved ones."

"And the dudes you're fucking," Karma shot back, giving Stephanie a pointed stare. "You should have told that dude how much he hurt you."

"Why? So he could throw it back in her face that she was too emotional when it was just sex?" I said, coming to Stephanie's defense. "No, fuck him."

"Are you OK?" Kara asked Stephanie.

Stephanie shrugged. "I am now. Yeah, it hurt. It still hurts, but I'm over it, I guess."

"So no calling them then, if shit pops off while digging into Lacey's new case?" Karma asked.

Stephanie laughed and shook her head. "Nah, I need a new drink."

"We all do," I said and stood up. Even though the topics were bound to be heavy this weekend, I was so grateful for the staycation with my girls. My guys had known exactly what I needed—likely Nico had—and I was so happy to have this time to catch up and unwind and be pampered.

Marcos

WITH MAYA OUT OF the house and Luke occupied with Nico, I took the morning to read my father's journal. It was time. Johnny had hinted at it long enough.

Inside wasn't what I was expecting, though. There were a lot of pages of abstract thoughts, like he was going for poetry but not quite. Then where would be a couple pages full of his thoughts on life and what was happening the moment. Those pages he dated at least.

One particular entry stood out a week or so before I was born.

Saw Lita this morning at the supermarket. She didn't see me, but she was looking ready to pop. She was a beautiful woman as usual, but something about her pregnant just made her glow. Oddly enough, I ran into Carmichael today too. He was leaving the restaurant when Jen and I walked in. We didn't speak, but I feel like the universe is trying to tell me something. I know Lita's having the baby soon. I wonder if it's really mine, and she lied about it to get money out of Carmichael?

There were more abstract thoughts following this entry, but after a couple pages I found another entry dated a couple years later.

I saw Lita today. She had her little boy with her in the supermarket. He must have been two or three by now. He looked so much like her, it was hard to tell who the father was. His eyes were blue, so he has to be Vince's. I don't think she'd lie about something like that to me. I hope she wouldn't.

Yeah, pop. Me too. I wished my mother hadn't lied about half the shit she had. Or I would have pushed her harder for more when I was older. By the time I was old enough to stand up to her, I didn't really care if I found my father anymore. I had found my own family in Jason and Nico.

I ran into Lita today. Her and Marcos were at the supermarket. The boy is her spitting image, but his eyes...there was something in his eyes that made me question if he was mine. I didn't confront her. She was pregnant and looked to be about ready to pop.

There was another entry from the same day down below some artwork.

God, the universe must really be trying to tell me something. I ran into Carmichael tonight. He had the balls to smirk at me. He told me that him and Lita were finally having their second child after all these years.

I shook my head and took a deep breath. Vince Carmichael had always been an epic asshole, that was no joke, but seeing the way he treated someone who was once his best friend just really drove home what a horrible person he was.

I kind of skimmed through the next couple pages, scanning for anything interesting. Lots of his thoughts and day-to-day happenings, but one entry caught my eye dated the summer I turned fifteen.

I saw Carmichael in Creekton today. The boys and I were doing a run and stopped off the highway to fill up and caught a glimpse of Carmichael walking out of the Devil's Psychos MC clubhouse, of all places. I wonder what the fuck bullshit he's up to now.

I gasped. That would have been twenty-five years ago. Buckley and Carmichael's dealings went that far back? For fucks sake.

I turned the page quickly.

I ran into Marcos tonight. He was running with a couple punk kids, looking like they were causing all the trouble they could. I was leaving the casino, and they were loitering around outside. I don't think he's eighteen yet. He was scrawny, looked a little under fed. I wonder if Lita and Carmichael ended shit? I wonder how she's doing.

I don't remember that. Though, if Mac went into Stella's, he wouldn't have worn his cut. There were no colors allowed in any of the Seratelli's establishments.

I turned the page until I found anything else.

I often wonder what life would have been like if Marcos was mine. Johnny and him are close in age, only a couple years different. I wonder how different Johnny might have turned out with a big brother to look up to and not just me and the club. Or maybe I'd have corrupted both sons, and all my pondering is for nothing. Johnny's a good big brother to the girls, but I think he'd have liked having someone else to grow up with.

I frown. It wasn't really anything profound, but the man had thought of me often. He was never sure enough that I was his to do anything about it, though. I didn't know what to think of Mac.

One thing being in this life has taught me is that people are never what they seem at face value. Everyone is deep and complex, despite how little you may know of them. There's no way to deeply know a person unless you spend every minute of every day together, and even then, you'll never know their thoughts at all times.

Another thing this life has taught me, is nothing is what it seems...ever. You have to dig deeper, you have to trust your gut. And if you can't, you have to set up your children to live a better life than you led.

I fucked things up tonight. I made a deal with Leonardo Seratelli to undercut the Bratva. Why? Because I thought I was going to set my children up to live a better life than I led. Seratelli informed me tonight that he's witnessed Vince Carmichael and Larry "the butcher" Buckley making a deal down by the Creekton docks.

How does that pertain to me? Hillcrest practically owns Mourningside County Jail and has strong ties within Illinois State Prison in Creekton. It means that if my son or our club ever needs protection on the inside, the Bratva is no longer our ally because I chose the Italians for profit.

In the end, I guess I was being greedy, wanting to leave a better legacy to Johnny, but the universe has a funny way of showing you what really matters. Or Vince Carmichael has a funny way of fucking me over, even after all these years.

Dax Hillcrest is a cockroach that won't die. He's wormed his way into the underbelly of Creekton with the help of Carmichael and Buckley. I fear for the future of Creekton and Mourningside.

I sighed heavily and closed the journal. There wasn't anything new that we didn't already know in there, but that last entry about coke deal was interesting. I'll have to talk to Johnny about it. I wonder what he thought about Mac's pondering on me growing up when he read it. Johnny's always been a straight-shooter with me, even when I probably didn't deserve it.

I think back to the time at the beach at Lake White Buffalo when Kara saw me in my cut for the first time—something I'd hidden from her all her life. Johnny hadn't though. He had been upfront with her on who he was, what he was. I had hidden a lot from my sister over the years.

I had done a lot of shady shit that I wasn't proud of, but lying to Kara about who I was will always be one of my biggest regrets.

It makes me wonder if I had been a better man, the kind of man that wasn't such a coward, would I have confronted Buckley sooner? Would I have stood up to him and my club, back then when Maya was being harassed by Hillcrest? Or would I have been a coward and let her go?

It was the deep and heavy soul searching that kept me locked in my room that morning. A melancholy mood that clung to me throughout the day. Reading Mac's journal might have answered some questions about whether my father ever thought of me, or wanted to know me—but those weren't answers I really needed.

I guess I was hoping to find the answers to myself in my father's journal, the deep-seated answers to who I was as a person. I was afraid those answers could only be found within me, and unfortunately, I knew exactly how to find them.

Only, I wasn't going to like the process.

Marcos

I had to admit the Ravager Knights compound was something of legends. Multiple out buildings surrounded the restaurant clubhouse. It wasn't just a clubhouse; no, it was a full-service restaurant that served the public. Something I was going to have to look into as we expanded our list of club properties.

The Pit was the regulation fighting octagon in its own building set at the back of the compound. It had its own full-service bar and concession stand, though there were no seats within the building. The concrete risers stepped down to the lower level, or pit, where the regulation size fighting octagon stood.

There wasn't a bad view in the house.

Not that I needed to see much, as my ass was about to be up that ring fighting in a moment. "So, what'd do you to land yourself here?" Leonard Seratelli as he stepped up beside me in the back of the Pit.

I glanced at the Mafia Don and smirked. "Was just being my charming self."

Leo's lips tipped up in the corner, like he was smiling. Probably the closest thing I'd get from the man.

"Hey, I wanted to say thank you, for everything you've done with rescuing Maya, and accepting Nico back into the family, and revisiting the deal with the Knights."

Leo turned to meet my gaze and finally smiled. "Nico was always part of the family whether he was here or not. But you're welcome for the other shit. You're not so bad, Candella." Leo held out a hand to shake.

I gripped his palm firmly. "Yeah, you're not so bad yourself, Seratelli. Just don't go be inviting me to family dinners."

Leo barked a laugh as Nico walked up. "Speaking of that, I want to see Maya and meet Luke. Your mom has been dying for things to calm down so you can bring them by. Bring them to family dinner."

"Is that an order?" Nico shot back.

"It's a suggestion," Leo spoke slowly, eyes twinkling.

"Then I suggest you let us use your boat for a family bonding trip. We need to woo our girl." Nico was ever the fast talker and deal maker.

When Leo laughed and slapped Nic's shoulder, I couldn't believe what happened. "The boat's yours, whenever you want it, the coke too. Bring Candella and Langford with you to dinner and we'll talk." Leo walked away from us, still laughing.

Utterly shocked, I turned to Nico. "Dude, what the fuck?"

Nic laughed and shook his head. "Guess we're taking Maya and Luke fishing!"

"And going to a Seratelli fucking family dinner," I grumbled.

Marcos

The fight in the ring with Johnny and I was a fun dance of trading punches. It was never meant to be serious, though I did let Johnny get a few hits in because I had wronged him, but by the end of it we were playfully jabbing each other and he ended the fight by locking me in a headlock and giving me a noogie. "Good fight, big brother."

My heart actually skipped a beat hearing him say that. I wrapped him in a hug and slapped him on the back. "Good fight, little brother."

I felt like I had healed a hole in my heart. I still had a lot more healing to do, but I would get there. I had the people around me to make me into a better man. I just had to listen.

Chapter Forty-Six

Axel

THE BASS POUNDED HEAVILY through the speakers, thrumming through my body as I stared out the open locker room door to the crowded warehouse beyond—and by doorway, I mean the gap in the strung-up sheets that blocked the view of the fighters from the crowd. There were tables as barricades on the other side of the curtains, where the merch teams were pushing their wares.

Phoenix sat in a folding chair to my right, while Blaze was out there selling our t-shirts—shit he made in his basement screen printing and vinyl cutting. It helped raise the money we needed to pay off my medical bills. After I caught a couple slugs against a rival out of state, I was still paying on the shit. The club had helped as much as they could, but Buckley was running shit then and didn't give a damn.

I had thought about mentioning to it Marcos now, but he had enough on his plate with cleaning up all of Buckley's messes, let alone all the shit with his girl. Nah, my president had enough to worry about—besides, I had this handled.

The music changed and my opener rang out, causing loud cheers to go up around the warehouse. Phoenix patted my shoulder, nodding his head to the music as we both stood up. We'd been through this a hundred times and we'd go through it a hundred more. These fights were a great way for us to earn cash quickly. After the decline in club activities, because Buckley killed most of our jobs, me and my boys had to do something quick, because the thought of having to live in the clubhouse was a living nightmare and not an option at the time.

Shit had calmed down since Marcos had taken over the club, but me and boys never felt completely comfortable at the club house to get any real sleep. It was too ingrained in us to look over our shoulders constantly.

Having a president like Buckley would do it to you.

I pushed the thoughts from my mind and prowled out of the makeshift locker room. The crowd went wild as I walked out. The MC's voice came over the speaker system, as the music dropped half a decibel. "Ladies and gentlemen, the moment you've all been waiting for!" the MC shouted through the microphone. "Axel 'The Mechanic' Jones!"

The crowd went wild.

"And in the other corner, all the way from downtown Chicago, the man, the myth, the legeeeennnd! Ronan 'The Ringer' Tiernan!"

I climb into the ring at the same time as my opponent. He was a large wide-chested man that had a notorious reputation. Rumor had it he was linked to the Irish Mob, but who knew if that was true. He had to be about my age though, with blond hair and sky-blue eyes that looked right through you.

I didn't give a damn about the notoriety or the rumors. Blaze had gotten me video footage of his previous fights and I had made sure to study them in the last couple of days. I knew that Tiernan dropped his left should when he swung, leaving his right side open. I knew that after a couple of hits, his anger would come out full force and he would lose all form and rhythm.

That was when I would strike.

I just had to bide my time. I could dance around him for a while. My stamina was a thing of beauty—something both Blaze and Phoenix helped me maintain, often times together. I just had to get through this fight and I could ask around for some dirt on Hillcrest.

Tiernan was an easy fight, but a steady rhythm of jabs and punches from both of us. While he kept me on my toes, he was also oddly predictable.

Blaze and Phoenix stood ringside, mostly quiet as they watched me. I kept an eye on them out of the corner of my eye as I dragged out the fight with Tiernan. Blaze would give me the signal when it would be time to escalate things. Everything was all about the show, after all. An intricate dance for the crowd, to earn us the most money.

I'd drag it out for as long as I could, unless the other fighter was overly aggressive, then I'd go for the K.O. ASAP. Tiernan seemed to be on board for dragging shit out, though.

Tiernan smirked, "You got green on this?"

"Like you don't?" I shot back, as we circled each other.

He chuckled. "I need information."

I almost paused, but the crowd cheered louder and I punched Tiernan in the ribs. I didn't hit him as hard as I could have, though. "What kind of information?"

He grunted in pain and side stepped my next punch. "Who runs the coke out of here?"

I laughed. "Even if I had that info, what makes you think I'd hand it over to you?"

Tiernan landed a punch to my shoulder and I grunted in pain. "I might have information you're looking for."

I narrowed my gaze on him, before I hit him back. "Then start talking."

"Make the fight worth my time," he grunted.

I growled and advanced on him, giving him what he asked for. Blaze and Phoenix shifted and glared my way for going against the plan, but this dude was toying with me. I needed to end him.

Tiernan grunted as I hit him in the ribs on his weak side. "Hillcrest has operations in Chicago."

I backed off, immediately. "What do you know?"

"I know locations, I know his men, I know his routes," Tiernan said, panting.

I bounced on my feet, weighing my options here. It was everything we needed.

"FINISH HIM!" someone behind me shouted.

Tiernan lunged at me, catching me across the face with his fist. My head jerked to the side with the force I hadn't expected.

"Fuck." I spat blood on to the floor.

Tiernan came at me again and I got serious. I blocked and jabbed and advanced on him. Going for his weak side, I drew his punches while I jabbed with my other fist.

He laughed. "Fucking finally."

We both settled into the zone then. I had to admit that his videos were child's play compared to what he was doing now. Clearly, he hadn't had a decent fight in a long time. Not that I had either, the dude was on fire, and I was getting hit as much as I was hitting back.

"After the fight," Tiernan grunted. "I'll tell you what I know, and you hook me up with who runs the coke."

"Deal, but I'm kicking your ass first." I smirked and upper cut his jaw.

He laughed and we fought harder. We gave it our best. It was clear that Tiernan hadn't shown his full potential in all the videos I watched. Blaze and Phoenix shifted again, I knew they were getting restless. The fight wasn't going as planned, but hopefully in the end it would pay off.

"We gonna call a draw?" Tiernan grunted, after I landed yet another hit to his ribs.

"You think the crowd's gonna go for that?" I shot back.

"Nah, but I'm not losing this one. I've got more intel than you can give me."

I bit back a retort, because he was right. If he wasn't lying to me about the information he had on Dax Hillcrest. I needed that information more than anything else. "I need assurances that you're not lying."

Tiernan huffed out a breath. "Hillcrest runs everything under a shell corporation, Summit Holdings. Dig into that and you should find what you're looking for."

I smirked and changed up fighting styles, there were no rules after all. I swung out my leg and caught him in the head with a roundhouse kick that sent him sprawling to the ground, stunned.

Standing over him, I waited for him to get up. The MC shouted into his mike and the crowd went wild. I crouched over Tiernan and snapped my fingers in front of his face. "You with me buddy?"

He grunted, his eyes blinking.

I put my hand on his chest in a mockery of a hold and glanced at my brothers. Phoenix raised an eyebrow at me while Blaze grinned.

Tiernan wasn't done, though. He caught me in the temple with a sucker punch that seemed to have come out of nowhere. "Fuck." I grunted and fell back on to the mat, my head ringing and vision swimming.

He scrambled over me and it became a wrestling match on the mats. I was still stunned, my head hurting, my body aching, while we grappled on the floor like a couple high schoolers. "Gonna have to my knock my ass out if you want it that easily."

I laughed. "Do you use the product you're asking for?"

"Nah, I'd already have you on your ass if that were the case."

"Doubtful."

We switched positions several more times, the crowd going wild every time one of us got on top. I was getting winded. I needed to get back on my feet and end this shit. He was a great opponent and I wouldn't give him the disrespect of throwing this fight. It would be a show down to the end.

Finally, I get back on my feet, leaving Tiernan to scramble after me. He grinned with blood covered teeth and lunged at me. I did another round house kick and catch him in the solar plexus—right below his sternum—and he stumbled backwards gasping for breath. I didn't give him a moment of recovery, though. Advancing on him, I aim another punch to his face. He lifted his arm in time to block me, but it left his left side open and I aimed my knee at his ribs, kneeing him hard on his weak side.

Tiernan grunted in pain and stumbled back breathless.

I moved in before he could catch his breath and did a spinning kick that caught him right in the temple. Tiernan went down like a bag of bricks on the mat. The MC slid into the ring and began counting. It didn't matter. Ronan Tiernan was out cold.

I stood back panting hard, only feeling a little guilty about how thing ended.

Axel

After the fight, I cleaned up in the makeshift changing room. I toweled off as much sweat as I could with towels I brought from home and poured a bottle of water over my head to wash my face of any blood that was leaking.

Blaze bandaged my face with a butterfly bandage above my eyebrow with a grin on his face. "Great fight, brother."

"Yeah, we gotta talk to Tiernan though. I gotta call Marcos." I grunted as I stood up.

"What's going on?" Phoenix asked, as he walked into the changing room.

"Tiernan is Irish Mob. He's looking for Coke. Said he has info on Hillcrest." I take a swig of my water and reach for my phone in my bag.

"Shit," Phoenix grumbled.

There was a commotion outside the changing room, I turned to look just as Marcos and Nico walked in the room. "Hey, I was just going to call you."

Marcos nodded. "Yeah, I thought I'd just come down. Sorry I missed the fight."

I shrugged. "No worries, but the other fighter was Ronan Tiernan. We need to talk to him."

"I'm not familiar with him," Marcos said.

"I think he's Irish Mob from Chicago. He says he has information on Hillcrest." I pull my shirt over my head as I talk to my president.

"Ronan Tiernan?" Nico asked, stepping closer.

"Yeah. You know him?"

"I've heard the name a time or two. Leo keeps tabs on prominent players." Nico nodded, glancing around the black curtained off space we had as our locker room. "How was the fight?"

"Good. He was fair. Wants a sit down with Leo, though. Looking for an in on the coke trade," I muttered.

Nico raised an eyebrow and Marcos crossed his arms over his chest. "What'd you tell him?"

"Nothing. He didn't mention Seratelli by name, was just looking for the coke supplier. I figured I'd run it by you. If we get coke back from Seratelli, we could make it one of our runs."

Marcos nodded his head once. "Something we can bring to the table. We need a sit down with Seratelli too. Where's Tiernan?"

"With the medic," Phoenix said. "Axel laid his ass out."

Marcos smirked. "Good."

I chuckled. "He fought clean. Wanted to trade information. I told him I was gonna kick his ass first."

Everyone laughed and Marcos nodded. "Alright. Well, let's go find him."

Phoenix led the way out of the locker room and down the hallway of black curtained off rooms, while we followed behind. He paused at the opening and spoke to someone before he motioned us forward.

I went first, taking in the small medical space. Ronan Tiernan was sitting in a chair next to the exam table. Two men moved in to block him as I entered with Marcos, Nico, and Blaze behind me.

"Leor," Tiernan barked in Gaelic, his accent strong. *Enough.* His men immediately fell back—well one of them did. The other man eyed Marcos suspiciously before he slowly backed away to stand to the left of his boss.

"Good fight." I nodded at Tiernan.

His gazed roamed over Marcos and Nico, before they flashed to mine. A small smirk pulled at his lips. "You too." He held out a hand to me, clearly not upset about the knockout.

I shook his hand. "Sorry about the head."

He laughed. "It was a good fight."

I grinned and dropped his hand. "My president, Marcos Candella and my VP, Nico Gage."

"My brother and second in command, Kierney Tiernan and my associate James McClintock." Tiernan waved his arm out to the two men glaring back at us.

Marcos and Nico moved forward and shook Tiernan's hand, then the hands of his men. "You guys with the IRA?"

Tiernan's men bristled immediately while Tiernan growled. "Hell nah." His Irish brogue thickening. "We don't deal with those cunts."

Marcos raised an eyebrow. "You have issues with them?"

"Let me guess, you run guns for them?" Tiernan asked, leaning forward.

Marcos nodded. "We might."

Tiernan barked a laugh and shook his head. "We don't have bad blood with Sullivan; we just don't run in the same circles. He runs a tight ship and you should remember that. There's a reason they call him the Butcher of Ireland. He's not to be fucked with."

Marcos nodded. "Yeah. I hear that."

"I don't care about your affiliation with Sullivan and his crew. I don't fuck with him if I don't have to." Tiernan said, shifting on his chair.

"I hear you have information on Hillcrest," Marcos said, changing the subject.

Tiernan smirked. "I hear you have a line on the coke trade."

Marcos stared hard at Tiernan, not giving anything away. "I might."

"And I might have information on Hillcrest," Tiernan shot back.

I rolled my eyes. The fucking dick swinging contest in these negotiations always killed so much time. I normally wouldn't interrupt my president in something like this, but time was of the essence here. "He said that Hillcrest has operations in Chicago. That he operates under the shell company Summit Holdings and that he knows locations of his operations."

Tiernan doesn't even look at me, like he wasn't surprised that I gave my president the information he spilled on the mat freely.

"We agreed that after the fight we'd exchange information." I glanced at Marcos.

He gave me a nod. "What are you looking regarding coke?"

"I need supply and delivery. We don't have the manpower to transport at the moment."

Marcos contemplated for a moment before he nodded, not even glancing at Nico. "I think we can help with that. We have a supplier that we handle distribution for."

Tiernan smirked. "Sounds perfect."

"What do you say we get out of here and have a drink? We operate out of Creekton." Marcos nodded to the door as he spoke.

Tiernan grunted and stood up. "Yeah, give me a few. Give me your number and text me the address. We'll meet you there."

The exchanged phone numbers and Marcos texted over the address to Satan's Palace, one of the club's establishments—something Trick and Ransom had purchased on behalf of the club. After we say our goodbyes, I shook Tiernan's hand again. "Great fight." He nodded at me.

"Yeah man, you too."

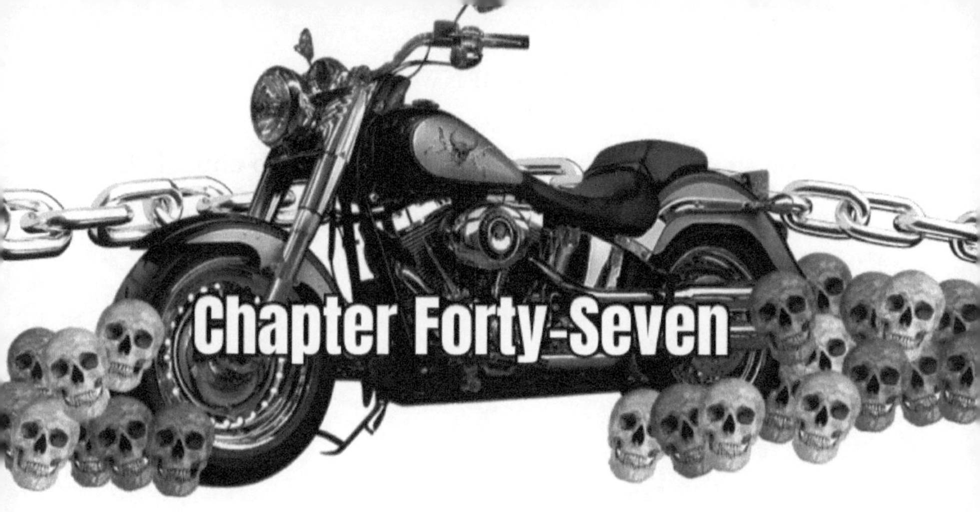

Marcos

"Good work, man." I slapped Axel on the back as we walked out of the warehouse that held the fight.

Axel nodded, a man of few words as usual. "You need me for the sit down?"

"Nah, unless you want to be there. I'll call Trick and Ransom for back up. Stone's home with Luke and Maya."

He shook his head. "Nah, I'm good. I need a shower. I hope he gives you what you need."

"Me too. Be ready for church if things roll fast." I glanced back at Phoenix and Blaze. The men nodded their heads at me.

I turned to Nico and nodded. "Ready?"

"For a sit down with the Irish? Always," Nico chuckled. "I texted Trick already. Him and Ransom are gonna meet us."

"Good."

Marcos

The ride to Satan's Palace is peaceful, if not a little chilly. Middle of October in central Illinois meant the riding season would be coming to an end soon. Nico gave Leo a call on the ride, and due to Bluetooth, we were both able to talk to him.

Dagger gave his cousin the run down and Leo agreed that Nico could make a deal on behalf of the family, and the Psychos could discuss their own deal for distribution.

Things were finally looking up. I only hoped that Ronan Tiernan was a man of his word, and that he wasn't just blowing smoke up our asses to land a coke deal.

We pulled into the parking lot of Satan's Palace. The bar and grill were around the corner from the Devil's Psychos clubhouse, so Nico and I parked at the clubhouse and walked over. As we were walking, I looked at the empty buildings between the two businesses and frowned. I paused as we passed a large empty lot.

"What's going on?" Nico asked, stopping beside me.

"Just thinking," I murmured.

"About?"

"Expansion dreams, brother. Expansion dreams."

Nico looked around and I could see it dawn on his face. "Build something like the Knights?"

"Maybe."

"It's a good dream." Nico patted my shoulder as we began walking again. The bright lights of Satan's Palace light up the otherwise deserted street. It was amazing that this place did so well, but because of its night club vibe after ten p.m. it really kept things exciting. The rooftop dining with a view of the river probably also helped. Something I would have to think about if I planned on buying the properties between the clubhouse and here.

The place was still busy, despite it being a Sunday night. We walk in just as Trick and Ransom pull up in front, so we pause to wait while they shut off their bikes and dismount. "Hey guys, thanks for coming." I slapped hands with them both, patting them on the back as we shook hands.

"Not a problem pres. Glad we could be of help," Trick said.

"You got a private room we can use?" Nico asked.

"We should," Ransom nodded. "Let's go talk to the girls."

He led the way to the bar where there were three ladies slinging drinks like their lives depended on it. Trick and Ransom were a couple of the most solid brothers the Psychos had. They'd always been great when I needed something, and they were never loyal to

Buckley in the sense that I had to watch my back. They were good dudes.

After talking to the bartenders, Ransom led us to a staircase on the right side of the room that led up to the VIP area on the second floor. On a Sunday night, the second floor was empty, as was the banquet room in the back.

When Ronan Tiernan and his brother Kierney arrived, one of the bartenders led him up to the VIP section and immediately took everyone's drinks. Ronan and Kierney settled into the booth across from us, their associate James standing near the stairs, where Trick and Ransom were standing by for back up.

"Damn, you look like shit, man," I said, cutting right to the chase. Axel really beat the shit out of the Irish man.

Ronan laughed and shrugged. "I'm good. Your boy Axel is a good fighter."

Kierney shook his head. "You'll have to excuse my brother; he's a touch off."

Ronan elbowed him in the gut and grinned. "My little brother wouldn't know what a good fight was if he was tossed in the middle of it."

Kierney rolled his eyes but chuckled.

I smiled, enjoying the comradery between the two brothers. I think we were going to get along with them well.

"Shall we cut to the chase?" Ronan asked, as our drink appeared. The bartender left and walked over to Trick.

I turned back to Ronan and nodded. "Yeah, seems like you know quite a bit about what I need to know. You work with Hillcrest?"

"Fuck no!" Ronan and Kierney yelled together.

"Fuck that cunt," Ronan spat, his Irish brogue coming out thick.

"He's a dirty mother fucker," Kierney added.

I nodded. "How do you know him then?"

"He fucked over a friend of mine. Made a deal with the mayor. Took a land project up from under him. He does dirty business and doesn't care who he hurts." Ronan took a sip of his drink.

"Yeah, he's been stalking our girl," I admitted, nodding at Nico.

"He kidnapped her for a while. We were able to get her back."

Kierney hissed. "That's damn lucky. I hear he's dealing in the skin trade."

"Trafficking, yeah. We killed most of his guys at a warehouse down south when we got Maya back, but Hillcrest has all but disappeared since then." I swig back my whiskey and nod at the waitress standing near the stairs.

Trick and James settled into their own booth to wait for us.

The bartender scurried over to the VIP bar and began making me a fresh drink.

"That's fucked up man. Your girl, she OK now?" Ronan asked.

"She's got her days, but she's a fighter. She's doing good," Nico answered.

I smiled and nodded. "She's learning self-defense and kick boxing, talking to a therapist. She's doing alright."

Ronan smiled, his lower lip cracking open. "That's great. I hate nothing more than then fuckers selling people. We'll help you any way we can. I wanna nail this fucker to the wall."

"Yeah, there's a long line of people that want in on his torture session." I nodded.

The bartender walked over and set down fresh drinks for everyone.

"Look into his shell company Summit Holdings. He's got buildings in Cicero and Englewood. You come to the city, and we'll help you take him out. We can ride around and do some recon before we figure out the best action plan." Ronan said.

I nodded slowly. "Ok. I'm gonna have my tech guy work on Summit Holdings. I need to bring this to my club, but potentially a recon trip would be viable. We'd need to move quickly though; I don't want this fucker getting away." I texted Jack immediately with the information.

"Absolutely. You and your guys can stay with me. I've got a place on Lake Shore drive, bring your girl. She can hit the sights while we work."

I smiled wryly. "I appreciate that. My son has school though. He missed a lot while his mother was kidnapped. He can't miss much more, I'm afraid. And my girl, we don't leave her alone without one of us, so I'll probably stay behind and send Nico and my enforcer Jason Langford north." I glanced at Nico, who nodded once.

"Ah, you have a son. How old?" Ronan's brogue popped out in the odd sentence that made me chuckle.

"He's nine. Almost ten. He's a good kid. Nic's teaching him how to fight. He's working through his anger over his own kidnapping at Hillcrest's hands and his mother turning herself in to save him." I sighed, not really sure why I was giving the man so much information. Ronan Tiernan seemed like a good dude though.

Both Ronan and Kierney cursed and shook their heads. "Jesus H. Christ," Ronan groaned.

I nodded. "Yeah, you can see why I'm gunning for Hillcrest."

"And we'll help you get him," Ronan said. "Talk to your brothers, talk to your tech guy. Let me know what you need and we'll help with what we can."

I nodded. "I appreciate that, man."

"What are you looking for in terms of weight for coke?" Nico asked, bringing the conversation around to back on topic.

Ronan and Kierney shot out some numbers, Nico nodded and countered an offer.

"And you're authorized to negotiate for the buyer?" Kierney asked, looking disgruntled.

"It's my family. You'll be going into business with the Seratellis," Nico said, eyes bouncing between both brothers.

"Shit," Kierney swore.

Ronan laughed again. "I had a feeling it was the Seratellis. That's fine. You a Seratelli?"

"On my mother's side. My cousin is Leonardo."

"Alright." Ronan nodded. "That works for us. And the Devil's Psychos will handle transportation north?"

"Yeah, for a price," I shot back immediately.

Ronan smirked. "Of course, let's hear it."

We negotiated the terms for a while longer before Ronan grinned and held out his hand. "Alright, good business."

I shook his head and grinned. "If only all business was this easy."

"It's only because he's had his head bashed in tonight," Kierney said. "He's a masochist in that regard."

Ronan rolled his eyes. "Nah, sometimes you just gotta fight shit out of your system. Fight or fuck."

"Amen," Nico and I said together.

Ronan and Kierney laughed, and we finished our drinks, toasting to a new friendship.

Chapter Forty-Eight

Maya

THE WEEK AFTER MY staycation with my girlfriends, I felt lighter and freer than I had in years. Even with Jason and Nico in Chicago doing recon on Hillcrest, I couldn't be happier. Marcos was home with us, Luke was in school, and my newly created group chat with my girls was popping off at random times of the days with random updates from my friends.

I had a permanent smile on my face.

Even my therapist commented on it when I was on the video session with her. She also reminded me that it was OK to feel sad tomorrow or later today if I felt myself dropping. Highs and lows were natural, but the biggest thing to remember was that my lows didn't have to be so low, because I wasn't alone. She still suggested that I check out a group session for victims of sexual assault, and I agreed to doing so one day soon, but for today, on this random Wednesday, I was going to enjoy it.

I danced around the kitchen, watching through the window as Marcos worked in the backyard. He was rebuilding the fire-pit that we used to have back there, as the previous owners had removed it. I was making soup in the kitchen while Luke was at school and I had a Halloween movie playing in the living room. It was a perfect fall day.

When the soup was done, I turned it off and headed out back to hang out with Marcos for a bit while he worked. I wrapped a flannel around me and slipped on some shoes before I headed out.

Marcos was busy digging out a base for a paver patio for our chairs to sit on while we sat around the fire pit in the middle. Eventually he would build a fire ring out of brick as well. "Hey, it's looking good." I smiled as I walked over.

He grinned and stopped working. "I sure am."

I smirked and leaned into him for a kiss. "So is now the time to ask for a pool since you're already digging?"

Marcos raised an eyebrow. "Now would be the time to ask for a pool. If my old lady wants a pool, then my old lady is going to get one."

My breath caught in my throat at his words. "Old lady?"

"You still have your Property Of patch?" Marcos asked, wrapping his arm around my waist and pulling me close.

I shook my head. "Nah, I left it here."

"Then Nico has it. Either way, we'll get you a new one if we need to. But you're ours again. Our old lady."

I grinned and put my hand on his sweaty chest to lean into him for a kiss. "My biker."

He chuckled. "You OK with the shit going on with Hillcrest?"

I sighed at the abrupt subject change. "I mean, I guess?"

"Meaning?"

"I don't know what to think of it all, Marcos. I just want it done. I'm so fucking happy right now, I don't want to think of that shit. I want to move on and live my life. Our life. Together."

Marcos nodded. "I hear you. After we finish him then, you won't have to worry anymore."

"Good. Now come eat me." I grinned up at him cheekily before I ran into the house with him hot on my heels.

Maya

Saturday morning, my guys were all home and acting suspicious. They told me and Luke to pack an overnight bag for a surprise they had.

"You can't just spring a surprise get away on me," I complained as I packed in the master bedroom.

"We did last weekend and you had no problem with it," Nico shot back.

"OK, you can't just spring a surprise get away on me two weekends in a row, Nicolai," I groaned.

He laughed and tossed half my shit out of my suitcase. "Let me dress you?"

My heart skipped a beat and I bite my lower lip. I nodded slowly.

He smirked and went into my closet. I watched him intently as he grabbed a black dress, a pair of strappy heels, and no under garments.

Next, he grabbed a black lace nightie with matching robe. He went over to my suitcase and packed it, then he grabbed me a pair of jeans, a t-shirt and sweater for tomorrow and tossed them in the suitcase too. In the bathroom he grabbed my toiletry bag. "Is this ready, or do you need to refill things?"

"Probably need a refill." I took it from him and set about doing that while he finished packing my suitcase.

"You're not going to tell me where we're going?" I called out to him.

"Nope! It's a surprise!"

"Fucking surprises."

"You love my surprises!"

"I do love your surprises." I grumbled as I walked out to my bedroom with my toiletry bag refilled. "You're seriously not going to tell me? Is Luke coming?"

"Luke is coming and Marcos helped him pack," Nico confirmed.

"Now I'm really worried. I need to double check they have everything." I walked toward the door and Nico stopped me, by standing in front of me and putting his hands on my shoulders.

"Little Dreamer, I need you to trust me." He gave me an exasperated look.

"I do trust *you*! I don't trust those to pack right," I laughed. "Can you at least double check they have everything if you won't let me?"

Nico huffed a laugh. "Fine, Dreamer. Fine. I will check on them. You will sit your pretty little butt down on this bed and not move until I come back! We still need to dress you to leave."

I looked down at my pajamas and sighed. "Nico." I shook my head.

He came back into the bedroom a moment later and I stood up and went into my closet. "I'm wearing jeans and a t-shirt, unless you tell me where we're going right now."

Nico rolled his eyes. "So dramatic, Little Dreamer. Fine. Jeans, but a cute sweater please. We're having pictures taken."

I quickly took in what he was wearing: black slacks and a black button down. His blond hair was trimmed around his shoulders and looked extra smooth. "Me and you?"

"Yeah, and everyone else. We're having family photos taken," Nico said.

I opened my mouth to say something, but came up short. I had nothing. No response.

"Made you speechless. Love that. Go get ready."

I jumped up from the bed and head into the bathroom to shower and get ready: hair, makeup, the whole nine yards. Once I'm ready, I changed into a maroon-colored sweater dress and black leggings with tan booties. Something casual and dressy at the same time.

Nico smirked when he saw me. "Hot damn, Little Dreamer. You look amazing."

"Thank you, you too."

We headed downstairs with our luggage and found everyone else waiting. All three boys are looking extra dapper. They're all wearing black, just like Nico, but they're all cleaned up as well.

Marcos's has grown out his hair and beard and he has it now styled into a faux hawk on his head and trimmed up goatee that just makes him look sinisterly sexy.

Jason's blond hair is styled in his usual spiky bedhead fashion that makes me want to run my fingers through it. His lip and eyebrow piercing glint in the morning light, making him look even hotter if possible.

Then my son, my beautiful son, was a spitting image of his father. When Luke saw Marcos growing out his hair for me, Luke had to do so as well. He really watched his father in all things, so it was no surprise that his hair was also in a faux hawk today, making my little man look so dapper and grown up.

"You guys look amazing." I grinned, tears welling in my eyes.

"Mom, why are you crying?" Luke asked, immediately walking toward me.

I smiled wider and hugged. "I'm just so happy, baby. Good tears. All my boys look so handsome." I rubbed his back.

He grinned. "So we did good?"

"You did great, baby. Are we ready?"

"Let's roll," Marcos said. He moved toward me. "You look great, Mi Vida." He pressed a kiss to my lips.

"Thank you."

Jason stepped in his place when Marcos moved out of the way. "I can't wait to tear this off of you later, Darlin'." He kissed me softly.

Nico chuckled from behind me. "Come on, Little Dreamer."

Maya

After family pictures at an outdoor venue on the river, where I had an amazing time, we drove down to the marina and Marcos parked the truck. "What are we doing here?" I asked, looking around.

Luke grinned excitedly. "Come on, mom! Let's go!" He quickly climbed out, following Nico, who had been sitting in the back seat with us.

I climb out and Jason grabbed my hand, lacing our fingers together. "Come on, Darlin', on to the next surprise."

Jason led me past the marina building and down the docks where there was a mix of small pleasure crafts mixed with larger boats until at the very end of the pier was a damn *yacht*. I didn't know how else to describe it, it was fucking huge, and Jason was leading me right for it. "What the fuck?" I asked him.

He smirked down at me and kept walking.

"Nico!" I shouted and turned to look at him over my shoulder.

"Eyes forward," Jason snapped, in that dominant commanding tone of his.

"Yes, sir," I muttered under my breath as I immediately looked forward.

Nico moved in front of us and led the way up to the boat—ship? Yacht? Yacht. Nico spoke to the guy standing at the entrance and he grinned brightly when they lowered a gang plank for us to walk across. I really didn't know my fucking lingo. All I knew was it was a big ass fucking boat and we were apparently going on it.

Nico went first and grinned at me once he was aboard. "Come on, Little Dreamer."

"Oh jeeze," I murmured and slowly walked across the very sturdy ramp they made from the main dock on to the boat that made the crossing very easy for someone in heels.

"Hello, Miss Henderson. My name is John Taverish. I'll be your Captain this weekend." The gentleman introduces himself.

"This weekend?" I looked at Nico with wide eyes.

"Mr. Seratelli sends his regards," Captain Taverish replied.

I gasped and Nico nodded. "He would like you and Luke to come to family dinner soon," Nico said.

"Cool boat!" Luke shouted as he stepped aboard.

I startled, forgetting they were behind us. I quickly moved out of the way so the rest of my guys could climb aboard.

"Surprise," Nico said, grabbing my hand and pulling me further in, where we were greeted by a full staff.

I stayed in awe all while we toured the Yacht—as the staff told me. They did a safety run down with life jackets and life raft locations. They showed us where the fire extinguishers were and how to call for help on the radio if anything were to happen to the crew.

Then one of the young men offered to take our photos on the boat and I about cried. "Whose idea was family photos? Because I love you forever," I declared.

My guys laughed, and the photographer snapped our photo. Then he started directing us into position and we had another photoshoot on the boat before we were under way.

"Drinks and appetizers will be served on the top deck while we prepare to set sail. Once we're underway, lunch will be served," a chef in a white coat said.

"Thank you," I smiled.

The photographer led us up to the top deck, snapped a couple photos and then brought us drinks. There were only a couple staff members on hand, so I assumed they were all trained in everything.

We sipped on our drinks while eating the most delicious mozzarella sticks and mac and cheese balls I've ever had. We settled onto the couches on the top deck and I kept staring around. "Isn't this cool, mom?" Luke asked.

"Yeah, babe. This is awesome."

"Oh!" Luke shouted as we pulled away from the dock. "Dad! Look!" Luke rushed over to the railing and Marcos followed him.

Nico and Jason slid in closer to me. "How you doing, Darlin'?"

"I'm great! This is amazing. How'd you manage this?" I asked.

"I asked. It was no big deal. We've worked things out with Leo. He wants to meet you and Luke soon, though." Nico wrapped his arm around me.

"Should I be worried?" I shifted against him.

"Nah. Leo and I worked things out." Nico squeezed my knee. "He's cool with Marcos again too. Life's good. Enjoy this weekend. We'll go home tomorrow evening."

"And what are we doing all weekend on this Yacht...with Luke present?" I questioned, coyly. I raised an eyebrow at him.

He grinned wickedly. "We'll make time. I promise. Tomorrow they're gonna show him how to work the boat. This afternoon we're going fishing on Lake White Buffalo."

"We're heading up the river?"

"Sure are, Darlin'. Lunch on the river while we navigate downtown Mourningside, then we'll hit the lake and get you some salmon. Luke had such a great time last time we went, but the whole time he kept saying how much you would love this."

I smiled and nodded. "I was a little jealous that I didn't get to go. Mostly because Luke loved it so much and I wanted to see him fish."

Jason set his hand on my other knee while we watched Luke and Marcos together. My heart felt full and whole, knowing they had a great relationship.

Nico

LUNCH ON LEO'S YACHT was a magical experience, mostly because Maya never once stopped smiling, even when she was quiet. The minute the boat headed up the Evermore River through downtown Mourningside toward Lake White Buffalo, she came alive. I knew she loved old architecture and one of the deck hands got on the PA and gave a little tour of the old buildings and the more modern ones. Maya ate up every single word.

I was so glad I hired the photographer to capture photos throughout the weekend.

We changed our clothes after lunch when the boat was far enough out into Lake White Buffalo. One of the deck hands was also a trained fishing guide—Leo had all the best people working for him, seriously.

Marcos bumped my shoulder as we watched Maya and Luke talking to the guide while the captain brought us further into the lake. It might not be as big as Lake Michigan, but Lake White Buffalo was no small lake. "This was a good idea."

"I know." I grinned at my brother.

"I've never seen her look so happy," Marcos said.

"She's looked this happy all fucking week. Like she's on cloud nine." I watch Maya's radiant smile as she looked over her shoulder for us.

I waved and Marcos smirked. "Let's go, brother."

Nico

Fishing was amazing. Luke and Maya each caught their own massive salmon, though Maya looked a little nervous reeling it in. When the guide hooked her up to the boat rail, she shot me a nervous glance, but Jason stepped in behind her and helped her pull back on the pole when she needed to, and the guide talked her through it all.

She was beaming when she pulled it over the side of the Yacht.

Luke screamed the whole time and when his reel went crazy. We were all right there with him, cheering him on. Marcos stood behind him to help pull back his rod if he needed it, but mostly let Luke do it all on his own.

"Hell yeah, Luke!" I called when he finally pulled it over the side of the boat.

"Good job, baby!" Maya wrapped her arm around him and hugged him to her side, while Marcos wrapped an arm around her shoulders. The photographer captured the moment of the little family without their knowledge. I couldn't wait for Maya to see the pictures when I got them back.

Maya

As the sun began to set and we finished fishing with more salmon in the freezer than I would know what to do with, Nico brought me into the large stateroom that the four of us would be staying in.

"Freshen up and change into the dress I packed," Nico murmured. He cradled the side of my face in his hand and kissed my lips softly. "Dress and heels, please."

"Yes, sir."

He growled playfully and kissed me again. "Oh, baby. I can't wait until Luke goes to bed."

"Me either." I kissed him passionately.

He broke the kiss all too soon. "Get cleaned up. Dinner's soon."

I take a quick shower in the ensuite bathroom, but don't wash my hair. I wash my body quickly and dry off. I reapplied my makeup and got dressed in the black dress and heels that Nico packed for me.

Finally ready, I headed up the stairs from the staterooms to the main deck where the back lounge area is encased in glass walls and looked out at the dark expanse of Lake White Buffalo—we were anchoring here for the night. I was grateful we weren't sitting in the open air as it was chilly out there once the sun went down.

My guys—Luke included—were dressed in their black dress clothes from that morning and I grinned when I saw them all looking so handsome again. "This is fancy," I said, motioning to the set table with a linen tablecloth and all made up with full place settings. "Remind me to thank Leo."

"You look fucking beautiful, Darlin'." Jason rose from the couch and pressed a kiss to my cheek.

"Thank you," I blushed.

One by one my guys all came over to kiss me—or hug me as Luke did—and told me I looked beautiful. Marcos's hand lingered on the open back of my dress, his fingers sliding over my bare skin. "Absolutamente hermosa luz de mi vida," Marcos rumbled in Spanish to me. *Absolutely beautiful light of my life.*

I blushed and kissed him softly.

Someone cleared their throat behind us and there was a waiter in a full tuxedo with white gloves ready to guide us to our table. "Please sit, we will begin serving soon."

It's hard to sit five of us at the table without someone at the head, so I'm a little surprised when Marcos guides me to the head of the table and takes the seat to my right, giving Luke the seat to my left. Jason and Nico sit beside them and smiled when I looked over.

The waiter came out a moment later and started setting down plates before each of us. A salad course. Of course, there were going to be more than one course at this dinner. I shouldn't have expected anything else. Thankfully it was a simple garden salad that Luke would eat as well. I could tell the ranch was homemade because it was divine.

The next course was a soup, a broccoli cheddar that was my favorite. I moaned loudly as I dug into the small bowl. I smirked as I watched my guys shift in their chairs. "Seriously?" Jason grumbled.

Luke and I laughed for very different reasons.

I was sad when I finished my small bowl all too quickly, but knew more food was coming. I couldn't fill up on soup and salad—even though I could very well make a meal out of that. Dinner came out a moment later, some kind of grilled chicken with a light sauce and a side of shrimp linguini and broccoli that looked awesome.

I glanced at Luke's plate and chuckled when I saw more mozzarella sticks and a cheese burger with fries. "You weren't going to try the chicken or linguini?" I asked him.

"And ruin this dinner for you? Nah." Luke grinned cheekily.

I shook my head. Smiling wryly, I turned to Marcos. He just grinned at me. "Enjoy the meal, Mi Vida."

I did. I enjoyed every single bite and didn't regret it. It all was absolutely fantastic. I couldn't help the couple moans that slipped out while I ate. Luke just laughed at me, while my guys gave me heated stares. I was playing with fire and didn't give a damn if I got burned.

After the meal, the staff cleared the table quickly and brought out the dessert plate. It looked like a sampler with small bites of cheesecakes and chocolate fudge and ice cream. "Oh, man," I groaned, eyeing the plate.

"Before you dig in," Marcos chuckled, grabbing my hand, "I have something I want to say."

I looked up into his warm chocolate eyes, wondering what in the world was more important than chocolate fudge.

He held my hand in his and pulled it toward him. "Maya, my life. Words can't describe how deeply I love you or how much you mean to me, to all of us." He glanced up at his brothers and Luke.

I squeezed his hand, my heart pounding in my chest.

"The last couple weeks, all of us living together in our home, have been a dream come true. You really are the glue that holds us all together and the light of our lives. I know it's too soon, I know we're just beginning to heal after everything that's happened, but Maya, there is no future for me without you or Luke in it." Marcos glanced at Luke and grinned.

Luke beamed back at his dad with all the love in the world on his face.

I swallowed thickly as tears began to well in my eyes.

Nico and Jason stood from the table and came up behind Marcos, just as he slid from his chair and down to one knee. He pulled a box out of his pocket and I gasped. My hands flew to my mouth, covering it as it dropped open in shock.

"Maya, life has no meaning without you in it. I refuse to go another day without making you mine—ours. Will you please do us the honor of marrying us?"

I try to choke back my sob, but it bursts out of me as tears pour down my face. "Yes! Yes." I reached for him, sliding off the chair to my knees in front of him. Sobbing, I fall into his arms, even as Luke cheered.

Marcos held me tightly, pulling me against him. "Mi Vida," he murmured, holding me against him. "Shh."

I reached behind him and pulled Jason and Nico closer, my hands holding theirs as I sobbed into Marcos's shoulder. Fuck, I was so happy, so fucking happy. I didn't even care if it was too soon.

I've wanted nothing more than this for the last ten fucking years of my life. I needed them more than I need air to breathe. The loves of my fucking life.

Luke joined the group hug, coming up behind me. "Mom, don't cry. It's a good thing, right?"

I chuckled softly and pulled away from Marcos and the guys enough to reach for my son and pull him into a hug with me and his dad. "It's a great thing, baby. I'm so happy, so happy."

Luke grinned and hugged me tight. "Then why are you crying?"

"They're happy tears, baby."

Luke looked exasperated and shook his head. "Doesn't make sense, mom."

We laughed, and I finally pulled back and wiped my eyes gently, mindful of my make up. Nico handed me a handkerchief, and I dabbed my face while Marcos opened the ring box.

"Oh my god," I gasped, when I caught a look at the ring.

"You like it? I got to help pick it out!" Luke grinned.

"I love it. You guys did good." I grinned as Marcos slid the ring onto my finger, both of us still kneeling on the floor. I looked at the ring in awe as it sparkled in the light of the room, making my finger look elegant and beautiful. "Perfect."

Eventually we get to our feet and Nico and Jason sandwich me between them, each taking their turn kissing me. "How will this work?" I asked, feeling overwhelmed.

"On paper, you'll be married to Marcos, but you're marrying us. We'll do our ceremony our way, and then submit the documents to the courthouse for Marcos," Nico explained.

Tears welled in my eyes again as I looked at him and Jason. "And you two are OK with that? I love all of you, I don't want you to ever think I don't."

"We're OK with it, Darlin'," Jason murmured. He kissed my forehead. "For the club, for legal reasons with Luke, we think it should be him."

"And when I have your children?" I asked.

Jason and Nico grinned sexily. "Then we'll give them our last name, and you'll have to have a million hyphens in yours."

I laughed and nodded. "We'll figure it out."

Maya

AFTER WE ATE DESSERT, Luke was excited to announce we were going to watch a movie on a projector screen. His enthusiasm was cute, and we settled into the couches while the staff quickly and efficiently cleared and broke down the table and chairs, moving things out of the lounge as a large screen lowered from the ceiling at the end of the Yacht, blocking the back glass wall.

The lights dimmed and Luke settled in between Marcos and I, his face set into a permanent grin. I knew how much this meant to him, that his parents were going to be together—be married. While he never voiced it, I knew he felt different from the kids at school because he grew up without a father.

Being in Mourningside the last ten months had really changed everything for not just Luke, but me too. Life was finally coming full circle, and I felt like I was finally healing from all the trauma I've endured over the years, not just my recent captivity with Hillcrest. I didn't allow myself to dwell on the negative thoughts. I just focused on the bright future we had ahead of us.

When the movie ended around eight p.m., Luke was already half asleep on the couch. We had a big day and I knew he was exhausted from all that fishing. I didn't bother to tell him how early it was still when I suggested he get ready for bed. He simply nodded and went down the stairs to the stateroom.

"I hope you're not planning on turning in early, Darlin'," Jason murmured into my ear, his voice low. It sent shivers down my spine. His voice always lured me in and turned me on. It made me want to submit and do anything he said.

"Wouldn't dream of it, sir." I kissed him sensually, opening my mouth as his hand came up to tilt my head. He deepened the kiss, making me moan.

"Mom!" Luke called from the stairs.

"Coming!" I called back to him.

"Not yet, but you will be soon," Jason growled and nipped at my lower lip.

I whimpered, my hands clinging to his dress shirt.

"Come on, Mi Vida." Marcos patted my thigh. "Let's put our son to bed."

I uncurled from the couch and got up. I swayed, slightly tipsy and grabbed Marcos's hand as we went downstairs. Luke was already brushing his teeth, so we went into his stateroom and turned down the bed and pulled out his PJs. "I'll give him those, you go slip into something more comfortable. Nico laid something out for you." Marcos murmured the words against my lips before he kissed me soundly.

"Yes, sir." I grinned and walked away.

In my stateroom, I slipped off the heels I'd been wearing and sighed as my feet relaxed on the plush carpet. Looking at the lingerie on the bed, I smirked and shook my head. Nico and his need to dress me like his little doll. There was a black see-through baby doll nightie, with a silk robe. It was sexy as hell and I would come back to put it on after I tucked Luke in for the night.

Hearing him leave the bathroom, done brushing his teeth, I left my room and walked down the short hall to his. He was already in the PJs Marcos had given him and was climbing into bed. Marcos stood next to the bed, ready to tuck him in once he was settled. I stood in the doorway with a smile on my face as I took in the simple domestic scene. It warmed my heart see Marcos be a father. He was such a natural at it and Luke adored him.

"Night, buddy," Marcos said, pulling the covers up around him.

"Night dad, love you," Luke murmured sleepily.

Marcos hugged him tight and then stood up and stepped out of the way so I could move forward. I smiled and walked over to Luke, leaning down to hug him tightly. "Love you, baby. Sleep tight."

"Love you too, mom. You liked your surprise?"

"Loved my surprise!"

"Good." He sleepily chuckled. "I'm happy you said yes."

"Me too, baby. Me too."

"See you in the morning."

"Yep. I love you."

"Love you too." Luke rolled over then and dozed off almost immediately.

I couldn't keep the smile off my face as I walked out of the room, only to pause when I saw Marcos standing in the doorway. I nudged him out of the way so I could shut the door behind me, before I leaned into him and kissed him softly. "Thank you for including him in buying the ring. It meant the world to him. I think he's going to remember that forever."

Marcos nodded, looking serious as his eyes roamed over my face, as if memorizing it. "I will too. I was serious when I said you are the light of our world. For all four of us, you are the sun we orbit. You give us life where we'd be empty. The three of us have been numb without you."

Tears gathered in my eyes for the hundredth time that night. "And I've been a shell of myself without all of you." I kissed him softly. "I'm gonna change."

"Take your time. Come back upstairs when you're ready." He patted my ass before he turned away from me and headed back upstairs.

I went back into the stateroom and into the attached bathroom. In the bathroom, I did my business before I freshened up my makeup a bit. All that sobbing surprisingly didn't ruin my eyeliner and mascara, but I was still a little blotchy. Using micellar water and a soft wash cloth I brought, I cleaned up my face.

After splashing cool water on my face, I fixed my eye makeup before I went out into the bedroom and changed into the nightie that Nico had laid out. It sure was a sexy number. Thankfully, he had thought ahead and packed me a robe. I hung up my dress before I left the room and quietly padded up the stairs.

The back lounge had been transformed while I was gone and a magical scene awaited me. The regular lights had been shut off, while fairy lights twinkled in the ceiling. I was amazed by the small LED lights set into the ceiling like stars in the night sky. Someone had strung up more fairy lights around the pillars of the ship and set twinkling battery powered candles on all the tabletops. The projector screen had been raised up and put away, showcasing the three walls of glass that had turned opaque to block our view.

It was breathtaking. Everything about the lounge was magical. Leo really had an amazing Yacht. I hoped we could borrow it again someday.

The large sectional had been pulled out into a bed that rivaled ours at home. Soft sheets and blankets covered it, making it a nest to snuggle into. My guys had changed their clothes as well, the three of them in nothing but black basketball shorts that hung low on their hips. Their bare torsos were on display, showing every chiseled inch.

I gasped as I took in the room and them. This whole weekend was utterly perfect.

"Come here, Darlin'." Jason held a hand out to me and I walked over to him, grabbing his hand. He led me around the couch to see the massive bed that was made in the middle of the room.

"Are we alone here?" I asked, glancing around the opaque glass walls and the doorways to the kitchen.

"The staff has been instructed to leave us alone for the night and there's an alarm on the stairs if Luke wakes up and looks for us. We'll be alerted before he walks up here," Jason said.

They really had thought of everything, damn.

"God damn, you're fucking gorgeous, Darlin'." Jason untied the belt on my robe and slipped it off my shoulders.

My fingers glided over the hard cut of his muscled abdomen, still in awe that these men were mine again.

Nico came up behind me and pressed his body against mine. His hands wrapped around my waist and skimmed over my lace-covered skin. I moaned and leaned back against his warm body as Jason stepped into me, molding us together.

"Tonight, I want to hear every filthy moan and whimper. Don't hold back." Jason's voice was low and gravelly. He nipped at my jaw and I gasped. "Say the words, Darlin'."

"Yes, Sir." I moaned the words and arched my back, pushing my tits into his chest and my ass into Nico's rock-hard cock that was nestled between my ass cheeks.

"There's a good girl," Marcos said from his spot sprawled on the cushions. "Get her naked."

Jason and Nico followed his instruction, slowly peeling the nightie up my body. Nico dropped to his knees behind me, kissing down my spine as he moved. My nightie went up and over my head while my panties slipped down my thighs. Nico kissed every inch of skin as he moved, teasing me.

I moaned loudly and grabbed Jason's arms to steady myself as Nico had me step out of my panties. Jason's skin was so warm and there was a slight chill in the air despite the glass enclosed room. I pushed closer to him and soaked up his warmth.

Nico came in behind me again, kissing his way up my spine as he stood up. He pushed my hair out of the way and sucked wet open-mouthed kissed into my shoulder and neck. Finding the sensitive spot behind my ear, he sucked a hickey there, making me moan loudly as I clung to Jason.

Jason dropped his head and followed Nico's lead, kissing my shoulder and neck on the other side until he too was sucking a hickey behind my ear. "Ohhh," I moaned.

"So fucking responsive," Marcos commented.

Was he still watching us? I had almost forgotten he was there. Jason pinched my nipples, and I moaned louder, arching between them. Fuck, the way they knew how to play my body like a fucking fiddle.

Nico's fingers slid between me and Jason, to pluck my clit.

My eyes were firmly shut and I let them control my body like they always had. They made it so easy to fall into our old roles. They made it easy to submit. Mastering my body was second nature to them, and I let it happen.

Panting and moaning, it was getting harder to stay standing. "Bring her here," Marcos ordered softly.

Jason and Nico moved as one, both sets of hands coming to my hips to lift me. My eyes flipped open, and I saw Marcos sprawled out on the makeshift bed, propped against the pillows looking like a king on his throne. He looked magnificent.

I wanted to crawl to him. I must have spoken the words aloud, because my guys chuckled and Jason and Nico set me down. Immediately, I dropped gracefully to my knees and seductively shimmied my hips as I crawled the short distance up to Marcos.

He smirked and cupped my jaw as I reached him. "Such a good girl."

Turning my head, I kissed his palm, showing him deference. I loved these men so much. As if sensing my thoughts, Marcos eyes softened. He pulled me closer to him by the hand on the side of my face. I went easily, straddling his hips, and leaned into him. Sliding my hands up his chest, I pushed into his warm body. A shiver went down my spine and Marcos frowned slightly. "Get over here and help warm up our old lady."

I gasped. Their old lady. My heart exploded in my chest. Tears immediately welled in my eyes. Fuck. I was getting emotional.

"Mi Vida." Marcos breathed the nickname as his arms came around me, holding me reverently. "Hey, why are you crying?"

I laughed lightly and shook my head. "I just...I don't know. It just hit me; I'm going to be your old lady again."

His eyes shone with love as a bright smile lit up his face. "Of course you're going to be my old lady. We're going to ink you the moment we get back. The wedding will come later, but there's no point in waiting for the ink."

I couldn't suppress the sob that broke out of me, and I tried to hide my face in his neck, but he pulled me back.

"Mi Vida, hey, it's OK. We love you more than anything. I'm sorry it took us so long to get our heads out of our asses. We should have inked you back then."

I shake my head as the tears pour down my face. Fuck, this was the least sexy thing on the planet. Why the fuck am I such a nutcase?

"You are not a nutcase." Marcos growled the words that I must have spoken out loud. Fuck.

"You are the best thing that has ever happened to all of us, Little Dreamer." Nico kneed his way over the mattress to fall against the pillows besides Marcos.

Jason pressed against my back and wrapped his arms around my waist, holding me tight as I covered my face because Marcos wouldn't let me hide in his neck. "We love you more than you could ever know, Darlin'."

"I'm sorry. I don't know why this is hitting me so hard. Fuck."

Finally, Marcos pulled me into his body and let me hide in his neck while I caught my breath. Feeling safe and warm nestled between Jason and Marcos, I calmed down and caught my breath.

"There you go," Nico murmured, grabbing my hand. "Take deep breaths."

I followed his instructions and breathed deeply. Keeping my eyes on Nico, I pulled him toward me. Lying flat on Marcos's chest, I pulled Nico into a passionate kiss. Nico cupped the side of my face he could reach and wiped away my tears. He pulled me up while still kissing me.

"There's a good girl," Marcos murmured. His hands wrapped around my breasts and groped and massaged me roughly.

I moaned immediately, closing my eyes as they quickly got me back into the mood. I needed them to fuck me; I didn't want to be this emotional right now. They were quick to make me forget, though.

Jason's hands glided around my waist, pulling me more upright as he slipped his fingers through my folds. Marcos's hard cock pulsed and twitched beneath me. Jason spread my pussy lips and slid me over Marcos's cock, coating it in my fluids. Marcos groaned and Jason sucked kisses into my neck.

Fuck, they really knew how to work my body. Nico continued to kiss me passionately, sucking my tongue into his mouth. I moaned lewdly and clung to Marcos's wrists to keep myself upright as he kept massaging my breasts and pinching my nipples.

"So fucking hot, Mi Vida," Marcos said.

Jason's fingers slid between mine and Marcos's bodies and spread me open further. He wasted little time in gripping Marcos's cock and lining it with my entrance. "You ready, Darlin'?"

I could only moan in response. Nico gripped the side of my face with his very large hand and held me in place. The kiss was breathtaking, and I was growing lightheaded, but he kept going.

Jason and Marcos worked together to lift me and impale me on Marcos's cock. I broke the kiss gasping as I was speared open. "Ohhh."

"Fuck," Marcos swore.

"There's a good girl," Jason murmured in my ear.

I shivered and leaned back against his chest. "So good," I whimpered.

My guys laughed softly. "Yeah, you are," Nico said.

Marcos gripped my breasts and Jason grabbed my hips. Together, they moved my body over Marcos's cock. I moaned and swiveled my hips, making Marcos cuss. "Fuck, Mi Vida."

I grinned and Nico grabbed my face again. "You gonna be a good girl, Little Dreamer? You gonna suck my cock?"

"Please." I licked my lips.

Nico smirked and pulled me down so I was leaning over Marcos and angled toward Nico's very hard dick. I opened immediately and sucked him to the back of my mouth.

Jason poured lube over my ass crack and began fingering my ass. I moaned around Nico's cock as Jason scissored open asshole. "Fucking hell," Marcos gasped.

"Wait until I fuck her." Jason chuckled. He didn't take too long prepping my ass. He always liked when I whimpered and stretched around his massive cock. Pulling out his fingers, he grabbed a towel while he lined up his pierced cock and starting pushing inside.

I whimpered around Nico's cock, the burn and stretch almost too much. Jason poured more lube over my crack and his cock, pulling out slightly only to push back in with more force.

Nico's hand slid through my hair, resting on the back of my head, not forcing me, but also reminding me that he was in charge here. It was so damn hot.

I loved every moment of them taking control of my body. I wasn't going to last long here. I barely had the thought as Jason bottomed out in my ass and my orgasm crashed over me. I shook and shuddered in the middle of the three of them. My eyes rolled back in my head as I moaned lewdly around Nico's cock.

Nico's hand fisted around my hair, keeping me in place as I breathed heavily through my nose. "Good girl." He spoke softly.

A shiver went down my spine. I fucking loved their praise.

Marcos and Jason only gave me a minute to come down before they began fucking me in earnest. Jason gripped my hips while Marcos groped my breasts, both of them maneuvering my body to fuel their own release.

"Fuck," Marcos muttered.

"Mmmhmm," Jason responded.

Nico began fucking my face, using my mouth and throat. It was all I could to do focus on breathing while Marcos pinched my nipples and Jason toyed with my clit.

"Those fucking barbells," Marcos swore.

"So tight." Jason groaned.

"Fuck, Little Dreamer. This mouth is divine."

I whimpered, another orgasm already building within me. I was mindless as they used me.

"Fuck!" Marcos shouted as he came, groping my breasts roughly.

My own orgasm shuddered through me as his warm cum filled me. I moaned loudly and barely swallowed in time as Nico swore and came down my throat. He bottomed out against my face, cutting off my breaths completely. "Shit, Little Dreamer," he swore, when I swatted at his thigh.

He pulled back immediately and I gasped for breath as cum trickled out of my mouth.

Jason fucked me harder, not giving me a moment of peace to catch my breath. "Fuuuuck!" he shouted. His hips shuddered to a halt and fell forward over my back, covering me with his body and pushing me into Marcos's chest.

Sandwiched between them and panting for breath, Nico's fingers traced over my mouth and scooped up his leaking cum. He pushed his fingers into my mouth, not giving me a choice but to clean up his fingers. "Good girl," he crooned.

I moaned and closed my eyes, resting my head on Marcos's chest.

Jason slowly pulled out of me, after kissing between my shoulder blades reverently. He stepped away and grabbed a warm washcloth. He cleaned me up and together Marcos and Jason lifted me up and settled me on the bed beside Marcos. "There's a good girl." Marcos's voice was soft as he wrapped his arm around my waist.

I curled into his side after Jason finished cleaning me up.

Nico grabbed a plush blanket off the back of the couch and tossed it over Marcos and me.

"This was the most perfect weekend," I murmured. I kissed his chest and nuzzled in, getting comfy.

His arm tightened around my waist and he kissed the crown of my head. "I'm glad, Mi Vida. We wanted to make this weekend special for you."

"Even if you're going off to kill Hillcrest?"

Nico chuckled. "Isn't that just the icing on the cake?"

I giggled and shrugged. "Maybe."

Marcos rubbed my back. "We're going to leave soon. We have a good window tonight and have a great alibi."

I nodded and yawned. "You'll be safe?"

"Of course, Darlin'." Jason came back to the bed and kissed my shoulder as he settled beside me.

"You have to leave soon?" I asked.

"Yeah. Why don't we get you settled into bed downstairs and we'll cuddle with you until you fall asleep?" Nico suggested. "Then hopefully we're back before you wake up."

I nodded. "Yeah, let's do that." I start moving before I can change my mind. I'm already on the cusp of sleep; it won't take me long if they're wrapped around me in a warm bed.

"Come on, Darlin'. Let's get you washed up for bed." Jason helped me up and together we head downstairs to the state room. We take a warm shower together, cleaning each other before he takes his time patting me dry with an extra fluffy towel.

I could get used to this kind of treatment.

Nico

LAYING IN A HEAP of bodies with Maya wrapped around me, I let out a breath and closed my eyes, feeling every bit of happy, content and satisfied. I savored it, because in another twenty minutes we were leaving. A boat would pick us up and take us to the north end of Lake White Buffalo, and from there a car would be waiting to take us to Chicago.

Maya snuggled in my arms. She fell asleep almost immediately after we all pulled out of her. We cleaned her up and I wrapped her in my arms and she was out.

Jason pressed a kiss to her shoulder, his hand rubbing lazily over her arm. "She's so fucking perfect," he murmured.

"Yeah, she is," Marcos said from across the room. He was already pulling out our duffels from the closet. "Come on guys, we gotta gear up."

I sighed and nuzzled my face against the top of Maya's head. I didn't want to leave her. I didn't want to leave her and Luke alone, even if they were going to be surrounded by Seratelli men...on a Yacht, in the middle of a giant lake.

Jason rolled away from Maya's back before I could muster up the energy to move. It had been a long day, but that had been the plan. Romance and adventure, and lots of orgasms. We wanted Maya so exhausted that by the time she fell asleep, she stayed asleep. We didn't want her to wake up and not be here for her.

Luke too. Thankfully he was a heavy sleeper and didn't get up often in the middle of the night.

I finally dragged myself out of Maya's warm embrace, careful not to jostle her. It took a couple minutes, but I was able to pull myself out of her arms without waking her. I started changing my clothes along with Marcos and Jason. The blackout clothing we brought would keep us hidden as we moved through the night.

As I was pulling my t-shirt over my head, my phone rang. I grabbed it out of my pocket quickly, not wanting to wake Maya. "Cousin," I answered.

"I need you." Leo's voice was hoarse.

Fear gripped my spine. My cousin did need anyone. "I'm here. We're ready to roll."

"Alessia was taken by Hillcrest. Her guard was killed. I'm sending a chopper to your pickup location instead of a car. Be there in twenty minutes." Leo hung up the call.

"Shit, we gotta. Alessia has been kidnapped."

Marcos and Jason both jerked their heads toward me. "What?"

"Her guard was killed and she's been kidnapped. Leo thinks it's Hillcrest. We need to move now." We quickly finished gearing up and then grab the duffels of weapons we had stored at the bottom. I glanced back at Maya sleeping peacefully, before we walk out the door.

We met with the captain before we left and he assured us that he and the staff would guard Maya and Luke with their lives. "The boat is ready for you," Captain Taverish said.

Five minutes later our captain for the small speed boat was hauling ass toward the northwest shore of Lake White Buffalo. Halfway toward the shore, the sound of a helicopter alerted us to Leo coming up from the south. As he passed us, a bright spotlight briefly illuminated our boat before they sped towards the rendezvous point.

Our boat slowed, the air heavy as we approached the shore. The small fishing boat was soon secured to a private dock and we climbed off quickly. We jogged toward the waiting chopper, still running. Leo opened the hatch as ran up and we quickly jumped inside. He barely had the door closed again, before he was instructing the pilot to take off.

It took the three of us a few minutes to get strapped in and headsets on. Once we were able to talk, Leo filled us in on his sister. "Her guard was supposed to check in at ten. When he didn't check in, I reached out to my men in the city. They went to her dorm and found the guard dead and Alessia gone. We don't know the timeline. My guys are pulling the security footage now. Last check in was at noon."

"Fucking hell," I swore. "That's a big ass window."

"Like I said, my guys are pulling security footage on the dorm now. We should know something soon. In the meantime, my guys are in position and ready to roll."

"Good. My guys are with the Irish at a warehouse on the west side. We're going to meet them there. You have issues working with The Irish Outfit?" Marcos asked.

Leo shook his head. "They're buying my coke, aren't they?" he deadpanned.

Marcos grunted.

Marcos

Thirty minutes later, the helicopter landed on top of a high-rise right on Michigan Avenue. I assumed it was Leo's building. We climbed out of the chopper and onto the roof. I ignored the height and the wind, following Seratelli toward the metal door. One of his guys in a suit held it open for us while we all stomped inside.

The noise difference inside was jarring as we rushed down a set of concrete stairs. Leo threw open a heavy metal door, and I followed, leading my brothers through a marble tiled hall as Leo lead the way through what I assume was his penthouse.

I didn't look around much at the modern space as we beelined for an elevator in the foyer of his open-concept living space.

Leo glanced over his shoulder as if to check that we were still there, then pushed the button on the elevator, which opened immediately. Down to the underground garage we went. "Give my driver the address for the Irish," Leo ordered as we climbed into the waiting black suburban.

I pulled out my phone and rattled off the address as my brothers climbed in besides me. Nico tossed our duffle in the back of the vehicle and we were off, tires pealing as the driver hastily drove away.

I texted the Psychos' group chat.

Marcos:

10 min out

The driver made it to the west side warehouse in six minutes. I quickly climbed out of the vehicle and headed for the entrance of the warehouse. Leo was ahead of me, just as in a hurry.

Near the door, Leo hung back and let me take the lead. I was walking into a room filled with my men and The Irish Outfit. Leo and Ronan hadn't been introduced yet; I would have to do that quickly.

Axel was on the door with Kierney when we walked up. "Pres." Axel nodded.

I nodded back and glanced at Kierney. "We're ready," he said.

"Good."

Kierney turned and led the way into the warehouse.

Inside, both crews were waiting. Ronan Tiernan looked up from where he was packing ammo at a table in the middle of the room. "Marcos, welcome," he greeted, his brogue thick.

"Ronan, this is Leonardo Seratelli, he's here to help." I keep all information about his sister being missing to myself. Leo could share that if he wanted to. "Leo, Ronan Tiernan."

Both men shook hands.

"Thanks for the coke." Ronan grinned.

Leo dipped his head in acknowledgement. "Thanks for buying."

Ronan chuckled. "Alright, your men outside?"

"Yes. You're ready?" Leo glanced around the warehouse and the soldiers mixed with Bikers.

Johnny Taylor walked over when I noticed him. "Brother," he greeted. We shook hands and slapped each other's backs. "Seratelli."

"Taylor." Leo nodded.

"Alright, let's move out!" Ronan called out.

A warrior's shout, raw and powerful, reverberated in the echoing warehouse as each man yelled their agreement.

Chapter Fifty-Two

Stephanie Stonewall

MY HEART RACED AS I backed up every file on my computer to an external hard drive. I backed it to my offshore cloud server first, then the hard drive. I already had the flash drive I needed to give to Jack Adams.

I wasn't safe.

They were coming.

They knew where I lived.

While the file downloaded, I packed more of my things into my suitcases. The whole house was packed up already besides my bedroom and office area, which were the same room. Once these files were downloaded, I'd be gone.

Hopefully before they found me.

"Come on, come on," I muttered watching the progress bar move slowly while I emptied my underwear drawer into my suitcase. I did the same to my sock drawer, not giving a fuck about orderly packing. I needed to get the fuck out of here.

I continued emptying my dresser into my suitcase. I had already done the closet. Garbage bags full of clothes filled my SUV. I was working on the dresser when one of my programs triggered an alert.

I'd been found.

I had to move fast.

I didn't know who they were; I hadn't had time to look into them yet.

I just knew it was time to go.

The computer finally stopped. I shut it down, tossed the hard drive into my suitcase and packed up my laptop into my briefcase with all my files.

My heart pounded in my chest. I needed more time. I didn't have it though. I couldn't stop. I grabbed what I could and zipped my suitcases. I'd live to see another day—hopefully.

Running through the house with my suitcase and my briefcase, I beelined for the garage of my humble home and tossed everything into my already loaded car. The garage door was still closed when I started my Caddy.

Once I hit the button, I waited the four seconds it took to open fully and flew out of the garage. I always backed into my garage space now. Force of habit from having four hot bodyguards living with me last year for the last threat.

Speeding away, I hit the garage button to close while looking around the quiet little neighborhood in the small farming community I lived in. There was no one around. That didn't mean they weren't watching me though.

I slowed to a relatively normal speed as I went through the quaint downtown and headed for the main highway. Once on the northbound ramp, I floored it.

I needed to make it to Chicago as soon as possible.

I needed Jack Adams.

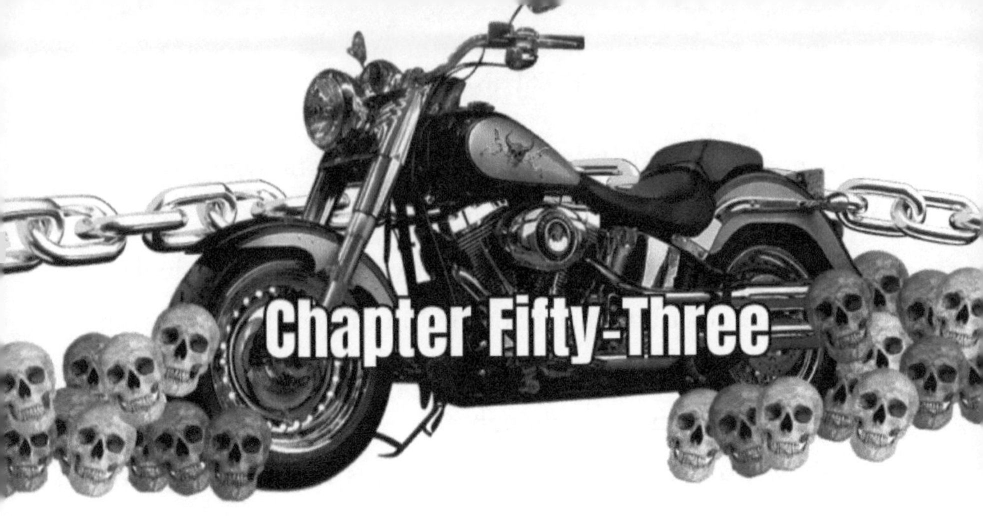

Chapter Fifty-Three

Jason

THE PLAN WAS SIMPLE. Two crews for Hillcrest's two main warehouses in both Cicero and Englewood. We had the manpower, we had the locations, and we knew where he was.

Jack Adams had come in clutch once again, when he had the information we gave him. Fucking shell companies made it so hard to trace people. Dax Hillcrest was well connected and apparently smart about his business as well.

Stephanie had been digging into Hillcrest for us, following the money, and found some even more concerning shit that I didn't want to think about. It didn't matter that this moment.

Right now, we had a location on Dax fucking Hillcrest and that was all that mattered. We were five minutes from his location and our men were fired up. We had split all crews fifty-fifty, so each crew had men at both locations.

I glanced at Marcos and Nico; they were both in the zone. We were locked and loaded and ready to move.

It was time for Dax Hillcrest to get what was coming to him.

We pulled into the industrial district of Cicero, Illinois rolling ten cars deep. Our driver pulled up in front of main entrance to the warehouse and things moved quickly. Jumping out, I followed Marcos, Johnny, Nico, and Kevin. Derrick hurried along behind me while we went with Tiernan and Seratelli, their guys leading the pack.

They blew the doors off the front of the warehouse with c-4. Smoke and debris flew through the air. Pulling my bandana up from where it was tied around my neck, I covered my face and followed through, just like we planned.

We'd spent all week doing surveillance while one of Tiernan's guys followed Hillcrest at a distance. Apparently, Tiernan has been tailing Hillcrest for a while. He knew his routine, his family, and his businesses all throughout Chicago and Cicero.

His family and businesses were in Cicero, while many of his warehouses were on the Southside of Chicago in the Englewood neighborhood.

Gun shots rang up ahead.

"Shots fired!" one of our guys yelled.

It was organized chaos after that. All of us geared up in Kevlar, we stormed through the doors and into the firefight. I killed two men across the room without batting an eye as we moved. "Fan out!" Tiernan shouted.

The warehouse was a winding maze with stairs leading up and down. It reminded me a lot of the warehouse we found Kara in not all that long ago. Pallets were stacked high with wooden crates, leaving isles to wind through and all too many damn places to hide.

My frustration amped up as more of our guys stormed in and we still didn't find anything. I tapped Nico's shoulder and nodded toward the stairs. As one, the two of us moved up them. "Behind you," Marcos said as he and Johnny joined us. I didn't look, but I was sure Kevin and Derrick were behind them as well.

Upstairs was a long dark hallway with too many doors leading off of it. I didn't care, didn't look back for back up. I pressed on. I needed to find that fucker and torture the fuck out of him for every fucking moment my woman had to endure at his hands.

I led the way down the hall, my brothers at my back.

Flashlights on our AR-15's lit the way. We searched every room we came across, top to bottom, moving like a military unit through the space. I knew the Knights were former military and Johnny eventually took point, leading us through the maze of rooms.

The deeper into the warehouse that we went and found nothing, the deeper my anger grew. I couldn't believe we hadn't found him yet. We had eyes on him this evening. Tiernan got the word that he was here. Where the fuck was the bastard?

There was shouting up ahead.

Johnny stomped faster down the hall.

Nico was on my ass.

"Got him!" Johnny shouted from up a head.

"Fuck yes," I grunted.

Marcos pushed forward, storming past me. I moved faster, running after them, Nico on my heels. There was more shouting and then gun shots.

I skidded to a halt outside a room at the end of the hall. Inside the room, Marcos was punching the shit out of Dax Hillcrest on the concrete floor. Hillcrest tried to fight back, but Marcos was clearly the better fighter.

Seratelli thundered into the room, pushing through Nico and I in the doorway. "Where the fuck is my sister?"

Hillcrest laughed and Marcos hit him again.

"Pres, let's get him up." I walked in the room, already pulling a pair of handcuffs from my pocket.

Marcos punched Hillcrest again and then forced him to turn over while he was still dazed and confused from his beating. Marcos shoved his knee into Hillcrest's back while he held his wrists together. I couched and slapped them cuffs on his wrists.

"Where the fuck is my sister?" Seratelli growled, kicking Hillcrest in the side.

Hillcrest grunted in pain but didn't say anything.

A cell phone rang shrilly, breaking through the intense show down between Hillcrest and Seratelli. Marcos climbed off Hillcrest and I quickly hauled the fucker to his feet while Marcos pulled out his phone. "Yeah? No shit. Fucking. Hell. We're on our way." Marcos hung up the phone and turned to Leo. "They found your sister. We gotta go." Marcos turned to me. "Take him back to Mourningside."

I nodded and Nico stepped in beside me. "We got him."

Axel

THE ENGLEWOOD WAREHOUSES WERE in the heart of the south side of Chicago. A place not welcome to outsiders or even safe for the locals that lived there. My brothers and I rode with Trick, Ransom, a couple of Ravagers Knights, plus the soldiers from both the Irish Outfit and the Seratelli family.

The mission had moved fast. Our guys blew the doors off the warehouse and stormed in, killing every single Las Serpientes man they came across. I led Blaze and Phoenix through the back of the warehouse and down a flight of concrete steps into the basement. Our AR-15's were strapped in front of us, the flashlight lighting our way. Trick and Ransom fell in behind us and we moved quickly and efficiently, clearing each room we came across and killing every man that moved.

Each room was set up as either a jail cell that housed dozens of naked women, or an empty room set up as a filming studio full of BDSM equipment that made my blood boil. I hated these fuckers with a passion. The women were all quiet, their eyes distrustful as they took us in. "We're looking for a woman, Alessia Seratelli."

Gasps went around the room, but they all shook their heads.

We moved on, kept moving. The lack of security down here was insane. Where were all their soldiers? Surely, they weren't all upstairs being killed by our guys?

The next room we came upon, a naked woman was screaming and fighting a man who pinned her down on the bed. Lights and film equipment were on and pointed at them, the red lights on and clearly rolling.

I didn't hesitate, I shot once, my aim true. The bullet penetrated the side of his skull, blowing half it off upon exiting the other side, splattering the poor women beneath him with blood and brain matter. Her screams took on a different tone and pitch as she became hysterical, trying to push the body off her.

I rushed forward, pushing the heavy jackass off her naked body. Thank God he was still dressed. I could only hope he hadn't had time to violate her yet. Blaze ripped the sheet out from under their bodies and quickly tossed it over the woman. I ripped off a pillowcase and got in her face. "Hey, hey," I said roughly, raising my voice to be heard over her screams. "Look at me."

She seemed to snap out of it. "You're OK. He's gone. He won't hurt you anymore."

Taking a deep breath, her crystal blue eyes were wide as she searched mine.

"Let me clean up your face." I held up the pillowcase.

She nodded slowly. "Who are you?"

"The names Axel. And you're Alessia Seratelli," I stated as I wiped the blood and brain matter from her face. I had a copy of her picture on my phone that Marcos sent out to everyone to help find Leo's sister.

"How'd you know?" she asked, her voice low and wary.

"My crew is working with your brother and his men."

"Leo's here?" Her voice grew more frantic.

"No, no, he's not here. He's at the other location." I tried to soothe her.

She calmed a bit, realizing he wasn't here. "I don't want to see him."

I froze. That was not part of the plan.

"Hey, beautiful. My name is Phoenix, let's get you upright." Phoenix helped her sit up and wrap the sheet around her body. "Why don't you want to see your brother?"

Alessia only shook her head in response, holding the sheet tightly around herself.

I sighed. This was not good.

Blaze stepped forward. "Alright, Alessia. We'll figure it out. I'm Blaze. These are my brothers."

Alessia looked wide-eyed between the three of us, her gaze taking in the leather cuts. "You're bikers?"

I nodded. "Like I said, our crew is working with your brother's men to rescue you and shut down Dax Hillcrest and Las Serpientes."

Phoenix crouched down beside the bed and rested his hand on the mattress next to Alessia, not touching her. "I have to ask before we move you, did he rape you? It looks like he was still clothed."

Alessia shook her head. "No one did. I fought back while he stripped me, but he didn't get a chance to get his clothes off." Tears well in her eyes as she spoke softly.

"Brave girl," Phoenix said. "Anything hurt?"

"My ribs are sore, I'm sure I'll have bruises everywhere." She sighed. "I'm OK to move."

Phoenix nodded and stood up slowly. Looking at me, he nodded toward the door. I followed him away while Blaze picked up her clothes from the floor. "Here, get dressed, we won't look."

We turned our backs to her as Blaze walked over to join us. "We've got to move out."

"She's adamant that she doesn't go back to her brother," Phoenix said.

"It's not our call to make. Seratelli wants his sister. We can't interfere." I rubbed hand over my scruffy jaw. "I'm gonna call Marcos and give him the update. We'll let him and Seratelli decide what to do."

"Don't tell my brother you found me." Alessia spoke from right behind me, her voice a demand.

I looked over my shoulder at her. She was fully dressed in a pair of blue jeans and a t-shirt, though I could tell they were some high-end brands and not your typical Walmart shit. "Not my call to make, Firecracker. I have orders to follow."

"You're not my brother's soldier, use your own damn brain. I don't want to be locked up in my father's mansion. Or worse, my mother's." Her voice grew more demanding and assertive as she.

"Again, not my call to make. If you're dressed, we're going to move out." I didn't give her a chance to respond as I walked off, leading the way out of the fucking basement of Hillcrest's sex dungeon.

I pulled out my phone and called Marcos immediately, letting him know what was going on. Him and Leonardo were outside the city in Cicero, but there were several Seratelli brothers here with us.

I heard her mumble under her breath and Phoenix laughed. Irritation rolled down my spine. Leave it to some prissy mafia princess to be all pissy about going home to her don of a brother. I need to call Marcos and Leo to get here faster. The faster they got here, the faster we would unload her to Leo, then help shut down this fucking trafficking ring.

We trudged up the stairs and out of the main warehouse, ignoring all the bodies on the ground. I glanced back, stopping briefly, wondering if we should shield Alessia from it—too late. She was already looking around in wide-eyed horror. As if having a dude's head explode in front of her wasn't bad enough, now she had to see the floor littered with bodies.

She crashed into my back as she took in the carnage. Startled, she looked up at me with wide doe eyes. Her crystalline blue eyes were so breathtaking, paired with her high cheekbones and full lips that were currently wobbling.

"Hey." I dropped my voice low and bent down slightly. At six-five, I towered over her barely five-foot frame. I cupped the side of her face, my hand so large compared to how tiny she was. I rubbed my thumb over her cheekbone. "Hey, it's going to be OK. Just look at me, OK?"

Alessia nodded, but her lower lip wobbled again.

Using her face, I pulled her into my chest, wrapping my arms around her. "Shh."

"ALESSIA!" a deep voice rang out across the warehouse.

Alessia startled, then started sobbing in my arms. "I don't want to go with him. Please don't make me go with him. Please, Axel, please." She clung to shirt, her fingers wrapping around the fabric and holding on so tight. She looked up at me with those crystalline doe eyes leaking tears and my gut clenched.

Mine.

I growled the word in my mind. My breath caught in my throat at the conviction of my thoughts. I nodded once at her. "Alright, Firecracker. We'll keep you safe."

I heard Blaze's and Phoenix's sharp intake of breath behind me, before Seratelli stormed over to us, his blue eyes wild. His black hair was in disarray, like he'd been running his fingers through the perfect coif.

"Alessia!" the man barked her name as he walked up to us.

Alessia clung to me and I hugged her tightly.

"Who the hell are you?" I demanded, not recognizing the man as a Seratelli brother.

"Fredrico Accardi. Who the hell are you?" He spat, moving closer.

Alessia clung to me tighter, telling me everything I needed to know.

"The Psycho that's going to kick your ass if you don't back the fuck up." I growled, baring my teeth.

It made him pause. He looked us over, Blaze and Phoenix flanking me, Alessia's face buried in my chest as she clung to me. He gritted his teeth. "Alessia, come." He barked the words like she was a dog.

Alessia shook her head and wrapped her arms around my waist, under my cut, clinging to me.

"She's not going anywhere with you."

Blaze and Phoenix closed rank in front of us, blocking Accardi's view of Alessia.

Fredrico glared as he looked over their cuts. "Biker scum."

I smirked. "Yeah, well. Good to see you and all. We're gonna go now."

"The fuck you are." Accardi took a step toward us.

Blaze stepped toward him, getting in his face.

"Come on, Firecracker," I murmured and nudged her along.

Alessia pulled away enough to be able to see where we were going, leaving one arm around my waist, her fist wrapped around the back of shirt. Her long brown hair fell forward, covering her face as she kept her head down, not looking at Accardi.

Whatever he had done to earn that level of distrust from the Seratelli beauty, was enough for me to instantly despise the man.

"ALESSIA!" He shouted her name after us.

"Come on, Firecracker. Let's get you out of here." I led her over to my bike, glancing back to see Blaze and Phoenix still squaring off against Accardi. "Ever ridden a motorcycle?"

Alessia wiped her face and shook her head.

"Alright, just hold on to me and we'll take it slow. I lean, you lean, got me?"

She let go of my shirt and finally looked up at me. Those fucking eyes killed me, a shot right through my soul. "Please don't take me to my brother. I can't face him yet."

I swallowed and nodded. "Alright. We'll go to my place." At my motorcycle, a Harley-Davidson Dyna, I pulled out an extra helmet from my saddle bag and turned back to Alessia. Placing it on her head, I didn't give her the chance to try to do the straps. I did them for her.

She didn't seem to mind though. Her eyes roaming over my face as I worked the straps through the d-rings.

Boots pounded on the pavement as Blaze and Phoenix jogged over. "He's going to get your brothers. We gotta go now if you don't want to leave with them."

Alessia's eyes grew wide and she nodded immediately. "Please."

"Let's go." I was shooting myself in the foot, probably betraying my club, but there was nothing I wouldn't do for those wide crystalline blue eyes.

Marcos

WHAT A FUCKING CLUSTER fuck. I shook my head as I listened to Leonardo rant and rave at Fredrico Accardi, his best friend. Leo was pissed and Accardi just screamed about my boys Axel, Phoenix, and Blaze.

I already called Phoenix, who informed that Accardi had made Alessia upset and she didn't want to go with him, so Axel took her home.

While I didn't blame the man for wanting to make the woman feel safe, it wasn't our fucking place to step in. Especially not when I just got shit squared away with the Seratellis.

"Fucking Christ," I muttered, watching the two men scream at each other in the corner of the warehouse. Accardi clearly didn't show Leonardo the respect he ought to show his Don.

"We need to go," Nico grumbled beside me. "Maya and Luke are waiting. It's going to be dawn soon."

I nodded. I'd been watching the clock myself, but I wasn't going to be the one to interrupt that fiasco.

"Accardi's a snake," Nico muttered, watching the two men.

"Yep," Jason grunted.

Finally, Leonardo punched his best friend in the face, sending Accardi sprawling because he hadn't seen it coming. Looming over the man, Leonardo growled a threat that I didn't hear, but his meaning was clear. *Fall in line.*

Seratelli turned away from Accardi and stormed toward me. I straightened, ready for the fall out, but Leo turned to Nico. "I'll expect the three of you at family dinner tonight." He glanced at me and Jason. "The chopper is ready for you. Get back to your girl." He walked away without another word.

"Fuck yes," I muttered. "Let's go home."

Maya

I woke late the next morning. The clock on the nightstand read nine a.m. and I groaned, wondering if my guys had made it back or not. I kind of expected them to wake me up when they got back on the Yacht.

Worry filled me. What if they weren't back yet? I scrambled out of bed, pulling on a night gown and grabbed a bathrobe out of the bathroom before I left the state room and flew up the stairs to the main deck—only to stop short when I saw Luke sitting with my guys, enjoying a hearty breakfast.

"Morning, mom!" Luke grinned brightly.

"Mi Vida." Marcos stood from the table and walked over to me, wrapping his arms around my waist as he pulled me flush against him. "Good morning, my life."

A smile pulled across my lips as I leaned into his touch and slid my hands up his chest. "Good morning." I kissed him slowly. "How did everything go?"

"As planned. We're going to family dinner, tonight."

I raised an eyebrow. I'd never been to a Seratelli family dinner before. Nico hadn't been on good terms with his family back then. "Should I be worried?"

"Nah," Marcos shook his head. "Be worried for me. I don't have a suit."

I laughed heartily at his confession. "I guess we're going shopping today."

"Sounds miserable."

"I bet Luke will look so handsome in a suit." I ran my fingers through his soft hair. "We should take more pictures."

"Didn't you get enough pictures yesterday?" he smirked at me.

I shook my head. "I have nine years of pictures to catch up on."

"That you do, Mi Vida. That you do. Come on, let me feed you."

With an arm wrapped around my waist, he guided me over to the table where he sat down and pulled me onto his lap. Nico and Jason grinned widely at me as their eyes roamed over my body.

I leaned back into Marcos's chest, feeling the warmth of his body as I smiled and said good morning to my guys.

There was nothing I loved more than the four guys right here.

Maya

Meeting Mrs. Gage was a dream come true. Teresa Seratelli-Gage was a beautiful woman, inside and out, and welcomed Luke and I with open arms. Immediately she brought me over to her little gaggle of women in the front room, while Luke joined his father, Jason, and Nico in the parlor where other family members mingled around a full bar—bartender included.

The mansion was crazy over the top and I couldn't stop staring around in awe at it all.

Teresa immediately dove into the history of the place, how it dated back to Leonardo's great-grandfather and had been in the family ever since. She also dove into the history and drama and familial relationships of everyone in the room, regardless of the fact that I likely wouldn't remember.

At dinner, Teresa sat beside Luke and me and filled him in on all the mischief Nico used to get up to as a kid—which fueled the rest of the family to chime in. It made for a laughter filled dinner that eased the tension that was clearly clinging to the men. Apparently, things hadn't gone according to plan on their mission. Or so Marcos had told me.

He'd said it was nothing to worry about. They had rescued Alessia, that was all that mattered. The fact that she didn't want to see anyone in her family was a different problem all together...and not really our problem.

My men did their part. And soon, I'd do mine. Or attempt to.

I wasn't all that nervous through dinner; despite knowing I would be ending Hillcrest's life after dessert. Maybe it was Teresa's stories and the family's laughter, or maybe it was the thought of my years of harassment and torment finally coming to an end. Either way, I wasn't that upset at the idea of killing Dax Hillcrest after I ate a five-course meal.

The dinner was spectacular; the presentation and fine dining felt like being at a fancy restaurant, while the food was simply magnificent. I had to stifle my moan after Nico's fingers dug into my knee the second time. His family laughed and Leo's mother told me she was glad I enjoyed her cooking.

After dessert, the ladies retired to the living room, while the men retired to the parlor. Leo led Marcos, Jason, Nico, and me down a set of stairs in the back hallway off the kitchen. I left Luke with Teresa, who was going to take him to tour the second floor of the opulent mansion, so he didn't feel out of place with the ladies while the men talked shop.

I held Marcos's hand as we stepped down the basement stairs. My nerves were starting to flare up. The idea of seeing him again just made my anxiety skyrocket. It wasn't killing him that I was having an issue with, but the idea of facing him again after everything.

At the bottom of the stairs, we turned toward the open cellar room, where several guys were standing around. I recognized Johnny Taylor immediately and Kevin and Derrick. There were a couple guys speaking with a thick Irish brogue that drew my attention. Besides the Irishmen were some of Leo's brothers who weren't at dinner. It was an interesting mix of different characters that made me realize just how many lives Hillcrest had affected with his fucking bullshit.

"Lass," one of the Irishman nodded.

I nodded back, unable to speak. I squeezed Marcos's hand tighter.

"They've been torturing him all day." Marcos spoke softly. "Honestly, we probably would have dragged this out longer, but I know you want it done."

I swallowed and nodded. "Yeah...sorry." I glance around at the room.

"Don't ever apologize for wanting Dax Hillcrest dead," Nico spoke up, his voice loud and clear through the cellar. He maneuvered past Marcos to stop directly in front of me. He cupped the side of my face, and I steeled my spine as every set of eyes in the room turned to us. "You've endured what no one should ever have to. You lived through a torture worse than anything. Worse than what these men have been inflicting all day. Don't you dare apologize for wanting that scum dead."

Again, I swallowed thickly as emotion clogged my throat and nodded. "Yes, sir." I breathed the honorific, my eyes solely on Nico's. His pupils dilated and a smirk tugged at his lips. God, I loved when my men got dominant, even if it was just to remind me that I was worth it.

"Ready?" Nico asked, his voice a soft growl.

I licked my lips. "Yes, sir," I said again.

A soft chuckle went around the room. I ignored them all, keeping my eyes on Nico.

"Way to steal the show, dick," Marcos muttered.

Nico smirked and kissed me. I closed my eyes and followed his lead, kissing him deeply until someone cleared their throat. Nico slowly pulled away, and I looked up at him feeling dazed as I always did when I kissed one of my men. "We'll be right there with you. No one is going to care if you can't do it, Little Dreamer. One of us will step in if you need us."

"I always need you," I murmured, softly. "All of you."

"You have us, Mi Vida." Marcos pressed a kiss to my temple.

"Always, Darlin'." Jason kissed the crown of my head, as he stepped into me from behind.

I let out a deep breath and squared my shoulders. "Alright." I nodded.

Nico turned away from me and nodded at Leo.

Leo looked at one of his brothers who were standing in front of the heavy metal door, and the man opened it slowly.

I walked through the doorway, my head held high as I took in the gruesome scene before me. Blood covered the floor and walls and the stainless-steel tables littered with different horrific tools, and there was an acrid burning scent in the air.

I took another breath as my eyes finally landed on Dax Hillcrest...or what was left of him. "Shit," I muttered.

Marcos chuckled softly. "Yes, the guys have been busy."

"You guys didn't take a turn?"

"We got a couple minutes in before dinner," Jason said.

Hillcrest was strapped unconscious to a medical exam chair in the center of the room. His head lolled to the side and his face was barely recognizable—someone had beat the shit out of him. The rest of his body was worse, though.

He was naked and someone had chopped off his cock and balls.

"His dick?" I gasped, feeling light-headed.

"That was me," Nico grinned darkly.

I gulp as my eyes widen in shock. "Nicolai!" I can't help the astonished laugh that escapes me.

"He won't touch what's mine, anymore." Nico simply shrugged.

"Which was why *I* took his hands," Marcos added.

It was then that I noticed both hands were missing. His wrists had been cauterized. That explained the burning smell.

"I cut out his tongue for all the threats he told you over the years," Jason said, his voice low and in my ear as he stepped in behind me once again.

His voice sent a shiver down my spine and made my core clench. Fuck, their love for me was such a turn on. Their utter devotion made me so happy I could cry. "You guys are so romantic." I can't help the laugh that bubbled out of me. I might have been in shock.

Jason's arms wrapped around me from behind and pulled me back into his chest, the heat of his body soaking into mine, making me realize how cold it was in the basement and I was only in a thin dress.

Marcos turned to me and pulled a pistol out of the back of his jeans. "I trust you know how to use this?" he asked as he held the Glock 9mm out to me, barrel down.

I nodded, because of course I did. I had guns of my own now. I wrapped my hand around the grip and brought it up to examine it. The safety was on, of course, and I quickly released the magazine to confirm it was loaded before I slid it back home.

"Do you want us to wake him up?" Marcos asked.

I swallowed thickly and nodded. "Yeah." I cleared my throat. "Yes."

Nico walked over to the stainless-steel table and grabbed a couple smelling salts and held them under Hillcrest's nose.

While I waited for him to regain consciousness, I took the moment to really look him over. Large swatches of skin were missing, like someone had taken a potato peeler to his body. There were cuts and stab wounds everywhere. Jason had mentioned earlier that they would have removed his finger and toe nails or drove needles under them, but as both hands were missing and all his toes were cut off, I couldn't see.

It didn't matter.

In the end, none of it mattered anymore. I wasn't even sure why I was bothering to have Nico rouse the bastard either. Jason said he cut out his tongue. He wouldn't be able to threaten me anymore.

Nico slapped Hillcrest's face roughly. "Wakey-wakey douche bag!"

Hillcrest woke with a whimper, struggling to open his swollen eyes. He turned his head and as his gaze landed on mine, I knew he was too far gone to understand a word I might say. Still, I tried. "We found your shell company. The Senator can't save you now."

His eyes narrowed on me, as if he was understanding what I said.

"You can't threaten me anymore. In the end, I won. You can't hurt me anymore." I raised my weapon and lined up the shot as a smirk pulled at his lips. Before he could make another move, I pulled the trigger, the recoil jarring my arm and the loud bang echoing through the quiet basement.

His body jolted with the impact of the bullet and blood oozed slowly from the wound.

With one clean shot through the head, Dax Hillcrest was dead.

Chapter Fifty-Six

One Month Later

Maya

LIFE IN THE LAST month had been bliss. Halloween was magical. I fucking loved my old Victorian Farmhouse. The guys had helped me decorate it to the nines. Every day it felt like a new decoration showed up. Luke thought it was hilarious. On Halloween, the five of us went Trick or Treating through the neighborhood, all of us dressing up and having fun with it.

Luke's tenth birthday party had been a hit. His best friends were able to come down from Chicago and spend the weekend hanging out and partying. Kara had come over with her guys, and so did

Slade and Karma. Stephanie had sent her love, but hadn't been able to make it...that was another story entirely.

Marcos had gone all out for Luke's birthday—all the guys had. They had gotten him the new gaming system that he wanted. Marcos and I had—after talking about it—gotten Luke his own cellphone. We wanted him to have a way to contact us when he was away, because he had joined the wrestling team through the local park district.

Thanksgiving had come and gone with a big dinner at Kara's, where she cooked for a small army of people. The mishmash of families that blended together so seamlessly was beautiful, and Luke was so good with his baby cousin Lilah. He'd really taken a shine to looking after her.

Even my mother had gone to Kara's for the holiday. We probably would never totally see eye to eye on most things, but our relationship was healing and so was my mother. Since my father's passing, it was like she was lighter. No longer weighed down by the stress of caring for him. She was walking better, going to physical therapy and even joining the local senior center to meet people. And of course, she had her little biker prospects to drive her around, much to her amusement—and mine.

Like I said, life was bliss.

Tonight, Luke was spending the night at Kara's while my men and I had a much-needed date night. Life might have been bliss, but we were all busy and all doing our own things throughout the days.

I had finally gone back to work at the women's clinic. My boss had been nothing short of amazing and understanding, but I was ready to get back into normal life again. The best part of it all was...I felt great. I felt normal. I felt happy.

Happy was such an understatement of what I truly felt though. I couldn't explain the emotions that coursed through me at the thought of my life now. My therapist had even dropped me back to once-a-month sessions, claiming I didn't need her anymore. I did—at least I felt I did—but I had come a long way in the last month.

I owed it all to my guys. They showed me the strength I held within me. While I'd been able to stand on my own two feet before, now I felt confident and steady. My men had showered me in love and supported me through every high and low.

They made me fall more in love with them every day.

Life was bliss.

Maya

"You look utterly breathtaking, Little Dreamer." Nico's voice was low and gravelly as his eyes roamed over the short leather skirt and tight black and red corset I wore. My tits were pushed up and my waist cut in, amplifying my curves. The sky-high heels only made my calves and ass look fantastic.

I had spent an hour on my dark sultry makeup, the smokey eyes and deep red lipstick only finished off the look. My curls were big and voluptuous tonight and I had made sure to take several pictures of myself for memory, because the whole damn look had taken forever to do.

"Fucking hell, Mi Vida." Marcos groaned as I walked into the living room where the three of them where sitting. They'd been patiently waiting for me, and I think I outdid their expectations.

Jason's eyes were glued to my tits, and I even saw him swallow and lick his lips in anticipation.

My heart thundered in my chest as I took in my men. They wore dress pants and black button-down shirts. Their Devil's Psychos cuts were nowhere to be seen, though they still wore their heavy boots with their dress slacks. It made me smile. I'd expected nothing less from them.

"You guys look hot."

"Not as hot as you, Mi Vida."

"Ready?" I asked, looking over them.

"Ready." Nico confirmed, holding up my long winter dress coat. Winter was upon us, and the end of November in central Illinois had turned blustery. While it hadn't snowed yet, riding weather was definitely over.

Maya

Sinister Desires was something out of an erotic novel. The sex club was off the charts in glamor and luxury. Black and silver accents everywhere, lots of velvet and silk coverings on the booths. Mood lighting was everywhere and there was plenty of deep booth space to sink back into the shadows. The main barroom was well thought out and breathtaking. There was a stage along the main back wall, and to the left of the room a long bar with all the top shelf liquor you could imagine.

Booths and tables filled the main space while cocktail waitresses and bartenders ran the room. It was a fully functioning restaurant as well as a sex club. From the website's pictures and descriptions, all the sex rooms or dungeon space was either upstairs or downstairs. Upstairs housed more private spaces, while the lower level housed the playrooms.

The building was an enormous warehouse turned into the club, and I could only imagine what all it housed. I knew my boys booked us a room downstairs in the dungeon space. I knew we talked about my current limits and ideas of what my triggers might be, but I truly didn't know until I'd be facing them...and I'd be facing them soon.

We enjoyed a delicious dinner tucked away in a corner booth that only had a pendant light over the table, leaving the booth itself a dark corner for us to touch and explore while ate our food. My men took advantage of my lack of underwear—something I had started doing again since moving in with them—by fingering me throughout our meal.

I was a panting keyed up mess by the time we finished eating and made our way downstairs. My eyes were wide as I tried to take everything in. Where upstairs was glamorous and luxurious with circles and soft edges, downstairs was industrial and sleek and modern. It still boasted the black and silver decor, but there were lots of chrome finishes and sharp lines. It was edgy and sophisticated.

There was a main room in the center, with a lot of heavy wooden equipment like a Saint Andrews cross and a stockade. There was a bondage table and breeding bench, several sex chairs with openings or space for toy attachments. Racks of toys and torture devices were placed strategically around the open space, allowing for a crowd of people to watch any given activity.

It was magnificent.

My mouth dropped open when I saw a woman on the breeding bench. Her legs were tied straight up in the air, with her ass hang off the edge, while her head hung off the other side of the bench. Two men plowed into her from both ends at the same time, right in the middle of the room. Her arms were tied to her sides by thick Shibari ropes and she was moaning loudly as they fucked her hard.

People loitered around the space, watching with fascination. I could feel my cunt clenching with need as I took in the scene. "Come on, Little Dreamer. We've got our own fun to find."

Nico wrapped his arm around my waist and led me away, down the opposite hall and away from the scene. I watched over my shoulder until I could no longer see them, and only then did I turn away, swallowing thickly.

I think I was going to like this place.

Marcos led the way down the hall past several closed doors until he paused in front of number fourteen and turned to look at me. "Remember, you tell us no tonight, and we stop. You say wait and we wait."

I nodded. "I'd like to use our safe words again."

The three of them straightened.

"Alright, Little Dreamer. If that's what you want."

"No degradation," I added. I bit my lip and watched the three of them nod at me.

"Of course, Mi Vida," Marcos murmured.

"Anything else?" Jason asked, his voice husky in my ear.

"No blindfolds." Most of this we've already discussed this week, but my nerves were frayed and I needed to repeat myself.

"No degrading our beautiful submissive, no blindfolds so she can watch everything we do to her body as we string her up." Jason's voice sent chills down my spine and I tilt my head back as his nose rubs against my neck.

I moaned softly.

"Come on, inside," Marcos ordered and pushed the door open.

I followed him in and took in the large space. The same industrial chic look was inside as well, with lots of thick wood and stainless steel or chrome accents. The racks were all wood with stainless steel bars. The benches were heavy wood with black leather padding.

The center of the room was an open space, though. Black and silver ropes hung from a set of heavy carabiners over the black I-beams in the ceiling. The hemp ropes hung loose, waiting for me to become a willing participant. Their presence was a calming balm for my soul that I hadn't expected. We may have spoken about my triggers and do's and don'ts over the last week, but I have no idea what they have planned. This was a surprise.

I smiled and reached for the ropes, grabbing them and inspecting them. Like with everything in the club, they were exquisite and very elegant. I looked up to find my men fanned out around the private room, watching me.

My heart skipped a beat and butterflies immediately erupted in my belly.

Jason stepped in front of me. Cupping the side of my face, he rubbed his thumb over my cheekbone as he stared intently into my amber eyes. His eyes were a stormy gray with their intensity as he gazed down at me. "I know last time we did this scene it didn't go well."

"Horrible, is a better word." I smiled faintly.

He chuckled softly, his voice a rasp that sent shivers down my spine. "Yeah, probably." Jason moved closer, his other hand resting on my hip. "We've learned a lot since then. Did you know Sinister offers sex education classes?"

I gasped.

Jason nodded before I could respond and continued. "They offer all sorts of classes during the day. BDSM for beginners, to master rope classes, all taught by experts in the field. The Seratelli brothers are very adamant about safety in their club."

I swallowed. I could only imagine.

"We've all been going to different Dom classes. From etiquette to the correct way to spank even. We've taken every class they offer."

My breath caught in my throat.

"We've been trying to be better for you. All of us," Jason said, glancing at Marcos and Nico.

Marcos and Nico moved closer, standing on either side of me. "We started seeing a therapist. A sex therapist, actually. She's a member here in the club," Nico said, rubbing a hand down on my back.

"She hosts group sessions a couple evenings a month. That's how we met her; we came when you were doing a girls' night with my sister," Marcos said. "We've been seeing her together and on our own, for the last month."

My mouth dropped open in shock. "What?"

Jason nodded. "Yeah, Darlin'. We wanted to learn everything we could about the lifestyle and learn exactly where we went wrong. There's so much we did wrong that night. Too much."

I bit my bottom lip. I didn't want to agree, I didn't want to ruin this moment. We'd talked about that night. I told my side; we didn't need to rehash it over and over. They knew things we were wrong, but the fact that they're digging into that night on their own—with a professional—was inspiring.

God damn. I fell more and more in love with them every damn day.

"We'd like a do-over, if we could?" Jason asked.

My eyes widened in shock. "Of that night?"

"Yeah, Mi Vida," Marcos murmured, nudging his nose along my neck.

"We're not going to be able to recreate it completely, obviously." Nico spoke up quickly. "There's no punishment scene. There never should have been something that intense. But we would like to do some impact play. And fuck you while you're suspended by our ropes. Your mouth and cunt open for our pleasure...and yours."

I had to swallow the drool pooling in my mouth. My pussy clenched and I stifled a groan. "Yes, please."

"I know we have a lot of come back from." Marcos said, his voice gravelly. "I know we need to rebuild trust and that will take a long time, but I hope you're comfortable to play with us tonight."

"I wouldn't be here, if I wasn't." I gently reminded him. Grabbing his hand, I brought it up to the side of my face that Jason wasn't touching. Marcos cupped my face and smiled as I pressed my lips to his palm. "I love you. All of you." I make eye contact with each of them as tears welled in my eyes. "You have no idea how happy you've made me. Actually listening, *hearing me.*" A sob broke out of me.

Jason pulled me into his chest by the hand cupping the side of my face. "Fuck, Darlin'. We didn't mean to make you cry."

I clung to him and tried to calm my breathing. I didn't want to be crying. Fuck, I was going to ruin my makeup. Taking a calming breath, I pulled away and quickly dabbed away my tears. "I'm good. I'm good."

"We don't have to do this tonight," Marcos said softly. "We can try again another night."

"No!" I quickly stepped out of their arms. "No." I grabbed the ropes and pushed them into Marcos's hands. "Please, sir." I looked up at him with doe eyes, then I slowly lowered myself to my knees.

I sat on my feet, keeping my back straight, shoulders back, head up. I licked my lips as I lowered my eyes to their intake of breath.

"Fucking hell," Nico groaned.

"Alright, Darlin'." Jason nodded.

"Our turn, Mi Vida."

Chapter Fifty-Seven

Jason

WATCHING MAYA GRACEFULLY DROP to her knees was the hottest thing I've ever seen. The trust in her eyes as she lowered her body, the slight smirk on her lips, like she knew exactly what she was doing to us. Fuck, she was a God damned Goddess, and I was ready to worship every inch of her body.

I turned to Marcos, watching as he swallowed thickly, his eyes never leaving Maya. I nodded at him as he met my eyes. Yeah, he felt it.

Straightening, Marcos nodded back and pulled on the ropes in his hands, giving them an experimental tug. They were of professional quality, already treated and conditioned—they would be soft against Maya's skin while holding up to the strength and quality needed for suspension play.

I took a step back and walked over to the chair next to door, so I had a direct line of sight as Marcos circled Maya with the ropes.

Nico took up post on the opposite wall, leaning back to watch closely.

Marcos's fingers dragged over Maya's skin in a sinful caress. She shivered as her skin pebbled with anticipation. She kept her posture and patience, though, while she waited. Marcos dragged it out, turning it into a sensual dance as he slowly touched and caressed, taking his time as he wrapped the rope around her ankle and calf, tying knots as he went. He created a harness out of the knots and rope as he worked her lower body.

Maya's breaths were still deep and languid. I made sure to watch for a hitch in her breath or any change in its rhythm. I made sure to keep cognizant of the scene as a whole—something I never did years ago.

Marcos and Maya fell into the zone, both of them falling into their sub and Dom space—neither of them fully aware of what was happening around them. It was why it was imperative that all of us stayed vigilant during the scene. There were too many variables.

As Marcos worked up Maya's body, he tucked her arms up behind her so she was grabbing her elbows, before he continued with the ropes. Once he created two separate harnesses out of the ropes and Maya's body was covered in knots over her clothes, Marcos tilted her head up to look at him.

From across the room, I could see how dilated her eyes were, how quickly she was already falling into subspace. His thumb ran over her lower lip and she waited for direction. "Good girl," Marcos murmured.

Nico shifted against the wall, adjusting his cock his in pants.

Marcos slid his thumb past Maya's lips and smirked. "Such an obedient little thing."

Maya whimpered and sucked his thumb, her cheeks hollowing out as her eyelids fell to half-mast.

Marcos pulled his thumb from her mouth and circled around her. He grabbed yet another rope and began looping it through the harnesses he made. Soon Maya was hanging from the I-beam, dangling in the middle of the room. Her hips and shoulders were hung from separate ropes, using carabiner's to be able to adjust her height or angle. It was a thing of beauty and Marcos was a pro.

"Hot damn," Nico groaned as he kicked off the wall and began to circle Maya's body slowly.

Maya lifted her head to look around the dimly lit room at us. She licked her lips as her eyes tracking Nico.

"Gentlemen, it seems we caught ourselves a toy to play with," Marcos said.

"We should have stripped her bare," I muttered, my voice raspy.

"We'll cut the clothes from her body when we need to." Marcos smirked.

Maya's eyes closed and her head fell forward, dangling.

Nico chuckled softly. "Look at this little dreamer all strung up for me to use. Plump lips and juicy ass just waiting to be taken." Nico flipped Maya's skirt up over her hips so her bare ass was on display, and gave it a healthy smack.

"Ohhh," Maya moaned.

I snickered and moved closer to her slightly spinning body. Grabbing a handful of her ass, I squeezed the glorious globe and slipped my fingers close to her asshole, teasing her. "Please," she whimpered.

"Mmm, what are our rules, Darlin'?" I squeezed her ass tighter.

Again, she whimpered. "Please, sir."

I patted her ass. "Better, but I asked you a question."

"Don't talk unless spoken to in a scene, always address you as Sir or Master, never ride share, and always text when I'm leaving work."

I grinned. "Good girl. And right now, you broke two rules."

She moaned and we laughed.

"Yeah, Darlin'. Time to receive your punishment." I walked over to the wall of paddles and picked up a pretty tame red padded flogger. I was going to warm her up with it, then Nico would come in and use his hand for a little extra stinging sensation, before Marcos will finish off the spanking session with something a little sharper—a Florentine flogger with all the whips trailing off the handle.

We were recreating that to a point. We were not going to go overboard with our spanking at all; hopefully we'd never do that again. I wasn't lying to her when I said we'd been seeing a sex therapist and also going to every single class that Sinister offered. There was a lot of learning we still needed to do, but I felt confident that we would only build a better relationship through it all.

"I want you to count and thank me for each smack to this luscious ass." I spoke deeply, keeping my voice gravely as I squeezed her ass again. I loved watching the shivers as they ran down her spine, my voice working through her body, turning her on.

"Yes, Sir." Her voice is soft, throaty. My cock jumped in my pants at the sound of it.

"That's right, Darlin'." I moved behind her with the red leather flogger. I rubbed the smooth surface over her ass before I swung back my hand and hit her smack on the ass with a heavy thud that made both ass cheeks jiggle.

"One. Thank you, Sir." Her voice came out breathy and made my cock fucking jump again. Fucking hell, I was not going to survive this without coming in my pants.

I hit her again, this time choosing the left cheek.

"Two. Thank you, Sir." Her voice was a little even breathier than before. "Three. Thank you, Sir."

I grinned and rubbed her ass, feeling the heat. "Doing so good, Darlin'. So fucking good for me, taking your punishment like a good girl."

Maya whined and lifted her head.

I motioned at Marcos and he immediately lifted her upper body so her head wasn't dangling anymore. I lifted her chin with my fingers and smirked down at her blown pupils. "Such a needy little thing."

She kept her mouth shut, but the look she sent me made me grin wickedly. Licking my lower lip, I raised my eyebrows waiting to see if she'd break another rule, but she didn't. I leaned into her face and pressed a kiss to her lips before I circled back around her and smacked her ass again without warning, harder than I had been.

Her gasp was music to my ears and I smacked her ass again before she could even count.

"Ohhh, four. Thank you, Sir. Five. Thank you, sir." Her eyes were closed as she panted.

I handed the flogger off to Nico who grabbed it immediately, while I slid my fingers through her very wet folds. "There's a good girl. So wet for us."

Maya moaned and swallowed thickly.

I pushed two fingers into her core and pressed on her front wall, circling her g-spot.

Again, she whimpered.

"Be a good girl for Nico and take your punishment. Remember, no coming until we say so." I pulled my fingers out of her as she panted.

It takes everything in me to step back and let Nico take charge of the scene. Maya's eyes tracked me as I walked back and leaned against the wall in front of her. She had no idea that Nico was behind her.

I kept my eyes on her, smirking slightly as I watched her chest rise and fall rapidly. The new upright position made her skirt fall around her hips again, so Nico had to aim for her upper thigh instead. The sound of his hand slapping her thigh rang out through the room and Maya jerked against her bindings as she cried out.

Nico waited.

Maya quickly spoke up. "One. Thank you, Sir."

"Good girl, Little Dreamer." Nico pulled up her skirt and tucked the hem into the waistband, holding it up and out of the way, leaving lot of bare skin on display. He quickly slapped her ass again, making the beautiful globes bounce.

Maya spun on her ropes, but Nico rested a hand on her shoulder and guided her back into place. "Two. Thank you, Sir."

Smack.

"Three. Thank you, Sir." Maya's breaths came out in softly whimpers and I had to check her face as she shifted against the ropes. She looked so serene, so at peace, even with the stinging pain from Nico's palm.

Nico alternated his next two hits, aiming for both upper thighs. Maya jolted and cried out, her eyes closed tightly.

"Four. Thank you, Sir. Five. Thank you, Sir." She panted and whimpered the words.

Nico grinned wickedly. "So fucking good for us." He roughly grabbed her jaw and kissed her passionately, claiming her mouth in a filthy kiss.

Maya moaned as he pulled away, her face leaning toward him as if she were chasing his mouth.

Nico laughed and stepped away, joining me against the wall. He propped a foot up on the wall and crossed his arms over his chest as he settled in for the wait.

Maya

My ass and thighs were on fire, heat radiating and a slight throbbing emanated from them, making my core clench down on nothing. Fuck, I needed to be fucked. I still had to go through Marcos's punishment if they were truly recreating that night.

It was hard to feel like I was strung up in our forest back at the house. With the lights down low, it was hard not to imagine the scene they had set, besides the fact that they left my clothes on this time and I wasn't wearing a blindfold or been drugged. OK, a lot was different, but my mind was able to fall into that subspace mindset and make believe.

Marcos walked over and stopped in front of me, a dark look in his chocolate eyes. "Mi Vida, you ready for your punishment?"

I nodded immediately. "Yes, Sir."

He smirked. Nodding slowly, he stepped away from me. "I found a whip I think you might like." He held up a standard leather whip with a million tines hanging from it.

My mouth dropped open with shock. It was a relatively standard whip in the BDSM community, but it was not entry level by any means—not that I asked for that. I was just surprised that Marcos was going there tonight.

He watched me carefully as I swallowed thickly. "You going to be a good girl for me, Mi Vida?"

I nodded slowly.

"What color are you, Maya?"

"Green," I murmured, my eyes still on the whip. I nodded again. "Green."

Marcos chuckled softly and trailed the ends of the whip along my cheekbone and I whimpered. "So responsive, so fucking ready to be fucked, aren't you, Mi Vida?"

I nodded vigorously. "Please, Sir."

Shaking his head, Marcos circled behind me. "Not yet."

The first lash of the whip had me arching. I cried out, squeezing my eyes shut. "ONE! Thank you, Sir!"

Marcos didn't play with me like the other had. He was quick and harsh with the five lashes he gave me.

I counted through all of them; my mind growing hazy with pain and need as I mumbled out my counts and thanks.

I felt like I was floating—well I kinda was—but my mind felt light and floaty. A dopey smile graced my face as Nico cupped my jaw and turned my head to face him.

"Beautiful dreamer." He grinned. "Such a good girl for us."

I licked my lips. I need a cock in my mouth, my pussy, my ass. I needed them to use my body.

"Ready for us, Mi Vida?" Marcos chuckled, standing shoulder to shoulder beside Nico.

"Yes, Sir." My voice was low and throaty.

"Such a good little toy for us," Jason said, walking over.

I tried to stifle my whimper, but I needed them. I was so fucking horny.

Marcos lowered my body and Jason gathered me into his arms. It would take Marcos sometime to untie everything; there was no need to cut the ropes. Jason carried me over to a padded bench on the left side of the room and sat down. He pulled me on to his lap, while he shifted back on the bench and then laid down with me straddling his legs.

"So fucking hot," Nico muttered.

Jason guided my body with his hands on my hips.

I smiled up at him, still feeling floaty.

Jason smirked and leaned forward to kiss me gently. "Such a good girl."

Marcos moved around us, carefully untying me. He was efficient and gentle as worked the knots. Kissing each new piece of skin he uncovered, Marcos showered me in love and aftercare. Jason helped lift me and maneuver me as needed, but he mostly kept me kneeling over his rock-hard cock.

Jason pulled his shirt over his head, exposing his muscular physique. I moaned and clenched my hands, needing to touch him but I still was tied up.

Nico walked over, gloriously naked and his rock-hard cock bobbing with each step. Salivating, I swallowed thickly. They were teasing me so much and I couldn't do a damn thing about it.

"Talk to me, Little Dreamer."

"Please, Sir. I need to suck your cock." I tried to lean toward him, but Jason and Marcos held me in place. I whimpered.

Nico laughed and slid his finger over my lips. "Soon, Little Dreamer. Soon."

Marcos pulled the last of the rope from my body and soon my hands were free. I wasted little time in reaching out to touch and caress Jason's abs and chest. His fucking muscles had only grown bigger in the last ten years.

Leaning forward I kissed my way up his abs while I made quick work of his button and zipper on his pants. I wasn't wasting anymore time here. My rules were no talking unless spoken to in a scene; there were never any rules about touching or taking initiative.

Jason moaned and lifted his hips, helping me take his pants off. God, I loved that he still went commando after all these years. His pierced cock was hard as nails as it sprung from his pants. Jason kicked off his pants and Nico gave him a helping hand as I leaned over him and sucked his leaking crown into my mouth.

I swirled my tongue around the head and then sucked hard.

"Fuck," Jason swore, jerking his hips.

I hummed around him and pulled off. Licking my lips, I got them extra wet before I sucked his dick further into my mouth, trying to take as much of his pierced cock as I could.

Marcos moved around us to stand directly in my eyesight as I sucked Jason's cock and began to slowly undress. I moaned, watching him intently. "Grab his balls," Marcos ordered.

My hand immediately gripped Jason's balls and squeezed.

"Fucking hell," Jason groaned. Sliding his fingers through my hair, he grabbed a hold of it with his fist and pulled me upright. He lifted me back up his body as he laid back on the BDSM bench and lowered me over his cock.

I looked away from Marcos to Jason's cock as he guides it into my pussy. I moaned, throwing my head back. My hands gripped his shoulders as I closed my eyes. Fuck, it felt so good. Each bar bell sliding into me set me on fire. Finally, I was seated on his cock, fully impaled.

"Such a good girl." Nico pressed his naked body to my back. "You going to take all three of our cocks tonight, Little Dreamer?"

"Yes, Sir." I moaned.

Lube was poured over my ass and Nico began working in his fingers. I was more than ready for them. I needed this.

"Please." I added.

Nico worked his fingers inside me, two of them, scissoring in and out. My fingers dug into Jason's shoulders as he held still for Nico to work my ass.

Marcos strolled toward us, buck naked as the day he was born. "You ready for this, Mi Vida?"

"So ready, Sir." I pushed back on Nico's fingers as he pushed them deep inside me.

Nico pulled out his fingers and Marcos tossed him a rag. He cleaned up before he climbed up on the padded benched behind me and lined up his cock with my ass and slowly started pushing in.

"Ohhh," I moaned. My head fell back on my shoulders and closed my eyes. Jason's hands slid up my body to my breasts and squeezed roughly.

Nico gripped my hip with one hand while he guided his cock in with the other. He groaned as he pushed deep into my ass. "Those fucking barbells," he groaned.

"You're welcome." Jason's voice was a sexy rasp that sent shivers down my spine.

Soon, Nico was pressed against my back, his chest warm and solid behind me. "So fucking good for us, Little Dreamer."

I whimpered.

"Yeah, she is," Marcos said. "You took your punishment so well, Mi Vida. Such a good little cock tease."

I whined and opened my eyes. Marcos was standing beside the bench, fully naked and stroking his very erect cock. I licked my lips as the need to suck his dick overcame me. My eyes roamed his body, taking in every inch of his muscular frame. Damn, my guys had all really bulked up in the last ten years. I was definitely not complaining.

"You need something, Mi Vida?"

I nodded hungrily, my eyes on his cock.

Marcos smirked and stepped closer. I felt a hand on my upper body, pushing.

"Then come here," Marcos said.

I was already halfway there. Letting Nico push my body forward, I laid on top of Jason's chest, making him shift his grip on my tits. He pinched my nipples as I reached for Marcos's cock and opened my mouth. I yelped slightly as I squeezed Marcos's cock roughly, making him groan, "Fuck."

I wrapped my lips around Marcos's cock and sucked him down quickly, opening my throat. Needing them to use my body, I swiveled my hips and sucked Marcos down to the hilt, only stopping when my face was pressed against abdomen.

My men all groaned as I worked their bodies in different ways.

"Fucking hell," Nico cussed.

"Tell me about it," Jason muttered.

"Time to take control." Marcos chuckled. He drew back his hips before he slammed back into my throat, fucking my face.

I moaned around his cock and he wrapped his fist through my hair, driving the face fucking as he began to piston his hips harshly.

Jason and Nico got the hint as well as they both gripped my hips and thrusted into me, figuring out their rhythm. They started a brutal pace, using my body as they saw fit.

It was so good. It was too good. I was moaning and writhing between them. I could barely focus on sucking anymore, but Marcos didn't seem to mind as he fucked my face.

Fuck, I missed this so much. I missed our life together more than I ever realized. I love these men with all of my heart and never want to live without them. Happiness settled over me as my orgasm tightened my core.

I moaned loudly as my body started shuddering and shaking as my orgasm crashed over me. My guys weren't far behind me, Nico and Jason cursing as my body squeezed their cocks.

The three of them roared loudly as they came, filling me with their cum.

It took them all a moment to catch their breath, before they slowly pulled out of me. Laying on top of Jason, he kissed the crown of my head while Nico kissed my spine and Marcos brought my knuckles to his lips.

Life might have taken us on a rollercoaster ride, but we found our way back to each other, brandishing balance in ways that we'll forever learn from. My men have made it clear to me that they're willing to put in the effort, and that's all I need.

Epilogue

Three Months Later

Maya

THE DAY WAS A flurry of running chaos and loud voices. Too many people asking me questions and touching my body all in the name of love and bliss. I was happy—I was. It was a magical day. I had officially married the loves of my life, but I felt like shit.

I woke up nauseous as fuck; every fucking scent had me rushing for the bathroom, and my boobs were sore as hell. On top of it all, I was crabby as fuck. Another pregnancy symptom that I would not so graciously rock for the rest of this first trimester—if this pregnancy was anything like the last one.

I didn't need a damn pregnancy test to tell me what this was, not when my guys had been trying to impregnate me for the last three months.

It was going to be the best wedding gift ever when I finally told them. First, I needed to get through the rest of these pictures. And the damn makeup artist needed to stop touching my face with every shot. Where the fuck did Nico find these women? They acted like this was a professional shoot; did they not see the damn leather cuts the men wore to the ceremony?

Fuck, I needed to calm the fuck down. I wanted these photos to turn out nice. I would look back at these years from now and remember that I was happy, even if my irritation was outshining it at the moment.

I took a deep breath when the makeup chick stepped away. We were taking a walk through the most gorgeous indoor botanical gardens I'd ever seen. End of February in central Illinois was no joke, but my guys had found me the most gorgeous indoor venue and pulled some strings to get me the date I wanted—I didn't ask how.

The ceremony had been absolutely magical and my guys had taken my breath away. During the ceremony I had said *I do* to all three of them and we all had exchanged rings, but on paper I was marrying Marcos. With Marcos being the president of the Devil's Psychos, it only made sense. I didn't necessarily agree with it, but in the end a piece of paper didn't matter - I was marrying my three men before God and our friends and families. That was all that mattered to me.

"Ready?" the photographer asked as we posed in front of a beautiful indoor waterfall surrounded by lush green plants.

"Yeah," the guys said.

The photographer begins taking pictures as we changed poses.

"I'm pregnant." I announced, watching my men.

Their faces immediately lit up, and the photographer grabbed the moment through each reaction.

"FUCK YES!" Marcos yelled.

"Hell yeah!" Jason cheered.

"Holy shit!" Nico breathed. "Seriously?"

I nodded as tears welled in my eyes. Nico cupped both sides of my face and brought his forehead down against mine. I could see his own tears lining his eyes. "You're gonna be a daddy," I murmured.

And he would be. The guys had made sure that only Nico came in my pussy for the last two months. They were diligent about making sure he was the next one to get me pregnant. The three of them had a damn plan for the next couple years. I had rolled my eyes at them, but I was ready for it.

I wanted this more than anything with them. All my dreams had come true.

"I'm gonna be a daddy," Nico gasped. He dropped to his knees and pressed a kiss to my stomach, while the photographer continued snapping photos.

Our happily ever after was just beginning, balancing out all the betrayal.

The End.

Want to read them get married in the extended epilogue?

Sign up for my Newsletter to get your copy today!

Loved the Devil's Psychos?

Please take a moment leave a review on amazon here!

Sign up for my newsletter here, for the latest updates and sneak

peeks on what I'm working on.

Follow me on social media!

amazon.com/author/methornwood

facebook.com/methornwood

instagram.com/midnightdreamingwriting/

goodreads.com/author/show/45144764.M_E_Thornwood

tiktok.com/@me.thornwood.author

https://twitter.com/ME_Thornwood

Ready for Stephanie and her bodyguards?
Check out Stephanie's story, coming 2026!
Pre-Order today!
Can't wait for Axel, Blaze, and Phoenix?
They're coming in 2026!
Pre-Order Today!

Also By M.E. Thornwood

Missed out on the Ravager Knights MC?
Start with Courting the Consequences!

Check it out here!

Choices have consequences, and some consequences cannot be undone.

FIGHTING TO SURVIVE IS all Kara Carmichael knows. Whether it was surviving the streets as a poor kid on the southside of Mourningside, Illinois or fighting the legal injustices in the court room, Kara prides herself on her ability to fight and win.

She also knows that every choice you make, has an outcome or consequence.

As the managing partner of the most prestigious law firm in the city, Kara had fought her way into a good life. She had made all the right choices.

Or so she thought.

When the Ravager Knights MC rolls into her law firm and kicks up trouble, Kara has a choice to make.

Fight the soul burning attraction of three rough and tumble bikers? Or fight for the prestigious job and gilded lifestyle she worked her entire life building?

Check out Reconciling the Consequences here!
Make a choice. Consequences be damned.
Kara made her choice, and the consequences of her choices left her burned and beaten.

After her father's hitman failed to kill her and her ex-boyfriend carried her body from the burning house, Kara wakes up in hospital... alone.

Without a home to return to, and her father still out for blood, Kara has only one choice left... beg for forgiveness from the three men whose hearts she deliberately broke. Or die trying.

Will Johnny, Derrick, and Kevin accept her apology and move on? Or will Kara have to face the consequences for her choices and save herself from her father?

Check out Embracing the Consequences here!

Not all consequences are bad. Some consequences are meant to be embraced.

Kara Carmichael knows first-hand that not all consequences are bad. She never would have met her boyfriends had her father not framed Mac Taylor for embezzlement and the list of other alleged crimes.

With her father locked away, Kara and her guys are faced with a new reality and a new family dynamic.

But when new threats and old enemies rear their ugly heads, new challenges are once again thrown their way.

Can Kara embrace the consequences for her actions or will it all come crumbling down around her?

Check out Brandishing Beginnings here!

They say trouble comes in three... as in the form of three rough and tumble bikers.

They make my heart race and my skin sizzle. They push my boundaries like no one else, introducing me to the dangerous world of the *Devil's Psychos* motorcycle club. And they're completely wrong for me.

When my college friend invites me to her family's home for the holidays, I didn't expect to see her brother Marcos—a gorgeous man I haven't been able to stop thinking about since we met—and he didn't come alone. His two best friends are hot as hell and downright dangerous... and they all want me.

One night I give into temptation. They teach me to submit, and it's hotter than I ever could have imagined.

Afterwards, I try to dismiss our passion as a one-time thing. But I can't stop thinking about Marcos's demanding presence and chiseled jaw. And Jason and his sexy piercings and sultry voice. And I miss the way Nico seemed to balance the two and always make me laugh.

When I need a place to stay, they take me in, and things heat up quickly. It turns out the three of them really like being in charge... and I find that I like that, too.

But a dangerous encounter reminds me of the risky world they live in—a world that could make me a target. For these guys, I'll risk losing my heart, but could that mean putting my life on the line as well?

Acknowledgments

Thank you to everyone that made this possible! I never thought I would be finishing up my second series and publishing my sixth book already. This is amazing. I want to give a shout out to the Smut Lovers Conference for always showing me tons of support and showing up when I come down to Florida. You guys are amazing!

As always, thank you to my husband. You are my rock, without you, I wouldn't be able to do this. Seriously, as I come out of my pneumonia trenches... you have been the rock that kept our home together.

To Jessica Baker! Thank you for always listening to me rant and ramble! And reminding me of my million tasks that I still need to. Thank you!

To my girl Megan at Cantina Book Club! Thank you for being my friend for the last 20 years! For listening and editing, for coming on this adventure of life with me.

Once again you readers, thank you so much for reading my books! I appreciate each and every one of you!

M.E. Thornwood is a contemporary Why Choose romance author that enjoys writing about dark themes, thrilling suspense, and hot hot spice. She loves her alpha males and the women who don't put up with them. Writing has been her passion since she was a little girl.

She lives in the Midwest with her husband and two children. When she's not writing, she's enjoying camping with family and friends, hiking with her kids, and reading books with her loveable fat cat Midnight.

www.ingramcontent.com/pod-product-compliance
Lightning Source LLC
Chambersburg PA
CBHW031234310726
48971CB00004B/1016